Jack's Lantern

THE WATCHMAKER REVELATIONS BOOK 2

MICHAEL L. HAWLEY

HELLBENDER BOOKS

an imprint of Sunbury Press, Inc.
Mechanicsburg, PA USA

an imprint of Sunbury Press, Inc.
Mechanicsburg, PA USA

Copyright © 2019 by Michael L. Hawley.
Cover Copyright © 2019 by Sunbury Press, Inc.

For information about special discounts for bulk purchases, please contact Sunbury Press Orders Dept. at (855) 338-8359 or orders@sunburypress.com.

To request one of our authors for speaking engagements or book signings, please contact Sunbury Press Publicity Dept. at publicity@sunburypress.com.

ISBN: 978-1-62006-837-3 (Trade Paperback)

Library of Congress Control Number: 2019954028

FIRST HELLBENDER BOOKS EDITION: October 2019

Product of the United States of America
0 1 1 2 3 5 8 13 21 34 55

Set in Adobe Garamond
Designed by Crystal Devine
Cover by Amber Rendon
Edited by Jennifer Cappello

Continue the Enlightenment!

chapter one

PRESENT DAY: October 2. New York City, New York—Lispenard Building

Jackie Lane sat at her desk and scanned the quiet, darkened room. She beamed. The light from the other high-rise office buildings penetrated the huge glass windows of her tenth-story office, as did the sounds of distant horns from the street below. The Lispenard Company, of which she was department vice president, occupied the entire tenth floor of the building deep in the heart of New York City, and the view from her swanky office of the streets and skyscrapers was incredible, especially at night. The entire wall was reinforced glass, adorned with high-end blinds that self-tinted according to the sun's movements. The room was spacious and uncluttered, and she appreciated the modern decor with matching metallic-and-glass office furniture. Contemporary paintings from a famous local artist complemented each wall. The only piece of furniture she favored over her unusually large desk was her executive chair "with unbelievable lumbar support," as she would remind anyone who'd listen. A large, cozy chair was a must, as she tended to work late into the night. All too often, instead of going home to her apartment five city blocks away, she merely slept on the soft leather sofa in the back room.

The huge, luxurious women's lavatory was equipped with showers and lockers that she used after her early evening workouts, so she purposely kept a toiletry bag and a few changes of clothes in her back room. Tonight had turned into one of those late nights, but she never complained; she even felt the

2 | Michael L. Hawley

evenings were her most productive times, thanks to the lack of interruptions. The stillness was refreshing.

"Damn!" she blurted out, suddenly realizing she'd left her cell phone in the lavatory after her workout.

"Everything all right, Ms. Lane?" a security guard asked as he popped his head into her office.

Jackie glanced up and smiled. She conceded that there was one evening interruption—Hank the security guard doing his evening rounds—but it was always at eight o'clock on the dot and lasted only ten minutes or so. He never lingered past that allotted time.

"Never better, Hank, thanks. I just remembered that I left my cell phone in the lady's lavatory, that's all."

"I didn't see it when I did my rounds," Hank commented, then glanced up at the ceiling. "Although I do recall hearing one in a locker."

"That's probably it," Jackie replied. "I'm sure I locked it up with the rest of my stuff."

Hank shook his head. "You work too hard, Ms. Lane. Always here late at night. You know what they say, 'All work and no play . . .'"

Jackie grinned. "But this *is* play for me, Hank," she replied. "There's nothing else I'd rather do."

Hank nodded. "Maybe," then he put on a big grin. "But I love my weekends, especially on poker night." He popped his head back out and stared down the hallway as if he heard a noise, then glanced back at Jackie, gave her a reassuring gaze, and waved as he left. "Have a good night, Ms. Lane. Remember, just give us a call if you need anything, and my cell phone's on that list."

"You too, Hank, and thanks," Jackie answered and went back to work. She paused again, briefly, listening as the night guard made an unusual amount of noise down the hall a few moments later.

Silence returned, Hank having handled whatever it was that had caused the short commotion, and the entire floor was hers again. As she worked, she lost all sense of time. She glanced at the clock and saw it was 8:20 p.m. She shook her head, amazed at how time just flew past.

Clunk.

Jackie popped her head up from her desk as she heard a quiet but distinct noise coming from down the hall. She tightened her lips as she stared at her open door. *I wonder why Hank is back over here at this time of the night,* she thought. She paused for a moment, listening. After a minute of silence, she shook her head and went back to writing. Although a little distracted now by the interruption, she actually felt at ease being alone at work since she knew building security was tight, with two security guards on duty at all times—in this case, Hank and Al. While one was walking the floors, the other was required to be at the desk. There were rumors that Al would doze off in the men's lavatory, but that was just office lore, Jackie was sure. Hank, on the other hand, was all business. If there were any issues, she would merely call Hank's cell, and he'd be up in no time. Besides, when she did choose to sleep in the back room, she would latch the deadbolt on the metal-framed door.

Clink, clang, clump.

Jackie popped her head up again at the sound down the hall. "Excuse me, may I help you? Hank?" she yelled at the top of her lungs, but her call was met with silence. *Strange*, she thought. *Hank would have answered me.* This time she got up to investigate the noise. She peeked into the darkened hallway. "Hello?"

Jackie entered the corridor apprehensively, repressing the fleeting thought to first call Hank as she quickly convinced herself it was a harmless situation. The last clamor sounded like a pot or pan falling into a sink in the office kitchen, a large room set up like a mini-cafeteria. Jackie's ears picked up the clatter of a two-way radio coming from the direction of the kitchen.

"It must be Hank," she muttered. She quickened her pace, and when she reached the kitchen doorway, she flipped the light switch and peered inside. Hank was out cold and lying on his side. Blood trickled onto the floor next to his head.

"Oh my goodness! Hank!" Jackie screamed in surprise, rushing to his aid. She crouched next to the security guard and shook his shoulder. "Are you OK?" she asked the unresponsive man, then she saw a huge welt on his forehead. Jackie looked down and noticed his wrists were tied behind his back. "What?" she blurted out, confused—and then it registered. Someone else had to have done this, and the hair stood up on the back of her neck. She immediately realized there was a third person on the floor—a person with less-than-friendly intentions.

In her peripheral vision, Jackie caught sight of a dark shadow flashing toward the kitchen door. She glanced that way and found herself staring straight into the eyes of a large man dressed in black, wearing a nylon mask and gloves, holding a pot, blocking the only exit to the room. His eyes were distorted by the pantyhose nylon pressing against his face, giving him a cadaver-like appearance. She could make out the man's grotesque, open smile behind the disguise. Jackie froze in fear as blood drained from her face.

The man laughed ominously as he stared at her then slowly approached.

She realized she was now the object of his unthinkable intentions; convincing him otherwise was not an option. She turned back to Hank, shook him, screamed his name; but he remained limp. Jackie glanced at the unconscious man's nightstick and grabbed at it, but it caught on its holster. She looked over her shoulder and saw that the approaching man was almost upon her, raising the pot. Jackie yanked on the nightstick with all her might. The nightstick released and she fell back just as the pot slammed down, missing her head but impacting her thigh. Jackie screamed in pain and crawled back, inching away from the assailant.

The attacker rushed her, grabbing her legs with his free hand and swinging the pot at her head. Unsuccessful, he paused momentarily, laughing. "Come here, plaything!" he teased. "Come here!" Then he leaped on her, swinging the pot.

Lying on her back, Jackie quickly raised her leg high, blocking the pot from impacting her head and entangling his arm behind her knee. She then swung the nightstick, which made direct contact with his head.

Thud!

"Ugh!" he belted out, momentarily relaxing his grip.

She swung again and again, but he buried his head in his arms as he advanced toward her. Although her strikes missed his head, they created enough confusion for her to obtain a slight advantage. She cocked her foot back and kicked him in the face, quickly pushed herself off the thick carpeting, and leaped toward the door.

He seized her foot, and she went down. "Where you going?" he yelled.

She rolled, bringing up the stick, and struck him square on the head.

"Ow! Bitch!" he shouted as he shook his head.

Jackie again leaped to her feet. This time, she successfully ran out of the room and down the hall. She glanced over her shoulder as he sprinted after her.

"I'll get you!" he screamed.

She raced to her office with the single-minded intention of making it to her back room and locking the metal door. *Is he getting closer? Will I have time to get into the room and lock it?* she thought to herself. She bolted into her office and straight to her back room. In her haste to swing the door shut behind her, she slid to the ground. Just as she climbed to her feet and grabbed the lock, the door handle turned and the door cracked open six inches, slamming into her foot.

Jackie fought hard to close it, screaming. At that moment, a fist came through the opening.

Whap!

Jackie felt a powerful impact against her cheek, and the room spun, then went dark.

The attacker watched as Jackie fell to the floor and onto her back, stunned by his punch. He moaned in excitement, knowing he now had the upper hand. He had her all to himself, and he loved it. The masked man entered the room and paused. He shivered in anticipation then slowly straddled her. He felt the warmth of his prey as he stared into her face for a few moments. Finally, he took off his nylon mask.

"Oh, you are a fine catch," he muttered to himself, breathing even more excitedly. He reached into his breast pocket and pulled out a knife and brought it to her face. Still breathing hard, the attacker continued to stare at her, taking in the moment.

"Where to start . . . where to start?" he spoke himself.

He froze as the barrel of a handgun jammed into the back of his head. He slowly turned and looked into the face of a man with intense, steel-gray eyes, who had a gun cocked and ready in his hand.

"Not today," the man holding the gun said in a deep, confident tone.

The attacker raised his hands above his head in a gesture of surrender, then dropped the knife, and three police officers rushed into the room and pounced upon him, ripping him off of Jackie and shoving him onto the floor. In seconds, he was apprehended, facedown, hands cuffed behind his back.

The man with the steely eyes re-holstered his handgun and approached Jackie's side. Crouching, he crooned softly, "Jackie. Jackie, you're safe now." He caressed her red, swollen cheek. "Can you hear me, Jackie?"

Jackie's eyes slowly opened, then she started screaming hysterically.

The man held her. "You're safe now, Jackie. The police are here." She gripped him intensely as she cried. Six more police officers invaded the room. He rocked her for a moment. "Come; let's get outta here."

Twenty minutes later, a New York City police lieutenant strode into Jackie's office and scanned the room, now filled with law enforcement officers. He glanced around the crowd, noticed three men in conversation, then walked with a deliberate step straight toward them.

"Dr. Dunham!" he called.

The man with the steel-gray eyes turned toward the lieutenant and smiled. "Hello, Lieutenant Sibley."

The lieutenant surveyed the room. "Well, Dr. Dunham, not only did you help us identify the serial killer—you just saved the life of his intended victim!"

Dunham grinned. "Maybe next time contact me a little sooner than a day before the offender had bragged about when his next attack would be. This kind of stuff is too suspenseful for my taste."

"Ha! We did!" Sibley replied with a big grin. "But you were off helping out some other serial killer task force, taking some other loser off the streets."

Dunham laughed.

"Seriously though, Dr. Dunham," Sibley continued, "how on earth did you break the case? We looked at the same evidence for weeks and nothing came up."

"Because he's the Watchmaker!" the detective standing next to Dunham blurted out. He put his hand on Dunham's shoulder. "What case hasn't he figured out?"

Dunham shot a glance at the detective, and then his face softened into a modest expression. "I wish it were that easy, Detective Howe." He turned back to Sibley. "Well, we had no idea who the offender was, except that his typology indicated a narcissistic sexually-based motivation. I merely exploited his ego and took this offender at his word that he was going to kill again tonight. All we had to do was identify his next intended victim—in this case, Jackie Lane—find her, then let him come to us. His bragging was his downfall."

"Dr. Dunham figured out how he selected his victims," Detective Howe interrupted excitedly, "which ultimately led him to our suspect's next target."

"Precisely," Dunham interjected. "As you know, it's all about patterns in the evidence, and your team found numerous patterns in this case. All of the victims were relatively affluent, athletic women, and the pattern I focused upon was their taste in art—specifically, paintings."

Sibley frowned. "Paintings? I don't recall the team identifying the victims' taste in art."

Dunham continued, "Well, lucky for our investigation, the offender murdered two of his victims in their bedrooms. I could see their wall paintings in the crime scene photos. With some further digging, we found out that the other two victims owned similar paintings." Dunham nodded toward the paintings on Jackie's office walls. "Just like these."

Sibley stared at one of the paintings, nodded, and gave a slight smirk. "Well, I'll be."

"This afternoon," Dunham added, "Detective Howe and I visited the art store where these were purchased, identified three potential future victims, taking into account the other patterns, and there you go."

"The other two were false alarms," Detective Howe added. "But we dispatched police to their residences." He shook his head. "This lady, Jackie Lane, was a bear to get a hold of. She wasn't answering her cell phone. He paused. "Fat chance you're going to get a direct line to the vice president of a company, although we eventually did, and building security wasn't answering, so we rushed here as fast as we could."

"Now that he's apprehended," Dunham interrupted, "we've discovered that the offender was an employee at the art store."

Sibley glanced around. "Where is the perp, anyway?"

"He's already downtown, Lieutenant," Detective Howe replied.

"Excellent," Sibley said. "Where is Jackie Lane?"

Detective Howe pointed to a lady seated in a chair with a blanket over her, being cared for by medical personnel. "That's her. She's off to the hospital soon."

Sibley glanced back at Dunham. "You know, Dr. Dunham, you didn't have to participate in the arrest."

Dunham grinned. "I know, but this task force stuff is in my blood now. I'm feeling my oats."

Jackie Lane rose from her chair and walked up to the four of them. "Excuse me, did I just hear that one of you is Dr. Dunham?"

Dunham offered his hand. "Hi, Jackie. I'm Dr. Dunham. How are you feeling?"

Jackie shook his hand and nodded. "Much better, thanks. Apparently, I still have to get checked out at the hospital, though."

"All for the better," Dunham replied.

Jackie pointed to a group of policemen. "I overheard them say you are the reason I'm still alive." Her eyes overflowed with tears. "I don't know how to thank you enough."

Dr. Dunham, evidently uncomfortable with the emotional nature of the situation, quickly shifted the direction of the conversation with levity. "Well, do you have large amounts of money?" he asked, jesting as he squeezed her hand.

Jackie laughed. "It looks like I have to go now," she said. "Thank you again," she glanced at the others, "everyone." Then she walked away with the medical personnel.

Sibley shook Dunham's hand. "Thank you, Dr. Dunham. A job well done."

"Now, it looks like I'll be able to get back to Virginia early," he paused, "but not until after I see the sights and sounds of New York City."

"It would be an honor if you'd allow me to escort you," the detective replied.

Dunham grinned. "I thought you would never ask."

chapter two

1570 AD: October. Old Ireland, Province of Connaught

The warmth of the hearth, the crackling and smell of the burning wood, and the flickering of dull firelight penetrated the room, invading Liam's senses. It created the illusion in his mind that all was well, but he knew better. Fear and turmoil ruled outside his front door and into the wood and boglands. An abrupt blast of wind from an oncoming storm caused the aged front door to shudder. He twisted around to face it, sword in hand.

"Do not leave us, Liam!" Aideen cried as she grabbed her husband's arm.

Liam relaxed and raised his shoulders, sheathed his sword, glanced at his two young children cowering on the bed, and turned toward his wife. "What do you expect of me, woman? I am the village chieftain. I owe it to our clan." He grabbed his long skean dagger and thrust it inside his belt.

"But this is the devil's spawn!" she bellowed. She draped around his neck an amulet tied on a thin cord. The stone was in the shape of a grotesque and ghostly face. "Wear this. It's blessed, and evil fears its own reflection."

Liam gently pushed her away to arm's length but left the amulet on. "He is no devil's spawn!" he belted out sharply, then threw his thick, goatskin shag-rug mantle over his shoulders. "This evil rogue is flesh and blood, and I will have his head and display it by the morn." A loud knock shook the front door. Liam glared at it. He rushed to the battened-down window and peeked through a crack.

"It is us, Liam!" a man outside yelled.

Liam unsecured the front door, opened it, and six similarly dressed men, wet from rain, barged in as a strong wind blasted in with them. The first man was massive, carrying a six-foot, two-handed axe, while the other five held javelin-shaped spears and daggers, two bearing shields, and one also armed with a bow.

"The others are waiting for us with Murtagh in his field next to the wood," the large man said.

Liam nodded. "Then we're off, Carrick," he commanded the large man, then shot a glance at his trembling wife. "Blockade the door!" he said firmly, then walked out with the six men in tow.

Cold rain pelted their faces in the dark, windy night as they hurried to Murtagh's field. After a few minutes, Carrick pointed out the others' lanterns. He roared over the wind, "There!" They quickly made their way to their comrades.

"We are ready, Liam!" one of the men blurted out excitedly.

Liam stared at them with confidence and determination. "We are twelve. It's time to avenge our four brethren and root out this vicious killer from the wood and bogs."

"Where is the friar?" another man asked.

Liam eyed him. "We are in no need of a monk, Quinlan! Yes, he is evil, but no more spirit than I." He turned toward Murtagh. "Show us where Aedan was slain."

A man, fear shining in his eyes, nodded. "Aye." He glanced at the other men. "Come, follow me. It's in the wood near the boglands to the north." They entered the woods, guided by a well-worn path dimly lit by their lanterns.

The trees tempered the raging wind, but Liam could see the rain reach the forest floor surely if somewhat haphazardly. Thunder shook the ground and lightning flashed above the trees. His men shifted their eyes excitedly at the edge of the lantern light, which created a barrage of moving shadows. "Courage, men!" Liam roared. "Take his heart, but leave me his head."

"Unfair, Liam!" Carrick laughed courageously as he wielded the huge axe. "Heads are my specialty." The laughter of the others roared above the gale.

"Sorry, old friend," Liam replied. "Tonight, he's mine." He glanced at the bowman. "Kian! Position yourself in the middle in case of an ambush. I want you to have time for a shot." Kian rushed from the back to the center. "Carrick, get behind Murtagh." Carrick nodded and moved to the second position.

"We are nearly there," Murtagh said. The path opened up to a slight clearing, but trees still surrounded them on three sides. Murtagh stopped and shined his lantern down in front of an old, half-dead tree. Blood, illuminated by the lanterns, could still be seen everywhere, and fragments of body parts and shredded clothing were strewn about. Murtagh turned toward Liam, his eyes wide open and his chin trembling with fear. "His body is gone!" he screamed then turned toward the darkness.

"The Will o' the Wisp! Hell's Lantern!" Kian shouted as the men looked around at the small glowing balls of light flashing in the darkness.

Crack!

Liam and the others faced a loud noise to their right. The silhouette of a massive body with broad shoulders shifted from between the trees. "Show yourself, coward!" Liam roared.

"Pharroh!" Carrick screamed their clan's battle cry, rushed the shadow along with two other men, and then disappeared beyond the lanternlight. Sounds of fighting resounded in the darkness, but moments later, the shouts of battle were replaced with screams of pain.

Then . . . silence.

Liam stared into the darkness. "Carrick!" he yelled. He approached, but now apprehensively. The others followed, weapons at the ready. From the blackness, a large object flew with tremendous force at Liam, but he ducked just in time. The object knocked over three men behind him. Liam gazed in horror as he realized the projectile that had sailed past him was Carrick's dead body. The next few minutes were sheer chaos as the fiend slipped past Liam and attacked his men. The strike happened so fast that he became confused as to which direction to move.

Then, the silence returned.

The lanterns, having been dropped to the ground in the midst of the terror, still glowed, revealing a mass of twisted, lifeless bodies steaming in the cold air. Liam realized he was now alone with an unbeatable, immensely powerful, otherworldly adversary hiding in the darkness. He heard a noise behind him, so he shifted his body, pointing his sword in the direction of the sound. His hands trembled. He shifted back to the other direction as he heard another sound. In an instant, the fiend had knocked Liam's sword out of his hands and lifted him off the ground by the shoulders. Liam, limp from the sheer power of the fiend's grasp, peered down but could not see its face in the darkness. *Was it human?* he briefly wondered. Unable to see into the eyes of his attacker, all he could do was reach for his dagger. The fiend's grasp tightened and ripped open Liam's tunic, revealing his wife's amulet, which then landed on its forehead. The fiend instantly let out a piercing scream, which gave Liam an opportunity to thrust his dagger into its neck. Liam fell forcefully to the ground, and as he turned to face his foe, nothing was there. He grabbed his sword, pressed his back into a large tree, and prepared himself for an attack, but nothing came. He sat, motionless, for what seemed like an eternity, but still no attack. Then he grasped the amulet, fingering it as he stared through the darkness. Exhausted from fear and defeat, he dropped his head, the rain still beating down above the treetops.

* * *

WEEKS LATER: Rome, Italy—Papal States

Father Francis Borgia, Jesuit superior general, stared anxiously out his window with his hands folded behind him, grasping a parchment, the papal seal easily discernible on the paper. He peeked down and wiped some dust off of his black vestment, then grinned slightly at the thought of the nickname his office was given: the Black Pope. It was true that the Jesuit superior general wielded great power in the Catholic Church because the office is invested with governing the largest men's Order in the Church, but 'black' was not in reference to anything evil in this instance. It was merely an unoriginal nickname because the pope was a powerful clergyman who wore white vestments, while the superior general wore black. A knock broke Father General Borgia's reverie, and he cast a glance at his door.

"Enter, please," he said.

A Jesuit priest entered. "You called for me, Father General?"

"Yes, Father Corel, please sit down," the father general replied, then sat at his desk, peering again at the parchment. "The Holy Father has given us a task—a task that our Order is best suited for."

"Oh?"

"The Holy Father has received word that evil is terrorizing the countryside of Ireland, a form of evil never before encountered and I fear beyond the reach of our usual method of exorcism." The father general explained: "It will require the skills, experience," he paused, "and special gifts of your team. It seems that a titan of a man has become possessed and now has the strength of many. Beginning last year, he has been ruthlessly murdering dozens of men, women, and even children in the night."

Father Corel shook his head. "I foresee some difficulty in restraining this man if we are to perform an exorcism, even with our charisms," he replied, substituting his preferred term for the aforementioned gifts.

The father general nodded. "The local friar sent word that an amulet he blessed saved the life of the chieftain. You might be able to take advantage of this. Seek the friar out."

"I understand, Father General," Father Corel replied.

"Time is of the essence, so please go as quickly as you can. Spend time in prayer."

Father Corel nodded. "Yes, Father General." He stood, bowed, and moved quickly to the door.

"And one more thing," Father General Borgia called after him. "Rumors are circulating through the local villages that even Satan has rejected this evil. If true, it may take more than an exorcism."

Father Corel stopped, turned, and stared at the father general for a moment, taking in what he had just been told.

"The Holy Father and I will be praying for you," Father General Borgia added, barely hiding his concern.

Father Corel bowed low and said, "I understand, Father General." He straightened, turned on his heel, and vanished through the door.

chapter three

PRESENT DAY: October 3. Fairfax, Virginia—George Mason University

Dr. Dunham sat down on a bench in the large park, which was situated in front of the anthropology building. He pulled out his iPhone and quickly scrolled through some emails, soaking up the sunny, cool, fall weather. His wife, Maggie, a professor of anthropology, had just returned from sabbatical in Ireland. She had been asked to give a lecture today on the history of Halloween. He knew she was excited about today's much-publicized presentation, and since he'd returned early from New York City, he decided to surprise her. Dunham checked his watch, ensuring he wouldn't be late for the lecture. With a few minutes to spare, he popped his head up and stared around at the beautiful park, its trees showing off their fall colors.

"Yeah, I just transferred here," a young lady remarked to her female walking companion as they passed by Dunham. "That campus was so huge I'd ruin a pair of tennis shoes every semester just by walking to class. It was too big."

"You'll love it here," the friend replied.

Their conversation quickly became inaudible to Dunham as they walked farther down the sidewalk. He stared straight ahead, deep in thought about a comment made by a serial killer, which had been nagging at him ever since his Niagara Falls Ripper case in Buffalo, New York, last year. Try as he might to ignore it, the comment was like a small pebble in his shoe; ever present and ever irritating. Although he had recently helped the Niagara Falls Serial Killer Task Force apprehend their elusive serial killer, the fact that this brutal murderer was immortal effectively played havoc upon Dunham's scientific worldview. This issue was not that he was face-to-face with an actual immortal. After all, immortality was lately theorized as a physical possibility, as long as the ends of DNA strands, called telomeres, repaired themselves—and that's exactly what occurred with the Niagara Falls serial killer.

Dunham's mental conflict with the whole scenario was the product of a related issue: realization that the supernatural just might exist. This Niagara Falls Ripper had told him, personally, that his immortality came from the same source as Dunham's amazing ability to apprehend serial killers: a divine spark. In this case, both he and Dunham had read from the same ancient document, releasing within each a supernatural gift. According to the Niagara Falls serial killer, if one reads from the *Ancient Book of All Knowledge*, one miraculously taps into one's own total inner knowledge. This divinely given knowledge was blocked off from the minds of humans eons ago when Adam and Eve were cast out of the Garden of Eden. Total knowledge is represented by the two great trees, and the Ripper had tapped into the Tree of Life, allowing him access to immortality—as well as the Tree of Knowledge of Good and Evil, allowing him to understand evil.

Dunham shook his head and tried to brush it off as coincidental hocus pocus, but two realities kept popping up into his mind. First, the Ripper actually was immortal; and second, Dunham himself had a perfect record rooting out serial killers. *Could it be true that I have a divinely inspired understanding of evil?* he asked himself. He glanced at the two young women who'd conversed near him moments ago, now hundreds of yards away. He thought to himself, *That young lady had a Midwestern accent, she called sneakers 'tennis shoes,' referred to a large campus, and had a green book bag with white stripes. Odds are she's from Michigan and just transferred from Michigan State University.* Dunham grinned. "Or, I'm just damn good at it," he bragged aloud to no one.

His iPhone chimed, and he read the notification. "Oh yes," he said to himself, quickly gathered his things from the bench, and rushed into the anthropology building. On the first floor, he saw a sign in front of a large, auditorium-style classroom, reading, 'The History of Halloween, presented by Dr. Margaret Dunham.' He noticed that the room was already darkened, then peeked in and saw Maggie speaking at a podium in the front of the lecture room. At the smile on her illuminated face Dr. Dunham beamed, knowing that she had a way of lighting up the room every time she spoke. He walked as inconspicuously as he could to the back of the room, his eyes locked on Maggie's slender frame; long, curly brunette hair; and oversized brown glasses.

". . . and Halloween," Maggie continued, "or Hallowe'en, or Hallow Evening, or All Hallows' Eve, regardless of name variant, was the pre-evening vigil and merriment that celebrated All Saints' Day. Knocking on neighbors' doors and begging for soul cake, while dressed up like departed souls and spirits, certainly did lead to today's trick-or-treating, but where Halloween falls on the calendar, as well as many Halloween customs, all dates back to ancient Celtic lore, to an eerily similar religious celebration of the Pan-Celtic religion of Druidism." Maggie paused, apparently having noticed her husband taking a seat in the back, and her surprise caused her voice to fade. She grinned from ear to ear, clearly touched by her precious husband's attendance at what she considered an important event.

"Hi, Dr. Dunham!" she announced proudly and waved to him.

Dunham grinned, embarrassed, but he waved back as dozens of heads turned toward him.

"Now, where was I?" Maggie asked herself. "Oh yes, Pope Gregory III, around 740 AD, placed the celebration of departed Saints on November 1. It is not a coincidence that he chose this date, coinciding with an earlier November 1 Celtic celebration called '*Sow-in*,' spelled 'S-a-m-h-a-i-n.' The name comes from Irish Gaelic and means 'summer's end.' This all-important religious and cultural celebration was not based upon the solar year with the solstices and equinoxes, but it marked the end of one agricultural and pastoral year and the beginning of the next. It was a time of plenty, with the harvesting of crops and slaughtering animals in preparation for the winter." Maggie grinned. "A perfect time for a party!" she belted out, and the audience laughed. "But it was also a time when their daily lives changed dramatically to a darker, indoor existence. It's not surprising that Samhain meant so much to the ancient Celts that they celebrated it with huge bonfires to bring back the light."

Maggie paused, turning her attention to something underneath the podium, and Dunham quickly glanced around the room. He noted that the auditorium was rather full, with a mixture of college-aged students and older adults. He glanced back at Maggie when he heard ghostly Halloween sounds emanating from the speaker and realized that she had donned a witch hat. The audience laughed again.

Maggie put on an evil grin. "But we're here to talk about Halloween, are we not? Curiously, Halloween is on October 31, and on not November 1, as All Saints' Day is. Well, for the ancient Celts observing a lunar cycle, the date began with the previous evening, or night preceded day, thus '*oidhche Samhain*' was the night preceding Samhain."

Maggie kept the Halloween sounds going and continued. "Our scary Halloween traditions of evil suddenly lurking in the shadows and having foggy mist in back alleys and behind gravestones in the form of demons, ghosts, ghouls, goblins, and witches flying in the night, find their origins with the ancient Celts." Someone dressed in a scary ghost costume walked slowly and ominously into the darkened room from a door to Maggie's side, causing the audience to point and giggle. The ghost, dressed in an oversized collapsed top hat and Victorian Age attire was covered from head to toe in white glow-in-the-dark powder, giving an eerie presence. The ghost eventually made his way to a wooden table positioned next to the podium and sat down. He then slowly turned his head toward the audience and maintained a deathly stare with his blackened eyes. Maggie grinned, broke from character, and said, "Wow, that glow-in-the-dark paint really looks awesome!" The ghost grinned but then regained his composure, and the audience laughed.

Dunham nodded approvingly. Maggie certainly could capture the hearts and minds of her audience.

Maggie glanced back down at the podium. "So, the ancient Celts believed that the boundary between summer, or the time of life and growth, and winter, or the time of death, was a religiously significant moment. They believed that the veil separating the realm of the living and the realm of the dead was at its thinnest during Samhain, which was why ghosts and even evil entities could slip into the realm of the living and roam the countryside. They also believed they could commune with their recently departed loved ones." Maggie turned and stared at the glowing ghost.

The ghost turned his head slowly toward Maggie. "What's happenin', sister!"

The audience laughed.

Maggie turned back toward the audience, smiling and shaking her head. "It was commonplace for families to set a place at the dinner table for the spirit of a dead family member."

The ghostly figure seated at the table then slowly waved to the audience, causing further laughter.

Maggie continued. "Many would even leave food on the front porch for good spirits and leave jack o' lanterns out to ward off evil spirits."

Dunham sat back and enjoyed the remainder of Maggie's lecture. She spoke more on the history of Halloween and the origins of customs, such as bobbing for apples and lighting bonfires, mixing it up with humorous interactions with the ghost.

After what seemed like a full hour of lecture and discussion, Maggie closed her binder, then paused, peering into the audience. "This concludes my—" Maggie stopped speaking and glanced over at the ghost, who was miming an irate emotion. Maggie chuckled. "*Our* presentation, and thus begins our next phase—the question-and-answer period." The auditorium lights gradually illuminated. "Are there any questions?" A hand quickly rose from the front seats.

Maggie pointed to the young lady.

"Hi, Professor Dunham," the young lady began. "How did the idea of carving faces in pumpkins and leaving them on the porch to scare away evil spirits come about?"

Maggie nodded. "In Old Ireland and Scotland, it was believed that evil spirits feared their own reflections, and the scariest evil spirit of them all was the spirit of Stingy Jack, who they called Jack of the Lantern, or Jack o' Lantern. They would carve a scary face onto a turnip, more specifically, a Swedish turnip, called a swede, and place it in their window or on the front porch to scare away Jack o' Lantern. The tradition came to America with the Irish and Scottish immigration. The American pumpkin was larger and much easier to carve, so it replaced the turnip and became the new canvas for the jack o' lantern."

"Who was Stingy Jack?"

"Legend has it," Maggie explained, "or at least one of the numerous versions of the legend, that when Stingy Jack was alive, he was a liar and a cheat. Satan heard about him and came up from Hell to take his soul. Stingy Jack, though, was intelligent and deceiving. He asked Satan if they could have a final drink before leaving this world. Satan agreed, so they went to a pub and had a drink. Stingy Jack, being 'stingy' with his money, asked Satan to transform into a coin in order to pay for the drinks. Satan agreed, and when he did, Stingy Jack put the coin into his pocket next to a small silver cross. This prevented Satan from changing back into his original form. Seizing the opportunity, Stingy Jack told

Satan he would free him only if he promised not to take his soul for a whole year. Satan reluctantly agreed, but when the time came, Satan called upon Stingy Jack again. This time Stingy Jack asked Satan to climb an apple tree in order to pick the best apple for Jack's last mortal meal. Satan again agreed, but when he was in the tree, Stingy Jack carved out a cross in the bark, and Satan was stuck in the tree. Stingy Jack told him that he'd let him out if he promised never to take his soul. Satan grudgingly accepted the terms and left Stingy Jack alone. When Jack eventually died, God refused his unsavory soul entry into Heaven, but when Stingy Jack went to Hell's Gate, Satan also refused, reminding him of their pact. He told him his spirit was doomed to forever haunt the forests and bogs of the earth. Stingy Jack asked Satan for a travel light, so Satan gave him a coal from Hell's fire. Stingy Jack had a Swedish turnip in his pocket, so he carved it out, added holes, and placed the coal in it, which made a lantern." Maggie paused and grinned. "So, when children would see the Will o' the Wisp ghost lights in the woods and bogs, parents would say it was Jack o' Lantern on the prowl, so beware!" Maggie shouted those last words, and the student who'd asked the question jumped in surprise, then giggled in slight embarrassment.

Dunham and the audience laughed along with her.

A hand raised and Maggie acknowledged the male college student. "Hi, Professor Dunham. Lately, on TV we see many ghost hunting shows, and it's interesting that those 'Will o' the Wisp' lights are extremely common. They call them 'orbs.'"

"That's right, these—yes? Another question about these mysterious lights?" Maggie asked as another hand shot up. She pointed at another young man, who nodded and quickly stood up.

"Hi, Professor Dunham, I'm in your Anthropology 350 class."

"Oh, hi, Ken. What is your question?" Maggie asked.

Ken beamed from his professor's personal recognition. He then glanced down at the group of college students he was sitting with. "Well," he said apprehensively as he glanced back up at Maggie, "speaking of orbs and Will o' the Wisp' lights . . ." He paused.

"Go ahead," Maggie said.

Ken glanced around the room. "It's still a Halloweenish question, so it seems appropriate, but when you were in Ireland recently, rumor has it that you saw an orb . . ." He paused again. "Er-r-r, what you reported as the Dublin Anomaly?"

Dunham sat up quickly, startled by the question. He looked to his wife and saw that Maggie's smile had left her face. He knew exactly what the young man was asking about. He remembered the day Maggie had Skyped him from Ireland, telling him about the incident. She was visibly upset and confused. As she and her team were cataloging their week's discoveries in the basement of the historical museum, surrounded by ancient Celtic artifacts, something unusual happened. He knew Maggie to be agnostic, more in the vein of atheism, so this event had wreaked havoc upon her natural worldview.

Maggie shot unnerved glances around the room, and as she realized everyone was waiting for her response, she replaced her frown with a tight-lipped subtle grin and nodded. "Yes, yes, the Dublin Anomaly. I forgot about that," she replied untruthfully, Dunham knew. "You're right, Ken; it is an appropriate time to discuss this. I'm of the opinion it was a coincidental play on lights, but my colleagues who also experienced it prefer to call it an anomaly, and even a ghostly encounter." She gave a sinister grin. "I'll let you be the judge." The audience laughed.

"It was late into the night and the museum was closed. My four Irish colleagues—Professors Quinn and Christie and their two graduate students—and I were the only ones in the building. We were all extremely exhausted. As we had our full attention on cataloging artifacts, I noticed Dr. Quinn staring at something at the far end of the room. She said nothing, but just stared. I peeked over to where she was looking, and I saw nothing, so I asked her what she was staring at. My question caught the attention of everyone else, so all of us then stared at Dr. Quinn, who was still watching, seemingly, nothing. She pointed and said, 'That artifact is moving.' I looked again at where she was pointing, and it certainly did seem like the artifact was moving. Again, though, we were exhausted."

"What did you do?" Ken asked.

"I didn't do anything," Maggie replied, "but Dr. Quinn's graduate student stood up and walked toward it. Just as he passed me, something awfully strange happened, which made him stop in his tracks." Maggie paused, complete silence hanging heavily as the audience waited for her to continue the story. "As I stared at the moving artifact, it stopped, and a tiny ball of light shot out of it and moved from left to right. As it flew by other small artifacts, they moved on their own." Maggie paused again. "We just sat there saying nothing for the longest time."

"And then what?" another audience member asked.

"Dr. Quinn broke the silence and said, 'What the hell was that?'" Maggie said in an Irish accent, which caused a few in the audience to laugh. "The graduate student then yelled '*slow shee*'! Which is spelled s-l-u-a-g-h s-i-d-h-e. A *sidhe* is a fairy, or spirit being, in Irish-Scottish lore, and '*sluagh*' is sometimes referred to as evil or cursed."

Dunham noticed many in the audience whispering to each other and nodding.

"Although certainly strange," Maggie admitted, "I did inform them that we probably set the artifact down unbalanced, and it finally gave. The 'orb' was merely light reflecting from the moving—or *falling*—artifact."

"So, what caused the rest of the artifacts to fall?" another audience member asked.

"That's what Dr. Quinn's graduate student asked," Maggie replied. "All I could say was that it was a mere domino effect from the first artifact. Ultimately, we all agreed to call it an anomalous event, hence, the Dublin Anomaly."

Even though Maggie had crafted the story in such a way as to entertain an audience seeking a spine-tingling tale, Dunham knew she left the most chilling part out—an experience she'd told no one but him. As the light had passed behind her, she distinctly heard a deep growl in her ear and felt something cold grab her by the throat, causing her to gag. Maggie said she froze in fear; then moments later the feeling was gone, and she could breathe again. Quinn and the grad student saw the light go into her, and it was only after she told them of her choking feeling that the grad student had exclaimed "slaugh sidhe." She'd told Dunham that she could explain away the choking sensation as a physiological reaction to the surprise of the "falling" objects, but she couldn't bring herself to divulge to the others that she'd heard the growl though—probably because she couldn't rationalize it.

"Are there any other questions?" Maggie asked. The excited buzz died down, and numerous audience members asked additional questions, which she handled expertly.

Dunham truly enjoyed his wife's presentation, and when the Q&A ended, he proudly joined the audience in approving applause. As the crowd departed, many approached Maggie and spoke with her briefly, so he decided to wait until the attention she received had waned to a few stragglers. A couple minutes later, Dunham left his seat, approached his wife, and waited for the last person to finish speaking with her.

"Thank you very much," Maggie said as the audience member walked away. She gave Dunham a big grin, then hugged him. "Hi, hon, I'm so glad you could make it. I thought you were still in New York?"

"It ended early," Dunham replied. "We apprehended the offender rather quickly."

Maggie smiled and grabbed his hand. "No doubt because of you."

Dunham brushed off her praise with a slight chuckle, then changed the subject. "Maggie, you are a master lecturer. Not only was the subject material expertly presented but you have an amazing ability to connect with your audience."

"Aww. Thank you!" Maggie replied. "It's easy to talk about a subject you love. It did seem like they enjoyed themselves."

At that moment, the man in the ghost costume approached Maggie and Dunham, but with the mask off. "Thanks again, Zack, for helping me out," Maggie said.

"Don't mention it, Dr. Dunham. It's certainly more fun than grading papers," Zack replied.

Maggie glanced at Dunham. "Zack, do you remember my husband, Dr. Edward Dunham? He was at Dr. George's retirement party this summer."

Zack shook Dunham's hand. "How could I forget? I pestered him relentlessly on profiling serial killers. Hello again, Dr. Dunham."

"It's nice to see you again, Zack," Dunham replied. "Are you enjoying your graduate experience?"

Zack nodded. "Love it!" he blurted out, then paused and grinned. "Except for grading papers." He raised his finger. "I was going to ask you, Dr. Dunham, being an expert on serial murderers, have you heard about this Boston serial killer?"

Dunham nodded. "Yes, but you probably know as much as I do. My knowledge about the case has only come from reading the newspapers."

"Oh?" Zack asked in confusion. "I thought the FBI was always involved in serial killer cases."

Dunham shook his head. "No, we're only involved in a supporting role. The task forces are comprised of local law enforcement. Most task forces do ask for our assistance though."

"But not in this case," Maggie interrupted, "and it bothers my husband to no end."

Dunham shrugged his shoulders. "I'm sure my office could assist—and we have offered."

"It's all about egos and personalities," Maggie added. "We have to deal with the same thing, even in anthropology."

Zack nodded. "You got that right. Well, I have to go. See you later." He turned toward Dunham and shook his hand. "Nice seeing you again, Dr. Dunham."

"Thanks again for all your help," Maggie called as Zack left. She glanced up at Dunham. "I'm starving. Wanna grab a bite to eat?"

"How about that Irish pub? I'm in the mood for the Dublin spirit burger and shadow fries," Dunham joked.

Maggie punched him lightly on the shoulder before linking her arm in his.

chapter four

FIVE YEARS AGO: County Roscommon, Western Ireland—Tulsk Inn Pub

"Guinness Stout," a rough-looking man said. He eyed the waitress as he settled into the booth.

"Anything else?" the waitress asked.

He glared at her from beneath the hood of his jacket. "Did I ask for anything else?"

Taken aback by his nasty response and intimidating stare, the waitress returned his gaze with a meek expression. "Uh, all right then," she replied, then walked to the bar, anger swelling inside her. "Another rude Yank," she quietly muttered to herself as she poured his drink from the tap. "Go back to America." When she finished filling up the glass, she grabbed a dirty rag, dipped the end in it, and swirled it around.

The hooded man in the booth reached into his pocket, pulled out some money, and laid it on the table. Moments later, the waitress placed the beer on the table, grabbed the money, and left quickly. He shook his head. *What a dreadful place,* he thought to himself. *This rich guy better pay me every penny he promised.*

A few minutes later, two men dressed in ragged jeans and old hunting coats walked into the pub, blending seamlessly with the local patrons. They spotted the hooded man, approached him, and sat in the same booth but on the opposite side. Simultaneously, they removed their well-worn traditional Irish hats—the kind with tweed narrowing to the tip of the brim, called "flat caps"—and plopped them onto the table.

One of the Irishmen glanced around and leaned toward the hooded man. "Everything's in order," he whispered nervously.

The hooded man raised his head and eyed the two Irishmen. He took a drink of his beer. "Is the digging gear hidden in the thorn bushes next to the cave?" he asked.

The Irishman hesitated, eyes clearly locked onto the fact that the hooded man was wearing thin latex gloves—an obvious indicator that the Yank didn't want to leave a trail of DNA. He nodded, then once more glanced around anxiously. "Do you have our money?" he whispered.

The hooded man gave him an intense glare but said nothing.

The Irishman stammered nervously. "I–I mean," he clarified, "this cave is a national historical site, and if we get caught digging in it, we go back to prison."

"You told me no one would be there at this time of night," the hooded man replied angrily.

"There won't be," the other Irishman interrupted apologetically. "We're just makin' sure we get paid."

The hooded man continued to stare at them for a moment, then reached into his pocket and pulled out an envelope, which he handed to the second Irishman. "Here's half, and when I acquire the artifact and make it safely back to the airport, I'll give you the other half." *Not that you'll live to see that,* the hooded man mused, smirking into his drink.

The Irishman nodded. "Are you riding with us?" he asked.

The hooded man nodded back. He didn't want to leave evidence of his rental car tire tracks anywhere near the cave. He'd parked it blocks away, near a drystone wall so common in this area. He took out a hanky, wiped his glass where his lips touched it, and then got up. "Let's go."

* * *

An hour later, they crouched in front of the entrance to the cave that was located in the middle of a rain-soaked field. The hooded man pointed a flashlight at the small entrance, obscured by thorny bushes. "This is the cave?" He asked, shocked, assuming a cave so important to people, albeit a long-forgotten ancient people, would be bigger. The opening was hardly large enough for a human to crawl into.

"This is Hell's Gate!" one of the Irishmen blurted out. "Fairies and evil spirits from the Otherworld use this as a doorway." He shook his head. "This is as far as I go." He crossed himself superstitiously.

The hooded man shined his flashlight into the man's eyes. "And you're not getting paid either."

The other Irishman rushed in front of his partner, himself now blinded by the hooded man's flashlight. "No worries! No worries. I told him he would be keeping watch out here, while I do the diggin'."

The hooded man held his flashlight on their eyes for a moment, then shined it back on the cave. "Let's go then."

The two slid into the tiny entrance and reached a small chamber surrounded by limestone walls, out of which groundwater seeped onto the floor. They listened for a moment, holding their breath; the only sound they could hear was the dripping of water. They continued walking through a small passage about thirty feet long, which then opened up to a high, narrow chamber.

"We need to go to the end," the hooded man said, and they continued for another hundred feet. The back of the cave ended in a pile of rubble. "Here's where we dig."

"What's in these stones?" the Irishman asked.

"Nothing," the hooded man replied. "These stones are blocking an antechamber."

After thirty minutes of digging, they did indeed break into another section of the cave. Once they'd enlarged the entrance enough to squeeze through to the antechamber, their flashlights illuminated what looked to be hundred-year-old wires and lights. The dank smell was even worse than the rest of the cave.

The hooded man shined his light to the very back of the room onto a large boulder. "Here," he pointed as they approached the boulder. "We need to move it."

With the assistance of shovels used as levers braced against the back wall, they successfully rolled away the large boulder, exposing a crack in the wall.

"What's this?" the Irishman asked, pointing to a metal box jammed into the crack.

"It's the reason why I'm here." The hooded man pulled it out. "Let's go."
The two slipped back through the antechamber hole and finally made their way to the first cave chamber near the entrance.

"Everything OK out there?" the Irishman yelled to the man keeping watch outside.

"Everything's quiet out here," the man replied.

The hooded man placed the metal box on the ground. "Shine your light down here," he ordered the Irishman. The light illuminated a holy cross adorned with a large red jewel blocking the small hinged door. Decayed leather straps were still wrapped around the box. He had been told by his wealthy benefactor not to open it, but the hooded man could not care less about what he had been told. Whatever was in it might be worth a lot more than what the guy was paying him. The hooded man used his knife to cut through the straps.

An ominous growling noise emanated from the back of the cave, causing the Irishman to flash his light from the box to the rear of the chamber. "What's that!" he yelled, backing up toward the exit.

"Nothing!" the hooded man yelled. "Shine your light down here!"

The Irishman hesitated, then reluctantly shined his light back on the box.

The hooded man inspected the front of the box for a moment, noticed a lock on the front of the small door, then jammed a large screwdriver into it. After a few minutes of twisting force, the lock popped. He fingered the door handle until it turned, and the door cracked open. Just as he lifted it, the small door flashed open and the hooded man was knocked off his feet. "Ahhhh!" he screamed as he was thrown back onto the limestone wall behind him. He fell to the ground with a thud.

* * *

Thousands of miles away in Vatican City, a Jesuit priest knelt with his head bowed, meditating in deep prayer in his quarters. He had been in the same position for hours, but because of years of discipline and conditioning, he was at ease. He felt a constant, dull pain, but he welcomed the suffering. It made him feel more spiritually connected to his prayerful intentions. Just then, his head instantly thrust back, his eyes and mouth fully wide open. The dull pain was replaced with intense, extreme anguish. His entire body tightened up as he seized. Seconds later, he passed out.

* * *

Back in the cave, the Irishman, who had seen everything in the beam of his flashlight—from the box door ripping open on its own, to a light shooting into the man's body, and then him getting thrown back against the wall—was stiff with terror. He gazed at the hooded man now lying motionless on his back, eyes closed. Sweating with fear, he stared unblinkingly at him. "Is he alive?" he muttered. He approached apprehensively, still not knowing if the hooded man was dead or alive, and he slowly bent down toward his face to see if he was breathing. He shined the flashlight into his co-conspirator's face.

The hooded man's eyes flashed open, revealing blacker-than-black eyes, and he thrust his hand up to the Irishman's throat and squeezed it. The Irishman gasped uncontrollably and dropped the flashlight as he tried to pull the hooded man's hand off with both of his. The hooded man maintained the chokehold as he sat up. His black gaze locked onto the Irishman's eyes, the hooded man listened for his victim's neck to break from the force of his grip. The Irishman went limp, and the hooded man dropped the body to the floor.

The other Irishman standing watch outside the entrance knew the two in the cave were in the closest chamber and about to exit, but they didn't come out when he thought they should have. He'd heard lots of commotion in the cave a few seconds ago, but still no one came out. Irritated, he yelled, "Let's be off now! It'll be light soon!" But no one responded to him. He shook his head and paced in anger. He suddenly stopped, thinking he heard a noise. In that instant, he was thrown with tremendous force and his head struck the ground. Slightly stunned, he shook his head, then spun on his bottom, shining his flashlight around. He saw nothing. Then, a bowling-ball-sized object rolled between his legs from the darkness. He backed off a bit, searched for where it came from, saw nothing, and shined his light on the object. It was the bleeding severed head of his partner. He screamed in terror and sprang to his feet, scanning the area for the person—or thing—that had attacked him and killed his partner. He stumbled backward, nearer and nearer to the vehicle. He paused and listened, but there was only silence. Just as he decided to turn and run, his head was jerked back, and he screamed in pain. A large knife penetrated his back, the tip thrusting out of his chest as blood spurted from the fresh wound.

chapter five

PRESENT DAY: October 4. Boston, Massachusetts—Boston University

College life as a freshman at Boston University was an entirely different world than what Rob Faulks was used to, especially hailing as he did from the suburbs of Buffalo, New York. It seemed like only yesterday he was walking the halls of his high school and then going home each day to see his mom and dad. Albeit a complete upheaval in his life, he loved every minute of his move to this new town. He was beginning to live out his adult life—and his dream of becoming a forensic scientist—and being accepted at this school was step one. Its PhD program had a great reputation in forensics, so since his high school academics gave him a full ride, he decided to start with an undergraduate degree in chemistry at this very school. It didn't hurt that his father was friends with the department chair.

"Rob, what time is it?" his dorm roommate asked without looking up from his studies.

Rob, studying as well, touched his iPhone. "Seven thirty," he said, then gave a slight grin. He loved dorm life and the people he'd met so far. His roommate, James Atkins, was a local Bostonian, had an excellent sense of humor, and would give the shirt off his back to a complete stranger. Rob and James had many similar physical characteristics: athletic builds though relatively thin, both around five foot nine, and each had light-brown hair. An interesting quality about James was his ability to attract women, yet he seemed not to even try. He was very comfortable speaking with women—with pretty much anyone, actually. Mr. Atkins owned a local lumber yard and had built amazing dorm room loft beds for his son and his lucky roommate. The beds were raised high off the ground with built-in desks underneath. James was just as serious with his academics as Rob was, which made for a perfect environment for both to excel. The room was silent as the two continued studying at their respective desks.

"Rob," James called out, still staring at his textbook.

"What?" Rob replied, also without looking up—they often carried on conversations like this.

"I have a serious question, which requires a serious and well-thought-out answer." He paused.

Rob waited for a moment, frowned, then glanced momentarily at James. "Well, what's the question?"

James nodded slowly. "Why would anyone want to live anywhere other than Boston? I mean, really; Boston is the measure of all things."

"Says the Boston-o-phile," Rob replied, still scanning the text. "I have to admit; I love Boston, but I do enjoy my Buffalo chicken wings."

"You do have a point there, Rob. Speaking of wings, you wanna order some—and maybe a pizza, too?"

"Let's do it," Rob replied, then thought about their two friends, Nick Tiedeman and Keith Allen, living across the hall. "Maybe Nick and Keith want some too."

James peered out their open door. "Nick! Keith!" he yelled. "Ya in for some pizza!"

"No onions this time!" Nick yelled back from across the hall. "Better yet, I'll call and order it!"

"I have an even better idea!" Keith interrupted. "It's Friday night, so let's get some fresh air and walk to Little Steve's Pizza near Fenway Victory Gardens! My eyes are bugging out from studying!"

Rob glanced at James, who raised a thumbs-up sign. "We're in, but why Little Steve's?" Rob called back.

"The love of his life works there on Friday nights!" Nick belted out.

"You better believe it! We'll be over in five minutes, just after Nick finishes rubbing my feet!"

"Shut up, you loser!" Nick responded. "He's on his iPad like he always is!"

A few minutes later, Nick and Keith walked into their friends' room. Rob shut his book and stood to greet Nick—who was well over six feet tall, thin as a rail, and had long, curly, brown hair—and Keith—a head shorter, on the hefty side, with sandy-blond hair—with a fist-bump each. Both roommates majored in computer programming and were brilliant—and each looked the geeky part as well, in his own way.

"Ready to go?" Rob asked.

Nick nodded at James, who was still studying. "Looks like your roommate isn't."

"Hey, I'm ready to go, my friend," James replied, "especially since Rob told me you were buying."

Nick belted out a laugh. "Keith has the rich parents. His dad makes mad money."

Keith stuck his nose up and closed his eyes. "We prefer to call ourselves 'financially unchallenged,' if you don't mind," he replied, raising a coupon in the air. "But we're cheap, too, so I have eight bucks and a coupon."

Rob laughed. "That's the real reason why you wanted to go to Little Steve's. You have a *coupon*!"

Keith smiled and nodded. "Yeah, but when you get a load of Brandi, you'll be glad we went."

"Does she even know you exist?" James asked.

"Of course not," Keith replied. "But I prefer our relationship this way. No high maintenance issues."

James shoved his schoolwork to the side and stood up. "Let's be off, gentlemen. I'm starving."

The four left the dorm and made their way to Little Steve's Pizza in fifteen minutes. It was crowded, but they found a dirty booth in the corner, which they bussed themselves and claimed as their own. A few minutes later, a waitress walked up to them, and they ordered their drinks.

As she left to retrieve their beverage order, Nick pulled out his iPad and started typing on it.

"So, which one's Brandi, Keith?" James asked.

Keith scanned the room. "Hm. Maybe she's not working tonight."

"Oh well," James replied. "At least you get to use your coupon."

"So, on this day in 1957," Nick interrupted as he stared at his iPad screen, "the Soviet Union launched Sputnik One, the very first artificial satellite."

Keith rolled his eyes. "That information and a buck fifty'll get you a cup a coffee."

"True," Nick replied, "but it seems that you're not aware of the significance of that launch."

"Oh?" Keith asked.

"The Sputnik launch freaked out Americans, that our Cold War nemesis, the Soviet Union, was more technologically advanced than we were, so we sunk billions into the Space Race. Tremendous advancement in electronics was a byproduct." He displayed his iPad. "We wouldn't have these beauties if it wasn't for the Space Race."

"He's right, you know," Rob added.

Keith narrowed his eyes at Nick and pondered for a moment before concluding, "I'm still better looking than he is."

The waitress came with their drinks, and they ordered wings and pizza. As the food was delivered and hungrily devoured, the foursome chatted casually.

"I'm not sure if I wanna go back and study," James said.

"Hey, we all need a head break from time to time. Besides, it's Friday night!" Keith answered, then paused at the sound of police sirens. All four glanced out the door. A police car passed by at a high speed. "I wonder what's up?"

James pulled out his iPhone. "Let's see." He scrolled. "My buddy's dad is a cop who works in the Fenway district. I'll see if his department has tweeted anything." James continued to slide his thumb across the screen as the other three watched. He popped his head up with a surprised look. "Holy shit! They found what they think is another October serial killer victim in Victory Gardens! That's just a block away!"

"Let's check it out!" Rob blurted out in excitement as he made to get out of the booth.

"Whoa! Whoa! Hold your horses!" Keith chimed in, clapping a hand on his friend's shoulder. "What if this serial killer guy is still around? I mean, don't these types always return to the scene of the crime?"

James shook his head. "Grow a pair, would ya, Keith! There're cops everywhere. The last thing he'd be doing is hanging around near the dead body. He's long gone by now."

"Come on, brother!" Nick encouraged. "I'll protect ya. I'll control-alt-delete his ass if he shows up. Computer geek power!"

Keith reluctantly high-fived Nick and slowly got out of the booth as the rest made their way toward the front door. "Oh, I feel secure already," he said sarcastically. "Well, if he's looking for his next victim and picks me, I'm holding you guys responsible!"

The four friends handed over their cash—and coupon—at the register, exited the restaurant, and turned left. As they approached the park, Rob noticed it getting darker due to the lack of building signs and streetlights in the area, and the higher concentration of trees, but the evening haze reflected the flashing lights of dozens of police cars. They could hear the sirens of additional police cruisers en route, and as the friends neared the scene, they realized they weren't the only ones with the idea of getting a better look. A small crowd had formed behind the parked police cars in an area just inside the main entrance to the park.

"This has got to be the place," Rob commented. "Let's go in the park and get a better look."

From their vantage point on the other side of the crime scene, just inside the park entrance, they could see that the police had an area completely blocked off with one section on the ground between two trees blanketed by a large tarp.

Rob pointed. "I bet that's the murder victim." He gazed at the crowd and the grounds. The entrance to the park garden just to the left was marked by two tall, thin granite pillars about ten feet apart connected by a horizontal granite crossbeam. "I can't believe they even let people in this far."

James took a photo with his iPhone. "You're right. I'll bet they move everyone out soon."

"You must be lovin' this, Rob," Nick said. "I have to admit, it's pretty exhilarating to be seeing an actual murder site."

"And to think," James added, "underneath that tarp is a victim!"

Keith's eyes opened wide. "What!" he yelled, as he stared at James.

"Cool!" Nick said excitedly, then lost his grin. "I mean, reprehensible, of course, but talk about sensory overload!"

"How do you know?" Keith asked James.

James lifted up his iPhone and wiggled it. "The police."

"This might not be a murder site," Rob replied to Nick. "The killer may have just dropped the victim off here. In that case, there'd be two crime scenes."

"That's exactly what happened," James said. "Assuming that the killer's following his own pattern of the last three years."

Rob glanced at James. "Oh yeah, you're from Boston, so you probably know quite a few details about this serial killer."

James nodded. "All I know is what's been in the papers and on social media for the last couple of years. Three years ago, in October, just before Halloween, he killed six people. He did it again each year after that, and it looks like he's doing it again this October. He kidnaps them, and three days later the police find the bodies."

"Just women?" Rob asked.

"No, it's a mix," James replied. "He started with this businessman; the president of some company." James then put on an evil-looking grin and stared at Keith. "The freaky thing about the killer's MO? He cuts the head off and places it next to the body."

"I've seen—and heard—enough," Keith blurted out nervously, shaking his head. "Homework is calling us. Let's go."

"You go ahead," Rob replied. "I'd like to stay here awhile."

Keith glanced at the other two, realizing that all three were going to stay. "Are you nuts? I'm not walking home by myself so this killer can follow me. It's safer here."

Rob shook his head. "This *so* reminds me of the Niagara Falls Ripper case back home last year," he said as another police car slowly made its way through the crowd.

"Oh, that's right!" Nick replied. "You're from Buffalo."

"Not only *from* Buffalo," James interrupted. "Rob helped catch the killer!"

"Awesome!" Nick exclaimed. "Did you shoot him?"

Rob stared at Nick. "No, you idiot. I helped break the case. I didn't apprehend him."

"What did you do?" Nick asked.

"Little did we know, the Niagara Falls Ripper was after my sister, Celine," Rob explained.

"Whoa!" Keith yelled. "Is she OK?"

Rob nodded. "Thanks to the Watchmaker figuring out she was his next intended victim. The killer was trying to make an elixir of life and wanted Celine's special O-negative blood."

"Sounds like a vampire," Keith replied.

"Well," Rob continued, "Celine noticed this creeper watching her at the theater she worked at, and when she told me about him, I thought this guy could be the Ripper, so my buddies and I followed him to his yacht."

"Why would you follow a known killer?" Keith asked.

"We didn't know for sure at the time," Rob replied, "and strangely, after being forced to meet the guy that night, we were then convinced he couldn't have been the killer . . . but he was! My part in it was just that we found out where he lived."

"So, who's this Watchmaker?" Nick asked.

Rob glanced around. "I'm surprised he's not around here right now, since Boston has a serial killer on their hands. The Watchmaker is the FBI's chief forensic scientist. A guy named Dr. Dunham. He helps out serial killer task forces, and apparently he's damn good." At that moment, Rob experienced an intense and uneasy feeling, causing the hair on the back of his neck to stand on end. He glanced around, and his eyes settled on an unusually thick grouping of trees. Against the park lights and swirling reds and blues from the cop cars, the trees cast eerie, long, dark shadows. He stared into one dark area on the other side of the police line, to the right of the victim, and caught a glimpse of a large section of the shadow shifting. Rob closed his eyes, shook his head, and stared back at the dark area. He could swear that the uneasy feeling emanated from that distant blackness; it was as if he could feel the presence of something evil. *It couldn't have been a person*, he thought to himself, since the shadow was so large.

Keith stepped forward and stared into the same dark area. "What? What are you looking at, Rob?"

Rob paused. "Uh, I dunno." Then he pointed. "Do you guys see anything under that tree over there? I know it's dark, but I thought I saw something . . . big."

All four stared apprehensively into the dark area for a moment, then James spoke up. "Nothing. Why? What do you think it is?"

Rob shook his head. "Not sure, but does anyone else have the heebie-jeebies?"

"Yes!" Keith yelled, raising his hand. "Can we go now?"

"Sure, let's get outta here," James said.

They started the walk back to their dorm, the darkened copse of trees to their right. Rob still felt uneasy, so he kept on staring into the trees as they walked.

"Stop looking in there!" Keith yelled. "You're freaking me out." At that moment, the friends heard a loud crack from within the trees, loud enough to be heard over the traffic. Keith jumped into the road and away from the tree line. "Holy shit! What was that?"

James laughed. "Oh, relax, Keith. I swear, you're the biggest chicken I know."

"A healthy fear of your surroundings is an evolutionary advantage, my young Padawan," Keith replied. "Just ask the gazelle." The tree line of the park abruptly ended as they crossed into the lighted commercial area. Keith sighed and muttered to himself, "The farther away from the park the better."

Curiously, the uneasy feeling left Rob as they entered the well-lit streets. He decided not to discuss the issue any further with his friends, but he couldn't stop thinking about it.

"Hey, James," Rob said, clearing his throat and shaking off his dissipating discomfort.

"Yeah?"

"Whaddaya say we look into this case further?" Rob asked. "Maybe we could help like I did in Buffalo."

James grinned. "I'm in. Nick, Keith, what do you think?"

"Sure," Nick replied.

"As long as it only requires my computer skills," Keith answered. "I'm not going to any rickety old building or graveyard."

Rob smiled broadly. "Deal."

chapter six

Dunham sat at a table in the cafeteria listening intently to Dr. Matt Holder, special agent in charge of the Forensic Analysis Branch of the FBI's Lab Division. Holder, thin, balding, and always wearing wire-rimmed glasses and a white lab coat, looked—and was—very academic. Dunham typically spent his lunch breaks with experts in other FBI departments, especially from the lab divisions like Holder's, in order to keep up with the advancements in forensic technology. Holder was his usual lunch partner, since the two worked so closely. Many of Dunham's subordinates worked in the Evidence Control Unit lab, a space under Holder's purview. Dunham quickly understood that Holder was frustrated about one of his new cases, as he had that case file in front of him.

"It's giving me a migraine, Edward."

"What's Dr. Wessel think about it?" Dunham asked.

"Wessel is just as stumped as the rest of us in the lab." Holder paused. "Actually, he gave me the idea to ask you, so I brought the case file with me to lunch." He half-jokingly gave Dunham a helpless look, complete with puppy-dog eyes. "Will you take a quick peek at it?"

Dunham nodded politely and accepted the file from Holder. "Of course I will. You know I miss working in the lab." Dunham opened the file and reviewed the documents and photos.

Holder sat back in his chair and smiled. "Speaking of the lab, Wessel and I believe we know why you're outshining your law enforcement colleagues on these serial killer task forces."

Dunham glanced up at Holder. "Oh, why?"

"You're one of the first serial killer specialists coming out of the forensic hard sciences," Holder explained. "The others hail from law enforcement or forensic psychology." He grinned. "You make us lab rats proud!"

Dunham raised his eyebrows as he returned his attention to the case file. "Perhaps you're right."

Jack Stride swung the cafeteria door open forcefully and rushed in, then abruptly stopped. With his index finger, he pushed his large glasses up on his nose and scanned the cafeteria. He spotted his boss and swiftly pursued that direction.

The dramatic entrance caught Dunham's attention, causing him to halt his review of the file and instead study Jack. He noticed that his thin, medium-height subordinate was still in his suit, top button unbuttoned with his tie loosened, auburn hair parted to the side. He was carrying a carry-on bag, so Dunham figured he must have come straight from the airport.

"Jack, welcome back. Are you joining us for lunch?"

"Thanks, boss. No, I just ate," Jack replied. "Hi, by the way." Then he glanced over at Holder. "Hi, Dr. Holder."

"How was your trip to St. Louis?" Dunham asked.

"Excellent . . . I think," Jack replied. "Is there any chance you and I could go over the case later?"

"What case?" Holder asked.

Dunham glanced back at Holder. "Jack was asked by the St. Louis Serial Killer Task Force to become a member."

"That's right." Jack pointed to Dunham. "Thanks to Dr. Dunham doing so well on local task forces—but presently too busy to join—the task force asked me."

Holder frowned. "You see! I let your team operate out of my Evidence Control Unit, and you guys get all the glory. How unfair is that?" he blasted jokingly.

Jack grinned. "Don't blame me. Blame him for being so good!"

Dunham laughed. "I'll be up to the office soon, Jack. I promised Dr. Holder I'd review this case file."

"That's right," Holder blurted out, grinning slightly. "So, get the hell outta here."

Jack laughed as he turned to walk away. "I'll see you soon, Dr. Dunham. Bye, Dr. Holder!"

Holder waved to Jack, but he was focused on Dunham. "So, what do you think, Edward? The deceased was a healthy, middle-aged female, yet the husband found her dead, lying in her bed after a nap. No obvious cause of death except the fact that her heart just stopped. She had absolutely no history of heart problems. He claimed she was complaining about a severe headache, so he told her to take a nap. The husband was giving her CPR until the medics came."

"The police have sent you stomach contents, blood, and urine samples in hopes of finding the cause of death," Dunham commented, then held up the photos to Holder. "So, why are these labeled 'crime scene photos'?"

"The investigators, and the family for that matter, suspect the husband may have murdered her," Holder explained. "Apparently, she was going to divorce him because of his history of infidelity, and since she was the daughter of a millionaire, he was going to end up with nothing. They suspect poisoning."

"Does the husband have any kind of questionable history?" Dunham asked.

"Yes, actually. His first wife died five years ago, and the cause of death was unknown."

Dunham paused. "So, the husband is a critical care nurse. Is that correct?"

Holder nodded.

Dunham studied the photos of the deceased, then concentrated on one in particular. "Do you have the chemical analysis results?"

"Yes, nothing unusual. They collected the samples on day one post-mortem."

"Did they freeze the samples?"

Holder shook his head. "No, why?"

Dunham placed the photo of the deceased in front of Holder. "We just might have a case of poisoning by injection."

Holder looked confused. "Nothing came up in the chemical analysis of her blood or urine."

"If my suspicions are correct, you wouldn't find anything, since the urine sample was not frozen." Dunham reached over and pointed to the woman's buttocks. "Do you see the two almost imperceptible tiny bruises on the victim's left buttocks?"

Holder studied the photo for a moment. "Yes."

"I believe these are well-placed needle-puncture sites," Dunham explained.

Holder took a closer look at the photo and gasped. "I believe you're right, Edward. Needle-puncture sites were off our radar screen since we initially saw no obvious marks and focused on poisoning through ingestion. Are you thinking this nurse would have the medical knowledge to inject a poison we don't normally test for?"

"Exactly," Dunham answered. "And the habit of a nurse would be to administer it in a normal injection area, like the buttocks. And succinyl choline, the paralytic drug used in surgery, fits the bill." He paused. "A critical care nurse would be very familiar with this drug."

"Now I see why you asked if the urine sample was frozen," Holder replied. "The half-life of that extremely reactive drug is only minutes, even seconds long. After a day or so, none is left in the body, post-mortem." He shook his head. "This means we're screwed."

Dunham grinned. "But the metabolite will be present; succinylmonocholine. It's the byproduct of the reaction. Luckily, they collected urine and blood samples prior to embalming the body, so if the metabolite is present, it would only have come from succinyl choline."

Holder beamed. "And this metabolite would not be detected in our normal analysis unless we were specifically targeting it."

Dunham leaned toward Holder. "You never were good at toxicology," he teased.

"Screw you, Dunham," Holder shot back in jest, then quickly got out of his seat, folding the file up. "Seriously though. Thanks, Edward. I'll let you know what we find. See ya."

Dunham sat back in his seat and watched Holder leave the cafeteria. Just as he exited, a woman in her late thirties with short, curly, jet-black hair and matching glasses rushed in. Heather Kennedy stared right at Dunham, clearly excited. One of his subordinate forensic scientists, Heather worked out of the Evidence Control room with Jack Stride. Dunham knew her as extremely organized and methodical, and he had to admit, she kept his absentmindedness in check.

"Hi, Heather."

"Hi, Dr. Dunham," Heather responded breathlessly. "Boston is finally knocking on your door."

Dunham sat up quickly, realizing Heather was referring to the Boston October Serial Killer case he was so interested in. "Oh?"

Heather nodded. "The public affairs officer for the Massachusetts governor is in the assistant director's office as we speak. He sent me here to get you." She handed him an iPhone and stared at him over her glasses. "He tried calling you, but of course, you left your cell phone on your desk."

Dunham reddened slightly as he stood up. "Of course. What would I do without you, Heather?"

Heather gave the impression that caring for him was bothersome, but he knew she loved rescuing him in small ways.

"I'll meet you back in the lab after my meeting," Dunham said as he started to walk away, but then he turned back. "Oh, Heather, Jack just came in from the airport and is waiting for me to give my opinion on his St. Louis case. Could you let him know what's happening?"

Heather nodded and hurried off.

Five minutes later, Dunham knocked on Assistant Director Peters' door and walked in. Peters was at his desk, and the public affairs officer was seated facing him on the opposite side. Dunham's boss was a tall, handsome, athletic, man always dressed in expensive dark suits. Although Peters rose in the ranks of the FBI as a special agent, he was very comfortable rubbing elbows with high-ranking elected officials in Washington, DC. Dunham thought Peters was the perfect liaison between the political decision-makers and federal law enforcement.

"Did you call for me, sir?"

Keeping his seat, Peters waved Dunham in. "Dr. Dunham, come take a seat."

Dunham sat next to the public affairs officer and nodded to her. He immediately noticed how attractive she was, especially in her form-fitting professional dress suit, glasses, and tied-back brunette hair. *The perfect image for a public affairs officer*, he thought.

"Dr. Dunham this is Anne Jackson, public affairs officer for Governor Brussel of Massachusetts." Both exchanged greetings. "She's traveled this far in order to speak with you personally."

"Yes, Dr. Dunham," Jackson began. "As you may know, the October serial killer has begun his fourth season of murder, mutilating someone on October 4 near Fenway Park, and he's just kidnapped someone else yesterday. The task force is still no closer to finding the killer than they were the first year."

Dunham nodded. "I am somewhat familiar with the case, but the FBI's not been involved, other than forensic testing on some physical evidence."

"That's why I'm here, Dr. Dunham," Jackson replied. "You see, the governor and the Boston mayor, Tom Grisanti, don't see eye-to-eye on this case. When the task force made no headway in the investigation last year, the governor contacted the mayor and challenged his decision not to involve the FBI. He specifically asked Grisanti why he hadn't contacted you."

"I did offer my assistance, they refused. I'm not sure why . . ."

"It's because of Dr. Gillespie, the famous criminal profiler," Jackson answered.

"The star of the *Criminal Profiler* television series that's been running for years?" Peters asked. "That criminal profiler?"

Jackson nodded. "None other, and if you've seen the show, you'll know he operates out of Boston. He is very close friends with the mayor and Superintendent of Police Andrew Sepanski. When the October serial killer began his second season of murders, the police superintendent got in front of the news camera shoulder-to-shoulder with Dr. Gillespie and announced to God and country that the famous criminal profiler was joining the serial killer task force."

"That wasn't a bad idea," Dunham commented. "Dr. Gillespie is one of the founders of modern criminal profiling. We in the FBI have been heavily influenced by him."

"Well, he's also an egomaniac, and you, Dr. Dunham, are the new wonder boy in violent crime investigation and serial offenders. Gillespie's been the king of the hill for decades, but his joining the team has gotten them nowhere. If you show up and solve the case, you may not only steal the show, but you'll embarrass the master in the process."

"I see," Dunham replied.

"That's only half of it," Jackson continued. "Now your involvement is a political disaster waiting to happen, in their eyes. Police Superintendent Sepanski—and the mayor by proxy—put all their eggs in the unsuccessful Gillespie basket. A publicly announced bad decision is political suicide, and it seems they did it. Sadly, the killer never being caught might be better politically—for them—than if you came and caught the killer." She paused. "The governor could care less about Boston politics, and honestly, is fed up with it, so yesterday, he directed the mayor to request you. He wanted me to get here first and let you know what you're up against."

"Quite the pickle," Dunham said.

"I hope this doesn't cause you to reject our request. We need you."

"Oh no, I would be honored to assist," Dunham remarked.

"I believe I have a solution where the mayor, superintendent of police, and Gillespie can all save face, and Dr. Dunham still gets involved," Peters said.

"Oh?" Jackson turned and leaned forward earnestly.

Peters glanced over at Dunham with his index finger pointed in the air. "Instead of Dr. Dunham joining the task force, we'll just have him operate out of the local Boston FBI office and be used in an advisory role. We'll tell them Dr. Dunham requests anonymity in order to work more efficiently."

Dunham nodded his agreement. "Special Agent in Charge Dean Carnie, of the Boston office, is a friend of mine. I'd love to work alongside Dean again."

"Excellent," Jackson replied. "I'll inform the governor that you're assisting with the case. It'll make his year. Oh, but it's best that the mayor does not know of my visit with you, so they'll still be contacting you to extend the invitation."

"I understand," Dunham replied.

Jackson stood up to leave. "And I'd recommend you emphasize the anonymity part. Thank you and goodbye, gentlemen."

As Jackson walked out, Dunham received a text and peeked at his phone. "Excellent!"

"What's excellent?" Peters asked.

"Dr. Holder asked for my assistance in a tough case," Dunham explained. "I told them if the blood and urine samples contained a certain metabolite, then the husband murdered the wife. He just texted me to let me know they found the metabolite. It looks like my assistance paid off."

"Why am I not surprised," Peters joked. "Have fun in Boston and say hi to Dean Carnie for me."

chapter seven

PRESENT DAY: October 9. South Boston, Massachusetts—Cathedral of the Holy Cross

Father Theodore Martin felt at peace kneeling in the pew of the cathedral as he finished his morning prayers. He gazed up at the cathedral's century-and-a-half-old Gothic Revival architecture with its high, vaulted ceilings, supported by massive white arches. *Marvelous*, he thought as he blessed himself and stood.

He left the chapel and made his way into the basement, then walked down a long hallway and into a small, austere room consisting of little more than a bed and a desk. His Eminence, the archbishop of Boston, presided here, but it was the parish's rector, the Most Reverend Patrick O'Farrell, who'd set him up with these temporary quarters. Martin had not expected to take up residence here in Boston for three years, but his task, assigned to him by the Holy Father himself, was far from accomplished. Father O'Farrell had been exceedingly kind, and so had His Eminence, as both understood the seriousness of his mission. O'Farrell, a fellow member of the International Association of Exorcists, was responsible for recommending Martin to lead this particular spiritual investigation.

Knock, knock, knock.

Startled, Father Martin peered at the door, walked over, and opened it to reveal Father O'Farrell with his usual kind grin. To O'Farrell's left was an older, shorter priest who seemed very familiar.

"Father O'Farrell," Martin said. "How are you?" As he greeted O'Farrell, it dawned on him who the other priest was: the president of the International Association of Exorcists, Father Andrea Giordano, the personal exorcist to the pope himself.

"Fine, fine, Father Martin." O'Farrell presented the older priest: "You remember Father Giordano."

"Yes, yes, of course!" Father Martin blurted out, then bent humbly. He dutifully kissed Giordano's hand. "I am honored, Father Giordano."

Giordano placed his other hand on Martin's face, then spoke in an Italian accent. "I am also honored, Father Martin."

"Please, come in," Martin said.

"Father Giordano has just come in from the Vatican," O'Farrell explained, "and wanted to meet with you, personally."

Martin nodded, visibly flattered.

"Have you been praying, Father Martin?" Giordano asked.

"Yes, Father. Twice a day, and often more."

"Good, good," Giordano said. "We are dealing with a malevolent spirit, freed from the restraints of the Evil One. Faith is our true weapon." Giordano glanced over at O'Farrell.

"As you are fully aware, Father Martin," O'Farrell added, "the murder run has entered its fourth year, and according to your reports, there has been little progress in the investigation—the task force's or yours."

Martin nodded. "Yes, Father. Perhaps I am not up to the task. Surely, there are others—"

"Nonsense!" Giordano interrupted angrily, then slowly smiled to ease the sting. "Father Martin, you are our best investigator," he paused for a moment, "and your charism is tailor-made for this anomaly; a true godsend."

"I understand, Father, but I have not had the opportunity to use my ability, my charism, as you say. The anomaly is extremely elusive, and I believe it's because the human host is someone with extraordinary skills."

"Father Giordano came to the same conclusion months ago, which, if true, requires someone with equally extraordinary skills to lead you to the anomaly," O'Farrell explained. "We have found such a man—the Watchmaker."

Father Martin tilted his head in confusion, aware of the Watchmaker's reputation but unable to make sense of his suggested involvement. "Forgive my ignorance, Father, but Dr. Dunham is an FBI special agent and forensic scientist. His superiors would never allow him to assist the Church in a spiritual matter."

O'Farrell and Giordano grinned. "We believe we have discovered a solution," O'Farrell said. "This is where Church affairs align with State affairs. The Massachusetts governor is very spiritual and has been a close friend of the cardinal's for years. We asked His Eminence if he would contact the governor and request that Dr. Dunham intervene in the Boston October Serial Killer Case, and he did. Word has it that the governor has just ordered the mayor to involve the FBI, specifically, the Watchmaker."

Martin nodded. "I understand. I will follow their investigation from a distance and just wait for Dr. Dunham to find the host."

"Precisely," O'Farrell replied.

Martin frowned. "They have no idea the destructive power of this evil spirit." He paused. "If they were aware of this, maybe they could be prepared. It might avert some unnecessary deaths."

O'Farrell shook his head. "I am sorry, Father. Our directives are clear. We need to keep this confidential, even from the FBI and the task force."

Martin took a deep breath then exhaled and nodded. "I will just have to keep close tabs on their progress and be ready."

"The Holy Father has great faith in you, Father Martin," Giordano replied. "May I join you in prayer tonight?"

"Of course, Father," Martin replied. "I would be honored."

chapter eight

PRESENT DAY: 9:15 p.m., October 10. Downtown Boston,
Massachusetts—Ghost & Gravestones Frightseeing Tour, Old Town
Trolley Stop #1

"Come on, Frank!" his wife, Betty, yelled in a high-pitched voice.

The obese man walked slowly across the Long Wharf toward his short,
chubby, middle-aged wife.

"The trolley will be here soon!" the curly-haired brunette called from fifty
yards away.

"I'm coming; I'm coming," Frank replied lazily to Betty as he stopped for
a moment and sipped on his soft drink. "It's not supposed to start for another
fifteen minutes."

A few minutes later, Frank finally met up with his wife, who was frowning
and standing at the street corner with over two dozen other people. He grinned
smugly. "See, Betty, I'm here." He took a sip of his drink again and glanced
around. "So, where is this haunted trolley, anyway?"

Betty pointed at the ticket counter across the sidewalk. "It's two trolleys,
and the guy behind the ticket counter said they'll be here any minute now."

Frank peered up into the night sky. "Clear sky tonight, and no wind. What
a perfect evening to traipse around in old graveyards. Not too cold either."

"Did you go to the bathroom, Frank?" Betty blurted out loud enough for everyone in the crowd to hear. "You know you have a bladder problem, and the tour is an hour and a half long."

"I'm fine; I'm fine," Frank replied, touching his stomach. "It's just that I think that fish gave me gas. My stomach's acting up." He belched.

The couple nearest to Frank and Betty frowned at each other, then casually moved to the other side of the crowd.

"Oh, here they come," Betty said. As she stared down the street, she could make out two old black trolleys trundling toward them. The first trolley blasted its horn, blaring an irritating but comical sound. As the trolleys abruptly stopped before them, she could see that they were filled with tourists, and everyone on-board was laughing and cheering. The first person out of the front trolley was a lady dressed in an old white wedding gown spattered with bloodstains. She had what appeared to be a long, bleeding scar along her neck. She was extremely animated, yelling at everyone to get their lousy butts off the trolley.

The people made their way down the steps, continuously thanking the lady in the wedding gown for such a great tour. After the last person left the trolley, she turned her gaze toward Frank, Betty, and the rest of the crowd waiting for the next tour.

"Aha! My next victims!" She pointed at everyone. "Don't move!" she ordered in a low, scratchy voice.

A man with what seemed to be a gaping wound on his forehead, dressed in a ghoulish costume, approached her ominously. She whispered to the man, then both slowly turned their gazes toward the group of tourists.

"Good evening, ladies and gentlemen," she said. "This fine gentleman next to me is Anthraxicon, the Death Bringer!" She paused. "He is our resident demon and has a taste for blood!"

Anthraxicon gave a deep bow. "It is a pleasure to meet you poor souls! I will be your tour guide in the back trolley; the Trolley of the Doomed." He pointed back to the lady in the white wedding gown. "And this fine lady is Constance Caskette!" Constance made a dramatic curtsey. "She is your tour guide in the front trolley, the Trolley of the Damned." He paused, then with an evil stare, he continued, "But I warn you now! Her first five husbands died on their wedding day, and she's looking for husband number six!"

At that moment she pinched Anthraxicon's buttocks.

"Ouch!" he screamed, grasping his rear with both hands and jumping forward. The crowd laughed as she gave a mischievous grin.

Constance pointed to the two trolleys. "Now, hop on the trolleys! Fine-looking gentlemen, up front with me please." She gave an evil laugh, then rubbed a male tourist on the shoulder. As Frank and Betty were about to walk onto the front trolley, Constance yanked Frank's drink out of his hands, surprising him. She flashed her darkened red eyes flirtatiously. "Want it back?" she asked, then bent toward him and whispered loud enough for Betty and everyone else to hear. "Then get rid of the broad and sit up front with me!"

Everyone laughed, and Frank merely stood there with a dumbfounded look on his face.

Constance hissed at Frank and gave the drink back to him. "Fine then! Get onboard with your lady!"

After a few minutes, everyone had boarded the trolleys, and they departed. Constance stood, holding onto the foremost pole located in the aisle between the two front seats. "Good evening, everyone, and welcome to Old Town Trolley's Ghosts and Gravestones Frightseeing Tour," Constance began in a deep, scary voice. "A tour like no other tour you've ever taken!" She walked through the aisle, eyeing each tourist as she spoke. "We are going to walk amongst the dead in nearly four-hundred-year-old burial grounds." She paused and thrust her face in front of one of the tourists. "You all will be kicking and screaming through Boston's haunted past as you hear about its darker side." She stared around the crowd with a wicked grin. "If you don't believe in ghosts, you will after tonight!"

After a five-minute drive, the trolleys stopped on the side of the road near an old cemetery. "Follow me, everyone!" Constance yelled excitedly. "It's time to mingle with the dead and experience mortal remains beneath your feet!" Everyone followed Constance into the old cemetery. Anthraxicon and his group met up with them, and Constance led the way while her colleague trailed in the back.

Betty glanced down at a gravestone. "Look, Frank. These gravestones have skulls with wings on them."

Frank nodded. "I bet the wings mean that their souls are flying into the afterlife," he replied.

Constance stopped. "Come around, everyone! Come around!" she yelled. Once everyone surrounded her, she began to speak. "You are standing in the second-oldest cemetery in Boston, the Copp's Hill Burying Ground, founded in 1659, but be careful!" She paused and glanced to her left and right. "Many a visitor has spotted a specter or two hovering in thin air, AND!" she screamed, "these gravestones are guarded by the ghost of Increase Mather."

At that moment, Anthraxicon leaped out from behind a large tombstone and screamed, "Blahhh!"

Startled tourists jumped back and screamed, then laughed once they realized it was the costumed ghoul joking with them.

Anthraxicon flashed a big grin, walked up to Constance, paused, then pointed animatedly at a tomb to the left.

"To your right, we have the Mather tomb, where Cotton Mather rests in peace next to his father, Increase." Anthraxicon crouched with his hands extended forward. "If one man could be blamed for the Salem witch trials and resulting torture and hangings, it's Cotton Mather!" Anthraxicon followed with a short but thrilling history lesson on the Salem witch trials. After fifteen minutes of Anthraxicon and Constance showing the gravestones of historical figures and expounding their scary, real-life stories, they led the tourists back to their trolleys.

A few minutes later, the trolleys stopped again, and everyone exited onto the sidewalk. Anthraxicon grabbed the old wrought-iron fence adjacent to the sidewalk, then pointed over the fence.

"Ladies and gentlemen, set your gaze upon a place where evil flourished in the past and abounds to this day! The Boston Common!" He paused. "Untold thousands are buried here. The Boston Common is the oldest public park in the United States, established in 1634 after the Puritan colonists bought this land from an Anglican minister named William Blaxton, who had been part of an earlier failed expedition to colonize America. The condition of the sale was that no private individual could own it; therefore, it became 'common' land." Anthraxicon stared into the face of one tourist. "But that's not why you're here!" He pointed toward Arlington Street. "For years trolley drivers have reported seeing ghostly apparitions in red coats, and just recently a mass grave of British casualties from the Revolutionary War was discovered at that very spot!" He paused and stared at the crowd. "Quite a coincidence if there's no such thing as ghosts." He turned toward Constance.

Constance pointed at a plaque in the park. "Up until the storm of 1769, a massive tree called the Great Elm stood at the very spot where you now see a plaque." She turned back to the crowd. "The Great Elm was used for public hangings of murderers, pirates, thieves, and—" she paused—"even witches. After the tree fell, they erected gallows in its place to continue the public hangings. If family members wanted a Christian burial, they had to publicly admit that their convicted family member was guilty. If not, the body was tossed in the Charles River." Constance motioned for Anthraxicon to continue.

"So, the family members would wait at night, secretly dig a shallow grave in or near the Common and bury their departed loved one!" He paused. "How do we know this? Because hundreds of bodies with broken necks have been found buried all around here!" He paused again for effect, then waved his audience back. "It's time to visit the Granary Burying Ground and mingle with the ghosts of John Hancock and Paul Revere."

Everyone boarded the trolleys once more, and the tour group continued to the cemetery.

Anthraxicon and Constance led the crowd of tourists through an Egyptian-style stone gate entrance to the Granary Burying Ground. It consisted of two stone pillars on each side, supporting an overhead horizontal stone block adorned with a motif of a winged skull. They walked through the cemetery and stopped deep inside at a large, flat illuminated monument. Aged gravestones and tombs surrounded the area.

A man in a Victorian-Age costume leaped onto the monument, surprising a few of the tourists.

"Good evening, ladies and gentlemen. My name is Jonathan Percival Goodspeed; mortician at your service." He took a deep bow, then faced the crowd. "You are standing in Boston's third-oldest cemetery, founded in 1660. Around you are 2,345 graves, but there are well over 8,000 people buried here!"

Frank frowned. "I don't get it. How can that be?" he asked Goodspeed.

Goodspeed grinned. "As generations of people passed on to the afterlife, the cemetery eventually filled up. Desiring to be buried at the Granary Burying Ground, family members would secretly dig up a gravesite and place their departed loved one on top of the current resident, creating a pancake effect of caskets."

Betty glanced up at Frank, frowning. "How disgusting!"

Frank nodded, then spotted a movement over her head between two distant gravestones. Silhouetted against the streetlights was the shape of a human . . . or two. As Goodspeed began to talk about the resident grave of Paul Revere, Frank continued to watch the silhouette. It soon became apparent to him that he was watching a man hovering over a limp body, doing something to the head or shoulders.

He eased toward Anthraxicon and Constance, who were sitting on a monument behind their patrons. When he approached, they both stared at him to acknowledge his attention. Frank pointed at the silhouette. "Is that part of the act?" Both glanced over to where Frank was pointing.

"Is what part of the act?" Anthraxicon asked as he glanced over. "Yes, that tall monument is John Hancock's gravesite."

Frank shook his head. "No, not that. Look to the left, just between the monument and the fence."

Anthraxicon stared in the direction Frank was pointing. "Oh, that." He watched the movement, then got up. "I don't know what that is," he said as he walked toward it.

While Anthraxicon made his way toward the distant streetlights, Frank saw that the man had vanished, but the body on the ground was still there. Seconds later, he saw Anthraxicon shine his lamp upon the body, and then quickly back off and fall back against a tree, clearly agitated. The faux ghoul stood motionless, staring straight ahead, then he shook his head quickly. Frank saw Anthraxicon pull out his cell phone, tap on it, then put it to his ear.

"Something must be up," Frank said to Constance.

"I'd think so, for him to break character," Constance replied, equally aware of Anthraxicon's unusual behavior. "Here he comes."

Anthraxicon rushed back. "Everyone!" he yelled. "Everyone, including you, Goodspeed. We all need to get back onto the trolleys at once! Hurry, and stay together!"

Constance and Goodspeed approached Anthraxicon. "What's up?" Constance whispered.

He stared into Constance's eyes, glanced at Goodspeed, and continued. "That person's dead; murdered!" he whispered anxiously. "And whoever killed them is still around!"

Constance and Goodspeed became noticeably anxious; Frank watched in stunned silence, mouth dangling open.

"Wait; how do you know they're dead?" Goodspeed asked.

"Let's go, everyone! Let's go!" Anthraxicon yelled, seemingly ignoring Goodspeed's question. But then he turned back to him. "Because her head is cut off, and there's blood still coming out of it!"

Goodspeed's jaw dropped, he glanced over at Constance, then he bolted in a full sprint to the closest trolley, Frank lumbering along behind the group of ghouls.

An hour later, Detective Lieutenant Nate Huff stood staring down at the victim, now surrounded by a team of crime scene specialists taking photos and collecting physical evidence. He was a tall, stout man with a prominent jaw line. Years of sailing in the harsh sun gave his face a tanned, worn appearance. He was no-nonsense and had little patience for ineptitude.

The Granary Burying Ground was now teeming with police officers and crime scene investigators, illuminated by the flashing, colored lights of dozens of police cars.

"Detective Sergeant!" Huff belted out. "Where's the profiler, Gillespie?"

Squatting next to one of the forensic experts was Detective Sergeant Brad Sadler, who stood up immediately when his boss barked at him. Sadler was of medium stature, balding, his remaining hair dark, his shiny bare scalp a subtle indication that he was nearing retirement. He knew Huff depended upon his knowledge and wisdom, which came from years of grueling detective work; he enjoyed this role. Sadler glanced down the hill at the entrance to the cemetery.

"He's coming up the trail as we speak, Lieutenant." Sadler grinned. "Oh great; he's got the police commissioner's yes-man as an escort."

Huff turned and spotted Dr. Gillespie and Deputy Superintendent Hurley making their way up the hill. "Indeed. It must suck for Gillespie, being the famous Boston criminal profiler, promising the public that he was going to take the lead and root out this October serial killer," he paused, "only to be the object of embarrassment after three years of endless dead ends."

"Oh, lay off him, will ya, boss?" Sadler replied. "It must be tough being the star of a TV show and claiming to be the only reason why incompetent detectives, like us, catch violent criminals."

Huff turned and grinned at Sadler. "You're worse than I am, Sergeant."

Sadler cocked his head. "Although, ya gotta admit. The guy's usually good at his job."

Huff glanced back at Gillespie and Hurley, still out of earshot. "It's too bad the egomaniac is not a team player and only rubs elbows with the top brass. I hear he's not too happy about the governor ordering our mayor to bring the Watchmaker in on the case."

Sadler waved to a nearby police officer. "Officer Crouch."

"Yeah, Sarge," Crouch responded, walking up to Sadler.

Sadler pointed at the crowd of pedestrians standing near the cemetery fence. "Grab a couple of officers and push the crowd back to the sidewalk. I don't want anyone trampling over evidence."

"You got it, Sarge." Crouch rushed off.

Huff fixed his attention upon Gillespie and Hurley as they neared. "Good evening, gentlemen."

Both Hurley and Gillespie nodded inattentively.

"Lieutenant," Hurley replied. Deputy Superintendent Hurley was a relatively tall man. He was dressed in a high-end suit and coat; his usual attire. His shoes shined so much they could reflect light even in the dark cemetery.

He and Gillespie walked by Huff and straight to the victim.

"What do you think, Dr. Gillespie?" Hurley asked.

Gillespie bent down, then glanced up at Huff and Sadler. "I apologize for being late, gentlemen. Problems with filming my next show. You'd think by now they'd know what I require in order to make a successful scene."

Huff shot a quick, sarcastic grin to Sadler, rolling his eyes. "None too soon, Dr. Gillespie."

Gillespie glanced over at the crime scene specialists cataloging the victim and searching for physical evidence. "All right; what do you have for me, and don't miss a detail."

"Well, Dr. Gillespie," one of the specialists began, "as you can see, the victim was decapitated, which by the blood flow pattern indicates that it was the cause of death; definitely not a post-mortem mutilation. Stab wound in the chest, and as expected, a rutabaga is stuffed in her mouth." He paused. "Estimated time of death is maybe an hour ago."

"Three witnesses caught the perpetrator hovering over the body about an hour ago," Sadler interrupted. As Gillespie glanced up at him, he pointed across the cemetery. "They were about forty yards away over in that direction, just past Paul Revere's grave. It was too dark to make out the details of the perpetrator, but streetlights in the distance allowed them to see he was doing something to the body. They could tell he was a large male. He vanished, and none of them saw which direction he left the crime scene."

Gillespie glanced up at Hurley. "Clearly, this is our October serial killer continuing his fourth season of victims. No mistaking his signature, especially the rutabaga jammed in her mouth." Gillespie glanced back at the victim and shook his head. "And just like the last thirteen crime scenes, there will likely be little evidence recovered. The methodical bastard. In all, no change to the pattern."

"Well, Dr. Gillespie, as usual, your criminal profile is rich in detail, so maybe this'll eventually break the case," Hurley complimented the TV star.

Huff's cell phone rang. "Lieutenant Huff," he answered, then glanced behind himself at an SUV parked in the road with its lights on. "Excellent, Special Agent Carnie. Come on up." Huff glanced back at Hurley, Gillespie, and Sadler as he put his cell phone away. "That was FBI Special Agent Carnie; special agent in charge of the local FBI office. He's got Dr. Dunham with him, and they're coming up."

A hush settled over the scene, and everyone at the crime scene abruptly stopped what they were doing, shot a quick glance at Huff, then stared at the two men coming from the SUV.

"Finally," Sadler commented.

Huff noticed that Gillespie and Hurley were frowning slightly, seemingly pretending to ignore Dunham's approach.

"Who contacted the FBI!" Hurley yelled angrily. "Did anyone get the police commissioner's permission?"

Huff shook his head in disgust. "I did, sir. I was assigned as task force leader, which means I make the call. You and I both know the mayor was directed by the governor to include them in the investigation. Did you want me to get the mayor into hot water? I can call him, if you'd like."

Hurley said nothing, glared at Huff for a moment, took out his cell phone, then turned and walked a short distance away.

Sadler snickered, impressed as hell that the lieutenant had balls of steel.

"Dr. Dunham is more than welcome to review my conclusions and further his criminal profiling knowledge base," Gillespie commented.

Carnie and Dunham approached Huff. "Lieutenant Huff, nice to see you again," Carnie said in a deep voice. "Although I wish it was under different circumstances."

Huff, a tall man himself, looked up at Carnie and scanned his appearance. Carnie was clearly a very athletic man. Not only was he probably six foot two, Huff thought, he had powerful-looking shoulders and a trim waste. He shook Carnie's hand and cringed in pain, but he grinned. "Nice to see you, Special Agent Carnie. Your grip is off though," he teased.

Carnie laughed. "Sorry, Lieutenant. Nice to see you, again."

"Still running those triathlons, I see."

"It's Cross-Fit these days."

Huff pointed to a thirty-plus-story office building just to the east. "So, why'd you drive here? The FBI office is a hundred yards away."

He pointed with an open hand toward Dunham. "I had to pick up Dr. Dunham from his hotel near the Wharf." He paused. "Lieutenant, I finally get to introduce you to Dr. Edward Dunham."

Huff shook Dunham's hand. "It's great to finally meet you, Dr. Dunham. I hope you can help out." He instantly registered the intensity in Dunham's eyes; a penetrating, all-knowing stare.

"Dr. Dunham," Carnie continued, "this is Lieutenant Nate Huff. He is head of the serial killer task force. Everything goes through him."

"It's nice to meet you, Lieutenant Huff," Dunham said.

Huff waved Sadler over. "This is my sidekick, Detective Sergeant Brad Sadler."

"Your reputation precedes you, Dr. Dunham," Sadler complimented. "It's a pleasure to meet you."

Dunham nodded. "You as well, Detective Sergeant."

Huff tilted his head at Hurley, who was still speaking to someone on his cell phone. "Over there is Deputy Superintendent Hurley."

Hurley turned at the sound of his name and waved them off impatiently.

"Dr. Dunham," Gillespie interrupted, still squatting next to the victim. "Come here. Come here."

Dunham glanced down. "Hello, Dr. Gillespie. I am honored to finally meet you," he said as he joined his new colleague on the ground.

Sadler leaned over and whispered to Huff. "Holy shit! Did you get a load of his friggin' eyes? It's like he knew I cheated on my diet today."

Huff smirked and nodded in agreement.

Dunham shook Gillespie's hand. "Thank you, Dr. Dunham. I hear your training has finally come to fruition. Congratulations on the Niagara Falls Ripper Case last year."

"Thank you, Dr. Gillespie. Strangely enough, you helped. We did a case study in 2005 at the FBI serial murder symposium on a particular case you profiled, which had amazing parallels with the case."

Gillespie nodded. "I'm glad to be of service. I have another book coming out soon. I hope that one comes in handy as well."

Huff grinned to himself, knowing full well that Dunham was purposely stroking Gillespie's ego, and it seemed to be working.

"Special Agent Carnie has briefed me on the October Serial Killer Case," Dunham explained, "and I read a general outline of your forensic behavioral assessment of the offender. Brilliant analysis, in my opinion." He pointed at the victim. "How does this compare?"

Gillespie paused to think, still staring at the victim. "I stand by those conclusions, and I see nothing here that alters them in any way." Gillespie gazed around the cemetery. "Let's start with the crime scene characteristics. The offender exhibits organized traits. It's clearly a planned secondary crime scene after kidnapping his victim, albeit this is where the homicide occurred. This pattern is nearly identical to his previous offenses. He kidnaps his victim, holds them for three days, then murders and mutilates them at a selected location; every one of them is outdoors, and most in a wooded location. The decapitated head is placed next to the victim's left shoulder, and a small portion of wheat and fruit are next to the right shoulder. All of the locations are in public, highly visible places like parks and cemeteries, which suggests he is attempting to instill fear into the public, increasing his feeling of power and control. Very methodical with a high level of forensic awareness." He glanced up at Dunham from over his glasses. "We believe he wears latex gloves because we see many smudge marks but never any fingerprints."

Dunham nodded. "Excellent. How about victimology?"

Gillespie continued. "The offender selects both males and females with no observable selection pattern in age or physical characteristics. This, plus the fact that there's no evidence of sexual abuse, pre- or post-mortem, suggests his motive is something other than sado-sexual. All of the victims lived in the area, spanning various socioeconomic backgrounds." He raised his finger. "A small rutabaga is jammed into the victim's mouth, post-mortem. I'm convinced that the rutabaga connects each successive victim with the offender's very first victim three years ago. He was the president of the Rutabaga Capital Management Company, a financial investment firm. This now seems to be his calling card."

Dunham nodded in agreement.

"We're keeping that piece of evidence out of the papers, Dr. Dunham," Huff interrupted. "If some correspondence shows up on our doorstep with the author claiming to be the killer and it mentions the rutabaga, then we'll know it's authentic."

Dunham nodded, then glanced over at Gillespie. "How about your offender analysis, Dr. Gillespie?"

"There are no apparent connections among the victims, other than all being Greater Boston residents." He shook his head. "No; he didn't know them personally," he paused, "and there's no indication of escalation of emotion at the crime scenes. This clearly fits into the 'stranger' category specific to the offender-victim relationship," he addressed the non-experts, "as opposed to the 'intimate' category."

Dunham nodded.

Gillespie cocked his head. "It's undeniably ritual, with no evidence of an evolving MO pattern or signature. The exact steps of the ritual are important to him, suggesting a strong belief system. He ended each 'killing season' on Halloween night." He shook his head. "The Halloween connection seems to suggest a belief in the authority of evil. If it's a satanic ritual it's unique, since it doesn't bear the hallmarks of any modern satanic organization, even the groups that promote human sacrifice. Lastly, the wheat and fruit seem to be some kind of harvest offering."

"Interesting," Dunham said, then paused. "How about schizophrenia?" he asked Gillespie.

Gillespie's eyes opened wide. After a moment of contemplation on the question, he regained his composure. "Nothing apparent, but things may develop as the evidence allows."

Dunham pointed his open hand at the victim. "May I?" he asked.

"Of course," Gillespie replied, then waved the forensic team off. "Everyone, give Dr. Dunham some room."

The other crime scene specialists moved out of the way as Dunham crouched closer to the victim. Everyone in the near vicinity abruptly stopped what they were doing and placed their full attention on Dunham.

Dunham first studied the body from top to bottom, noting the knife wound in the chest area and the decapitated head next to the left shoulder, then shifted to the right shoulder and examined the wheat and fruit. He looked up at Gillespie, Huff, and everyone else. "Just as Dr. Gillespie has concluded; this is a satanic sacrificial murder, but with no connection to any modern Satanists. The offender is offering a sacrifice to Lucifer—or Satan, the fallen angel—and with an unusual level of biblical knowledge."

"What do you mean?" Huff asked.

"Modern atheistic Satanists worship nature, not Lucifer, so they don't offer sacrifices as this offender is doing. Certain theistic Satanists do, but Halloween is of no real significance to them, nor is there any evidence here of their flavor of ritualism. The offering of wheat, grapes, and figs was given to God by Cain, the eldest son of Adam, but it was rejected, preferring instead the animal sacrifice offered by Abel. Along with the human sacrifice, this offering of wheat and fruit would certainly please the enemy of God. Also, notice that there are six heads of wheat, above one fig, with six grapes at the bottom." Dunham glanced up at Gillespie, Huff, and Sadler. "Is this consistent at every crime scene?"

Huff looked over at Sadler and Gillespie. "I'm not sure."

"I believe so," Gillespie answered.

"Why?" Huff asked. "It's not like a six-six-six satanic number pattern."

"Well, if this pattern is indeed consistent at each murder site, then there's a reason behind it," Dunham explained. "The very oldest existing ancient texts of the Book of Revelation do not have as the mark of the beast the numbers six, six, six. Instead, it is written as six, one, six." Dunham pointed down at the wheat and fruit. "Here we have six heads of wheat, one fig, and six grapes. It might not be a coincidence."

In his peripheral, Dunham saw Sadler catch Huff's eye, and the two nodded and grinned at each other.

Dunham turned his attention to the victim's head, took out a flashlight and magnifying glass from his pocket, and examined her mouth. "That certainly is a rutabaga, and I see the three circular cuts in it."

"The rutabaga in each victim had cuts on it, but none were alike," a forensic expert said.

Dunham analyzed the cheekbones. "What?" Dunham popped his head up and scanned the area, illuminating it with his flashlight; then he studied the face again. "Lieutenant Huff, where were the eyewitnesses positioned when they spotted the offender?"

Huff turned and pointed at the flat monument. "Forty or so yards back there, and no one saw him leave."

Dunham turned in the opposite direction and stared into a dark area between the front fence and the adjoining building.

Sadler leaned closer to Huff. "I think he's onto something," he whispered.

Huff nodded and took a step closer to Dunham.

Dunham turned toward Huff. "There is a minute amount of white powder on the victim's cheek. If Dr. Gillespie is correct that our offender always wears gloves, these gloves might be the source of the powder. Since talcum powder is used inside medical latex gloves," Dunham stood up and paused, "it seems he may have taken his gloves off in order to touch the victim's face. If so . . ." He thought for a moment, then stared at Huff. "Do you have an alternate light source available? One that emits 300 nanometer wavelength UV radiation?"

Huff glanced toward the other forensic experts. "Do we?"

"Yes, we do," a crime scene specialist responded. "It's in our van."

"Well, get it!" Huff yelled impatiently.

The man nodded and rushed to the van.

"What are you thinking, Dr. Dunham?" Special Agent Carnie asked.

"Well, women's makeup fluoresces under high-energy UV radiation, specifically between 290 to 310 nanometers. The normal blacklight sold on the market does not emit in this range, since it's hazardous to human health." Dunham glanced again at the darkened area. "I believe our offender took his gloves off in order to touch the victim's face, and in doing so, some of the talcum powder landed on her cheek. If he has women's makeup on his fingers, he may have left his glowing fingerprints as he departed the scene. I see a wrought iron fence connecting the front fence to this building."

"That's the historical Park Church," Sadler interrupted.

Dunham continued, "These buildings to the right seem to block any obvious escape from the cemetery, while the front fence to the left is spiked, making it difficult to jump it." Dunham pointed to where the front fence connected to the church. "If the offender attempted to make the quickest and easiest escape possible, that section of the fence would have been his path. Notice there are no spikes on it."

Deputy Superintendent Hurley walked up to Gillespie, then whispered to him. Gillespie nodded in response, but both maintained their silence.

The crime scene expert returned with the alternate light source.

"I see where you're going with this, Dr Dunham," Huff replied and turned toward the man with the light. "You, light up that fence with the blacklight, and concentrate on the corner section." He glanced around. "I want a dozen eyes on it, so, everyone, follow him." Multiple specialists and police officers, including Sadler, followed the specialist to the fence.

"It's nighttime, so the fluorescence should be bright!" Dunham yelled.

"This is a tourist area, so we might see a few latent fingerprints," Hurley pointed out.

"Well, the good news for us," Dunham replied, "is that this crime scene isn't in a powder room." At their confused faces, he continued. "Women tend to touch up their makeup when they're near mirrors and sinks—like in a restroom—not outside, where touching their face would mess up their makeup, with no mirrors around to fix it." Dunham watched the forensics and police personnel as they scanned the fence. "There may be fingerprints, but they likely won't fluoresce. Even so, we're looking for male latent fingerprints. And if we do find one, we can compare the composition of the makeup with the victim's makeup."

"I'm curious, Dr. Dunham," Gillespie began, as all of the attention was now on the man with the alternate light source. "Why did you ask me if the offender showed tendencies of schizophrenia?"

"I believe your analysis is spot on, Dr. Gillespie," Dunham explained, "and two of the offender behaviors he exhibits seem to conflict with each other. First, the offender's forensic awareness is so acute that he shares behavioral tendencies with physical scientists—attacking everything methodically. Conflicting with this is his clear motive of ritualism. The last people to embrace anything ritualistically are physical scientists. I should know—I fit into this category. One of his personalities is a thinking rationalist, and the other is a heartfelt idealist."

Gillespie nodded slowly. "Hmmm."

"Reinforcing this," Dunham continued, "is the fact that the offender seems to put so much effort into protecting himself against being identified at the crime scene, but then recklessly takes his gloves off to touch her face."

"We got one!" Sadler shouted from the fence. "And it's a beauty!"

"Yes!" Huff hollered with excitement. As everyone rushed toward the fence, Huff saw that Hurley had his cell phone to his ear, most likely updating the police superintendent.

Huff held everyone back as the crime scene photographer took photos of the fluorescing fingerprint from multiple angles. "Send those latent fingerprint photos off immediately!" Huff ordered. "I want those submitted to every fingerprint database out there."

"Including the FBI's IAFIS database," Carnie added.

"Especially the IAFIS database," Huff replied.

"I'm sending them off to the lab electronically as we speak, Lieutenant," the photographer replied as he tapped on the back of the camera.

Carnie raised his hand. "And don't forget CODIS; that is, of course, if you do collect any DNA off the print or on the victim's cheek. Our DNA database increases daily."

"We have a plan, folks!" Huff yelled. "Let's get busy!"

"Congratulations, Dr. Dunham," Gillespie said in a reserved tone.

Dunham nodded and pointed toward Park Street. "It seems the offender exited in that direction, so maybe we'll get lucky and catch him on a street security camera."

"I already have officers on it, Dr. Dunham," Sadler interrupted.

"Great," Dunham replied.

"It seems the offender planned his escape route well," Gillespie interjected. "On the other side of Park Street is Boston Common; a large, nicely forested park with few security cameras."

"There's a traffic camera at the intersection just in front of the church, so if we do get lucky, it'll be from that one," Sadler added.

Gillespie nodded approvingly. "This offender seems to have an affinity for forested areas."

"Then it wouldn't hurt to search every inch of the Common," Huff remarked.

"Lieutenant Huff," Hurley said as he glanced toward the cemetery entrance. "I see the press is here. I don't want them anywhere near this print."

Huff nodded. "Detective Sergeant!"

"Already on it, boss," Sadler said as he dragged a few officers with him.

Dunham glanced over at the press flooding the front gate. "For the time being, Lieutenant Huff, I'd like to keep a low profile." He exchanged nods with Carnie and glanced back at Huff. "Special Agent Carnie and I will be leaving. May I come to the task force headquarters and look over your files on the case?"

"By all means, Dr. Dunham. I'll have the files ready for you first thing tomorrow morning."

Dunham and Carnie turned to leave. "Thank you, Lieutenant, although, I'll need a few days before coming in. I have some FBI records I'd like to look over first. I'll call you if I find anything."

"Even better," Huff replied. "We may have the results of the print analysis by then."

Dunham waved at everyone as he departed. "I hope to see everyone again." Lastly, he waved to Hurley and Gillespie. "Gentlemen."

Hurley joined Gillespie, and the two watched as Dunham entered Carnie's vehicle. "I didn't see anything special about him."

"We just lifted a fingerprint from the serial killer, sir," Huff replied from behind Hurley.

Hurly glared at Huff, apparently having overlooked him before commenting to Gillespie.

"The Watchmaker did more in twenty minutes than the entire task force has done in three years. I'd say that's special," Huff muttered as he walked away.

chapter nine

**PRESENT DAY: October 11. Downtown Boston, Massachusetts—
FBI Field Office, One Center Plaza**

Dunham reached the sixth floor of the tall office building, showed his identification at the front desk, and made his way to Special Agent in Charge Carnie's office. Carnie was sitting at his desk, dressed in his FBI physical fitness T-shirt and sweatpants.

Carnie, who was speaking on his cell phone, noticed Dunham at the door, gave him a smile, then waved him into his office. "Guess who just walked into my office?" Carnie asked the person on the other end of the line. He nodded. "That's right. I will." Carnie handed the phone to Dunham. "Someone wants to talk to you."

Dunham accepted the phone with a curious look at Carnie.

"Dr. Dunham speaking."

"Dr. Dunham!" the voice on the phone yelled. "It's great to hear your voice!"

Dunham beamed as he recognized the speaker. "Detective Riggs!" The last time he'd seen Detective Riggs was last year in Buffalo, New York, while working on the Niagara Falls Serial Killer Case. The task force commander had assigned Detective Riggs to Dunham for the duration of time he spent in Buffalo, and they'd developed a strong friendship. "How are you?"

"Couldn't be better," Riggs replied. "Buffalo's not the same without you though."

"I enjoyed Buffalo—I miss it," Dunham said. "Maggie wants to visit some-time and see Niagara Falls."

"Set it up!" Riggs yelled through the phone. "You certainly have a place to stay."

Dunham nodded. "I'll keep it in mind." He glanced over at Carnie. "So, how do you know Dean Carnie?"

"We're members of the same aikido organization, Wadokai. He's a fellow chief instructor for the organization—another fourth-degree black belt."

"Small world," Dunham replied.

"I told Dean to get you on the mats," Riggs said. "I worry that someday you'll need it. And besides, you promised me you'd try it!"

"I did, didn't I," Dunham admitted, and glanced over at Carnie. "Actually, I fully expected this fitness nut to get me off the couch, so I started jogging in preparation."

"Dean'll keep you fit for sure," Riggs agreed. "Gotta go. Take care, Dr. Dunham, and keep in touch."

Dunham nodded. "I will. Take care yourself, and say hi to Captain Johnson for me."

"Sure will," Riggs answered.

Dunham handed the phone back to Carnie.

"I'll see ya at summer camp, Riggs," Carnie said. "Take care." He hung up and looked at Dunham. "Perfect timing, Dr. Dunham. As you can see, I'm in my PT gear. A couple years ago, headquarters have me approval to teach aikido to the department." He reached down, grabbed a gym bag, and handed it to Dunham. "Now that I'm under orders from Riggs, it's time you try aikido. I figured you wouldn't come here with your sweats, so here's your PT gear. Follow me. We've got mats in the gym."

Dunham followed Carnie out. "I'm ready, but I didn't bring a pair of sneakers."

"Won't need 'em," Carnie answered. "We practice in bare feet for safety reasons."

After Dunham changed his clothes, they made their way to the gym in the basement, and Dunham saw through a huge glass wall about twenty fellow FBI agents wearing physical fitness gear, waiting for the class to start. Some were sitting or lying on the mats, and others were already practicing martial arts. When Carnie opened the glass door to the gym, the agents spotted Dunham, immediately stopped what they were doing, approached, and gave him a friendly greeting.

Carnie grinned. "Wow, it's like I brought a celebrity or something."

"And the Watchmaker isn't a celebrity, boss?" one of the agents asked jokingly.

Carnie laughed. "So true." He clapped his hands. "OK, line up!"

Everyone lined up into rows, and Dunham followed suit. Carnie was in the front directing their stretching and warm-up.

Carnie glanced over at Dunham. "After stretches and warm-ups, we're going to practice rolls and falls. Where people generally injure themselves on the mats is incorrectly rolling out of a technique being applied to them. It's mutual welfare and benefit to both the person applying the technique *and* to the person having the technique applied to them to roll out properly. The better you can roll out of or fall from a technique, the more aggressively the other person can apply the technique."

After twenty minutes of warm-ups, Carnie had everyone sit on the side. "Dr. Dunham, I'd like you to sit this out and watch." He called up six students, who surrounded him. "We call this *ryokatatori randori*, which is kind of like 'bull-in-the-ring' practice in football, where everyone attacks the guy in the center." He nodded to his students, who then attacked him in full motion, both hands forward. As a student made contact with Carnie, trying to grasp him at the shoulders, the agile instructor simply pivoted out of the way on one foot like a door opens on its hinges. The attacking student was thrown by Carnie in the same direction he'd charged, then merely rolled out of the throw and turned around to attack again. After one student was thrown, another attacked. Carnie was constantly throwing and turning, throwing and turning. After a few minutes, he clapped, and the students stopped attacking and sat down.

Dunham grinned. "And you think I'm going to do that! My bones'll break."

Carnie laughed, panting slightly. "Eventually, you will! If someone unexpectedly rushes in and attacks, the usual response is to back up. The problem with this is backing up is much slower than rushing forward, and you'll end up on the short end of the stick." He pointed his finger up and scanned the entire group. "Now, if someone attacks you with excessive energy, you can effortlessly manipulate that energy and throw him with it by merely turning and using your foot as a pivot point." He called a student forward. "I'll do it in slow motion in order to break down the important points."

Dunham studied Carnie's every move and felt this was simple enough that even he could do it.

"Dr. Dunham!" Carnie called. "Are you ready to try it?"

"As ready as I'll ever get."

"OK," Carnie announced to everyone, "grab a partner and practice the specifics of the technique, and then we'll group together and work on multiple attacks."

The practice went on for a full hour, and most of it dealt with pivoting out of the way of a charging attacker. After performing the technique what seemed like hundreds of times, Dunham felt like he could actually apply it in a real situation.

"Great class, everyone!" Carnie yelled to signal the end of the session. "Remember, one of the reasons we practice this time and time again is to achieve an automatic response to an attack. If we have to think about what technique to apply as someone is attacking, it's too late. It must automatically flow out of you." He paused to take a sip from his water bottle. "Dismissed, everyone. Have a great rest of the day."

Dunham walked up to Carnie and said, "Great class, Dean. I learned so much."

"Thanks, but remember, it only works if you've practiced it enough so that it's second nature."

Dunham grinned. "OK, OK; I'll keep on coming." He followed Carnie to the elevator. "So, do you mind if I study your October serial killer file?"

"Of course not," Carnie replied as they entered the elevator. "I've been thinking. Now that you're hanging your hat at our Boston field office for a while, is there any chance we can set up a few training courses so you can teach my agents? It's all they're talking about."

"I'd be delighted," Dunham responded as the elevator doors closed.

chapter ten

**PRESENT DAY: Evening, October 11. Boston, Massachusetts—
Boston University, Mugar Memorial Library**

Rob glanced up from his studies and noticed that the three others at his library table—James, Nick, and Keith—had their complete attention on their smartphones. He stared around at the students at the rest of the tables and realized that over half of them were also staring at their own cell phones. He shook his head. "I wonder what college students did before the invention of the smartphone?" Rob asked facetiously. "I'm sure they actually studied or something."

James popped his head up, then glanced around at the other students. "Well, it does make for a quiet library environment if we ever do study."

"It's not just us," Nick chimed in quietly, still staring at his phone. "It's all Americans. I read about a recent study where they placed a group of Europeans in a room for an hour—all strangers—and observed their behavior. Most merely sat patiently, while some struck up conversations. Then they placed a group of Americans in a room, and ninety percent of them immediately pulled out their smartphones for the entire period." He finally looked up from scrolling. "It's the American way, Robbo. Embrace it."

"Shhhhhh!" Keith shushed the three as he typed away on his phone. "You're interrupting me working on my YouTube business. I need to pay for college, you know."

Nick shook his head. "I can't believe YouTube is paying you for your how-to videos."

"What's this how-to video thing?" Rob asked in a whisper.

"Ignore Nick's pessimism, gentlemen," Keith replied. "He's just jealous he didn't figure it out for himself. The video's getting thousands of hits per week, so YouTube advertises on it and pays me. It's that simple. I can make mad money if I can figure out how to go viral."

"What's this one about?" Rob asked.

Nick snickered. "Tell him, Keith."

Keith glanced at the three of them and stated proudly, "It's a how-to video on self-defense for geeks," he paused, "or who I call 'the computer-savvy gentleperson.'"

Nick burst out laughing, causing students in the library to glare at their group. He leaned toward Rob and James. "Keith couldn't fight his way out of a paper bag; scared shitless of his own shadow. And he's an expert?"

Keith raised his shoulders smugly and closed his eyes. "I beg to differ, my envious friend. You see, the technically literate communities are wanting for the expertise of a brainiac lethal weapon, such as myself." He leaned back with a grin. "Who cares if I'm slightly deficient in experience. It's a huge market, and I'm providing a level of emotional comfort for them." He smirked at Nick. "Score."

"What happens when they find out the hard way that your advice doesn't help?" Rob asked.

"Oh, it works all right," Keith declared. "I repeat; I'm a lethal weapon. Just ask me. Besides, what they don't know won't hurt them." Keith bobbed his shoulders. "Well, maybe in this case it will, but statistically speaking, they'll never have to use it anyway."

"Hi, James," a young lady greeted, beaming as she approached the table. She tossed her hair to one side.

James sat up. "Oh, hi, Tammy," he replied, then glanced at Rob, Keith, and Nick to silently indicate 'Gorgeous, am I right?'

He smiled, and Tammy blushed. "How's it going?"

"Great," Tammy responded in a flirty, singsong voice, then twirled the end of her hair. "Are you going on the Halloween hayride this weekend?"

James raised his eyebrow. "Only if you're there."

Tammy blushed again and glanced over at Rob, Nick, and Keith. "Hi, guys." She eyed Rob. "Rob, Sarah's going, too. Are you coming?"

Rob looked up at Tammy, redness creeping into his own cheeks, then glanced over at James. "Umm, yes. I'm going with James."

Tammy smiled widely again. "Great." She turned, then glanced back and waved at James. "I'll see ya later, James."

All four watched Tammy as she walked away. She glanced back again and giggled as she noticed they were watching her.

Nick turned to Keith, while pointing at James. "Serious score."

"How do you do it, James?" Keith asked. "Every time I'm with you, some hot girl is hitting on you."

James snickered. "They recognized quality, Keith. What can I say?"

"You do realize there's a how-to YouTube video in the making, don't you?" Keith replied.

James laughed. "I'll think about it."

"It's your pheromones," Nick explained confidently. "Although odorless, they attack the olfactory system in females, and in your case, your scent convinces females your genes are superior to other males' genes, sparking a subliminal desire to copulate and produce fit offspring."

"You have a way with words, Nick," James replied.

"Since we're no longer studying," Rob interrupted, "how about we figure out this October serial killer?"

"OK," Nick said, "but how are we going to figure out something that the police haven't already thought of?"

"Cause and effect," Rob responded simply. "Forensic theory states that every effect, i.e., the crime scene, leaves behind a trail of physical evidence to the cause, or the killer. The police just haven't found it, yet."

"Causality," Nick understood.

"Exactly," Rob replied, "and combine this with evidence outside of the crime scene, like, eyewitness testimony, profiling, suspect alibis—and the case is solved."

Keith glanced at Nick and shook his head. "I get causality and CSI stuff, but we don't know what the police know. It's like fighting with one hand tied behind your back."

"True, but a lot of information's been released to the public, so let's start there," James interrupted. "We know the killer ends his yearly murder spree on

Halloween. Maybe if we discover the reason behind this, it might be the trail that leads to the killer."

"Don't you think the police thought of that?" Keith asked skeptically.

Rob pointed his finger at Keith. "You guys constantly brag about your brilliant computer skills. Are you telling me you can't find something that these computer un-savvy police haven't?"

Nick and Keith paused, then both opened up their laptops. "Well, if you put it that way," Keith replied, "let the genius-ness begin." He paused. "Where should we start? Talk to me, Goose."

"Well," Rob began, "in order to discover the effect, we need to look at patterns in the evidence, such as every killing year ending on Halloween, as James pointed out. So, what's the Halloween connection?"

Keith typed on his laptop. "Here's something . . . an article in the *Boston Herald*, and this investigative reporter proposes three theories. First, the killer is narcissistic and is seeking as much publicity as he can, so he's mutilating and displaying the victims in popular locations and ending his killing season on the popular Halloween. Second, the killer revels in the public fear that he's producing by killing his last victim on scary Halloween each year. Third, the murders are satanic sacrifices since the victims have been displayed on the night evil spirits roam the earth."

"Oh, I like the last one," James said. "He decapitates his victims, and that is certainly an evil act."

"Problem," Keith remarked. "The very first reader post below the article has a very interesting statement. All Hallows Eve, or our Halloween, is a connection to Heaven, not to Hell. It is the Eve before All Saints' Day, when the Church honors the saints. Also, the Halloween tradition of evil spirits roaming the earth predates All Hallows Eve and finds its origins in an ancient Celtic harvest celebration called Samhain," Keith stumbled over the correct pronunciation, 'sow-in.' "A satanic sacrifice requires Satan, which is a Christian tradition, and really has no connection to roaming spirits. Halloween is not really connected to Satan."

"I don't think that's a big issue," James replied. "Nowadays, everyone connects Halloween and evil spirits with Satan."

"I agree with that," Keith said.

"Satanism is a bit more complex than we think," Nick interrupted. "I'm on Wikipedia, just as a starting point, and apparently there isn't just one kind of

Satanism; there are dozens." He paused. "There is one common thread, though. They're all anti-Christian, and since individualism is a vice in Christianity, it's a value in Satanism; hence the reason for its diversity."

"So, we may have a rogue Satanist," James commented. "A lone wolf makes sense."

Nick continued, "They group Satanists into two categories, atheistic Satanists and theistic Satanists. Atheistic Satanists are 'anti-God' but aren't necessarily 'pro-Satan.' They worship nature. Reverence to Satan, or Lucifer, happens with the theistic Satanists, and if we're talking ritual sacrifices, then it's them." Nick paused as he read further. "Some call themselves, 'The Order of the Blah, Blah, Blah,' and others are called, 'The Temple of the Blah, Blah, Blah.'" Nick paused again. "Oh, here's an order that publicly promotes human sacrifice." He shook his head. "But there's no connection to Halloween."

At that moment, three young men approached their table. They had their coats on with their bookbags hanging over their shoulders and rolled up sleeping bags behind their backs. The tallest walked up to Rob. "Dude, how's it going?" he asked loudly, eliciting a few angry stares from around the room.

Rob glanced up. "Hi, Seth, Tyler, Jeff." He eyed the sleeping bags. "Where're you guys going?"

"It's Halloween season, bro," Seth replied. "Remember that cemetery everyone claims is haunted? You know, the one that's in the Guinness Book of World Records for the largest stone wall?"

"You guys aren't going to stay overnight in a cemetery, are you?" Keith interrupted.

Seth gave Keith a huge grin, bobbing his head up and down. "Affirmative, my man. Experiencing a taste of the supernatural is a huge adrenaline rush."

"The local serial killer just decapitated someone in a cemetery," Keith reminded Seth. "That's the last place I'd want to be at; not even in the daytime."

"One must not be a prisoner of fear, Keith-ster!" Seth explained philosophically. "Life is too short."

"It's not my fear that's the problem, Seth-ster," Keith replied. "It's the life being cut too short!"

"Do ya think you'll make contact with the other side?" Rob asked.

Seth pulled out his K-2 meter. "Oh, we will, all right, Rob-banski, and we plan on making first contact by 'smoke 'em da peace pipe.'" He slid a bowl and small baggie of weed from his pocket and leaned closer to Rob, turning his cupped palm for the group to see, before tucking his paraphernalia safely away. "I'm gonna ask if these ghosts wanna smoke up," Seth whispered, then laughed, with an occasional snort.

Another one of the young men approached Rob and showed him a photo on his smartphone. "Robbo, check out these light orbs over the gravestone."

Rob peered at the screen and nodded. "Tyler, this is seriously cool."

"You dudes need a break from studying," Seth commented. "How about you join us?"

Rob, James, Nick, and Keith all stared at each other, then shook their heads.

"Sorry, not tonight, Seth. We're busy researching," James answered.

Seth pulled out an audio recorder. "Are you sure? We're gonna try and pick up some EVPs—spirit voices."

"What if one of these spirits is evil and wants to . . . I don't know rape you or something?" James asked, glancing around after realizing he'd gone a bit shrill with his last few words.

Seth chuckled. "No worries, bro," he replied, then pulled out a tiny Bible and a cross. "We're prepared for all facets of the supernatural. I've been watching *Ghost Hunters*, *Ghost Adventures*, and a few others."

"There's a harvest moon out tonight," Nick interrupted. "It's a full moon, so do you have any silver? The wolves are howling."

Seth lost his smile. "Shit. I didn't think about werewolves." He glanced back at Tyler. "Do you have any silver, man?"

"Back at the dorm," Tyler replied.

Seth's smile returned. "Let's go get it." He turned back toward Rob and waved. "Later, dudes!"

Rob turned to James, Nick, and Keith. "Hope we don't see those guys on the eleven o'clock news."

"Not a chance," Nick answered. "If the killer gets even ten feet from them, the billowing marijuana smoke'll give him such a case of the munchies, he'll ignore them and go straight to Denny's."

Rob snickered. "Right. Back to the October serial killer. I think it's clear we're dealing with one serial killer, so if it's a satanic ritual, I agree, he's a loner and not part of a devil-worshipping cult." Rob paused. "But the Halloween thing. Why? It's gotta be more than just connecting the two because of evil spirits."

"Maybe he's pissing on the Christian tradition of All Saints' Day with human sacrifices to Satan?" James theorized. "That would make Lucifer happy."

Rob shook his head. "But if that was his motive, wouldn't it make more sense to then do it on Christmas or Easter? They're clearly more important Christian holidays."

James nodded. "I see your point."

"Maybe it isn't satanic after all," Keith suggested as he typed. "Maybe it's part of that Celtic Samhain festival." He popped his head up. "There's a group that celebrates it to this day—Wiccans." Keith paused. "Yes, here it is. Wicca is the modern witchcraft movement, and they certainly do celebrate Samhain!"

Rob's eyes opened wide as he grinned excitedly and leaned forward. "Maybe you're onto something, Keith. Do they perform human sacrifices on Halloween?"

Keith shook his head as he read. "Far from it. Wiccans see no need for sacrifice of any kind, apparently. Here's their creed: 'Nor do I demand aught in sacrifice, for behold, I am the Mother of all things, and my love is poured out upon the earth.' They claim sacrifice, especially human sacrifice, is repugnant to them."

"They murder, don't they? I thought witches ate kids?" James asked.

Keith glanced up at James, then back to the screen and shook his head. "These Wiccans spend an awful lot of time explaining why they're not Satanists and why the Hollywood version of witches is wrong," Keith explained.

"I see why the police are stumped by this guy," Nick commented. "This is going to be more difficult than I thought."

"Screw it," James blurted out. "Let's grab some pizza."

Rob opened his mouth to speak, then noticed Nick and Keith already had their laptops closed and had grabbed their bookbags. He sighed as they stood and zipped up their jackets. "I guess it's pizza then."

Seth drove into a cul-de-sac where, between two houses, a large open field butted up against a four-foot-high stone wall in the back. He turned his lights and engine off. "Here's the place, dudes. We can park here, jump over the wall, and go right into the cemetery. This is the old section, so it's gotta be full of our spirit brethren."

"That full moon's bright, man," Tyler noted. "These neighbors might see our car and get suspicious."

"Hey, if we get kicked out, so what. At least we tried."

"Let's do it, bros," Jeff replied.

Seth took the keys out of the ignition, and they got out, carrying their sleeping bags and backpacks filled with their gear. "Don't turn your flashlights on until we go over the wall, gentlemen," Seth directed.

After a short trek through the open field, they jumped the stone wall then turned on their flashlights.

"This moonlight is scary," Jeff remarked. "Lots of shadows."

"The perfect ambiance for a ghost adventure," Seth commented, then pointed between a group of crumbling tombstones and the tree line of a small patch of woods. "Here's a good spot."

"Actually, we don't even need flashlights in this moonlight," Jeff said, still stuck on the topic.

"We should've brought a tent," Tyler thought aloud.

"Bro," Seth replied, "we need to be open to the elements to better connect with the spirits."

"Yeah, and have a bat or something shit on my face when I'm sleeping."

Seth snorted and laughed. "Right when you're snoring, so the bat shit hits your tonsils!"

"With my luck," Tyler added, "it'll shit on my forehead and I'll scratch it and spread it all over myself. I'll wake up painted in shit from head to toe."

They tossed their sleeping bags and gear in a pile on the ground. An owl hooted in the woods.

"What was that?" Jeff asked nervously, shining his flashlight toward the sound.

"An owl, dude," Seth said, exasperated. "Grow a pair, will ya?" He turned to the group. "Get your equipment out, gentlemen." Seth pulled out the K-2 meter, Tyler grabbed a digital camera, and Jeff turned on a digital audio recorder. "Start taking pictures of those gravestones, man. If we see a light orb over one of them, we'll do an EVP session over it."

Tyler nodded. "Good idea." He took photos of the gravestones, then he scanned the images. "Nothing so far."

"Keep on snapping, man," Jeff directed.

Tyler took another photo, then reviewed it. "Hey, there might be something!"

Seth and Jeff stared at the photo. "Good enough for me. Let's do EVP," Seth suggested.

Jeff pushed the audio recorder button and gave Seth a thumbs-up.

"OK," Seth began. "Spirit brethren from the spirit world, come hang with us."

"I don't think they know what, 'come hang with us,' means, bro," Tyler commented.

Seth nodded and started again. "Spirits from the spirit world, reveal yourselves to us!"

Tyler shook his head and whispered, "Dude, I bet you're creeping them out. They're probably hiding from you now."

"Ugh," Seth grunted. "Take some more photos, bro. We'll try again."

They spent a half hour taking photos and recording and listening to the audio recorder for voices.

"So far nothing, bro," Tyler stated.

"I don't understand," Seth commented. "It works on TV."

A tree branch cracked behind them, followed by the sound of rustling leaves and heavy footfalls.

"What the—" Jeff blurted out.

"It's a raccoon, man," Seth replied.

"Dude, that sounds a lot bigger than a raccoon," Tyler commented nervously.

"Relax, my man," Seth said confidently. "It's probably more afraid of us than we are of it." He paused and raised the K-2 meter. "Let me try this now."

"What's that K-2 thing supposed to do, anyway?" Jeff asked.

"Spirits give off electromagnetic energy," Seth explained, "and this meter senses it and lights up if we get a spike of energy. If it's a lot of energy all five lights light up." He paused, staring at the K-2 meter. "So far, nothing's happening."

They heard rustling of the leaves again, causing all three to turn around to face the woods, and at that very moment, the K-2 meter lit up to half intensity.

"Shit!" Seth blurted out.

The noise in the woods stopped, and the K-2 meter's lights simultaneously blacked out. "That's freaky, man."

"Don't tell me a raccoon can do that!" Tyler yelled as he aimed his flashlight in the direction.

They heard a deep growl coming from the woods, and the K-2 meter lit up again. All three froze in fear. "Uh," Seth started, "must be a coyote or something?"

"Sooo, raccoons can't light up the meter, but coyotes can?" Tyler asked facetiously.

"I vote we get the hell outta here," Jeff blurted out.

"I've had enough," Seth commented. "Let's go." They quickly tiptoed over to grab their sleeping bags and bookbags. The K-2 meter lit up, but this time at full intensity.

"What's going on?" Seth whispered as the meter maintained its reading.

"Look!" Jeff yelled. He pointed at a human-shaped silhouette slowly walking toward them from the woods.

All three quickly grabbed their gear, bolted over the stone wall, and ran to the car. Seth searched frantically for his keys. "Where'd I put my keys?"

Tyler glanced back at the stone wall. A dark shadow faced them from where they'd just jumped over the wall.

"Hurry!"

It placed its hands on the wall.

"Let's go! It's coming!"

Seth found his keys but dropped them in the excitement. "Shit!" He picked them up, pushed the unlock button, then all three jumped in. As Seth started the car, Tyler and Jeff glanced over at the wall. The dark figure was now standing in front of the wall, with its full attention on them. Seth backed up, put it in drive, spun the tires, and drove off at top speed.

"Dudes, what the hell was that?" Seth asked, panting.

"I think James was right, bro," Tyler replied, shaking. "That thing was an evil spirit. I could feel it in my bones."

"I think I pissed my pants," Jeff commented, then glanced out the back window. "Maybe that thing was just a man . . . some dude messing with us."

Tyler glanced over at Jeff. "Then explain the K-2 readings."

"It's too bad we didn't get a photo of that thing, man," Seth added. "No one's gonna believe us."

chapter eleven

Dunham walked through security, then up to the officer at the front desk
and presented his identification. "Good morning. Special Agent Dr. Edward
Dunham. Detective Lieutenant Huff is expecting me."

The desk officer's eyes opened wide. "Dr. Dunham!" he said excitedly, then
stood up and shook Dunham's hand. "It's great to meet you, sir. I'm Officer
Whitford. Yes, Lieutenant Huff just spoke with me on the phone, and he's
been waiting for you. Come in, come in." Whitford buzzed open a metal door.
"Take the elevator up to the fourth floor. He'll be waiting for you in front of
the elevators."

"Thank you, Officer Whitford," Dunham replied.

When the doors opened on the fourth floor, Lieutenant Huff and Detective
Sergeant Sadler stood before him.

"Dr. Dunham, how are you doing?" Huff greeted Dunham warmly and
shook his hand as the two exchanged pleasantries.

Sadler reached out and shook Dunham's hand. "Nice to see you again, Dr.
Dunham."

"You too, Detective Sergeant."

"Did you see Dr. Gillespie and the superintendent of police on the news
this morning?" Huff asked.

Dunham shook his head. "No, I'm sorry. I haven't had the opportunity to watch TV."

"They held a news conference on the October Serial Killer Case," Sadler continued, "and made it public that there was a break in the case."

Dunham frowned. "I'm not sure that we want to inform our offender that we might be onto him."

Huff stared at Dunham, showing no emotion. "The mayor, superintendent, and Gillespie have a slightly different agenda than the task force has, Dr. Dunham. The earlier you know about this, the better."

Dunham nodded. "I believe I know where you're going . . . I was informed of this by the governor's advisor. I hope they didn't release what the break was."

Huff shook his head. "They didn't, but they certainly hinted enough." He paused. "Screw 'em." He turned around and waved for the other two to follow. "Come, let's get to the task force office."

After a short trip down the hall, they entered a large room with open office spaces, busy with activity. Dunham couldn't help but notice that dozens of officers stopped what they were doing and stared at him.

Huff also noted everyone staring at Dunham: "This is the investigative division. You can certainly tell detectives are a curious bunch." Huff stopped at a large adjoining office space. "Here we go," he said and motioned Dunham into the task force office. "This is excellent timing, Dr. Dunham. The fingerprint analysis is in." He paused as he handed Dunham the folder containing the results. "But, sadly, we haven't found a match."

"Oh? I'm surprised," Dunham replied. "Serial offenders generally don't begin a massive killing spree from a life of law-abiding normality. Usually, they've had run-ins with the law." He paused to peruse the file. "And it's been cross-checked with the FBI database?"

Huff nodded. "Oh, by the way, would you like something to drink? Tonic?"

"Yes, please," Dunham replied, then gave a slight grin. "Lately, I've worked all across the country, and Boston is the only place where I hear soft drinks referred to as tonic. A Diet Coke is fine."

"There's an interesting history as to why many Bostonians, especially the older generation, call it tonic," Sadler responded. "In the nineteenth century, carbonated beverages were used medicinally, thus, they were called tonics. When Dr. Pepper introduced the soft drink, it was a carbonated beverage, therefore, used for medicinal purposes. It was only natural to call it tonic."

"How interesting," Dunham said as a clerk handed him his drink. "Thanks."

"I still believe this guy's fingerprint is in some database. Since this is our only big lead, I've assembled a team of officers dedicated solely to finding it," Huff explained. "Who knows, maybe the guy's a foreigner."

"Was any DNA collected off the fingerprint?" Dunham asked.

Huff shook his head. "No, nothing; at least not yet, anyway."

"The good news? We can now compare the offender's fingerprint to anyone on our suspect list," Sadler interrupted. "That's huge."

Huff typed on the computer. "Absolutely, and the traffic camera at Park Street did indeed capture a couple of images that might be this guy, though they're a little grainy and from a distance. Check it out."

Huff turned the screen so Dunham and Sadler could view the images on the computer monitor.

"The left screen is at 9:42 p.m., and we see a couple making their way toward the Granary Burying Ground from the wooded area across the street in Boston Common. The right screen is at 10:28 p.m., and we see what appears to be the same man—now alone—walking toward the Boston Common wooded area from the cemetery. I've looped the video."

Dunham pointed his finger at the screen. "Assuming this is the offender, it doesn't help that he's wearing a dark wool cap over his face, but he certainly is Caucasian, with the appropriate stature."

"The clothes on this woman with him match the clothes on the victim. It's gotta be him!" Sadler exclaimed, then pointed to the image of the woman. "Her head is hanging, and her legs don't seem to be moving. It looks like she's unconscious . . . but if that's the case, this guy must be extremely powerful. He's holding her off the ground at his side, with one arm!"

"I believe you're correct, Detective Sergeant, and her feet are not dragging at all," Dunham agreed. "He must be quite strong."

"Did you photograph the crowds at each of the crime scenes?" Dunham asked. "Since these images give us a general description of the offender, maybe we can see if he's in the habit of returning to the scene of the crime."

"We have," Huff replied, then slid a large manila folder across the table. "Here they are." Sadler and Dunham reviewed the photos.

"I see a couple of potentials, but no one wearing the same dark wool cap, yet."

"If we scan these photos and send them to the FBI lab," Dunham explained, "we can use a facial recognition program that'll help us spot our offender if he's in the crowd."

"Great," Huff replied.

Sadler peeked over Dunham's shoulder at the photos in his hands, then pointed at someone in the top photo. "See that priest? Strangest thing; he asked me if you were in the Granary cemetery."

"Oh?" Dunham replied, then studied the image. "I don't recognize him, and I'm certainly not acquainted with a priest from Boston. That is strange. What did you tell him?"

"I told him nothing," Sadler responded, "but the officer standing next to me pointed you out." He paused. "His description bears no resemblance to the image of the killer."

"I agree," Dunham switched photos and reviewed a couple of others. "Here he is again at one of last year's crime scenes."

Sadler and Huff leaned toward the photo in Dunham's hands.

"Well, what do ya know," Huff commented. "Very observant, Dr. Dunham. I wonder why a priest—if he is a priest—is so interested in the October Serial Killer Case?" He paused. "Maybe one of his parishioners has confessed?"

"Intriguing, boss," Sadler responded. "I'll visit the Catholic parishes around Boston. See if we can't locate this curious priest."

"Don't stop there, Sergeant," Huff said. "I'd also check out other religious denominations. Don't Lutheran ministers wear the collar too?"

"I'll check it out," Sadler replied, pulling out his smartphone, a yellow legal pad, and a pen. He tapped on the phone's screen, waited for the results of his search, and began jotting down a list of churches to visit.

Dunham glanced up at the office wall and noticed two large maps of Boston and the surrounding area. Both had a dozen or so red pin markers on them, all in different locations. Around each pin was a date and time, handwritten in pen. He pointed up to the maps. "What's this, Lieutenant?"

"Oh, the map on your right shows the locations of all the October serial killer murder sites, and the left map shows the locations where our perpetrator first kidnapped his victims three days prior," Huff answered. "So far, we don't see any patterns that'll help us out. His hunting ground is clearly Greater Boston, and his murder sites are, too, just at separate locations."

"Interesting."

"Most are no more than seven miles from Boston, with the exception of one just west of Needham near the Waban Arches Bridge." Huff approached the map and pointed at Highway 95, which surrounds Greater Boston. "Notice how almost all of the pins are on the Boston side of Highway 95?"

"Central Boston is clearly our offender's anchor point," Dunham concluded.

"A large percentage of the murder sites are near rivers and bridges, but not enough to call it a pattern. Other sites are nowhere near a river."

Dunham continued to stare at the maps, focused primarily on the murder site map. "So, our offender commits four murders per year, and your map shows that there is no obvious geographic pattern, other than the murder sites being in and around Boston." He paused. "I do see that he selects at least one murder site within the city limits of Boston each year."

"We noticed that, too," Huff interrupted.

Dunham pointed at the map. "I see in year three, there were two murders in the city of Boston."

"I'm not sure what to make of that," Huff replied.

Dunham nodded. "Hmm," he mumbled, then focused his attention on the kidnapping map. "Lieutenant, may I photograph these so that I can spend some time studying the locations?"

"By all means, Dr. Dunham," Huff agreed as he turned back to his computer. "Sadler, come over here. Let's see if we can spot our killer in the crowd. I'd love to be able to apprehend him the next time he murders."

As Sadler clicked off his phone and joined Huff, Dunham took a photo of the kidnapping map, then tapped on his iPhone. "Lieutenant, is there somewhere that I can take a private call?"

Huff popped his head up and pointed to a small adjoining room. "Sure, use my office."

Dunham rushed into Huff's office and touched an app on his phone titled, 'Secured,' then dialed a phone number and put the phone to his ear.

"One Alpha Charlie," a voice answered at the other end of the call.

"Winfall, one, eight, eight, eight, eight," Dunham replied.

"Our crypto-translators are in sync, and this connection is now secured," the voice said. "Good afternoon, Dr. Dunham. Please ensure no one is within earshot. How may I help you?"

Dunham peeked back at the officers in the other room, still huddled around the crime scene footage, oblivious to his call. "Good afternoon, Big Brother. I just sent you a photo of a map with the locations of where the October serial killer has kidnapped his victims. Each location is labeled with the date and time."

"Yes, I have it," Big Brother acknowledged, "and I'm downloading the information as we speak."

"Great," Dunham replied. "My guess is that some, or most, of the victims were carrying their cell phones with them at the time of their kidnappings. Maybe the cell phone GPS data might reveal something."

"Excellent thought, Dr. Dunham," Big Brother replied. "Just one moment please."

Dunham could hear him typing on the other end of the phone.

"How's my favorite town been treating you, Dr. Dunham?" Big Brother asked.

"I've only been here in Boston a couple of days, but I love it."

"If you haven't had the clam chowder, I highly recommend it."

"Oh yes," Dunham agreed. "I've had some, and I will be having more."

"I see all of the kidnappings occurred throughout Boston and surrounding suburbs, but always within the boundary of Interstate 95," Big Brother observed. "It looks like Interstate 95 circles Boston at a radius of six-to-eight miles from downtown."

"Yes," Dunham agreed, "and I'll be curious to see if the GPS data reveals any spoke patterns identifying a central location."

"We have a little luck, Dr. Dunham," Big Brother interrupted. "Seven of the victims had their cell phones on them, and each one matches the location and date of that victim's kidnapping recorded on your map."

"Is there a geographic history track of the cell phones after being kidnapped?" Dunham asked.

"There is, but it's a bit complex at first look," Big Brother answered, then paused. "OK," he paused again, "in each case, the very next location after the kidnapping is a stationary GPS signal for more than a day. Some are multiple days. The next location after that is the signal terminus, and in three cases, it's the very same location."

"Interesting, so the signal stops completely," Dunham remarked.

"The very last time—ever. Either the phone was destroyed, or the batteries merely went," Big Brother explained.

"Are you able to identify the central location for the three cases?" Dunham asked.

"Already on it. It's a city dump. The fourth cell signal terminus is another dump site, but in Medford, just north of Boston." A pause. "Yep, the fifth terminus is also a dump site," he paused again. "And this one's in South Boston."

"Separate dump sites," Dunham said. "I bet the last two are dump sites, as well." He thought for a moment. "Before the offender murders his victims, he holds them for three days somewhere. Could it be at these dump sites?" he asked himself aloud. "Or . . . Big Brother, could you check if the stationary location immediately after the kidnappings has a large garbage dumpster located there?"

"I see where you're going with this, Dr. Dunham," Big Brother replied. "And yes, there's a dumpster at that very location. The particular one I'm seeing now is in the Boston Navy Yard."

"It looks like our offender kidnaps his victim, leaves the scene of the crime, stops a distance away, then discards the cell phones in order to hide his tracks," Dunham surmised. "Our offender is aware of GPS tracking."

"I do notice another pattern, Dr. Dunham," Big Brother interjected.

"Oh?"

"In each kidnapping case south of the Charlestown River, the GPS signal travels over the Charlestown Bridge before finding its way into a dumpster. All of the stationary signals north of the Charlestown Bridge are along Highway 60, with the signals moving easterly."

"Excellent, Big Brother. Are you able to plot this on the map?"

"You'd be amazed at what I can do, Dr. Dunham," Big Brother replied confidently. "Already done, and I'm sending the photo to you now."

"Excellent. As usual, you've been invaluable."

"No problem, Dr. Dunham. Contact me if you need anything else."

Dunham hung up, then pulled up the photo that Big Brother had just sent him. He rushed back to the task force office where Huff and Sadler were still at the computer. "I have something, Lieutenant. Do you have wi-fi on this computer? I want to send you an email."

"Sure," Huff said, then rattled off his email address.

Dunham typed in the address on his phone's email app. "I'm sending you the photo I took of your kidnapping map, but there've been some additions to it; courtesy of the FBI."

When Huff pulled up the attachment on the screen, Dunham explained, "What you're looking at superimposed on your kidnapping map is GPS tracking data on the cell phones of these seven victims at the time of their kidnappings and a short period of time thereafter until their signals ended." He pointed at the screen. "These were the only victims who had their cell phones on them when they were kidnapped. Notice how the cell phone signals were stationary for a day or so, but then moved to their final location."

Huff's eyes widened and he pointed at the screen. "All three signals stop at the same spot!"

"That's a dumpster," Dunham answered, "and so are the rest of these." He paused. "The signals then terminate at major dump sites."

"He's holding his victims at dump sites?" Sadler asked.

"Maybe," Dunham replied, "but this pattern seems to suggest that our offender kidnaps his victims, leaves the location in a hurry, but then stops near a dumpster and throws out any personal possessions belonging to the victims, before taking them farther on."

Huff sat back from the computer screen. "That's exactly what this shows, which also means he's probably disposing the victims' clothes and any other personal items at these dumpsters." He paused. "If this is the case, he must be using a van or something with lots of space in it." He shook his head. "Chances are slim to none that we find their possessions at a huge dump site."

Sadler's head popped up, then he grabbed a folder and searched through it. "Boss, do you remember me interviewing a lady the first year, who claimed to see a white van rush away from the crime scene? Here it is; a Connie Marotta from Sudbury."

Huff nodded. "Of course; a dead end at the time, since there are thousands of white vans in Greater Boston."

"I believe we can take advantage of this, if we act quickly and if our timing is right," Dunham replied.

"What do you mean?" Huff asked.

Dunham pointed to the map. "Notice that there are two consistent bottlenecks. Any time our offender has kidnapped someone south of the Charlestown River, he's driven over the Charlestown Bridge north before he dumps their possessions. Any time there's been a kidnapping north of the river, he dumps their possessions along Highway 60, so it looks like he's traveling on Highway 60, and the pattern suggests that was he traveling east."

Huff studied the photo. "Indeed."

Dunham continued, "We know he ends his year by kidnapping someone on October 28, three days prior to Halloween, and he's likely to attempt one prior to this. If we get lucky and someone calls in the kidnapping, we might be able to intercept him at one of these two bottlenecks, assuming he's using a white van."

Huff beamed with excitement. "I know of three cases where 9-1-1 received a phone call about a kidnapping within minutes of the event, so this just might work." He paused. "I'll send out an alert immediately, and we'll set up a task force meeting for tomorrow to coordinate." Huff glanced at Dunham. "Will you be able to make it? Everyone wants to meet you, anyway."

Dunham frowned slightly as he thought about the mayor and police chief not wanting him to be involved in the first place—to protect the reputation of Dr. Gillespie. "Will that cause issues for you with your superiors? I believe they want me to keep a low profile."

Huff shook his head. "Dr. Gillespie never shows up to our meetings. I'm not sure he even knows where the task force office is. He spends his time filming for his next episode." Huff waved dismissively. "Besides, I could give a shit."

Dunham nodded. "OK, I'll be there. Just let me know what time."

"Salem," Sadler blurted out, as he stared at the computer monitor.

"What about Salem?" Huff asked.

"The offender's taking his kidnapped victims to Salem," Sadler answered. He pointed at the screen. "Crossing the Charlestown Bridge takes him to Broadway Road, which turns into the Salem Turnpike. Traveling east on Highway 60 meets the Turnpike, and then it's a stone's throw away to Salem."

"Or the town just prior to Salem—Lynn," Huff replied. "Nice catch, Detective Sergeant."

Dunham nodded. "I believe you're right."

"Well," Huff added, "I believe we'll invite the Salem Police Department to tomorrow's meeting and we'll most likely add them to the task force." Huff glanced over at Dunham. "Dr. Dunham, the investigation's going in a positive direction thanks to you."

Dunham grinned and pointed toward the wall, then at Sadler. "Thanks, although it was your kidnapping map that started this. It's all about teamwork."

Huff raised his eyebrows. "It's too bad Dr. Gillespie doesn't know that."

chapter twelve

PRESENT DAY: October 14. Salem, Massachusetts—Brewer Hawthorne Cove Marina

Old Anthony Berber enjoyed retirement onboard his forty-eight-foot yacht. He lazily read the paper on the deck, the yacht moored in the Brewer Hawthorne Cove Marina. *Salem, Massachusetts, certainly is a relaxing place*, he thought, *compared to the hustle and bustle of New York City and a life in the finance and investment office.* He pulled off his soft-brim hat, scratched his bald head, frowned, and stared around the famous Salem marina. His frown deepened at the eyesore: a large warehouse butting up to the marina just thirty feet away from his yacht.

"Stop staring at that building," his wife, Dorothy, blurted out as she climbed up to the top deck of the yacht carrying two glasses filled with lemonade. "You're gonna give yourself heartburn again."

Anthony shook his head. "I don't see why they gave us this slip, situated just feet away from this god-awful warehouse. We pay good money for a season pass."

"You're the one who wanted to dock our yacht at such a famous marina," Dorothy replied as she handed him his drink. "All the good spots have been taken for years."

Dorothy pointed in the opposite direction at an old, well-kept wooden building. "Are you gonna come with me to the House of the Seven Gables, Anthony? You said you would."

Anthony dropped his gaze to the paper again. "I dunno."

"We've been here all summer," Dorothy argued, "and only two feet away is a piece of early Americana. You know I love Nathaniel Hawthorne. That's the very building that inspired his novel, *The House of the Seven Gables*."

"*The Scarlet Letter* was his best work, anyway," he grumped.

"What do you mean?" Dorothy replied angrily. "*The House of Seven Gables* is full of family curses and witchcraft. You like that sort of thing. Besides, I hear the building's haunted."

He glanced at the old wooden mansion. "I guess it does have seven gables."

Dorothy glared at him.

"OK, OK!" Anthony replied. "Let's go after lunch."

Dorothy beamed. "Now you're talking. I'll make some sandwiches." She turned and marched happily back into the cabin.

Anthony continued to read his paper, then permitted himself a small grin. He shook his head, taking pleasure in putting a smile on Dorothy's face. A few moments later, motion in his peripheral caught his attention, and he watched as a white van pulled to the front gate at the entrance of the neighboring warehouse. The gate and the warehouse garage door opened up simultaneously, and the van quickly vanished inside the building. The gate and the door closed behind it. Anthony went back to reading his paper. A few minutes went by and then he heard a noise emanating from the warehouse, which enticed him to squint at the small window on the warehouse wall. He could see the curtains—which he remembered as being generally closed—were now open, and inside the warehouse he could make out a man jostling around in the white van. There was a blue van behind that. The man seemed to have something covering his face, Anthony noticed, before the man ducked out of the window's frame of view. Strangely, this spiked his interest.

As he watched, Anthony's curiosity grew, and the newspaper dropped to his chest. He fixed his eyes on the window and waited for the man in the warehouse to come into sight again. In less than a minute, he stopped in full view, facing to the left, looking down. He seemed to be wrapping something up. Anthony now realized what was on his face: a scary-looking rubber Halloween mask bearing the visage of a deranged clown.

Creepy, he thought. The man suddenly popped his head up, then turned and met Anthony's eyes. Surprised and embarrassed, Anthony lifted his paper, pretending to read. He didn't want to peek back at the window and get caught being nosy again. He read a full article in the paper, but curiosity finally got the better of him. After what he thought was five minutes, he glanced back at the warehouse window. The man in the deranged clown mask was now positioned at the window, staring right at him, which immediately sent shivers down Anthony's spine. Anthony quickly turned his head and pretended to read his paper again, but he now knew this strange man was watching him. He slowly rose from his reclining chair and tried not to hurry into the yacht's cabin. "Let's eat in the kitchen, Dorothy!"

* * *

Anthony glanced up at the bedroom clock and read that it was eleven p.m. He could feel his eyes finally getting heavy from reading the latest book on wealth management. "Are you almost ready for lights out, Dorothy?"

"I guess so," Dorothy responded as she closed the magazine she'd been reading. She glanced down to the right and read the cover of her husband's book. "I'll never understand why that work stuff still interests you. I thought you were retired."

"You know, I was pretty damn good at identifying gaps in subsidiary company financial plans and strategies. And you know that's why, even after I retired, I couldn't say no to contracting as a troubleshooting consultant." He began reading again. "Can't quit it. It's in my blood, dear."

"Hmm," Dorothy replied, not quite understanding, even after all these years, exactly what it was he did at his firm.

"If I inspected a company and found out that the weakness was in personnel, I wouldn't think twice about firing an entire executive team," Anthony continued. "Serves 'em right for being stupid bastards."

"Sounds mean to me," Dorothy said. "I have no idea why I married such a heartless man."

Anthony grinned. "Because you love the lifestyle I can afford. How many people live in a mansion and spend their summers on a yacht?"

Dorothy nodded and grinned back. "A match made in heaven." She set down her magazine on the nightstand. "Ready for bed?"

Anthony put his book down and turned the light off.

Dorothy preemptively put in her earplugs to drown out her husband's inevitable snoring and nestled her head on her pillow. Within minutes, Anthony drifted off to sleep.

* * *

Anthony woke up from a dead sleep to a dark, quiet room.

What woke me up? he thought. He felt like he had been sleeping for quite some time, then he peeked at the clock and saw that it was just past two o'clock a.m. He reached over and gently grasped Dorothy's arm. Anthony quickly realized something was wrong. Her arm was cold and stiff when he touched her. He reached to his right, turned on the nightstand light, and turned back toward Dorothy.

Wide-open eyes. Gaping mouth. Motionless, pale body.

Aghast, he glanced over at the door to the bedroom and his fear morphed into terror. Occupying the doorframe was the man in the deranged clown mask. Anthony turned pale as the blood left his face, then he felt an intense pain in his chest—the same pain he'd felt when he'd had a heart attack years earlier. At that moment, the masked man advanced toward him with amazing speed and shoved him onto his back. The masked face just inches from his own, his attacker laughed ominously. It was as if the man knew he was having a heart attack and used terror to exacerbate his condition. As Anthony gasped for air, the masked man growled, then slowly covered Anthony's mouth and nose, suffocating him.

Anthony's fear turned into darkness, then calmness, and, finally, oblivion.

chapter thirteen

PRESENT DAY: October 15. Westford, Massachusetts—Witch's Woods

The resident assistant on Rob's floor was bundled up in fall-weather attire, pacing back and forth in the hallway. "Come on; come on, everyone!" the RA belted out. "The bus'll be here in just a few minutes. I don't want anyone to miss the haunted hayride! It's gonna get cold tonight, so dress accordingly! And no alcohol! RAs get fired for that sorta thing!"

"You ready, Rob?" James asked as he wrapped his scarf around his neck.

"All set," Rob replied, then glanced toward the door. "Nick! Keith! You guys ready?" he yelled.

"We were born ready, Robbo," Keith called from the hallway as he appeared before their door with an overconfident strut, wearing a thick, oversized leather jacket, holding onto a wide-brimmed hat. "I believe it's time to transform into Indiana Jones, gentlemen." He donned the hat and tugged his shirt down over his exposed, slightly hefty midsection. "Yeah, I know what you're thinking, my jealous friends—perfection."

James laughed. "Sick, Keith—sorry, *Indy*. It's an honor to be in your presence."

Keith opened the door to James' closet. "James, do you have another one of those sexy scarves? It'll complete my irresistibility."

James grabbed another scarf and threw it at Keith. "Have at it, my friend," he said. "I gotcha. Just bring it back in one piece."

"Thank you, kind sir," Keith replied, bowing. "The ladies will appreciate it."

"Let's go; let's go!" the RA yelled from the hallway.

"We're off!" Rob said, and the three walked into the hall. As they did, Nick met them from his room, wearing only a short-sleeve shirt and jeans. He was clutching his iPad, as usual.

James shook his head and pointed into his room. "Nick, get back in there and get your coat. You're gonna freeze your *cojones* off," he scolded.

Nick turned around obediently and stepped back into his room. He waived his hand in the air behind him. "Yes, Mother."

Seth, Tyler, and Jeff rushed past Rob, James, and Keith, clearly excited about the haunted hayride. Seth clapped Rob on the shoulder. "Dude! Time for some mad fun!"

"You better believe it!" Rob replied excitedly.

"I didn't think you guys were gonna come after your brush with death at the graveyard," Keith interrupted.

"Oh contraire, Keith-ster!" Seth shouted over the growing din of students flooding into the hall. "We faced our fears and came out of it better men. We now yearn for the adrenaline rush of horror!"

"You should be a speechwriter, Seth," James complimented dryly.

"Rock on, bro!" Seth replied, opening the door with one hand and throwing up a sign of the horns with the other.

After some effort to quiet them, the RA counted each student and checked them off on a clipboard. "OK then, let's catch up with our female guests from the second floor and be off. We're supposed to meet them in the cafeteria. Let's go, gentlemen!"

Keith rubbed his hands in excitement. "Accompanying ladies to haunted attractions is the best. They get the shit scared out of them, and when they scream, they hold onto you, and you give 'em comforting hugs. Next thing you know—passionate sex."

James smirked. "Outstanding, Keith; I see a YouTube how-to video in the making."

Keith grinned. "I like the way you think. This could be huge." He strutted with overblown confidence. "I may ask you to video a few of my moves."

Nick joined them, now wearing a winter coat but still holding onto his iPad. "All set."

Rob grinned and shook his head. "Do you feel naked without that thing?"

"No telling when a smartphone just won't cut it, Brother Rob," Nick replied.

As they took the stairs to the first floor, Rob glanced at James. "What is the name of this haunted hayride?"

"It's called Witch's Woods in Westford, just outside of the 495, about a thirty-minute ride," James replied. "You'll love it. Besides the hayride, it's got three haunted houses, a live fire show on a stage, food, scary creatures walking around you all the time; everything." He leaned closer to Rob. "I can guarantee it's going to scare the shit outta Keith."

Keith glanced at James. "Did you say food?" He turned to Rob. "He said food, didn't he?"

When they reached the cafeteria, the co-eds were standing around waiting for them. James spotted Tammy talking with a blonde girl with glasses and long, straight hair. "Tammy!"

Tammy turned and beamed. "Hi, James. I like your scarf."

James put his arm around her, then held her hand. "Thanks."

Keith popped his hands up in mock disgust. "Uh, Tammy? How about mine?"

Tammy giggled. "Of course, Keith; yours too." She glanced over at Rob. "Rob, remember Sarah?"

Rob nodded and waved to Sarah. "Oh, yeah. Hi, Sarah." Rob noticed that Sarah wore very little makeup; she was naturally pretty. *She dresses and acts kinda nerdy, but she's pretty hot*, he thought. It didn't bother him that Tammy was obviously trying to be a matchmaker and hook them up.

"Hi, Rob," Sarah replied. "I remember reading about you in the Niagara Falls Serial Killer Case last year."

Rob, taken aback by Sarah's response, beamed at her recognition of him. "Yes, are you interested in that sort of thing?"

Sarah nodded. "I'm majoring in psychology, and eventually I'd like to get into criminal profiling, especially with violent offenders. Their pathology is so foreign to me. I'm intrigued at how a human being doesn't have the ability to sympathize with another human being."

As Rob and Sarah delved into conversation about serial killers, Tammy elbowed James and they exchanged knowing smiles.

"My interest is in the forensic sciences, but profiling has always intrigued me," Rob continued.

A large girl, nearly six feet tall, dressed in a scarecrow costume, complete with a bow made of straw sticking out of her hair, ran into the middle of the assembled group. "Who's ready for some scary fun! Yeaaah!" She gave a group of girls a big hug.

"Whoa!" Nick blurted out, taken aback by her overwhelming stature and rambunctious presence.

"That's Bobbie Jo," Tammy said. "She's in charge of floor morale."

Keith nodded with a huge grin. "That's a whole lot of woman!"

The RA for the girls' floor waved her hands. "Bus is here, everyone! Time to go!"

"Come on, guys!" Bobbie Jo screamed.

As everyone left the cafeteria for the bus, Rob casually walked along with Sarah. "Dr. Dunham concluded that the Niagara Falls serial killer was an aggressive narcissist."

"Dr. Dunham's the Watchmaker, right?" Sarah asked.

"That's right," Rob replied. "The police had nothing but good things to say about him. He was the one that really broke the case."

"I hear you guys are studying the October Serial Killer Case," Sarah said. "I've been looking into it, too. I'd love to get into the mind of that killer."

"Maybe we can compare notes," Rob suggested.

Sarah beamed. "I'd like that."

Their conversation continued as they made their way onto the bus. James and Tammy sat together, and Rob sat in the seat in front of them. Sarah slid in next to him as she said, "I see this Boston serial killer as a narcissist, in the sense that he cares about nothing but his own agenda, but his motive seems to be different than the Niagara Falls serial killer. It's kind of a ritualistic motive; an evil sacrifice to Satan, maybe."

Rob nodded excitedly. "That's exactly what we concluded." He glanced over at James, then Keith and Nick, who were sitting together across the aisle. "James, Keith, Nick, and I read up on the different types of Satanists and compared them to the available evidence. His MO doesn't conform to any of the groups of Satanists promoting sacrifice, so we concluded that he's not part of any satanic group, but he's doing it on his own."

Rob and Sarah's conversation lasted the duration of the thirty-minute ride. As the bus drove into the entrance of Witch's Woods haunted attraction and stopped between the parking lot and ticket office, everyone piled out. The two RAs made their way to the front of the group. At that moment, a zombie actress pushed a baby carriage straight through the group as if she were completely oblivious to their presence. Rob's RA laughed and shook his head. He waved his hands. "All right! Everyone, take your tickets out and follow us!" They filed as a group toward the ticket office.

Nick noticed another scary-looking actor dressed in a ghoul-like creature outfit, making his way toward the group. "Hey, check out all the creatures among us! There must be a dozen of them roaming around the crowd. Keeping everyone entertained while they wait for the hayride and haunted houses, I bet."

Another actor dressed as a crazed prison inmate approached a lady from behind. She screamed in surprise, then laughed uncontrollably to her friend. Keith quickly placed himself on the other side of James and Tammy. "Not cool," he announced in a higher-pitched voice.

"Wow," Rob mused aloud, to no one in particular.

"What?" Sarah asked.

Realizing he'd obscurely addressed his surprise, he pointed at the entrance to one of the haunted houses. "My sister, Celine, was attacked by the Niagara Falls Ripper last year at a huge haunted attraction. She's OK, but how coincidental that we're discussing another serial killer *and* we're at a Halloween attraction."

"I'd be freaked out if I were your sister," Sarah replied. "The whole fun about Halloween attractions is to experience the horrific and deadly, but without the deadly part. If you were to find out later that the deadly part was put back into the equation . . ." she glanced around at the Halloween actors scaring the customers, then moved closer to Rob. "I hope these actors were all vetted."

Rob laughed as he spotted Keith screaming and running away from a close encounter with a zombie character, right into the comforting arms of Bobbie Jo.

"We'll really never know, will we!"

After a fifteen-minute wait, they boarded a large wagon lined with bench seating and filled with hay. The whole thing was hooked up to a tractor, idling loudly. Their guide sat in the middle of the wagon and informed them he was seated this way for his own safety and to be heard by all. Rob noticed that everyone was loud and in high spirits, then glanced over at Keith sitting on Bobbie Jo's lap, believably feigning fear. Rob reached to his right and tapped James' knee. "James! Check out Keith!"

James and Tammy glanced over and laughed. Then James pointed at Nick and said, "Check it out."

Rob glanced over and saw Nick tapping away on his iPad, with two other guys peering over his shoulder. "That's so Nick!" Rob yelled over the noise of the crowd. "Once a gamer, always a gamer!"

Without looking up, Nick gave Rob a thumbs-up.

The tractor jerked forward and began to move in a relatively slow and bumpy pace, headed toward a section of poorly lit woods. At the entrance to the woods, Rob saw three cloaked female figures hunched and huddled around a large cauldron over a burning fire. The wagon stopped just feet away from the figures.

"Beware of these witches, folks!" the guide barked out. "Who knows what flavors their broth!"

The witches cackled as they stirred the contents in the cauldron. "We need more meat!" one of the witches yelled, then all three faced the wagon.

The crowd laughed.

"They're creepy!" Sarah said to Rob.

The witches slowly approached the wagon, cackling and making cannibalistic comments. Just before they reached the nearest side of the wagon, a huge ogre character jumped onto the wagon from behind the crowd, growling at the top of his lungs. The actor must have been well over six feet tall and over 300 pounds. The wagon shook from his jump. This surprised everyone, causing most to scream, some to fall off their benches, and all to laugh hysterically. Sarah grabbed ahold of Rob, screaming, and Rob held her, acutely aware that Sarah was in his arms. Rob was never comfortable interacting with a girl he liked, so the darkness was actually comforting. He could tell Sarah enjoyed his company just as much as he enjoyed hers, which actually made him feel at ease. He glanced over at James, who always seemed in his element around attractive women, and decided to watch how he behaved with Tammy to gain some helpful hints. After a minute of fun bantering between the witches and the ogre, the tractor started moving again, now entering the woods.

"Prepare yourselves, everyone!" the guide yelled. "We are now entering the haunted forest!"

As they approached the forest, Rob glanced up at a large Haunted Forest sign and noticed that the trail ahead was lit in dull light.

"How cool!" Sarah commented, pointing in front of the tractor. "Look at all the ground fog. I bet they use dozens of fog machines."

Out in the woods, Rob spotted a half-dozen motionless, hooded figures with glowing red eyes. Speakers in the distance bellowed howling noises.

"Beware of werewolves!" the guide said, staring around in the dim light at all the hayride patrons. "Keep your arms inside the wagon!"

The wagon came upon three decrepit shacks, two on the left and one to the right, shrouded in billowing fog. Strategically placed hidden lights glowed from within the gloom. Rob could hear howling from inside the shacks to the left. The tractor stopped between the decrepit buildings on either side. Moments later, a screaming man rushed out of the largest shack wearing torn, bloodstained clothing.

"Help me! Help me! They're after me!"

Two monstrous werewolves hot on his tail, growling and howling, charged the man, attacked him, and dragged him back into the shack. Everyone on the wagon laughed excitedly, their complete attention on the old cabin. An instant later, a third werewolf jumped onto the wagon from behind, leaning directly over Tammy, who was now screaming in hysterics. The other two werewolves left the shack along with the man in bloodstained clothing, the latter now wearing a wolf mask, as if he had begun to transform into a werewolf. As the four werewolves taunted the hayride patrons, the tractor moved forward. The werewolves scurried back into the shack.

"I nearly pissed my pants!" James yelled as he gasped for breath.

Tammy leaned on James, laughing excessively. "I think I did pee my pants."

"Prepare yourselves, everyone!" the guide yelled. "We are now deep in the haunted forest! Somewhere is an ancient cemetery rumored to house the undead!"

"Ohhh, this is going to be sick, dudes!" Seth blurted out. "I can't wait!"

"Speak for yourself!" Keith retorted, holding onto a happy Bobbie Jo.

Rob noticed a lighted area through the trees a few hundred yards ahead and could make out a few gravestones. He pointed and said to Sarah, "That must be the cemetery." As the tractor neared the cemetery, Rob could see it was covered with lighted ground fog, just as the werewolf shacks were. The shadows created by the hidden lights beaming on the dozens of various-sized gravestones made the scenery even scarier.

"How cool!" James exclaimed.

The entrance to the cemetery was a huge, wrought-iron open gate with a large arched Cemetery sign looming over their heads. Next to the gate was a man in a large black cloak holding onto a black scythe with a long handle and a large, curved, sickle-like blade on the end.

"Watch out for the gatekeeper . . . or grim reaper!" the guide warned.

As the tractor pulled the wagon past the gatekeeper, the hooded figure's head followed the caravan ominously, his body motionless.

Sarah tapped Rob on the shoulder. "I wonder if the October serial killer thinks of himself as the grim reaper, harvesting souls for Satan."

Rob glanced back at the grim reaper, then turned toward Sarah. "You know, I bet you're right!" He paused for a moment. "The reaper selects souls because they are about to die. I wonder what his agenda is?"

"Maybe it's not who it is, or which soul, but just any soul, as long as it's harvested in October," Sarah surmised.

Rob nodded. "Could be, or maybe *who* it is, is important. Maybe we should take a look at the names of all the victims and see if we can come up with anything."

"We should also look at the locations where they were murdered. Maybe there's a pattern," Sarah added.

"Right! We'll have to put our heads together on this," Rob replied.

The tractor stopped near the center of the cemetery. Rob peered around at the gravestones on both sides of the trail. The graves themselves were difficult to see in all the ground fog. Owls hooting mixed with other Halloween noises blaring in the distance. Rob could make out the sound of a door creaking open, followed by more creaks. He watched as mummies and zombie-looking creatures climbed out of coffins and graves. The zombies and mummies then converged upon the wagon with their arms stretched out in front of them, moaning and groaning. A couple of girls screamed at the top of their lungs, and everyone one got out of their seats and crowded the center of the wagon where the guide was perched. As the creatures stretched their hands across the floor of the wagon attempting to grab someone, the crowd screamed and laughed. After a few minutes of terror, some feigned and some bashfully real, the tractor moved forward again, and soon they were out of the cemetery. After a few more close calls with witches on broomsticks and a family of inbreeds, the wagon finally made its way out of the woods and headed back to the ticket area.

James leaned toward Rob and Sarah. "Hey, you guys want to come with Tammy and me to get some pizza? Just the four of us?"

Rob turned toward Sarah, who smiled and nodded.

"Sure," Rob answered.

"Cool!" James replied and turned back toward Tammy, continuing their conversation.

Rob felt a nervous flutter, realizing this was a date; something he was very inexperienced at and uncomfortable with. At that moment, he felt Sarah slip her hand into his. He glanced back at her and saw her beaming. He smiled. *I think tonight will be all right*, he thought to himself.

chapter fourteen

PRESENT DAY: October 17. Southside Boston, Massachusetts—Al's Used Cars

Al Folgers walked into the automotive garage of his used car business and eyed a car that was up on the lift. His mechanic was underneath the car, turning a wrench. Thin and balding with wire-rimmed glasses perched on his nose, Al carried a clipboard and a half-eaten sub. His favorite working attire was a pair of second-hand suit pants, an oversized sleeveless white shirt, and a cheap clip-on tie—and today was no exception. He believed it gave him an advantage in closing a sale with the class of 'clientele' who visited his lot. Besides, he was too cheap to pay good money for clothes.

As he made his way to the car, he took a bite of his sub and stepped right into a puddle of oil, which then splashed onto his pantlegs. He dropped his clipboard as he swore and grabbed his pants with his free hand. Oil smeared from his pants to his hands, which then spread to his light-blue tie as he grabbed it, creating a thumb-sized dark-brown stain. He pulled out his hanky and wiped the stain, which only made it worse.

"Damn it, John, you pinhead! I told you to clean this spill up!" He picked up his clipboard and wiped it with the napkin he had wrapped around the sub.

John glanced over at Al and snickered. "You want the car repaired on time or not?"

Al walked up to the car's front tire and stared at the tread. "I should've fired your drunk ass years ago." He shook his head. "Too bad your wife's my cousin. She'd nag me night and day if I did. Be useful and take these good tires off and put shitty ones on, then put the good ones on that Corolla out front!"

John kept on wrenching underneath the car. "Someday one of these customers of yours'll find out you're ripping them off just to sell those piece-of-shit lemons you have out front."

Al shook his head. "Those used cars out front make more money than this auto shop does." He started back toward the office. "How else am I gonna pay for your drunken stupors and kiddie porn habit?"

As her boss walked into the office, Al's secretary swung her swivel chair around to face him. He shook his head and scowled.

"Stop looking at me with those buggy eyes, Jan. You creep me out."

"That credit collector called again," she responded in a high-pitched, nasal tone. "Someday you'll have to pay 'em, ya know."

Al ignored her. A flash from the big front window drew their attention as a white van drove into the lot. A man in a hood got out of the driver's side of the van and walked up to a used car. "Screw those collectors," he said as he stared at the man. "I know what I'm doing, so keep on telling them I'm unavoidably detained."

Jan shot an irritated look at Al, then followed his gaze to the man checking out one of the used cars. She glanced back at Al. "Well, are ya gonna go out there or not?"

Al glared at Jan. "Shut up and mind your business." He peered back at the man in the lot. "Do your own job, and don't screw it up this time," he said, then left the office.

Jan glared at Al as he sauntered toward the man in the lot. She brushed under her chin and flicked her fingers forward in a rude Italian hand gesture. "*Marón!*" she muttered angrily. She went back to her typing for a moment, then peeked back out the window at Al, who had just reached the customer. She didn't know why, but something about the man caught her interest, so she kept watching the interaction. *Strange how the man seems to hide his face in his hood*, she thought. She noticed that the man had his back to Al and was staring into the side window of a used car as Al spoke to him. Then, it happened. The customer turned and faced Al, grabbed him with one hand around the neck and picked him up completely off the ground, then punched him, causing Al to go limp. Jan popped up from her chair, stunned. In an instant, the man dragged Al to the back of his van, threw him in, closed the door, then rushed to the driver's seat. She shook her head.

"John! John!" she screamed, then grabbed the phone and dialed 9-1-1.

John rushed into the office. "What! What's up!"

Jan pointed a shaky finger at the van, now making its way out of the lot, the phone pressed to her ear. "That man just knocked Al out and kidnapped him!"

John glanced out the window, then rushed out the front door into the lot. He stopped running as the van pulled out into the street and drove away. John ran back into the office.

"Hello, I just saw my boss get kidnapped by a man in a white van!" the secretary screamed into the phone, then glanced up at John.

"I didn't get the plate number," John blurted out, then watched out the window at nothing as Jan spoke to 9-1-1 dispatch.

Jan hung up. "They're on their way." She stared out the window. "Oh my God! What just happened?"

John shook his head. "Looks like he scammed the wrong person this time."

* * *

Detective Sergeant Sadler popped his head into Lieutenant Huff's office. "Boss! A person's just been kidnapped by a man in a white van only minutes ago!"

Huff shot up from his desk. "Shit! Where?"

"Southside Boston. We've got units on their way to the bridge. One's there already."

Huff grabbed his jacket and rushed to the door, and he and Sadler bolted out of the office.

* * *

Patrolman Ed Haggerty went through the red light at a high speed, his lights flashing and siren screaming. "This is it, Cal!" he yelled excitedly to his partner. "I can feel it. We're gonna catch this October killer bastard!"

Cal peered out the window nervously. "Be careful, Ed. You're driving wicked fast."

"We're all right," Ed replied. "I don't wanna get there too late." He pointed in front of the car. "There's the bridge."

The center of the Charlestown Bridge had supports made up of steel girders and frames, which blocked Ed's view of the other side. When they reached the end, he noticed that two patrol cars had beaten them there and were strategically positioned on both sides of the road. The police officers had just pulled a white van over, and the driver was already out of the car. Ed eased the cruiser across the last few feet of the bridge and slowly drove up to the police officer waving him over. Cal lowered his window.

"Stay in your car, Ed!" the officer directed. "As we pull over white vans, I need you ready if someone attempts to flee." He pointed at the van on the side of the road. "We just cleared that one. More help's on the way, but the problem is, he should be here any second."

"You got it, Sarge," Ed replied, then pulled his car off to the side and backed in, engine running. Not ten seconds later, a white van appeared on the bridge, just passing by the center steel girders. "Here's one coming!" Ed yelled. The van abruptly slowed to a stop even before it reached the end of the bridge, causing the vehicles behind it to stop. Ed could now hear car horns blowing.

"Oh, he sees us for sure!" Cal yelled.

Ed nodded. "For him to stop like that, Cal, it's gotta be him." Ed pointed at the van. "There's no way he can back up outta there with all that traffic jammed up behind him, and he can't get over the centerline wall and fence between his lane and the outgoing traffic even if he wanted to try to escape in the outbound lane."

"Yeah! Unless . . ." Cal replied, his voice trailing off as he spotted a small break in the wall.

The police radio buzzed with activity. In an instant, the white van accelerated forward, then made a sharp U-turn into the outgoing lanes through the small break in the wall, nearly colliding with the oncoming traffic. The rapid screech of brakes from the vehicles trying to avoid the van caused another road jam.

"Shit!" Ed yelled, turned on his lights and siren, then accelerated onto the bridge into the oncoming traffic, keeping near the centerline in order to needle through to the small break in the wall. He heard the sergeant call on the radio about the suspect's U-turn. The oncoming traffic slowed to a crawl and attempted to move out of the way of Ed's patrol car. He was nearing the break in the wall, but the traffic wasn't budging fast enough.

"Come on! Come on! Move over!"

"10-31, 1-November-1 in pursuit," Cal announced over the radio. Two other police vehicles got right on Ed's tail and followed him through the traffic, single file.

"All patrols, suspect vehicle has been blocked at the south side of the bridge! Suspect's door just opened," a voice over the radio announced. "1-November-3 on the scene with another unit; request immediate assistance."

"Got him!" Ed blurted out. After a few seconds, he finally reached the break in the wall and darted into the outgoing lanes. "Yes!" As he passed the center steel support frame, his view opened up and he saw the white van blocked at the end of the bridge, nose-to-nose with one police car and jammed into the road wall by another. Traffic was at a standstill, but the left lane was open. The police vehicle lights were flashing, and both had their doors open, as well as the driver's side door to the white van.

Something's wrong, Ed thought.

"Oh my God!" Cal shouted, then grabbed the radio. "All patrols, 10-00, officers down! Officers down!"

Ed saw exactly what Cal responded to on the radio. Multiple police officers were lying motionless on the pavement near the opened driver's side door of the van. They sped toward the scene. Drivers on the bridge had their doors open, half out of their vehicles, pointing to the opposite side of the van between two large buildings just beyond the bridge. Ed parked the car, and he and Cal rushed out of their vehicle, pulling their handguns from their holsters. Other police officers jumped out of their vehicles and joined them.

"He ran over there!" a driver yelled. "He attacked the police and ran over there!"

"I'll go!" Cal yelled, then sprinted in the direction the drivers were pointing.

Ed scurried the other way to the assist the downed police officers. He checked the pulses of the motionless officers as additional officers arrived on the scene.

A police sergeant zipped up to Ed, who was just staring at the police officers lying on the ground. "Haggerty!" the police sergeant yelled at Ed, the latter clearly in a daze.

Ed slowly turned his head toward the police sergeant, then looked at the fallen police officers again. "They're dead, Sarge. Malone, Haskill, Johnson, Vasquez . . . all dead."

"Did you see it?" the sergeant asked.

Ed shook his head slowly, still staring. "That's the strange thing," he continued. "We heard Malone on the radio saying they had the van trapped, and within minutes we made it over the bridge." He paused. "The guy didn't have time to take out four cops, let alone armed, experienced officers."

"Sarge!" a police officer screamed from the back of the white van, the back door now opened.

The sergeant wheeled his body in the direction of the van. "What?"

"Someone's tied up in the back of this van!" the police officer replied. "Alive!"

* * *

Forty minutes later, Lieutenant Huff stood behind the white van, staring in at its interior. He glanced around at the police tape that sealed off the entire area and watched police divert the high volume of traffic around the scene.

Sadler approached him.

"Check this out, Detective Sergeant," Huff said and pointed inside the van. "The entire interior is lined with plastic."

Sadler scanned the inside of the van. "Smart bastard. We've got units searching the area and have an APB out. Doesn't look good."

"Hopefully forensics can find something inside the van," Huff said, then peeked over at the medical personnel surrounding the four dead officers. "Now he's a cop killer, too." He glanced around. "Detective Sergeant, where's the witness, that lady driver?"

Sadler pointed to the woman speaking to a police officer. "That's her, Lieutenant. Her name is Anna . . . Dragovitz, or something."

Huff turned and headed toward the witness, followed by Sadler. The woman glanced up at Huff.

"Hi, Anna. My name is Detective Lieutenant Huff. I know you're giving a statement to the patrol officer, but do you mind telling me what you saw?"

Anna nodded. "It was out of a horror movie," she explained in an eastern European accent. She pointed to her car, which was thirty feet away from the white van. "I stopped my car when the police cars jammed the van into the fence." She dropped her head and took a drag of a cigarette, her hands shaking.

"It's fine," Huff said reassuringly. "Please continue."

"The man in the van got out and put both of his hands on the van, like he was going to be arrested. The first thing the police did was lunge from their cars and point their guns at him. One of the policemen came up to the man and put handcuffs on him."

Sadler and Huff glanced at each other, both confused.

"The other policemen ran up to them and . . ." Anna paused. "It was like he never had the handcuffs on. His hands came from behind his back, then everything was a blur." She took another drag, exhaled, but didn't continue speaking.

"Go on, Anna. It's OK," Huff said.

Anna stared into Huff's eyes. "I saw him ferociously attack each policeman, and they fell like dominos in a matter of seconds." She pointed between the buildings to the right. "Then he ran that way."

"Did you get a good look at the man?" Sadler asked.

Anna shook her head. "He had a hood covering his face." She glanced over at the policeman who was receiving her statement. "I told the police officer that he was definitely Caucasian, medium height, and he had no mustache or beard that I could see."

"Thank you, Anna. You've been very helpful." Huff nodded at the witness, then the officer, and then he walked away with Sadler.

"Are we to believe this guy broke his cuffs?" Sadler asked in disbelief.

Huff shook his head. "Ah, they must not have secured them." He paused. "If I didn't know any better, I'd say this guy put his hands on the van in a submissive gesture just to lure the officers toward him before he attacked."

"If that's true, he knew he'd be able to escape from the cuffs."

A police officer approached Huff and Sadler. "Lieutenant, strangest thing. The vehicle is registered to a Samuel Heflin at 235 Broadway, Cambridge, Massachusetts." He shook his head. "But there *is* no Samuel Heflin at that address. Never was."

"Go on," Sadler replied in disbelief.

The police officer pointed to the van. "So, I checked the VIN on that van, and it was reported stolen four years ago out of Salem." He paused. "I think this guy stole it and faked the registration."

Huff nodded to the police officer. "Makes sense to me. Good work." The officer nodded back and turned away. Huff glanced over at Sadler. "Last time I checked, registering a vehicle in the state of Massachusetts is a rigorous process; matching VIN numbers with vehicles and multiple IDs. Odd."

Sadler nodded. "This is getting stranger by the minute." He pointed to a police officer, who was speaking to a pedestrian. "The sergeant just told me that the police were on the scene in less than two minutes. How could this guy do all this in only two minutes?"

"Maybe it was actually longer than two minutes."

"That's what he said," Sadler replied. "And Anna's recount of the events supports it."

Huff shook his head. "I don't know what to say." He glanced over at the man found in the back of the van, who was yelling at the two medics who were trying to treat the bump on his head. "Let's talk with . . . who's this?" he asked Sadler.

"Al Folgers," Sadler replied as he stared at his pocket notepad. "He owns a dive used car lot on the south side. He's been in and out of civil and criminal court for questionable business practices for years."

"How'd you know all that already?" Huff asked.

"I arrested that shady character three years ago," Sadler replied as they approached him. "Don't forget a face."

The medic treating Al turned toward Huff, shaking his head in frustration. "He's refusing medical treatment here and refuses to go to the medical center."

"Mr. Folgers, my name is Detective Lieutenant Huff, and this is Detective Sergeant Sadler. How are you feeling?"

"Fine," Al replied. "I just got cold cocked. Not like it's never happened before."

"You are a witness in an ongoing homicide investigation, Mr. Folgers," Huff explained, "so, you have a couple of choices. You can either go to the hospital and get medical treatment and we can interview you there, or you can refuse medical treatment and come straight to the station. You will not be released on your own recognizance for a while."

Al glared at Huff, then glanced over at the medics. "I'll go to the station. I'll be damned if I'm going to pay some huge medical bill."

The medic approached Al with a clipboard. "Sign here, then here, stating that you refuse medical assistance."

"I ain't signing shit!" Al yelled.

Huff nodded to the medic. "I'll take responsibility. You can go."

The medic rolled his eyes, then walked away with his partner.

"So, did you get a look at the man who did this?" Huff asked.

Al touched the bruise near his eye, cringed, and shook his head. "No, he had a hood over his face, and it happened so fast. He wasn't any bigger than me, but he was strong as an ox." Al glanced at Sadler. "He picked me off my feet with one hand!"

"I want you to think back, Mr. Folgers," Huff requested. "Were you ever in contact with anyone or did anything happen recently that could possibly be related to you being kidnapped?"

Al shook his head again. "I piss people off all the time, but not enough for someone to do this." He paused. "At least, I don't think so."

Huff turned around at the sound of a small commotion to see Dr. Dunham showing his credentials to a police officer, then heading straight to the white van. "Thank you, Mr. Folgers," Huff said. "Soon you'll be taken to the station." Huff and Sadler turned toward Dunham.

Sadler snickered as he watched Dunham inspect the van with his latex gloves on. "Just like a bloodhound on a scent, our Dr. Dunham."

"All the better," Huff replied as they reached the van. "Good afternoon, Dr. Dunham."

Dunham turned around. "Ah, good afternoon, gentlemen. I apologize for not greeting you before diving right in, but this van just might lead us to our offender." Dunham paused respectfully. "I see he's now murdered four police officers."

Huff sighed and nodded. "So, you heard he got away," he said and shook his head. "Shit! So close."

Dunham stopped and stared at the shrouded police officers lying on the ground. "Not close enough," Dunham replied gravely, then glanced over at Al Folgers. "Is that the intended victim?"

"Yes," Sadler answered. "Al Folgers."

"We need his clothes for a forensic analysis," Dunham explained.

Despite the serious moment, Sadler burst out laughing. "Oh, he's gonna love that. The guy's got a *real* sunny disposition."

"The van's registered under a false name," Huff explained, "and the VIN matches a van that was stolen four years ago—just before our serial killer began his October murders."

Dunham paused and stared at the van's ceiling for a moment. "That takes some strategic planning and access to resources." He scanned the interior. "Depending upon what we find, this van will not only help us ID the offender, but it just might give us physical evidence connecting many of the murders."

Huff noticed something under the driver's side visor. "What do we have here?" he asked.

Dunham opened the visor and pulled out a remote with a keypad. "Hmm. A wireless remote garage door keypad." He paused. "We'll definitely have to dust for latent prints."

Huff raised his eyebrows. "Maybe we could contact the manufacturer, get the passcode and frequency, then try to activate all the garages around the Salem area?" He shrugged his shoulders. "That's like finding a needle in a haystack, but it's something."

"Excellent thought, Lieutenant Huff," Dunham said. "Even if it becomes logistically impossible to arm the entire police force with garage door openers, at least we could use it on any hot leads or to eliminate suspected locations."

Huff noticed that Folgers was being led away to a police cruiser. "Detective Sergeant, let's get back to the station and interview Folgers. Maybe he'll remember something important."

Sadler nodded.

"I'm going to hang out here for a while and help out forensics," Dunham stated.

"Didn't expect anything different, Dr. Dunham," Huff answered.

* * *

Hours later, Al Folgers' secretary, Jan, was sitting at her desk, staring up at the corner of the room, watching the flat-screen TV. She glanced out the window and watched a police car pull into the used car lot. The back door opened, and Al exited then rushed into the office. He walked by Jan without even acknowledging her, opened up a drawer, and pulled out a bottle of whiskey. He sat in his chair, took a big swig, and stared at the TV.

"It's been all over the news—four cops dead," Jan stated. "They say you may have been kidnapped by the October serial killer."

"Bullshit," Al blurted out. "It was a couple of Johnny Rizzo's thugs. Looked like Caine; I'm sure of it."

"The TV said there was only one man, and that's all I saw kidnap you," Jan replied.

Al shook his head. "One man couldn't do all that kind of damage. Those witnesses have their heads up their asses. The other guy must've been in the passenger seat." He touched the bruise on the side of his face and grimaced. "I told that asshole, Rizzo, two days ago I'd be getting the money." He sat up out of his seat, opened his safe, pulled out a handgun and holster, and concealed it behind his belt and pants. "I'll be ready next time." He sat back down with his head back.

"Wow, your neck's all red," Jan noticed.

"No shit, Sherlock," Al responded sarcastically, then took another swig. "The nut grabbed me by the neck and lifted me off the ground. I thought my head was going to pop off."

Jan threw her coat on, grabbed her purse, and walked to the door. "Why don't you go home too?" she suggested. "Lie on the couch and drink more whiskey or something."

Al shook his head, still staring at the TV. "If I know Rizzo, since he didn't get a piece of me, he'll take it out on my property. I'm staying here a while . . . introduce them to my forty-five caliber if they show up here."

"Suit yourself," Jan replied, then slammed the office door behind her.

Al took two more gulps, belched, rubbed his neck and writhed in pain. Within twenty minutes he'd passed out, snoring as loudly as the TV was blaring. A jarring motion woke him up. He felt like he was being lifted. By the time he came to his senses, he was outside, slung over the shoulder of a powerful man who was walking away from the building, Al bouncing along like a ragdoll.

"Wha . . . ? Hey! What the hell!" Al tried to wriggle out of the man's grasp, but his efforts were in vain. He reached for his handgun in his hip holster, but it was gone. "Let me go!" he screamed, flailing his arms and striking the man in the shoulders and back of the head, but the man completely ignored his assault. "Hey, I've got the money for Mr. Rizzo in the safe in my office. I'll get it; just let me down."

The man remained silent and continued toward a dark-colored van. He opened up the back, flung Al from his shoulders and into the back of the running van, then knocked him out with another punch to the head.

Al's body rolled limply into the van's interior wall as the driver signaled and turned out of the lot, leaving the scene at exactly the posted speed limit.

chapter fifteen

Dunham popped his head into Lieutenant Huff's office and spotted the lieutenant and Sadler hunched over an open folder lying on the desk.

"Is it true? Al Folgers was kidnapped again—the same day?"

"That's exactly what happened," Huff replied, "but no one reported him missing until first thing this morning. The secretary claims she and the mechanic thought he just stayed home recuperating from the attack, until one of them saw his car parked alongside the dozen other cars in the used car lot."

"Determined evil soul, isn't he," Sadler added. "This killer was hellbent on kidnapping Folgers and had the balls to do it, even though the entire police force was on high alert."

"I believe this confirms two suspicions," Dunham surmised. "First, his selection of victims is not random, and second, the dates of his kidnappings and sacrifices have meaning to him."

"The traffic camera at the intersection next to the used car lot recorded a van leaving his place at 3:24 a.m.," Sadler interrupted.

Dunham nodded. "He's planning a sacrifice in two days."

Huff shook his head slightly. "He planned on kidnapping him before midnight, so doesn't this mean the sacrifice'll be tomorrow?"

"Originally, yes, but if I'm correct," Dunham answered, "three days between kidnapping and sacrifice is crucial in his mind."

"Why do you suppose this guy's waiting three days every time?" Sadler asked.

Dunham nodded. "If we accept that the offender is offering his victims to Satan, or Lucifer, it actually makes sense. Christ died on the cross, and three days later he rose from the dead—death to life. The offender may be attempting to appease Satan by performing an 'anti-resurrection' after three days—life to death."

Huff nodded. "That does make sense."

"Do we know if Folgers owned a cell phone?" Dunham asked.

"Yes, but his secretary said he didn't want anyone calling him, so he never carried it." Sadler handed a file to Dunham. "Multiple latent prints were discovered in the white van, all from one individual; identical to the print pulled at the Granary Burying Ground."

"At least we know Folgers' kidnapper is our man," Huff said.

"Anything else?" Dunham asked.

"They're still analyzing a few fibers, hairs, and some soil they discovered in the van," Huff answered. "I'll let you know the results once I get word." He handed Dunham a clear plastic bag.

Dunham studied the contents. "Oh, the wireless garage door keypad from the van. What did they find?"

"Besides fingerprints," Huff answered, "the manufacturer claims that this particular remote keypad was sold at a hardware store ten miles west of Salem."

Dunham nodded. "Excellent; confirms the geographic patterns of the victims' cell phones."

"Sure does," Huff agreed. "Now, the manufacturer identified the frequency of this particular remote and claims it's not a common one, but he also said that they have no way of determining the passcode once it gets changed from the default factory setting, as in the case with this one. All they can do is reset it."

Sadler leaned over and tapped the remote. "We've purchased a dozen of these with the same frequency and rushed them to the Salem Police Department this morning."

Huff grinned. "Looks like my idea is coming to fruition. Starting today, they're pushing the buttons as they drive along the streets."

"Hopefully, within the next day, we'll get a hit," Dunham said then stood up. "I was actually on my way back to Virginia to visit my wife, but I'll have to postpone it until after the suspected day of his sacrifice."

"Fly her in," Sadler suggested. "Everyone loves Boston."

Dunham thought for a moment, then nodded. "Funny you should say that. Maggie was hoping for just that. I believe I will have her visit, although not just for social reasons."

"What do you mean?" Sadler asked.

"My wife is an expert on Celtic studies, which includes Halloween," Dunham explained. "Maybe she can shed some light on the significance of October 31. We have yet to connect his satanic sacrifice to this date."

Huff walked over to the wall maps displaying the locations of kidnappings and sacrifices by the October serial killer. "Let us know what your wife says, Dr. Dunham." He stared at the map. "In the meantime, any thoughts on where his next sacrifice'll be? Maybe we're missing something here."

Dunham joined him at the maps, paying particular attention to the map with the sacrifice locations. "These locations do have meaning to our offender, so maybe there is something. Do you have photos of each location?"

"I got it," Sadler replied, opening a folder, then spreading a number of photos on the table. "I'll separate them by year." As Sadler placed the photos on the table, Dunham studied them.

"There are a few patterns we identified," Huff began. "All are outdoors; most are near a stream or river, maybe a bridge; and many are in or near forested areas."

Dunham stared at the fourteen photos, slowly shifting his gaze from one to another. At one point, he backtracked and glanced between a couple photos in particular. "It's interesting that the Eliot Memorial Bridge and Paul's Bridge, both in Milton, the Echo Bridge near Newton . . ." He stopped mid-sentence, shifting his attention to the other photos. He glanced up at Huff and Sadler.

"What?" Huff asked.

Dunham grinned. "I believe I found another pattern."

Huff and Sadler crowded him.

"What is it?" Huff asked.

Dunham pointed at a photo. "Notice the stone archway." He paused. "Every time our offender has committed a murder-sacrifice near a bridge, the bridges are made of stone or some earthen material in the shape of supporting archways." He stared at Huff and Sadler. "You're looking at a doorway."

Sadler pulled two of the photos. "How about the locations not anywhere close to a bridge or river, like the Granary Burying Ground murder site and the war memorial?" He pulled a third photo. "And the Victory Park murder site?"

Dunham pointed at one of the photos. "Notice the stone entrance to the cemetery, with a horizontal stone piece supported by two vertical stone pieces. Here it is again at the Victory garden, and a similar stone feature at the war memorial." He paused. "Stone doorways."

"Well I'll be," said a surprised Sadler. "This asshole is picking his sites near stone arches or door-looking features."

Huff typed on his computer. "Problem. I just Google mapped the science museum murder site, and I don't see anything remotely resembling a stone arch or door." He paused. "Just a big dinosaur."

"Hold it," Sadler interjected. "Check out across the street under the train tracks—arched stone supports. That's less than fifty feet away from the murder site."

Huff grinned. "Why, look at that." He glanced up at Sadler. "We need to contact task force members from the surrounding jurisdictions immediately and identify any locations in their particular areas that have these stone arches and doors."

"Excuse the pun, boss," Sadler replied, "but this sounds like a monumental task."

"So it is, Detective Sergeant, but thanks to Dr. Dunham, we have our first pattern that just might lead us to this killer's next site."

At the sound of a commotion taking place just outside the task force room, all three turned in the direction of the loud voices.

"What's this all about?" Huff asked.

"All I want to do is talk with him!" a male voice yelled.

Sadler shook his head and glanced at Huff. "That's Sergeant Friedman." He eyed Dunham. "He wants to speak with you, but I won't let him."

"What does he want?" Dunham asked.

"Last year, his wife was attacked and murdered in his home," Huff explained. "The case remains unsolved to this day. It was a clear case of robbery, and we believe his wife was at the wrong place at the wrong time."

Dunham frowned and shook his head. "How sad."

"She was found next to the screen door in the kitchen, which exits into the back yard," Sadler added. "She sustained blunt-force trauma to her skull, and forensics identified the murder weapon as the perpetrator's boot."

"As you can guess," Huff added, "since he's one of our own, we left no stone unturned at the time. Forensics was extremely thorough throughout the entire house, and we interviewed everyone within a few blocks of their house in all directions—the neighbors, delivery guys, dog walkers, everyone—and we came up with nothing."

"We did get a partial print, but it wasn't enough to ID anyone conclusively," Sadler interrupted.

"Actually, Lieutenant Huff," Dunham said, "if you don't mind, I would be more than happy to look at the case file. Of course, I'm not sure how much help I'll be. It sounds like your department covered everything."

"OK." Huff nodded. He walked over to the door. "Bring Sergeant Friedman in! Dr. Dunham would like to speak with him!"

A distraught man in uniform walked slowly into the room. Four other police officers followed him. Huff place his arm around his shoulders. "It's all right, Sarge."

Dunham stood up and greeted the widower. "Hi, Sergeant Friedman. They informed me of your wife's murder. I'm so sorry."

Friedman paused and composed himself. "Thanks, Dr. Dunham. I know you're busy, but is there any way you can review this case folder? Maybe we missed something."

Dunham nodded. "Of course, but I can't promise anything."

The officer to Friedman's right handed Dunham the case file.

Friedman nodded. "I know, I know, but it would mean a lot to me," he glanced at the other officers, "to us."

Dunham opened the folder. "Are the autopsy results in here?"

"Yes," an officer replied.

Dunham glanced up at everyone. "Give me some time. I'd like to review everything; crime scene management, evidence collection, documentation, photos, sketches, even the reconstruction. Anything I can do to help."

Friedman nodded. "Thank you, Dr. Dunham," he said quietly as everyone but Huff and Sadler left the room.

"How about some coffee, Dr. Dunham?" Sadler asked.

Dunham nodded. "Sounds great. Just cream, please."

"I'll go with you," Huff said to Sadler. "Dunkin' Donuts?"

Sadler nodded as they left the room.

Dunham opened the file, read the reports, spread the photos out, and studied each one. He surveyed the photos of the crime scene and Friedman's home. After about thirty minutes, Huff and Dunham returned with the coffee. Dunham continued to review the contents of the case file.

Another thirty minutes went by. Huff glanced at Sadler. "Look how zoned he is," he whispered.

"He's in his element," Sadler replied.

Another few minutes went by before Dunham glanced up a Huff. "This investigation certainly was thorough. My initial assessment is that I agree with the conclusions that the offender's agenda was robbery. I see no evidence of a personal agenda against Sergeant Friedman's wife or Friedman himself, and there was an unusual amount of time invested by the offender searching for items of worth after the murder. If his agenda was personal and he was attempting to hide his tracks in order to make it look like a robbery gone awry, we would generally see conflicting physical evidence in a rush to leave the crime scene." He paused. "I don't see this."

"Our thoughts exactly," Huff responded.

"The fact that you found a partial print means he wasn't wearing gloves," Dunham added, "so I'm surprised he didn't leave more latent prints."

"We noticed he tried to wipe down everything," Sadler said.

"Albeit an impersonal crime," Dunham commented, as he re-read a statement, "the offender clearly knew when to enter the home. The surprise for the offender was that Friedman's wife stayed home from work on that day."

"Dr. Gillespie came up with that very same conclusion," Huff replied.

Dunham read the autopsy report, then studied the victim photos again. He pulled the head injury photo closer, studied it, then scanned the photos of the home. He grabbed the photo of the entrance hallway. He glanced up at Huff and Sadler. "She was initially attacked in the hallway, but the attack continued into the kitchen."

Surprised by Dunham's statement, Huff and Sadler rushed behind him. "Forensics didn't come up with that! How do you know?"

Dunham pointed at the wounds on the victim's face. "Do you see these small, repetitive marks partially hidden by the tread marks?"

Huff nodded. "Yes."

"These are not part of the tread marks from the boot," Dunham explained. "The medical examiner probably thought these were subsequent scuff marks, but I've seen these marks before." He paused. "On my own face."

"What?" Huff asked.

Dunham grabbed the hallway photo. "As a young teenager, I was hit in the head with a baseball, and for weeks, I had these marks on my forehead. I believe what we're looking at are baseball stitching patterns, and when this idea popped into my head, I looked through the crime scene photos for baseball paraphernalia." He handed Huff the hallway photo and pointed at one spot. "Notice the trophies in the hallway trophy case. There's a baseball." Dunham turned around and caught the attention of a police officer walking by. "Could you bring Sergeant Friedman back in here please?"

She nodded, then walked away.

Huff scrutinized the photo. "It certainly does look like she has a baseball stitching pattern on her face, but I'm not as confident as you are. I can see it being a scuff mark too."

"It's just a suspicion. I know forensics dusted for prints in the trophy case, but nowhere does it say they collected any trace evidence with the vacuum."

Friedman rushed into the room. "Yes, Dr. Dunham."

Dunham handed Friedman the hallway photo. "Sergeant, do you still have that baseball in the trophy case?"

Friedman nodded. "Yeah, it's been sitting in there for years."

"Were there any other baseballs in the trophy case?" Dunham asked.

"No; just that one. I caught it in the stands at a Red Sox game when I was a kid."

"Are you aware of anyone handling it recently?" Dunham asked.

Friedman shook his head. "No, no one. No one has touched it since I put it in the trophy case years ago."

"As you may know," Dunham began, "'Touch DNA' is the process of collecting minute amounts of organic material, such as skin cells. We collect samples with a forensic vacuum and collection filters."

Friedman glanced over at Sadler, confused. "Do you think this guy touched my baseball?"

"Yes," Dunham answered. "I believe your wife was initially attacked in the hallway when our offender was searching through your trophy case for valuables, then the fight ensued to the kitchen," Dunham explained. "If I'm correct, she probably surprised him, so he grabbed the baseball and struck her with it, then placed it back in the trophy case. This would cause not only his DNA to be deposited on the ball, but also her DNA. Even if he wiped away any fingerprints, skin cells still might be on the surface."

Huff spoke to Friedman. "Sergeant, would you please escort a criminal investigation team to your home and have them collect that baseball? Make sure they have the forensic vacuum and filters."

"Yes, sir!" Friedman beamed, tears glistening in his eyes, as he and four other police officers rushed out of the office.

Huff turned toward Dunham. "Thank you again, Dr. Dunham."

"Now, we may not come up with anything," Dunham warned.

"Regardless, you just made his day," Huff said. "Hope hasn't been in his life in a long time; even if it's only short term."

"If it's a dead end, I'll spend some more time on the case. I have a few other ideas."

"We can't thank you enough," Huff replied.

"Back to the October serial killer's taste for stone arches and doors," Dunham said. "Maybe my wife can shed some light on this too. I bet there's a connection."

"Enjoy your time with your wife, Dr. Dunham," Huff said, "because your life is about to get real busy real fast."

* * *

South Boston, Massachusetts, Cathedral of the Holy Cross

Father Martin kneeled in the pew in the main chapel, deep in prayer. A few minutes later, he sensed someone kneeling next to him, unusually close. He opened his eyes and glanced over at Father O'Farrell, also deep in prayer.

After a moment, O'Farrell blessed himself, opened his eyes, and leaned toward Martin. "My apologies for interrupting your prayer, Father Martin, but could you come to my office after your morning session? There seems to have been a slight break in the case, which may interest you."

Father Martin signed the cross. "Excellent timing, Father. I've just finished."

As Martin and O'Farrell were seating themselves in the latter's office, O'Farrell pointed to the iced tea pitcher on his desk. "Would you like some iced tea, Father?"

"No thank you, Father," Martin replied.

"Well, it seems that Dr. Dunham has had success in advancing the investigation, almost to the point of our subject's capture a couple of days ago . . . only for the offender to have escaped a roadblock."

"As expected in both cases—Dunham's success and our subject's escape," Martin replied. "Did the suspect kill anyone during his escape?"

O'Farrell nodded. "Four police officers."

Martin glared at O'Farrell. "Father, I warned you this would happen. They have no idea what they're up against."

O'Farrell shook his head. "Our instructions are clear, Father Martin. We are in no position to question their decision." O'Farrell paused until Martin nodded in agreement.

"My apologies, Father," Martin replied.

O'Farrell smiled kindly. "They have possibly identified Salem as the general location of where our subject operates out of."

"Salem," Martin responded. "Interesting. A place of unholy history."

O'Farrell nodded. "Since it's expected that our subject will be sacrificing his victim in two days, the task force, along with the Salem Police Department, is making a concerted effort to find it. You might want to visit our Salem parish tomorrow in order to be there if they are successful."

"Yes, Father," Martin replied.

"And Dunham has discovered how our subject selects the locations of his sacrifices, although the connection to *Porta infirni proxime* is still foreign to them, but he is a smart man. He'll soon make the connection."

Martin nodded, then stood up to leave. "I understand, Father. I'll keep you informed."

chapter sixteen

PRESENT DAY: October 19. Salem, Massachusetts

Salem Police Officer Norm Gross aimed the remote at a garage door of a passing building and pushed the button, but nothing happened. He glanced over at his partner, Officer Robert O'Donnell, who was driving the patrol car. "RJ, this is gonna be like finding a needle in a haystack. I've pushed this thing literally a thousand times, and nothing's happened."

"It's the only thing we have to go on, Norm," RJ replied. "Nothin' else makes sense."

"Bullshit," Norm blurted out. "This guy kills on Halloween and he's from here—Salem. It screams one thing: witches. He's part of that witch religion. What do ya call it?"

"Wicca."

"Yeah, Wicca," Norm repeated. "These Wiccans think Salem is holy ground because of the witch trials." He paused. "You know, these witches are into Satan with their witches' hellbroth and eating babies, and apparently, the October murders are satanic sacrifices as per the Watchmaker himself." He pushed the button at another garage door, but again nothing happened. Norm raised his hands in frustration.

"You watch too many movies, Norm," RJ replied. "I can see 'em into satanic rituals and all, but eating babies?" He shook his head. "Besides, rumor has it that this remote garage door thing is the Watchmaker's idea."

Norm scowled. "Ah, that came from Detective McCafferty, right? Consider the source. Would the Watchmaker be making us do this kinda shit?"

RJ shook his head. "McCafferty's not the only Salem detective on the serial killer task force. This came from Griffin."

Norm stared out the window. "I say we go to that Wiccan priest." He glanced over at RJ. "You know, the one who runs that witch museum, Halloween Place, or whatever, on Pickering Wharf."

RJ shot a glance back at Norm. "What? How do you know he's a Wiccan priest?"

Norm pushed the button at another garage. "The wife went there this summer. Some cousins came into town, so she did the tourist thing with them. I saw a photo of him wearing a satanic pentagram necklace! How about them apples?" Norm pointed out the front windshield. "It's just a block down there on Wharf Street. Come on."

RJ drove silently, contemplating Norm's suggestion. "I dunno."

"Hey, there's probably garage doors around that area, anyway." Norm paused, staring at RJ. "Come on, RJ; let's do it. We'll just ask a few questions. That's all."

"You gonna behave?" RJ asked.

Norm grinned and held up his hand. "Scout's honor."

RJ turned the police car toward Wharf Street. "OK, but if this guy puts a curse on my family, it's your ass."

Within a few minutes, RJ pulled onto Wharf Street in the Pickering Wharf outdoor shopping area. Wharf Street was in a block-long U-shape on the coastline, and on each side were separate buildings with storefronts. The large redbrick sidewalk gave it an open, spacious atmosphere. RJ pulled into a parking spot in front of the Halloween store, which was decorated on the outside with seasonal items, most prominently numerous pumpkins. Overhead was a large Halloween sign painted black with orange letters stating, 'Hallowe'en Town.'

"Pickering Wharf's pretty empty," Norm commented as they got out of the cruiser. "Not many tourists today." Norm entered the store, RJ trailing behind. He scanned the long, narrow room, which was dominated by a glass showcase counter. Black shelves displayed touristy Halloween items for sale. He noticed that the walls were adorned with objects he associated with witchcraft: stuffed bats, birds, black cats, and even rats. There was a framed picture of a pentagram. In all, the room had a macabre feel to it. The only thing missing were people;

the store seemed to be empty. In that moment, an elderly lady popped her head up from behind the counter, startling Norm and RJ.

"May I help you?" the lady asked in a very nasal tone.

"Yes, we'd like to speak with the owner," Norm replied.

The lady walked around the counter, putting on a jacket and throwing her purse over her shoulder. "He's in the museum." She walked toward the museum entrance. "Mr. Ellsworth! Two police officers are here to see you! I'm leaving now! Bye!" she called as she walked out of the store.

"Bye, Ethyl!" Ellsworth yelled from inside the museum. "Come on in the museum, Officers!"

"Hello!" RJ yelled as he and Norm neared the museum entrance. The sign over the doorframe stated, 'Hall of Witches Museum.' He glanced over at Norm and waved at him to follow. "Come on; over here." RJ and Norm slowly entered the small museum. On each side of them were lighted wax displays of witch-related scenes. To the right was a forest scene with a large black cauldron surrounded by three grotesque, evil-looking, green-skinned witches.

Norm pointed at the scene and glanced at RJ over his glasses. "See? I told ya," he whispered.

"That's our scene of misconception," a man at the top of a rickety old ladder answered. "Hi, my name is Brian Ellsworth. I own the place." He started his descent, but halfway down the ladder he stumbled.

RJ rushed below him and grasped the ladder. "Be careful!"

Ellsworth moved more cautiously the rest of the way. "I'm fine; I'm fine." He glanced up at the two officers. "What can I do for you? Have we done something wrong?"

RJ grinned. "Other than using a ladder that you should have thrown out years ago, nothing, Mr. Ellsworth," he replied kindly, then glanced over at Norm. "We've actually come here for your assistance; for information."

Norm noticed Ellsworth's pentagram necklace, then glanced over at the wax witch scene. "What're these witches cooking?" Norm questioned with an edgy tone. "Something satanic?"

"This is the Shakespearian image of the three evil witches from *Macbeth*, huddled over a brewing hellbroth," Ellsworth responded calmly, clearly used to this kind of reaction. "It surely was satanic, but the reason why we have this display is to explain how witchcraft was incorrectly associated with the Devil's work centuries ago, and we've inherited this misconception to this day."

"We?" RJ asked.

Ellsworth nodded, turned, and waved the two police officers over. "Yes, please follow me." He approached another forest display of a woman engulfed in foliage, sitting next to a horned creature. "*Wicce*, means 'witch' in Old English, and 'Wicca,' means 'wizard' or 'sorcerer.' It is also the name given to our spiritual belief system. Our goal is to better understand the earth and nature and affirm the divinity in all things." He pointed to the woman. "We believe the whole cosmos is alive and connected—something scientists would call the web of life, really." He paused. "It's a very organic view."

Norm pointed at the horned creature. "What's up with the horned demon?"

Ellsworth smiled slightly. "Just as Christianity is expressed physically by the actions of Jesus, we cannot be fully expressed without a godhead, and a dualistic one at that." He pointed at the models. "The woman is our mother goddess, and the male is our horned god. It's sort of like the concept of yin and yang. She represents the earth, moon, and stars, while he represents the sun, forest, and animals."

RJ nodded. "I think I get it, actually."

"They're our physical embodiments of the life force manifested throughout all of nature; the reason why your physical body lives," Ellsworth replied. "Now, in the Christian sense of having one all-powerful creator, we do believe in a 'prime mover.'"

"So, are you good or evil?" Norm asked bluntly.

"Our morality is guided by the Law of Three," Ellsworth answered. "All benevolent or malevolent actions return three-fold." Ellsworth paused, but Norm was confused by his response and raised his eyebrows. "If we do something morally good," Ellsworth continued, "we will receive good three times over. If we do something bad, we will receive something bad three times over. So, we are good."

RJ glanced over at Norm. "That certainly doesn't sound satanic."

Ellsworth nodded. "In a sense, we Wiccans believe we are the counterweight to Satanism. We consider satanic magic as 'black magic,' while our magic is 'white magic.'"

Norm pointed at Ellsworth's pentagram necklace. "So, what gives with the pentagram around your neck?"

Ellsworth nodded as he grasped his pentagram. "Ah, you believe this to be a satanic symbol." He shook his head. "The satanic symbol is an upside-down pentagram, while ours is right side up with the single point of the pentagram pointing to the zenith. A beautiful example of the antithesis to Satanism." He glanced back at RJ. "I believe you came here because of the October serial killer, am I correct?"

Norm shot a glance at Ellsworth in surprise. "Yeah, how'd you know?"

"I don't get many police coming into my store asking about Satanism," Ellsworth explained, "and the October serial killer is dominating the news."

RJ nodded. "Very astute, Mr. Ellsworth, and you've helped us out immensely with this crash course in Wicca, but we've taken up enough of your time."

Mr. Ellsworth suddenly seemed very anxious.

"Speaking of the October serial killer, I'm glad you're here, Officers," Ellsworth said, then hesitated.

"What do you need, Mr. Ellsworth?" RJ asked.

"I've been advised not to speak with you, but I must." He paused. "You see, there's a tenuous bond between white and black magic and the powers manifested through them." He paused again. "Ever since the murders began three years ago, I've been feeling the evil presence responsible for them. It's an evil like I've never felt before. Powerful."

RJ nodded with a neutral expression.

Ellsworth shook his head. "I know this sounds unbelievable, but I have a sort of telepathic ability to sense an evil presence, and my gut tells me this evil resides within a few blocks of here." He pointed north. "I believe the presence is somewhere near the marina."

RJ nodded, then shook Ellsworth's hand. "Thank you, Mr. Ellsworth. We'll certainly check this out." He and Norm turned to walk out, but RJ stopped and glanced over his shoulder. Ellsworth was climbing back up the old creaking ladder to continue his repair. "Oh, Mr. Ellsworth, if you can feel his presence, can he feel yours?"

Ellsworth, visibly concerned, merely nodded and started working on his repairs.

Once they left the store, Norm jumped into the car as RJ started it. "You don't believe that crap, do you?"

"Not the telepathic business," RJ replied, "but he certainly convinced me these Wiccans have no love lost for this killer."

Norm nodded. "Yeah, I guess I was wrong about Wiccans, but hey, we had to ask 'em."

They drove by the marina, and both cops scanned the area.

"Looks good to me," RJ joked. "And I'll be damned if I'm going to spout off at the station that a witch priest told me he *feels* the killer's nearby."

As they continued by the marina, Norm aimed the remote out the window and pushed it a few times. He glanced over at RJ, who gave a quick glare. "Hey, ya never know!"

Twenty minutes later, Ellsworth was still on the ladder working on the same repair job. He heard the front doorbell jingle, signaling that someone had just walked into his store. He stopped his work and listened, and at that moment his mind flooded with fear. The blood drained from his face as he realized that what entered his store was not a customer.

"How did he know so quickly that I spoke to the police?" he whispered to himself, then climbed down the ladder and rushed to a hidden closet next to the display of the horned god and mother goddess. He closed the door, holding onto the hammer he'd been using, and mumbled a protection chant: "If spirits threaten me in this place, fight water by water and fire by fire, banish their souls into nothingness and remove their powers until the last trace, let this evil being flee through time and space." He repeated the chant just under his breath, over and over.

After a few minutes, he stopped chanting and listened. He heard nothing, but the throbbing of the blood flow in his head was seemingly amplified by the darkness of the closet. He felt the intense presence of the evil entity dissipate to a tolerable level. A few more minutes went by and he heard only silence. He slowly grabbed the door handle and cracked the door open. In an instant, the feeling of the entity returned, the door swung open, and someone picked him up off his feet and threw him into the wall. Stunned by the impact, Ellsworth shook his head. He opened his eyes as he sat up, then saw a man in an evil-looking clown mask walking slowly and confidently toward him. He belted out his chant, "If spirits threaten me in this place, fight water by water . . ."

The masked attacker stopped just as Ellsworth spoke the chant. Surprised, the attacker tried to move forward again, then again. He screamed in frustration from behind his mask, but still he could not advance upon Ellsworth.

". . . and fire by fire, banish their souls into nothingness," Ellsworth continued.

The attacker shook his head, picked up the hammer that Ellsworth had dropped, and threw it at him.

As Ellsworth brought his arms up to block the approaching hammer, he inadvertently stopped chanting, and in an instant the attacker grabbed him around the nose and mouth, the clown mask inches from his face. Not only was it now impossible to chant, Ellsworth couldn't breathe. He grabbed the attacker's wrists in order to wrench his head free from the grasp, but to no avail. His terror turned into hysteria as he realized he was being choked to death. Within seconds, his vision dimmed. As he was losing consciousness, he wondered who he would reincarnate into as his soul entered another stage of existence.

Just as Ellsworth went limp, the attacker snapped his neck. He glanced around and noticed the ladder, so he picked Ellsworth up and dropped his body underneath the ladder. Once satisfied, the masked man hovered over the body, opened Ellsworth's mouth, placed his hand over it as if he were suffocating him, then chanted in a deep, low voice. Satisfied, he walked casually out of the museum.

chapter seventeen

PRESENT DAY: October 19. Boston, Massachusetts—Quincy Market

Dunham slid a couple shopping bags off Maggie's shoulder. "Here, hon, let me carry some of these bags for you."

"Thank you, dear." Maggie sighed happily. "I just love Quincy Market—especially the shopping!"

"That's why I suggested it, dear," Dunham said. "Are you hungry yet?"

Maggie nodded and glanced over at Sam's Café at Cheers. "I am, actually. How about here?"

"I've never eaten here," Dunham replied. "Doesn't look too busy. Let's do it." They entered, chose the outdoor section, sat down, then ordered drinks.

"Oh yes, it's nice to get off my feet for a bit," Maggie commented, then took a sip of water. She glanced up at Dunham. "So, how's the investigation going?"

"Well, we've made some inroads, and as I was telling you earlier, we expect something to happen tomorrow, late in the evening."

"Sounds like you're busy," Maggie said. "Maybe I should've come some other time."

Dunham shook his head. "Nonsense; it fit your schedule. And there's actually a professional reason why I wanted you to come too."

"Professional reason?" Maggie asked. "What do you mean?"

"I need to pick your brain," Dunham explained as he pulled out an envelope stuffed with folded papers. "If you recall, the offender has ended his killing spree on Halloween night each of the last three fall seasons, and there's every reason to believe he'll continue this pattern this fall. Also, it's clear his motive is sacrificial, specifically satanic."

"Yes," Maggie interrupted, "I recall you telling me about the six-one-six connection." She leaned forward with a grin and placed her hand on his. "Brilliant deduction; something only my husband would have figured out."

Dunham nodded, beaming. "Why, thank you, my dear."

"I'd love to help, but what can I add?" Maggie asked.

"Well, the problem is Halloween—an area of your expertise," Dunham explained. "Theistic Satanists, which our offender certainly is, do not consider this date significant, at least not significant enough to make the final seasonal sacrifice on that day." He took a drink of water. "Now, Satanism is an extension of the Christian tradition, while I recall you saying Halloween finds its origins with the Celts and Druidism in a festival called Samhain. Am I correct?"

"You are," Maggie replied, "but the Insular Celts, or the Celts from the British Isles, were more or less Christianized by the fourth, maybe fifth century. The Church believed that the way to win over the hearts and minds of these pagans and convert them was to express Christianity in the language of that country through their specific culture and customs."

"So, what are you saying?" Dunham asked.

"This was a time when cultures in the British Isles celebrated much of Christianity through pagan traditions—a melding of Christianity with, in this case, Druidism," Maggie explained. "You can see it with the Celtic Britons, and the king of these Britons, King Arthur."

"King Arthur and the knights of the round table?" Dunham asked.

Maggie nodded. "Yes. Even though the Christian Knights of the Round Table searched for the Christian Holy Grail, they still received advice from a Druidic priest, Merlin the Magician, and had nature spirits, like the Lady of the Lake, who repaired Arthur's sword, Excalibur."

"I see," Dunham replied. "So how about the Halloween connection?"

"The customs and daily lives of Insular Celts revolved around the agricultural and pastoral calendar, including their festivals, and the most significant was Samhain," Maggie continued. "It marked the end of the harvest season and beginning of winter, so the Church supplanted Christian holidays on the dates of the pagan festivals. For the celebration of Samhain, where evil spirits walked the earth and the spirits of loved ones came home for dinner, the Christians supplanted All Hallows Eve, where families celebrated a departed patron saint defeating evil spirits."

"I get why the Church would choose such a spiritual day since they're attempting to connect with the departed saints."

Maggie nodded. "Supplanting worked for the most part, but allowing Druidic customs while still abiding by the dogma of the Church certainly caused some issues as well. When the Church, including the protestant denominations, believed pagan customs went too far, they put their foot down."

"Oh?"

"Common practice was to identify something as satanic," Maggie explained, "such as the evil spirits roaming the physical world during Halloween."

Dunham grinned. "Ahh, I see."

Maggie nodded. "They punished these practitioners, and the side-effect of this reaction was the reverence to Satan by certain outcasts." Maggie paused. "I have a suspicion that your October serial killer practices this type of Early Christian Irish Satanism—a melding with Druidism."

"Why Early Christian Ireland?" Dunham asked.

Maggie glanced around with her hands up. "Not only did the culture of Early Christian Ireland hold this particular October 31 – November 1 celebration so dearly, look what city this is—Boston!" she exclaimed.

"I don't follow . . ."

"Boston has the highest concentration of Irish descendants than any other major city in the US," Maggie explained. "I think around twenty percent Irish." She tilted her head. "Of course, that's just an educated guess."

Dunham raised his eyebrows. "Hmm, very convincing, Maggie." He returned to the envelope. "I believe I have something that just might reinforce your suspicions." He paused as she took the envelope. "I printed photos of the crime scenes, but I blocked out the victims. I didn't want to disgust you. Instead, I made a few observations about the victims."

Maggie studied the material, then shot a quick glance at Dunham. "Hon, I understand why you consider these murders satanic sacrifices, but they're also consistent with Samhain sacrifices, specifically the single stab wound to the chest and the decapitation; another connection to Druidism and October 31."

"The Druids had human sacrifices?" Dunham asked.

"Generally not," Maggie explained, "but recent evidence suggests it did happen. Typically, the Samhain sacrifice was an animal—usually a pig. In the cases of human sacrifice, each exhibited a stab wound to the chest, with the head decapitated."

"Hmm," Dunham mumbled, then pointed at the photos. "Another consistent pattern at each murder site is a stone archway or door-like structure near each victim. When the murders were near a bridge, it's an archway. The rest of the victims were near a door-shaped stone structure."

Maggie stared at the door-shaped stone structures. "Dolmens," she blurted out.

"Dolmens?" Dunham asked.

Maggie nodded. "Yes, dolmens are door-like or tabletop stone structures. The Druids considered them dwelling places of spirit people, sometimes tombs, or even portals to the supernatural Otherworld—most active during Samhain. In Ireland and Scotland, it was a place where the spirit peoples of the Otherworld, called '*ees shee*,' spelled a-o-s, s-i, dwelled, a connection between the physical world and the spirit world."

"Aos si?" Dunham asked slowly, echoing his wife's 'ees shee' pronunciation and raising his eyebrows to confirm his effort.

Maggie nodded. "Fairies," she continued. "Although not like Tinkerbell in *Peter Pan*. These fairies, or 'Fair Folk,' were a dwarflike race of spirit people feared by the Irish and Scottish, even to this day. They could take physical form but could disappear in an instant when threatened. Usually only people with the gift of second sight can see them. There's even evidence of actual dwarflike pre-Celtic peoples that inhabited the hills of the British Isles, which may have spawned this belief. An example of one you may have heard of is the banshee, a fairy woman who announces the coming of death by wailing. They also lived in the caves and hollow hills called fairy mounds."

"So, the stone archways would be considered dolmens as well?" Dunham asked.

Maggie pointed her finger in the air. "Yes, stone archways, and any earthen archways, like at the entrance to a cave, were also considered portals to the Otherworld." She grinned and paused. "This certainly is a pattern consistent with this melding of religious traditions."

"Sooo," Dunham thought aloud, "the offender—influenced by Druidic tradition—is sacrificing to Lucifer, then using these earthen portals to send the victims' souls to Hell."

"*Porta Infirni*," Maggie specified. "The Gates of Hell." She sipped her drink. "One limestone cave in Ireland, nicknamed the Cave of the Cats, had first been a portal to the Celtic Otherworld, and after the Irish became Christianized, it became Hell's Gate."

"And the significance of completing the final sacrifice on Halloween is that it's a Samhain sacrifice. Is that right?" Dunham asked.

"Think about it," Maggie replied. "The whole idea of a sacrifice is to carry a request to the supernatural world, and the most efficient time to do this is when the boundary between the spirit world and physical world is thinnest."

Dunham took a gulp and beamed. "Thanks, hon; you've been very helpful."

Maggie grinned as she read over the menu. "Glad to help, but I'm not sure how much I have."

"You've helped me connect this Satanist to Halloween, and it's definitely confirmed my suspicions about how our offender selects his murder sites," Dunham explained. "As we speak, the task force is identifying all potential locations." He paused. "I'm also going to contact the An Gara Siochána, Ireland's FBI. Maybe this guy's a transplant. I've never heard of a US citizen with Irish descent practicing in this way. It's almost like he's a product of this culture you speak of."

Maggie extended her menu toward Dunham. "Very true, dear; only he lives in the wrong century." She pointed at the menu. "Time to order."

He took the menu. "Thanks." He read for a moment, then snickered. "Well, I'll definitely not have the rutabaga casserole."

"Why not?" Maggie asked. "It looks good to me."

Dunham glanced up at her. "Oh, I forgot. I didn't add that particular detail to the crime scene evidence in the papers I gave you." He set the menu on the table. "Each victim's decapitated head had a small rutabaga shoved in their mouth. Dr. Gillespie believes it's a calling card, since the very first victim was the president of the Rutabaga Capital Management Company." He studied his menu and nodded. "Logical connection."

Maggie frowned and stared at Dunham.

Dunham glanced up. "What?" he asked, now aware that Maggie's body language suggested she disagreed.

"Do the rutabagas have faces carved in them?" she asked.

Dunham paused as he recollected the markings on each rutabaga. "There were definitely multiple deep markings on each rutabaga, localized on one side." He nodded. "I believe they did!"

Maggie shook her head. "I don't know about the killer using the rutabaga as a calling card," she explained, "but this is exactly what a spiritually-minded serial killer grounded in Old Irish tradition would think of. Rutabagas are Old Irish jack o' lanterns."

Dunham sat up, realizing that Maggie may have discovered something vitally important to the case. "Go on."

"Well," Maggie began, "in Old Ireland and Scotland, the gourd of choice for the jack o' lantern was the rutabaga. Using pumpkins only began in America." She paused. "I talked about this at my lecture, remember?"

Dunham shook his head. "I remember you talking about it, but you said it was a Swedish turnip or something."

"Exactly," Maggie answered. "That's what a rutabaga is. They also call it a swede."

"That certainly does reinforce the Halloween connection." Dunham thought for a moment. "But I thought jack o' lanterns were used to ward off Satan's evil spirits. I'd think the offender would be inviting them to his offering."

Maggie nodded. "True, but he seems to be Old Irish, so maybe he's referencing the origins of this, the spirit of the nasty Stingy Jack doomed to roam the earth." She tilted her head. "Strange, though, the more I think about it. According to lore, his soul was rejected by Satan, and you're saying this killer exalts Satan."

"Or, didn't you say the Will o' the Wisp light orbs over the bogs were also called jack o' lanterns, meaning the offender might be using these rutabagas to represent an evil spirit?" Dunham asked.

"Yes," Maggie answered, then shrugged her shoulders. "Still doesn't make sense though." She snickered. "Then again, my expertise is not in understanding the mind of a serial killer. That's yours."

Dunham sat back in thought, then glanced up at the waiter who'd just approached to take their order. "It doesn't make sense to me, either," he said to Maggie. "Maybe he's trying to taint the released soul of the victim before Satan takes it. I'll speak with Dr. Gillespie about it, but first, let's order." His phone rang and he answered, "Dr. Dunham," pointing at his selection on the menu.

Maggie ordered for her husband and herself and asked for more drinks.

"Excellent!" Dunham replied. "And a match too?" He paused. "Great. Thanks for letting me know, Lieutenant. Bye." He hung up and glanced at Maggie. "That was Lieutenant Huff. I helped out on a local unsolved murder case yesterday morning. The wife of one of their Boston police sergeants was murdered in their home."

"Oh, how sad."

Dunham nodded. "I suggested they perform a DNA test on a baseball, which I thought the offender may have touched, and it worked! Not only did it have this man's DNA on the surface, it had the wife's, confirming that she was hit with it. What's really damning is that her makeup was on the ball, conforming to my theory that her face was in contact with it as opposed to her accidentally grabbing it."

"Great!" Maggie exclaimed. "Well, for the theory—but that poor woman . . ."

"They found a match in the national database too," Dunham explained. "A man who's coincidentally serving time in prison for robbery and attempted murder a few months ago."

"Well, at least this'll give the sergeant some closure," Maggie suggested.

"Very true, Maggie," Dunham agreed. "Their department needed it too."

Maggie grinned. "I bet you can do no wrong with them now!"

"I certainly do get free Dunkin' Donuts coffee," Dunham replied, grinning.

chapter eighteen

PRESENT DAY: October 20. Boston, Massachusetts—Boston Police Headquarters, October Serial Killer Task Force Office

Huff scanned the large room packed with task force members from each participating jurisdiction. Everyone was unusually active, moving about, speaking with one another, coordinating, and comparing notes. He was just as excited as they were, since today was the day that the task force had the best chance of apprehending the October serial killer.

"Listen up! Break's over!" he belted out. "I'm almost finished." Most sat back in their seats, but conversations continued at a dull roar. "So, we've identified a total of—" he shot a glance at Sadler.

"Fifty-eight!" Sadler replied, shouting over the low mumble of conversations.

". . . fifty-eight potential locations that this guy might use as his next murder site!" Huff raised his hand. The crowd finally went quiet. "One thing is for sure, ladies and gentlemen; he's doing it tonight, and it's going to be in one of your districts."

"Report back with anything suspicious, immediately!" Sadler interrupted. "We'll have people ready to respond along every major thoroughfare from here to Salem." He paused. "We're gonna catch this asshole."

The chatter picked up again, everyone clearly anxious to get started.

"Cameras have been set up everywhere!" Huff added, then turned toward Dunham, who was sitting at a front table. "Do you have anything to add, Dr. Dunham?"

Dunham stood up and the room immediately went silent, so much so that he was slightly taken aback by the instant change in the noise level.

Huff grinned slightly at the quiet reverence afforded to Dr. Dunham. He glanced over at Sadler, who was grinning back. "If you haven't heard yet," Huff announced, "Dr. Dunham has been assisting us on the sidelines. Any breaks in the case are directly attributed to him." He noticed heads coming together at each table, striking up whispered conversations, clearly about Dunham.

Dunham stood next to Huff and turned toward the crowd. Everyone immediately stopped their side conversations and the room went silent again.

"Good morning. It's a pleasure to work with you on this case. We have a few leads, and we'd like to take full advantage of what we have, as in the case of these dolmen-like structures." He paused. "Keep your eyes out for vans of all colors parking near your particular identified locations. Our offender is extremely methodical and ritualistic, and most likely he feels comfortable with the use of the same style vehicle that he used to kidnap his victims. Also, evidence suggests that our offender parks a distance away from the kill site, so watch for two males walking together with one seemingly in control of the other."

"Wait for backup!" Huff interrupted. "We all know what happened three days ago." He glanced around the crowd, whose faces showed visible anguish at the mention of the fallen. "This guy is incredibly dangerous when trapped and has no fear of police presence—even armed officers." Huff paused. "Any questions?"

No one raised their hands.

"Dismissed, and good luck!"

As everyone left the room, a number of law enforcement officers made it a point to shake Dunham's hand. "Nice people," he said to Huff.

Huff nodded as he scanned the departing crowd. "They all want to catch this guy in the worst way." He glanced back at Dunham. "How about you accompany us tonight, Dr. Dunham?"

Dunham nodded. "I was hoping you'd ask."

"Any recommendations on where we position ourselves?" Huff asked.

Dunham glanced up at the map. "Anywhere between here and Salem."

"Perfect," Sadler answered as he approached them. "Eight of the fifty-eight locations we've identified are in that area. How about we join in and stake out one of these sites with the local police?"

"Excellent," Dunham replied.

* * *

Evening, October 20. Nahant Island, Massachusetts

Nahant Reserve Police Officer John Decker parked the patrol car on Swallow Cave Road next to the marina entrance. The road was dark, with few streetlights; the trees lining both sides of the road made it seem even darker. Wind swirled around, picking up the fallen leaves. He glanced over at his partner, Reserve Officer Alan Halley, who had his eyes closed and his head reclined on the seat. "Remind me why we volunteered for this all-night stakeout duty, Al?"

"Because we're getting paid," Al replied without opening his eyes. "Besides, with all the department cuts, the full-timers have their hands full. I think we're down to seven patrol officers now. This is a boon for us reservists."

"Yeah, well I hope to crap that this October serial killer doesn't choose Swallow Cave for his next murder site," John grumbled. "I have to work tomorrow night, and I do not want to spend tomorrow stuck in paperwork all day."

Al opened his eyes and shook his head. "I don't see how Swallow Cave made the list. There's never been a murder near a cave. Besides, he'd be an idiot to choose this cave." He pointed up the road at the dead end. "There's only one access to the cave at the end of this road, then there's a wicked drop down a rough, rocky cliff, with the cave entrance right on the waterline. He'd have to traverse this entire path in complete darkness—dragging a body no less."

John nodded and pointed behind them. "And there's only one road off this island. Too risky getting trapped."

Al glanced around the car. "Let's hedge our bets. Keep the car running and have the lights on. This is the only road to the cave access, so if he does come, he'll see the patrol car and get cold feet."

John nodded. "Now you're thinkin', Al. Should be easy for us to spot a van coming down this road anyway." He glanced over at the marina, which was well-lit and crowded with people in costumes. "Check it out, a Halloween party."

Al turned his head slowly, still reclined on the seat. "I bet they have coffee." He paused as he eyed the party. "Hey, what do ya say I go get some?"

John nodded. "I'll take some, but don't hang out too long showing off your uniform to the rich ladies."

Al grinned as he opened the door. "It's one of the perks of the job, Officer Decker." He closed the door and walked toward the party. As he neared the bar, he spotted a very attractive female bartender and approached.

The bartender glanced over, and it seemed to take her a moment to realize that the uniformed officer wasn't just a patron in a Halloween costume. She addressed him politely: "I'm sorry, Officer, is there something wrong?"

Al shook his head, putting on an air of authority. "Not at all, miss. I'm here in the capacity to protect and serve. My partner and I have orders to sit in front of the marina all night." He scanned the shelves behind the bar. "Do you happen to have any coffee?"

"Certainly do," the bartender said, then handed Al a basket. "Grab some sugar and cream."

"I'll take two coffees," Al answered.

The bartender nodded, left, and a minute later returned with the coffee.

"How much do I owe ya?" Al asked as he reached for his wallet.

"On the house," the bartender answered, "and there's more where that came from. We'll be open till two."

Al nodded, then winked at her. "Much appreciated. It'll be a long night." He grabbed the coffee and left the party. As he walked around the front of the car, he eyed his partner in the darkened interior, and he could see he had his head reclined on the seat with his eyes closed. As Al got to his side of the car, he put one of the coffees on the roof and opened the door. He grabbed the coffee then slid into his seat, leaving his door open.

"Hey, John. Wake up and take your coffee," Al demanded.

John didn't answer.

Al glanced over at him. "John?" He pushed on John's shoulder, which caused John to slump over. Realizing his partner was unconscious, Al sat up quickly, accidentally spilling some of the coffee. "What the hell?" He shook his partner's shoulder and whispered urgently, "John? John!" to no avail. As Al reached for the radio to call for assistance, he glanced around in panic and caught sight of a glint of red down the embankment, just off the road. He leaned forward, squinting, and in a split second he realized with a sinking feeling that the glint of red was the reflection of a taillight belonging to a dark van parked in the shrubs.

The moment he pressed the button on the radio mic, a hooded man reached through the door, grabbed Al's head and, in one smooth movement, snapped his neck.

The second officer went limp and slumped on top of the first. The hooded man calmly walked to the van, parted the shrubs, and got in. He drove down the road a quarter mile, parked, and shut off the lights and engine. Then he got out, opened the back, and dragged out an unconscious man, threw him over his shoulder, casually walked the path to Swallow Cave, and vanished into the darkness.

* * *

Late evening, October 20. Boston, Massachusetts—Boston University

Rob glanced around the cafeteria, aware of its emptiness due to the late hour. Although some students sat at a few of the long tables, most were empty. He stared at Sarah's hand so warmly placed upon his knee. Sarah didn't notice him gazing at her because her attention was on her studies. Ever since getting together at the haunted hayride last week, they rarely left each other's side. He loved it and was amazed at how much he and Sarah had in common.

Across from them were James and Tammy, their attentions on each other appearing to make studying difficult. Through the cafeteria doors came Nick and Keith, sauntering toward them with their bookbags slung casually over their shoulders.

Rob waved. "Nick, Keith, take a seat."

"Brother Rob," Keith whispered, then glanced over at James. "Brother James." He beamed at Tammy and Sarah. "Hello, gorgeous ladies."

Tammy chuckled. "Hi, Keith."

Keith placed both his hands on the table. "Tonight's the night, team. The October serial killer kidnapped his third victim three days ago!" he whispered excitedly.

Rob nodded. "Yeah, we were just talking about it. How wild that he kidnapped this guy, the police stopped him, he got away, then that evening he went back and kidnapped him again."

"That can only mean one thing," Sarah interrupted. "He chooses his victims."

Nick placed his laptop on the table, opened it, and turned it on.

"How does he choose them? That's the question," James added.

"According to the *Boston Globe*, the police haven't released the name of the victim yet," Nick interrupted.

James pulled out his cell phone. "I'll find out. I bet my buddy's dad knows."

"Let's focus on victimology," Rob interjected, "specifically, *how* he selects his victims." He paused. "Sarah and I were thinking about this. We originally concluded that the only pattern was living near Boston, but now that we know he selects them, there must be something else." Rob shook his head. "Remember, he's appeasing Satan. Something makes him believe Satan would approve of his choice of victims."

"Al Folgers," James blurted out, looking up from his cell phone screen. "That's who my buddy says the killer kidnapped. He owns a used car lot."

Nick glanced over at James, then continued typing on his laptop.

"I dunno," Tammy said. "It freaks me out knowing that this killer's on the loose." She kissed James and got up. "Gotta go. I'll see you guys," she said turning to leave.

"I'll see ya later, babe," James replied.

"Nothing." Nick interrupted, his search apparently having failed.

"What's up?" Rob asked.

"A while ago, I did an internet search with the names of all the victims, but nothing ever came up," Nick explained. "I didn't expect much, actually, since the police would've done the very same thing. I just added Al Folgers' name to the list, and again nothing came up."

Rob thought for a moment. "Wait, aren't there databases from BU's library we can search that the police probably don't have access to, or wouldn't probably think to use?"

Nick started typing. "Yes, and some're searchable for us students." Nick paused. "Here's the Oral History and Family History database." He paused again. "What? McGarrity?"

"McGarrity? There was no victim with the name McGarrity," Rob said.

"Right, but I got a hit with Al Folgers and one of the other victims in our Family History database. The McGarrity Family Crest site."

Rob got up and rushed behind Nick, peeking over his shoulder. "McGarrity Family Crest."

Nick pointed at the screen. "Apparently, there's an Al Folgers from Boston whose mother's maiden name is Gerty, a variant of McGarrity. On the same page is the name of the victim Jamie Geraty, another name variant of McGarrity."

"Might be nothing," James said.

"Don't speak so soon, James," Nick replied. "I just clicked through a few more pages and found the name of the victim Ashton Bitter, son of Annette McGarrity Bitter." He paused, then continued, his tone of voice growing more excited. "Here's another—Thomas Geright, another name variation. They're all from Boston!"

Rob stood up straight, still staring at the screen. "This is getting *too* coincidental!" Everyone had gotten out of their seats and were all huddled around Nick's laptop screen.

"Here's another!" Nick blurted out.

After fifteen minutes of searching the website, Rob sat down, staring at the wall with his jaw hanging open. "You did it, Nick. This McGarrity Family Crest website has every one of the victims."

"I can't believe you guys discovered how the October serial killer selects his victims," Sarah commented.

"I can see why no one figured it out until now," Nick said. "Actually, this database is also available in the Boston Public Library system, but even if the police did check it, each name is on a separate page, so searches wouldn't have come up with anything. Luckily, Folgers is on the same page as Jamie Geraty."

"What's he have against the McGarrities?" Keith asked.

James' cell phone dinged to signal an incoming text, and he peeked at it. He shot up from his seat. "They just found Folgers' body!" He read further. "At Swallow Cave!"

"Where?" Rob asked.

"It's a grotto on the coast, twenty minutes northeast of Boston," James replied. "Who wants to go? I'll drive."

Rob and Sarah rushed up to James, but everyone else remained seated. James grinned. "Keep the home fires burning, gentlemen."

* * *

Late evening, October 20. Nahant Island, Massachusetts

The waves crashed behind Huff's back. He shined his flashlight around at all of the crime scene specialists and law enforcement officers bracing themselves between the rugged cliffs and the ocean. "By all means," he screamed over the roar, "be careful! Don't get caught in the waves!"

Near the victim, a crime scene specialist held his flashlight aloft, illuminating the scene. He glanced up at Huff and Sadler. "The signature clearly indicates the October serial killer! Decapitation, chest wound, everything!" He moved so Dunham could get a better look.

"It certainly looks like Folgers!" Dunham yelled.

"OK then!" Huff yelled. "This is just too dangerous! Other than the necessary crime scene specialists, let's assemble topside!"

As they made it back up the cliff, Dunham noticed that the police had sectioned off the entire dead-end section of Swallow Cave Road. What used to be a dark section of road was now lit up by the flashing lights of dozens of police cars. All of the neighboring homes were lit up, and the residents were either peeking out of their windows or standing outside. He saw an older gentleman within the taped-off section, heading their way.

"I see Dr. Gillespie's made it," Sadler said.

"Hello, gentlemen," Gillespie greeted them. "Is it the work of our man?"

"Certainly is," Huff replied as he took out his smartphone, "but I don't recommend you walking down the steep cliff tonight." He handed Gillespie his phone. "Here; I took a bunch of photos of the victim."

Gillespie grabbed the phone. "Thanks." He swiped through the photos, enlarging certain ones for a better view. "It certainly looks like it. I hope the conditions down there don't destroy any potential evidence."

"Although the bastard got away," Sadler interjected, "the fact that he used one of the sites we predicted means we're figuring him out."

Gillespie glanced over his shoulder. "I see he murdered two more police officers in the process."

"If it wasn't for one of the guests at the Halloween party down the street noticing them slumped over in their police car," Huff surmised, "it might've taken days before we knew he killed his next victim down there in that cave." He glanced over at the huge mansion just a hundred feet away then at a nearby police officer. "Officer!"

The police officer turned around. "Yes, Lieutenant?"

"I see the owners of this residence on their front porch. Go ask them if they have a security camera pointed in this direction," he ordered. "Maybe we'll get lucky and catch the killer's entrance or exit down this path."

The police officer nodded, then rushed toward the owners.

Dunham shook his head. "I'm sure he made it back to Salem even before the party guest called 9-1-1."

"Well," Huff added, "it looks like we have eight days before he kidnaps his final victim of the season. Maybe forensics'll find something."

Sadler nudged Huff's coat sleeve as he stared into the crowd. "Boss, I think I see that priest."

Huff whipped his head around, then spotted him. "Well now; let's have a chat with the good Father, shall we, Detective Sergeant?" Huff and Sadler rushed away.

Dunham glanced over at the priest but stayed with Gillespie.

"I've been reading your reports, Dr. Dunham," Gillespie said, "including this morning's. We're lucky that your wife is so well versed in Celtic studies. She's a brilliant academic."

Dunham grinned. "Maggie watches your show all the time, Dr. Gillespie. She's going to love the fact that you gave her a compliment."

"Please tell her . . ." he replied, then trailed off. "Dr. Dunham, I believe I've come up with something."

Dunham turned his body toward Gillespie. "Oh?"

Gillespie pointed his finger. "Do you recall our discussion about the schizophrenic behavior our offender exhibits?"

Dunham nodded.

"Well, I think he believes he is possessed by an evil spirit, and his actions are expressing both personas."

Dunham paused in thought, then nodded. "How interesting," he replied, realizing Gillespie might be onto something. "This would eliminate the paradox."

"I'm sure he's convinced that the evil spirit is directing the ritualistic behavior, while by nature, he's a pragmatist attempting to be methodical about it," Gillespie added.

Dunham thought for a moment, then raised his eyebrows. "Not only am I convinced you are correct, Dr. Gillespie, strangely, I think I know which evil spirit he believes he's possessed by."

"Oh?"

Dunham nodded. "Recall that my wife made a convincing argument that the rutabaga is actually a jack o' lantern, and if so, it would be the perfect symbol for the evil spirit of Stingy Jack, a.k.a., Jack o' Lantern."

Gillespie nodded slowly. "I am aware of the Halloween tale, and it certainly does make sense, Dr. Dunham." He paused. "Now, how can we exploit this knowledge to our benefit?" Both were silent, contemplating Gillespie's question.

A police officer approached. "Dr. Dunham?"

Dunham turned to him. "Yes?"

"A young man claims he knows you and says he has critical information specific to the case," the police officer explained. "He says he's Celine's brother? I believe that's what he said . . ."

"Robbie?" Dunham grinned and turned toward the crowd, scanning, then spotted Robbie with two other young people just behind the yellow tape. "Excuse me, Dr. Gillespie. I'll be right back."

Dunham approached them, making eye contact with Rob.

"Hi, Dr. Dunham."

"Hi, Robbie!" Dunham replied, grinning. "It's great to see you again."

Rob blushed slightly. "It's Rob now."

Dunham noticed James and Sarah grinning. "Sorry about that, Rob." He changed the subject. "So, why are you in Boston?"

"I'm a student at Boston University. I'm in line for the PhD program in forensics." He glanced over at James and Sarah. "This is my roommate, James, and this is my girlfriend, Sarah."

"Hi, James and Sarah." Dunham noticed Sarah glancing over at Rob, beaming after he said, 'girlfriend.' He shook their hands.

"It's an honor to meet you, Dr. Dunham," Sarah replied. "I remember you solving the Niagara Falls Serial Killer Case last year."

Dunham pointed to Rob. "Thanks to Rob and his sister. How is Celine, anyway?"

"She's doing great," Rob answered. "She'll graduate next year."

"So, forensics!" Dunham exclaimed to Rob. "Great field. That's how I got my start. Keep the FBI in mind."

Rob beamed. "I plan on it, Dr. Dunham. Sarah's planning on going into criminal profiling."

Dunham gave Sarah a big smile. "Excellent." He pointed over his shoulder. "There's Dr. Gillespie."

"Yes, I recognized him immediately," Sarah replied.

Dunham glanced over at James.

"I have less-aggressive aspirations, Dr. Dunham," James said. "I'm a business major. I just want to own three or four manufacturing companies and half of Boston."

Dunham laughed. "I can tell by your accent you're a local Bostonian. Proud of your hometown, no doubt." He turned back to Rob. "The police officer said you have some critical information on the case? Sounds like you're still working on serial offender investigations on the side."

Rob nodded. "We found out how the October serial killer selects his victims."

Dunham's eyes opened wide, then he glanced at all three students. He lifted the yellow tape. "Come, follow me. Sarah and James, you too." He brought them over to a more private spot. "So, what've you found out?"

Rob glanced over at James and Sarah. "Well, a computer savvy friend of ours, Nick, and his roommate, Keith, have been helping us out. We came up with the idea to search the Boston University Oral History and Family History database—"

"Rob came up with the idea," James interrupted.

Rob nodded and continued. "We then plugged in the names of the victims, and we got a hit that just so happened to connect two of the victims, which led us to look deeper. Every one of the victims' names is on one massive website called the McGarrity Family Crest."

Dunham pulled out his iPhone and typed on it while Rob spoke.

"We figured that no one identified the site before because the site's not accessible from the regular internet, and also each name was on a separate page—until Al Folgers was kidnapped."

Dunham glanced up at Rob. "We didn't release Folgers' name yet. How did you know he was kidnapped?"

"Well," James interrupted, "my buddy's dad is a cop." He clenched his teeth and bounced nervously on the balls of his feet. "He probably wasn't supposed to tell me that, but he knew we were doing some amateur sleuthing . . ."

Dunham nodded as he continued to operate his iPhone.

"You won't be able to look it up from here, Dr. Dunham," Rob pointed out. "As I said, the database is not connected to the public internet."

Dunham showed Rob his iPhone screen. "Is this the website?"

Rob stared at Dunham's iPhone screen and grinned. "Wow! How'd you do that?"

Dunham snickered. "I'll tell you when you join the FBI." He scrolled down. "I think we can exclude coincidence. Brilliant job, all of you." He paused. "Did you come up with any ideas as to why the offender's selecting his victims from this site?"

"No, not a clue," Rob admitted, "other than he has a vendetta against the McGarrities, or he just randomly selected this group of people since hundreds of them still live in the greater Boston area."

"We still think he didn't know any of his victims personally," Sarah added.

"Very astute," Dunham replied and thought for a moment. After a short pause, he decided to open up to them with some information. "There is evidence of an Irish connection, so I'm inclined to believe he's got some kind of vendetta against this family lineage. I just sent this info to my lab, and they'll analyze the entire site. Also, Dr. Gillespie has concluded that our offender believes he is possessed by an evil spirit." He glanced back at Rob and held out a pen and notepad. "I must go, but do you mind giving me your number, just in case I need to contact you?"

Rob beamed. "Of course." He hesitated. "Uh, may I?" Rob held his hand out for Dunham's phone instead of the notepad.

"Oh, of course." Dunham chuckled. "Better to skip the middleman." He waved the notepad and put it away, along with the pen. "I suppose my penchant for losing things precedes me," he said as Rob entered his number into Dunham's phone contacts. "Heather, one of my assistant forensic scientists, would appreciate your more direct approach since she's not here in Boston to keep after me."

Rob smiled and handed the phone back.

"Rob, Sarah, James," Dunham began, "you've been immensely helpful, and hopefully this information will allow us to break the case before the killer selects someone in eight days."

"Do you mind if we keep on investigating?" Rob asked.

"By all means," Dunham replied. "Please keep everything I've told you in confidence."

"Absolutely," Rob responded solemnly, and Sarah and James nodded.

"One last thing," Dunham added. "We believe our offender operates out of Salem, so if you find any connections with this, let me know." He grinned at Rob. "Rob, you breaking the big cases is becoming a habit. Say hi to Celine for me. Take care." He shook their hands and walked back to Gillespie.

"How cool that you know the Watchmaker, Rob!" Sarah said.

Rob grinned. "He's a real nice guy."

"Did you see his eyes?" Sarah asked James. "How intense!"

James nodded. "No wonder he's the best."

Rob grinned proudly. "Yup."

chapter nineteen

**PRESENT DAY: October 22. Downtown Boston, Massachusetts—
FBI Field Office, One Center Plaza**

Dunham stood on the edge of the workout mats panting from the morning aikido workout with Special Agent in Charge Carnie and the other special agents. He felt pretty good about how he'd been progressing. For the last week, Carnie taught only three techniques, then drilled them into Dunham and the others. Carnie told them that it's better to be good at three techniques than lousy at a dozen. The special agent was teaching them a bull-and-the-matador-type technique. An attacker charges, and once he makes contact, you act like a door opening up and pivot on one foot. While pivoting out of the way of the attacker's energy, you grasp under his elbows and effortlessly heave him in the same direction of his momentum. *Easier said than done*, Dunham thought to himself, but after hundreds of times performing the technique, he knew he was catching on.

"OK!" Carnie called out, then clapped. He waited for everyone to sit down on the sides of the mats. One of the special agents raised her hand, and he pointed to her.

"Sir, where might this particular attack be applied?"

Carnie nodded and pointed to two special agents who then joined him on the mats. "One example is during a multiple attack situation." He asked one special agent to be in front of him, about ten feet away, and the other to be behind him. "Now, both of you attack me at the same time, but only half-speed so you don't get hurt." As they rushed him, he advanced on the front attacker, blended and pivoted, and sent him flying into the attacker behind him. Everyone, including the attackers, laughed.

"You never fight two people at once," Carnie explained. "Two on one are bad odds, so attack one and, in this case, throw him into the other." He then directed both special agents to be in front of him, about ten yards away, one just in front of the other. "Attack," Carnie ordered. As the two darted forward, Carnie quickly threw the first attacker away with the same blending technique, then caught the second attacker's head, causing his feet to fly out from underneath him. Carnie faced the special agents.

"Notice that I did not apply a technique on the first attacker, other than throwing him out of the way. If I'd tried to, the second attacker would have had the opportunity to help his buddy out, and it would have been a two-on-one situation. If I throw the front guy away and eliminate the back guy, the first one must spend the time getting up and turning around before he can attack again. He might even have second thoughts about attacking again." He paused again. "Notice it's always the better odds; one-on-one."

Over the intercom, a female voice called, "Special Agent in Charge Carnie, the gentlemen from the task force just arrived."

"Thank you, Angie!" Carnie responded. "Show 'em to the video conference room. We'll be right there!" He glanced over at Dunham. "It looks like Lieutenant Huff and Detective Sergeant Sadler are here for the video conference." He nodded to the group. "Dismissed, everyone, and great job today."

Carnie crossed the mat as everyone began to leave. "You're a natural at this, Edward. You should think about continuing aikido when you get back to Virginia."

Dunham got up slowly, cringing with muscle pain. "I love it, but I'm almost fifty."

"It's never too late to start," Carnie encouraged. "We have a few black belts in the organization who actually started in their fifties."

Dunham nodded as they made their way to the elevator. "You know, I believe I will. Maybe Maggie'll want to try it, too."

"We have a Virginia club in our organization not too far from where you live. The dojo instructor's a great guy," Carnie said as they entered the elevator. He pushed the button, and the door closed.

They made their way to the video conference room, where Huff and Sadler were waiting. "Good morning, gentlemen," Carnie greeted.

Huff stood up and shook Carnie's hand. "Does the FBI always work in sweats?" Huff teased. He glanced over at Dunham. "Hi, Dr. Dunham."

"Thanks for meeting us here, Lieutenant," Dunham responded, then nodded to Sadler.

Sadler scanned the video conference room, which had comfortable leather-cushion seats with high head rests, the chairs arranged in the shape of a mini-theater. "Gorgeous room." He then pointed to the six-foot screen at the front. "How can I get one of these?" he joked.

"Talk to the mayor," Carnie joked back.

Huff leaned over toward Dunham and handed him a *Boston Globe* newspaper. "Speaking of the mayor, word has it he's steaming mad. The press has found out you're involved in the case."

Dunham took the paper. "Not good." He opened it up to the front page and saw the article above the fold.

"Nahant Chief of Police Tina Randall spilled the beans," Sadler interrupted. "She even told the paper you're the reason why we've been picking up so many leads lately and nearly caught the killer during the Folgers kidnapping."

Dunham shook his head. "We were quite clear to everyone not to mention my name."

"Oh, it wasn't a slip up," Huff explained. "Chief Randall knew damn well that the mayor and our police superintendent didn't want you involved. She's getting him back." He paused. "You see, the chief's husband is a council member for Nahant, and he was in Boston two years ago for a local government pow-wow. He got a speeding ticket, and our police superintendent wouldn't help him out. To top it all off, they cited him for no seatbelt and an expired registration. Not exactly the leniency he'd expected, considering his position and his wife's clout."

Dunham shook his head. "Angering the mayor is one thing, but more importantly, the offender might now see that we're not completely blind to his motives and actions. Let's hope he doesn't change his pattern of behavior."

"Nothing we can do about it now," Huff replied. "What do you have?"

Dunham nodded. "If you recall, two nights ago at Shallow Cave I told you I sent my team at the FBI lab the McGarrity website information that the college students discovered, and I also asked them to contact law enforcement in Ireland. Yesterday, my team asked to set up a video conference at nine o'clock this morning," he glanced at his watch, "which is in just a few minutes."

"Sounds like they found something," Carnie interrupted.

Dunham received a text and glanced at his phone's display. "It looks like they're ready."

Huff pushed a button on a remote and the six-foot screen lit up. Two figures came into view; a man and a woman. "Hi, Jack; Heather," Dunham greeted. "We see both of you. Can you see and hear us OK?"

Jack nodded. "Yes. Good morning, everyone."

"You know Dean Carnie, and to my left is the head of the task force, Lieutenant Huff, and to my far left is Detective Sergeant Sadler." Dunham glanced over at Huff and Sadler. "These two head my team. Jack Stride and Heather Kennedy."

After the pleasantries, Jack began. "I headed up a team of analysts, and we decided to use a mathematical search algorithm and apply it to the McGarrity Family Crest website. Because of its time-critical nature, our first goal was to generate a probability list of whom the offender might select next by prioritizing the hundreds of names throughout the seventeen pages."

"Any success?" Dunham asked.

Jack nodded. "I think so, but keep in mind we've only come up with probabilities." Jack pressed a key on his end, and the right-hand side of the screen displayed photographs of ten different people with their names underneath each. "On the screen are the top ten names in order of highest probabilities. The top on the list, with a 71% probability, is a Sudbury resident, Ashley Geraghty, an employee at the Apple retail store in the Cambridgeside Galleria Mall. Her parents retired and moved to Florida, and she has a sister in New York City. She lives with two friends."

"The twenty-eighth of October is a weekday, so I bet he'll attempt to kidnap her at the mall," Huff surmised.

Dunham nodded. "I agree. Every kidnapping that's occurred on a weekday occurred somewhere other than at their home."

Huff stared at the screen. "The second potential victim on the list has only a 48% probability." He glanced at Dunham, Carnie, and Sadler. "If this algorithm got it right, Ashley Geraghty's our next potential victim. We need to set up round the clock protection on these ten for the twenty-eighth, with the heaviest protection for her."

"I say we set up a trap and use this lady as bait," Sadler suggested, then paused, "with her permission of course."

"She might not go for it," Carnie responded. "And for that matter, you'll need to inform each and every person on that website that they might be targeted by the offender. Prudence dictates they leave the area on that day."

"Agreed," Huff replied, "but she'll also need to know that if she does bow out, he'll most likely go after her at another time."

Dunham nodded. "Evidence suggests that our offender follows his intended victim, and in order for him not to suspect our discovery, I think we should use an undercover task force member to make contact with her. Maybe at the mall."

Huff nodded and grinned. "Excellent." He glanced over at Sadler. "Let's set up a task force meeting this afternoon and coordinate it."

"Already in the works, boss," Sadler replied, typing a calendar invitation on his iPad. He then glanced over at Dunham with a slightly confused expression. "So, a bunch of college kids figured this out?"

Dunham grinned. "Rob is an amazing young man. He was instrumental in discovering the identity of the Niagara Falls serial killer last year."

Sadler glanced back at Huff. "Let's get him on the team!" he said semi-facetiously.

After a slight pause, Dunham turned to Jack's image on the screen. "Great job, Jack." He turned in his chair. "What do you have for us, Heather?"

"Hello, everyone," Heather greeted as she pushed a button and an Irish newspaper article popped up on the right side of the screen. "My task was to contact the Irish authorities and attempt to identify any cases that might possibly be connected to the October serial killer, and I believe we may have hit pay dirt."

Huff sat forward to get a better look at the newspaper article.

"On the screen is a newspaper report of an unsolved murder in Western Ireland, specifically County Roscommon, eight months prior to the very first Boston murder," Heather explained. "The mutilation of the victim is identical to our October serial killer victims: decapitation, with one post-mortem stab wound in the chest." She tapped a few keys, and a number of crime scene photos popped up. "Local law enforcement provided me with a volume of information on the case, and here are some crime scene photos." She paused. "There are a number of differences though."

"Oh?" Huff asked.

"First, there were two victims, and neither was kidnapped three days prior to their murder. Second, there was no wheat, grapes, and fig offering."

"I don't see the second victim in the photo, Heather," Dunham commented.

Heather brought up another series of photos. "He was inside the cave."

Dunham sat up in his seat, staring at the cave entrance in one photo, and the victim inside the cave lying next to a shoebox-sized metal container in another.

Heather waited as Dunham studied the photos of the cave. "I thought you'd be interested in the cave, especially since the last victim was killed next to the entrance to a cave."

"What cave is this?" Dunham asked.

"They call it the Cave of the Cats."

"Cave of the Cats!" Dunham blurted out in shock. "This is the second time I've heard about the Cave of the Cats this week." He glanced over at Huff. "My wife explained to me that this particular cave was considered Hell's Gate to the early Christian Irish, and before that the ancient Celts believed it was the entrance to the Otherworld." He paused. "Maggie referred to this cave in reference to our offender's desire to sacrifice his victims next to the stone door-like structures."

Huff's jaw dropped. "Holy shit."

"There's no question that this double murder is the work of our offender, and the difference between the Irish murders and the Boston murders could be attributed to the Cave of the Cats being ground zero." Dunham paused, staring at the photos of the cave. "Dr. Gillespie is convinced that the offender believes he's possessed, and if true, it seems this belief began with his visit to the Cave of the Cats five years ago."

"Other than those belonging to the two victims, there were no latent fingerprints discovered at the crime scene," Heather explained. "There were tire tracks, but they were from the vehicle owned by one of the victims. It was discovered near the road." She grabbed a sheet of paper from in front of her. "We've checked flights between there and Boston just before and just after the double murder, but so far, we've come up with nothing."

Carnie pointed to the metal box. "Heather, could you enlarge the image of that metal box?"

Heather enlarged the image and continued. "The authorities believe this ancient artifact was what was excavated from the back of the cave. The shovels you see in the photo near the victim were used to dig into an antechamber to the cave. The artifact was taken from behind a large limestone boulder in the back of that antechamber." She paused. "Because of this, they attributed the murders to a tomb raiding gone awry."

"I see a cross on the door of that box. A holy relic," Dunham observed, then glanced over at Huff and Sadler. "And we have a priest at every crime scene?"

Huff nodded. "Maybe there's a connection; although when we interviewed him at Swallow Cave, we were confident he merely had an interest in the case, nothing more."

"What, again, was the priest's name?" Dunham asked.

Sadler responded, "Father Theodore Martin. He claims he was temporarily assigned to the Cathedral of the Holy Cross in South Buffalo three years ago. His parish is in New York City."

"How coincidental, being assigned to Boston when the murders began." Dunham glanced up at Heather. "Heather, could you quickly look him up and see what his background reveals?"

Heather nodded as she typed. "How interesting. Of the numerous Catholic affiliations Father Martin belongs to, he's a member of the International Association of Exorcists."

"Now that *is* interesting," Dunham commented. "Maybe the Church came to the same conclusion as Dr. Gillespie?" He glanced over at Huff and Sadler. "While the two of you focus on the potential victims, I believe I'll give Father Martin a visit."

chapter twenty

PRESENT DAY: October 22. Boston, Massachusetts—Boston University

Rob popped his head up from his studies and watched Sarah tap on the screen of her laptop. He was sitting on the leather-cushioned couch in his room, her legs strewn over him, while she used one of the large armrests to support her back. James was studying at his desk under the loft.

"So, James," Rob called out. "What're you gonna be for the dorm Halloween party?"

James shook his head. "Not sure yet." He paused. "Maybe I'll use my bed sheet as a toga and go as a Roman citizen. How about you?"

"I have that black cloak and wizard hat I bought after the hayride," Rob replied.

"Sarah?" James asked.

Sarah glanced up at James, then at Rob. "Well, if Rob's going to be a wizard, maybe I'll be a witch." She glanced back at the laptop screen. "Let me see what the Halloween stores have to offer. Maybe I'll drag Tammy with me and pick something up."

Keith barged into Rob's room and plopped himself down on the reclining chair, then beamed at Sarah. "Hi, Sarah," He said in a seductive tone.

Sarah smirked. "Hi, Keith."

"Keith, what're you gonna be for the Halloween party?" James asked.

Keith grinned. "I have a huge brown sack, so I'm gonna go as a dirt bag. Everybody says I have a dirty mind, so I need to promote my image." He glanced over at Rob. "So, you spoke with that famous FBI guy, the Watchmaker, huh? How cool is that! I guess you weren't lying, Robbo."

Rob grinned. "Thanks for the confidence, Keith, and his name is Dr. Dunham."

"What's Nick going as?" James asked, still stuck on the Halloween party.

Keith glanced over at James. "A bag of computer chips; does it every year." Back to Rob: "The Watchmaker sounds cooler. It shows that he's the man. Was he impressed with us?"

"He was," Rob replied, "and he said we might have just saved the lives of future intended victims. He's asked us to see what else we can figure out."

"I'm there, Robbo," Keith replied smugly. "Just say the word." He sat up, now anxious. "Um, you know, as long as it doesn't involve sneaking around dark alleys searching for the killer."

Rob grinned. "I say we go through the McGarrity website and figure out which McGarrity descendent this serial killer's gonna go after on the twenty-eighth."

Keith shook his head and waved his hand. "Nick and I were going crazy with that. There are hundreds of names on that huge website, and so many possible ways he could choose from them." He sat back. "Yeah, we hit a roadblock."

"That's because you didn't have me helping out, Keith," James interrupted.

"OK, Brother James," Keith replied.

"Let's get together after dinner," Rob suggested. "What do ya say?"

"Sorry, computer lab tonight," Keith answered. "But I'll stop by later."

"Hey, check this out," Sarah said, staring at her laptop screen. "I've been looking up ideas for witch costumes, and I came across this Salem Wiccan website. Apparently, their high priest, a Brian Ellsworth, died at his Halloween store in Salem last week. Even though the police believe he broke his neck by falling off of a rickety old ladder while doing repairs, these Wiccan followers are convinced that the October serial killer murdered him. The website also talks about the suspicious deaths of an elderly man and woman on a boat at the neighboring marina."

Rob shook his head. "Certainly doesn't follow the signature of this killer; no decapitation, abdominal knife wound, or satanic ritual." He paused. "I don't get how they'd think so."

James turned around and faced Sarah. "Why *do* they think so?"

Sarah continued. "They say here that their high priest was powerful enough psychically to feel the presence of the evil spirit that possesses the October serial killer. The evil spirit, though, knew this, since he could feel his presence as well."

"Oooh-kaaay!" Keith blurted out in a doubting tone.

"It says here that his followers warned him not to speak to the police, since the killer would immediately pick up on that, and when he did inform them last week, the killer retaliated and killed him." She glanced up at Keith. "Apparently, the last people to see him alive were two police officers who went to his store and questioned him on the case."

James turned around again. "It takes all kinds."

Rob stared up at the ceiling in thought and raised his finger.

"Uh-oh! Rob's onto something," James said.

Rob glanced over at James and grinned. "So, hear me out. What if there's an element of truth to this?"

"You're saying we need to believe in this hocus pocus crap?" Keith asked.

Rob pointed his finger. "No; but what if the killer *believed* this high priest witch, or warlock, could sense him?"

"I think you're smokin' up with Seth, Robbo," Keith joked.

"Don't you remember what Dr. Dunham said?" Rob asked, then glanced at Keith. "Well, not you, Keith, because you weren't there." He glanced at James and Sarah. "Dr. Dunham said the criminal profiler has concluded that the offender thinks he's possessed by an evil spirit." Rob paused, and everyone sat in silence. "And, Dr. Dunham also told us that they believe the offender hides out in the vicinity of Salem, and if the killer does indeed hide out near this Halloween store, there's a good chance they've seen each other."

Keith nodded. "I guess if he did kill this guy, his motive would have been different than his usual ritual sacrifice motive, therefore, there would be no reason to decapitate."

"Why not suffocate him and give the task force no reason to believe he was the killer?" Rob speculated.

"Slow down, everyone," James began. "It's still a stretch, and the only people claiming a connection between this death of the warlock and the serial murders are a bunch of modern-day witches. The police don't seem to believe it."

"James is right, you know," Keith added. "I don't think I'd bother the Watchmaker with this one."

"At least not yet," Rob replied. "How about we visit the Halloween store and the marina and investigate ourselves? We're going to Salem for Halloween at the end of the week anyway, so we'll get to know our way around. And, Sarah, you could get your costume while we're in town."

Sarah smiled in agreement.

James nodded. "Actually, we're gonna be in that very location." He grinned. "Hey, why not? Let's do it."

chapter twenty-one

PRESENT DAY: October 24. Boston, Massachusetts—Cambridge, Cambridgeside Galleria Mall

Ashley Geraghty's manager, Anne Strassburg, was speaking to a new employee. The new girl had blond hair, similar in color and length to hers, but her hair was a bit curlier; and she seemed to be about the same age—mid-to-late twenties. Even though the new employee was as thin as she was, she was buff; clearly into physical fitness. She was wearing a Bluetooth headset and carrying a clipboard, so Ashley concluded that the new employee was assigned to customer service. Ashley glanced back at the customer she was working with and handed him a new iPhone. "Here you go. You're all set. All your information has successfully been transferred from your old phone to this one."

"Thank you so much," the customer replied. "Quick question. Should I always charge it to one hundred percent each night, even if it has a relatively full charge?"

Ashley shook her head. "No, especially with a new phone, the battery needs to be drained to ten to twenty percent before charging, but when you finally do charge it, always do it to one hundred percent."

The customer nodded.

"Eventually," Ashley continued, "do this as part of your monthly battery maintenance. Also, the phone should be turned off at least once a week." The customer thanked her again, then left. Ashley turned in time to see her manager approaching with the new employee.

"Hi, Ashley," the manager greeted and presented the new employee. "This is Samantha Bronson. She's our newest customer service rep."

"Nice to meet you," Ashley greeted and shook Samantha's hand.

"Nice to meet you, too, Ashley," Samantha greeted back.

"Instead of taking on the next customer, Ashley," her manager explained, "I'd like you to take an early lunch at the food court and give Samantha the ins and outs of the tech department." The manager handed Ashley a credit card. "It's a working lunch, so it's on the store."

Ashley grinned. "Cool! Thanks, Mrs. Strassburg." She turned to Samantha. "Come on, follow me." She walked behind the technical service desk, grabbed her purse, and they left the store.

As they exited the Apple Store, Samantha glanced around. "The last time I was at the mall was years ago. It's so beautiful." She marveled at the gorgeous high-end interior décor. The center was open, with the stores on both the first and second floors visible. Huge, off-white pillars connected the first and the second floors, rising all the way to the glass ceiling. The shiny brass of the handrails and rail supports throughout the mall glinted in the sunlight that streamed in through the clear ceiling.

"I love working here," Ashley replied, "especially because I love to shop!" She snickered.

"Me too," Samantha said, then pointed up at some mall workers on ladders. "Hey, check it out. They're already adding the Christmas decorations."

Ashley grinned. "Why not? Christmas shopping begins about now."

They made their way around a prominent escalator to the food court, the ever-present upbeat shopping music swelling around them. When they entered the food court, they were assaulted by smells from multiple cultural foods, especially Italian and Thai. The walls and ceilings in the food court were adorned with bright neon lights, and tables filled the center of the large area.

"What a great selection of food," Samantha commented.

Ashley nodded and scanned the restaurants in the food court. "So true. Everyone comes here for lunch. Even though it's not peak shopping time, look how crowded it is."

"Oh, I see. Everyone here is on their lunch break," Samantha said, acknowledging that most of the people in the food court were in professional attire. "This place seems to be an excellent location for lunch for many of the employees in the white-collar businesses surrounding the mall."

"People use it as a 'third place' to hang out too. So, what are you in the mood for?"

"Greek, actually," Samantha replied, pointing to a Greek fast-food restaurant.

The two ordered their lunches and sat down together at a table. Samantha glanced around, then leaned forward. "Ashley," Samantha whispered, "let me explain why I'm really here."

"What do you mean?" Ashley asked, confused.

"My name is Samantha Bronson, but I'm not a new employee for Apple. I'm actually undercover Boston PD assigned to the October Serial Killer Task Force."

Ashley's jaw dropped slightly. "Oh my," she whispered, eyes locked on Samantha.

"Now, don't be alarmed," Samantha began. "Apple Store management is fully aware of and has approved of my being here."

"OK, but why are you here?" Ashley asked.

Samantha paused, taking a small bite of her gyro. "My assignment is to protect you, Ashley." She paused again. "You see, we've discovered how this serial killer selects his victims, and according to the FBI, there's a 71% probability that you're his next target." She watched the color drain from Ashley's face, clearly stunned by the news. She leaned toward Ashley. "Don't look now, but four of these people sitting at the food court, eating lunch, are also well-armed undercover police officers assigned to you."

"Do you think the killer's here?" Ashley asked.

"We're not sure, but even if he is, he's not going to try anything for another two days," Samantha explained, "and he never varies from his pattern of behavior." She paused. "We do believe he follows his targets around prior to kidnapping them, hence, the reason why we're undercover."

Ashley sat back. "Oh my," she repeated, clearly unprepared for this kind of news—as if anyone could be.

"The best way for us to keep an eye on you," Samantha explained, "while not giving away our discovery that we've figured him out, is to have me act as a new employee who you coincidentally befriend. This *alternative plan* is for me to hang out with you this entire week, and even be invited to your apartment and mingle with your two roommates, Janette and Dayna." She paused. "Outside your apartment will be multiple task force members, twenty-four/seven."

"What do you mean by alternative plan?" Ashley asked.

"The most important thing, Ashley, is your safety, which means our first recommendation is for you to leave Boston entirely, at least until after Halloween. This is our first plan." She glanced around. "Do you have a place to go?"

Ashley nodded. "My sister lives in New York," she paused, "but if I'm targeted, won't he just try again later? I don't want to move away from Boston permanently, especially because of this guy."

Samantha nodded. "We believe so, and not only you but others . . . which brings us back to the alternative plan—a trap." She leaned forward. "The problem is, it would involve you. Ultimately, this is the most permanent alternative for you and the others . . . trapping this guy and getting him off the streets—and we finally have the opportunity to do it."

"Screw this bastard," Ashley whispered sternly. "Let's do the alternative plan."

Samantha grinned. "Great, but any time you wanna back out, let me know and we'll call it off. This is a real-life threat."

Ashley bit her lower lip and nodded. "What do I need to do?"

"Well, we'll have constant surveillance on you at home," Samantha continued, "but the offender also kidnaps his targets away from home, mostly at work." Samantha glanced around. "In this case, here at the mall." Samantha subtly slid a small, coin-sized object toward Ashley. "Keep that in your pocket at all times. It's a GPS tracker, just in case the unthinkable happens and you get kidnapped."

Ashley covered it with her hand, slid it off the table, and slipped it into her pocket. "You guys think of everything."

"In the unlikely event you do get kidnapped, put it in your mouth the first chance you get; even swallow it if you can." Samantha glanced around. "After our offender kidnaps his targets, he first drives off but then stops somewhere and throws their clothes and personal possessions in the trash. Including your cell phone, so Find My iPhone won't help us then."

Ashley smiled briefly at the mention of the familiar Apple feature, then nodded. "Got it."

"So, we're going to handle this in two phases," Samantha explained. "Today and tomorrow will be surveillance. You run your life as usual," she grinned, "now with me involved in everything you do. At work, you're going to also wear the Bluetooth headset like your manager and the customer service reps, starting today. It'll allow you to keep in constant communication not only with me but with the entire security team."

"I can do that," Ashley confirmed.

Samantha nodded. "Apple asks that your manager be connected as well."

Ashley grinned. "How convenient for us that wearing a headset at the Apple Store is not going to raise a red flag to the killer."

Samantha glanced around. "On October 28, the day we expect our offender to kidnap his target, we go into phase two. I'll let you know what that entails later."

Ashley pressed her palm to her forehead. "Wow, this is so surreal. I feel like I'm in a movie—a scary movie."

"I know, Ashley," Samantha consoled. "But we need to be careful. Look up and laugh like I just said something funny." Ashley let her hand fall away from her face and the two laughed lightly. "Just making sure we don't look like we're discussing anything *too* serious, on the off chance we're being watched. I don't want you to feel paranoid, but we can be smarter than him if we work together and keep our cool. I'll be with you every step of the way, and I'll be damned if that guy's gonna touch you."

Ashley grinned and sighed, taking a sip of her lemonade. "You're right. I think I—*we* can do this." She glanced over Samantha's impeccable posture and muscular physique then looked down at her own slender frame. "Maybe after all this is over, I'll have to start hitting the gym." She laughed again. "You're pretty ripped. I'll bet that guy doesn't realize the threat you pose to him!"

Samantha chuckled and sat back in her chair. "So, if I'm gonna be able to pull off this customer service thing, I'll need to know a little bit about what you techs do in the back. I'm ready to listen."

For the rest of the lunchbreak, Ashley explained the operations at the Apple Store and gave a brief overview of the technician job. After about ten minutes, Ashley threw her purse over her shoulder. "That's about it. Ready to go back?"

"Thanks, Ashley," Samantha said. "I believe I'm ready to try this Apple thing out."

Samantha glanced over at Ashley as they walked back to the Apple Store. "Who knows? Maybe I can do this for a second source of income."

"I love working at the Apple Store," Ashley commented as they turned the corner and met a crowd of people moving in both directions. Ashley glanced at her watch and shouted to Samantha, who was a few people away, "The post-lunchbreak rush!"

"I feel like a fish swimming upstream!" Samantha commented, bumping into a few businesspeople in the throng.

After a few moments, the crowd thinned out and Ashley and Samantha continued to make their way to the Apple Store, now only two storefronts away. Ashley abruptly stopped, grabbed her wrist, then scanned the ground. "Shoot! My watch fell off!" She moved back toward the food court still scanning the ground.

Samantha followed, helping her search the area. "What a bummer."

"It must've caught on someone in the after-lunch rush."

"Was it expensive?" Samantha asked.

"No, not at all, and the elastic watchband was real loose," she answered. "My Apple Watch is being repaired, so I was wearing this old one just because I'm so used to having something on my wrist. Ya know?" She paused and waved her hands. "Ah, forget it. I'll have to wait till my Watch comes back from the Repair Center." She shrugged and the two headed into the Apple Store.

* * *

Behind the escalator, a man wearing a hooded jacket glared at Samantha and Ashley as they entered the Apple Store. He wore an ominous grin under his hood as he expertly flipped a lady's watch around in his fingers, clearly proud of his pick-pocketing skills. He stopped flipping the watch and stared at its face. He quickly changed the date and time on the watch to October 28, 10:00 p.m., then purposely left the dial out, ensuring that the hour and minute hands no longer moved. He pulled out a folded-up rubber clown mask from his large jacket pocket, rolled the watch in it, then put it back into the pocket. He glanced up, peered around the mall, then exited through the first-level parking garage.

chapter twenty-two

**PRESENT DAY: October 24. South Boston, Massachusetts—
Cathedral of the Holy Cross**

Dunham parked a few hundred yards from the entrance to the cathedral and exited his car. His plan was to meet with Father Martin, unscheduled, and speak with him personally, so he decided to visit in the evening, well after dinner. As Dunham walked through the dark streets, he noticed that the area was unusually empty, seemingly devoid of human presence, aside from an occasional vehicle driving through. The swirling of fallen leaves hitting the pavement and buildings added chilling sound to the desolate atmosphere.

Dunham neared the church and marveled at the Gothic architecture. When he entered the large chapel, he saw a lone person praying in front of the image of Mary. Lit candles flickered in front of him. Just then, a priest entered from a door on the right and made his way through the chapel. Dunham caught priest's eye and waited as the priest placed some items on the massive marble altar, then turned and casually approached him.

"Good evening, Dr. Dunham," the priest said with a kind grin, as if he were expecting him. "It's a pleasure to finally meet you."

Dunham nodded. "I'm sorry, you caught me at a disadvantage. Are you Father Martin?"

The priest shook his head. "No, I am Father O'Farrell, the parish rector. I recognized you from a photo I saw on the front page of the *Boston Globe*. Father

Martin is under my direction but is not in at the moment." He pointed to the last pew. "Come, sit. Perhaps I can be of service." O'Farrell approached the pew. "Father Martin and I share the same interest in the nefarious activities of the October serial killer."

Dunham realized that Father O'Farrell would be very likely privy to anything Father Martin knew, so he decided to sit and chat with him instead. "Actually, you just might be able to assist me, Father. As you're most likely aware, the head of the serial killer task force, Lieutenant Huff, spoke with Father Martin at the latest crime scene."

O'Farrell closed his eyes and nodded deeply. "Yes, Father Martin informed me of this." He lost his kind smile and shook his head. "I hope you're not considering Father Martin as a suspect. His heart is pure, I assure you."

Dunham shook his head. "No, of course not, Father; although we would be remiss in our duties if we hadn't considered, well, everyone."

O'Farrell nodded and regained his kind expression. "Perfectly understandable."

"Recently, we discovered an unsolved double murder event that occurred in Ireland five years ago—" Dunham noticed O'Farrell's grin vanish again—"at the Cave of the Cats, and we believe it was the work of our offender." Dunham paused. "Next to one of the victims was a shoebox-sized metal box, a holy relic with a cross on the door."

"I see," O'Farrell said.

"I am aware that Father Martin is a member of the International Association of Exorcists—" Dunham took notice of O'Farrell's lips tightening—"and we have a suspicion that our offender believes he became possessed in that cave; a cave referred to as 'Hell's Gate'?"

O'Farrell nodded. "I see where you're going with this, Dr. Dunham." He took a deep breath. "I, too, am a member of the International Association of Exorcists." O'Farrell glanced up and watched the lone parishioner in the chapel pass by them on his way out of the church. O'Farrell continued, "We in the association have made a vow to try and stamp out possessions by the Evil One, and his minions, wherever they occur in our designated areas of authority. Just as you have your suspicions of a possession—or the killer believing he's possessed—we did as well, three years ago. Father Martin came from New York City in order to assist me, since my position as the rector of the parish here where the archdiocese, His Eminence, works out of, is a busy one."

"I understand," Dunham said.

O'Farrell nodded. "Are we convinced that this serial killer is truly possessed?" The priest shook his head. "Not entirely, but I'm sure you're less concerned about true possession than if we have information on the identity of this killer."

Dunham nodded. "Yes."

"No, nothing," O'Farrell began. "We're in the dark as to who this killer is too." He paused. "Actually, we were hoping the task force would discover his identity, which is the reason why Father Martin has been at all of the crime scenes. Once discovered, we were going to determine if he's truly possessed or not."

"I see," Dunham muttered, then pulled out a business card and handed it to O'Farrell. "Thank you for your time, Father. Based on what you've shared with me I don't need to see Father Martin, but if he has anything else to add, please have him contact me."

"I certainly will, Dr. Dunham." O'Farrell stood as Dunham did. "We will be praying for you and the task force."

Dunham left the church and made his way back toward his vehicle. Outside, the area was still eerily desolate, with only one vehicle traveling down the street. However, it wasn't quiet; rather, the wind howled as it whirled down the empty street. Dunham wondered if it was always like this in this neighborhood. When he reached his car, he pulled out his key, then paused and glanced around in the darkness. Something was wrong. He noticed a large trash compactor truck slowly making its way toward him with its light shining in his face. He had the strangest feeling he was being watched and examined by something unsettling.

In an instant, Dunham was picked up and hurled headfirst with tremendous force. He slid across the hood of his own car and directly in front of the oncoming truck. The strength of the attacker was unbelievable, which threw Dunham into a slight state of shock. His recent intensive aikido training unconsciously kicked in, and he stuck his hand out in front of himself and rolled through the throw as he made contact with the road. The momentum put his body out of the way of the moving trash compactor, but the truck was so close it clipped the heel of his shoe, popping it off his foot. He rolled to his feet and turned to face the attacker, just as Carnie had drilled into him, in the event that the attacker followed up with a second attack. This was exactly the case, and as Dunham stood up, the attacker was on him—but this time, Dunham was prepared and turned out of the way on his left foot, like the opening of a door on it hinges.

The attacker rushed him so fast that as Dunham pivoted, the man's momentum carried him past Dunham, and Dunham grasped the attacker's elbows, following through with the throw, causing the attacker to twist uncontrollably in midair. The attacker went flying into the sidewalk near the opening of an alley. As he got up, Dunham got a good look at him. He was a man similar in size to himself, wearing a hood that partially blocked his face. Dunham could clearly make out what was appeared to be a Halloween mask of a deranged and bloody clown. Dunham whipped out his handgun from its holster and aimed it at the offender. "Facedown on the pavement!" Dunham shouted with authority.

The attacker faced Dunham, growled, and approached Dunham slowly and deliberately.

He's not afraid of me pulling the trigger, Dunham thought to himself. Just as he was about to do just that, the attacker stopped and craned his neck to look at something behind Dunham. From fifty feet behind him, Dunham could hear a man's voice chanting in a language that sounded like Latin. Dunham watched as the masked attacker collapsed to his knees, covered his ears, and screamed. The chanting got louder, but at that moment, the attacker stood up and rushed into the dark alley. Dunham turned around and eyed the chanting man, some thirty feet away but rapidly closing the gap. Without stopping, the priest rushed by and ran into the dark alley after the attacker.

Dunham rubbed his eyes, slightly dazed and confused at what had just transpired. He found his shoe, put it on, got to his car, and locked the doors. He contemplated on calling for assistance, but a moment later, the priest came out of the alley and approached. Dunham pressed a button and his driver's side window automatically rolled down.

"Are you all right, Dr. Dunham?" the priest asked.

Dunham nodded, rubbing his shoulder. "I think so." He paused. "You must be Father Martin?"

"Yes," Martin replied.

"I'm not sure that was too smart, running into that dark alley after this guy," Dunham commented. "He was unusually powerful and threw me like a rag doll."

"He wasn't hiding out in the alley," Martin explained. "He ran through it to his car at the other end and drove off. He's out of the city limits by now." He glanced up at Dunham. "Father O'Farrell was correct. The October serial killer saw you in the paper and was going to try and eliminate the only threat to his plans—the Watchmaker. I've now been given the additional responsibility of protecting you."

Dunham shook his head, momentarily reeling from information overload. "Wait." He pointed into the alley. "You're saying that guy may have been the October serial killer?"

"No," Martin said, still panting, "I'm saying he *is* the October serial killer."

Dunham rubbed his ankle. "I'm at a loss here. You're saying you were assigned to protect me from a ruthless, powerful, violent serial killer? That's not a job I would not expect for a man of the cloth, but I was indeed attacked, and you certainly did protect me . . ." he paused, "by chanting in Latin?" He couldn't wrap his agnostic head around this spiritual reality.

Martin nodded. "That's about it, Dr. Dunham, although I was too far away to impress upon him all of my influence. But that was a beautiful maneuver. Maybe you don't need my protection."

"Luck, Father Martin," Dunham responded. "It's still not registering with me why Father O'Farrell tasked you to be my bodyguard. There seems to be more to the story."

Martin seemed to study Dunham for a moment. "I've been ordered not to speak to you, Dr. Dunham, but I believe we are now overcome by recent events." He glanced behind himself at the church. "You need to know everything, but I would prefer not to discuss this here."

Dunham nodded. "How about some coffee?"

"Maybe you should get medical attention first," Martin suggested.

"I'm fine," Dunham responded. "I've been told of a nice twenty-four-hour diner, just down the road from here."

"Sounds good," Martin replied.

Dunham unlocked his car's passenger door and Father Martin got in. After a ten-minute drive to the all-night diner, they sat in a booth and ordered coffee.

"Seriously, Dr. Dunham," Martin commented, "few have ever successfully lived through an attack by this man, let alone thrown him."

"I've had intensive training recently," Dunham replied, "and it's paid off."

"Do you recall how the man who attacked you immediately dropped to his knees as I was speaking Latin?"

Dunham nodded, then shook his head. "I do, but I'm not sure what I saw."

Martin glanced around the diner, then leaned toward Dunham. "I have a special divine gift," he whispered. "A gift from the Holy Spirit. We in the

Catholic Church call it a charism." He paused. "It's a very unique charism; one that allows me not only to recognize the presence of evil but to have a certain level of control over it."

Dunham remained silent and stared at Martin, listening intently.

Martin glanced down and shook his head. "It's most effective when I clear my head of all sin, which is another reason why I spend hours a day in prayer. Also, it's proximal—meaning, I need to be near the evil spirit in order to gain complete control. Being twenty or thirty yards away, as I was tonight, only gives me limited control." He glanced up at Dunham. "You see, Dr. Dunham, the October serial killer truly is possessed by an evil spirit, although, one that's outside of the ranks of the Evil One." He glanced around. "He's a rogue entity, which, in a way, makes him even more dangerous."

"So, you know who the killer is, meaning the man who is possessed by this spirit?" Dunham asked.

Martin shook his head. "No; what Father O'Farrell told you in the chapel is true; he just didn't tell you everything. We've been ordered not to speak to law enforcement; a directive straight from our Holy Father's personal exorcist, our exorcist association's leader." He paused. "You see, you are correct that this killer was in the Cave of the Cats five years ago. When one of the thieves opened up the metal box, he released the evil within it, which then immediately possessed him. A priest at the Vatican with a very sensitive charism sensed the release of this spirit immediately. We just don't know who was possessed."

Dunham nodded but stayed silent.

"Once the killings began four Octobers ago," Martin continued, "we knew this was him, so I came here to recapture the evil spirit. Only, he has proven to be much more elusive than we expected, and we suspect it's because of the craftiness of the human host."

"Hmm. That certainly would explain why our offender exhibits both idealistic and pragmatic behavior."

Martin stared at Dunham with a grave expression. "They make a perfect killing machine. At the onset, the plan was to follow the task force and be there when they attempt to capture him, but the task force found themselves in way over their heads." He pointed his finger at Dunham. "His Eminence finally convinced the governor to get you involved."

Dunham grinned slightly. "Interesting." He paused. "So, you were aware that there was a holy relic that was buried in the back of the cave?"

Martin shook his head. "Not until the ancient container—which was sealed by a blessing—was opened. After the Vatican priest became aware of the presence of this evil spirit, once it escaped its bondage, they went into the archives at the Vatican library and discovered the story behind this evil spirit. They learned how it had terrorized the local Irish clans while possessing a massive man. How a team of Jesuit priests successfully trapped it in the container, then buried it in the back of the cave in 1570 AD."

"How did they trap it?" Dunham asked.

Martin took a deep breath. "Not without difficulty, apparently . . ."

* * *

November, 1570 AD. Old Ireland, Province of Connaught

Liam rested his head on the table as he sat, completely exhausted. He was fully dressed and armed, absently grasping the pendant his wife had placed over his neck before the fateful evening when he came face-to-face with the monstrous entity.

"You must eat more, Liam, and regain your strength," his wife demanded. "The friar will be here soon with the priests. Help has finally arrived to rid our lands from this evil, and you must be strong enough to do your part."

Liam raised his head and stared at his wife. "Priests are no match for this . . . thing. The friar brings hope for our clan where there is none. The countryside has been decimated."

"Then why do you hold onto your blessed pendant so?" his wife pointed out. "The power of God saved you. Our neighbors are now protecting themselves against Jack o' Lantern."

Liam sat in silence, contemplating his wife's words. He nodded, then glanced up at his wife. "You are wiser than your years, my wife." At a loud knock, he turned toward the door.

"Liam, it is Friar O'Neil," came a muffled voice from outside.

Liam glanced back at his wife and took a deep breath, then looped the pendant over his head and around his neck. "God be with us. I will be back at a late hour," he said courageously and rushed out the door. He saw the friar holding onto a dimly lit lamp, standing next to five hooded priests. All were wearing dark brown robes tied with a rope around the waist. One carried a small metal container slightly larger than the lamp.

"Liam," the friar said, then pointed to the closest priest. "This is Father Corel. He and the others made the trip from Spain."

Liam, a full head taller than all of them, merely stared at the assembly as Father Corel nodded in greeting.

"They do not speak our language, yet I can interpret," the friar explained. "I told them you know where this evil is. They have spent hours in prayer this morning in preparation."

Liam nodded and glanced up at the sun nearing the horizon. "I will take you there now. Prepare for a two-hour journey on foot through the wood and boglands to the north." He nodded to O'Neil. "We will need your lamp."

The friar relayed the message to Corel, who nodded, then spoke to O'Neil. O'Neil glanced up at Liam. "They will still need your sword. Once they release the evil spirit from within the wretched man, he will attempt to mutilate us with the same ruthlessness as his master. They are the same now."

"I will take pleasure in slaying it," Liam replied, then guided everyone toward the woods.

As they made their way by a number of homes, Father Corel gestured toward gourds in the windows with carved faces in them; some were lit up.

O'Neil acknowledged Corel's attention on the gourds. "The face of the Jack O' Lantern, Father," he explained in Spanish. "They believe evil fears its own sight." He paused. "The pendant Liam wore around his neck when he was attacked by this creature had the face of evil on it, and it saved him. I tried to explain to everyone that it was my blessing upon the pendant that the evil spirit could not bear, not the frightening face, but tradition is strong in these lands."

"I received word this morning that this evil is terrorizing our neighbors to the north," Liam announced. "We will ask locals where it is hiding out."

O'Neil shared that information with Corel, who replied back to O'Neil, who said to Liam, "Once we are near the evil spirit, Father Corel will be able to locate it."

As the sun set, the group continued along the darkening path. O'Neil walked with Liam and lit the way with his lantern. As they broke through some trees, a few homes came into view, though they were not lit up by the customary lamps and hearths. Instead, the front doors were torn off their hinges. In front of the first home were the mutilated bodies of the residents. The priests made their way to each dead body they saw and said a brief prayer.

Corel pointed toward a path in the woods and spoke to O'Neil.

"That way," O'Neil relayed to Liam, who led the way. Minutes later, a large dairy barn came into view in the moonlight. Father Corel grasped Liam's arm, alerting him to stop. Corel pointed at the barn and whispered to O'Neil. O'Neil leaned closer to Liam and whispered, "Father Corel informs me that the evil still inhabits these walls."

Corel whispered again as the four other priests approached the barn.

"He said you and I are to stay behind him at all times, until he needs your sword," O'Neil explained.

As they neared the barn, the priest holding onto the metal container handed it to Father Corel, then the four of them separated and slowly surrounded the barn, chanting softly.

"They are chanting in Latin," O'Neil whispered to Liam.

Corel turned and whispered to O'Neil.

"The evil is aware of us, so be prepared for anything," O'Neil said as he pulled out a hidden dagger.

Liam unsheathed his massive sword.

Once the four priests surrounded the barn, they chanted louder. Corel glanced at Liam and O'Neil. He marched fearlessly into the barn, repeating the same Latin chant, O'Neil and Liam on his heels.

As Liam entered the barn just behind Father Corel, he heard a piercing scream, and in the light of O'Neil's lantern, he saw the silhouettes of a number of cows moving about, clearly agitated. Father Corel advanced forward toward the commotion, chanting even louder. Then he saw the titan of a man on his knees. The man dropped the severed head of a victim so he could cover his ears with his hands, growling and gasping. The man then retrieved the bloody head and heaved it at Corel, but Corel merely ducked and continued his chant. Corel neared the large man, and as he did, he opened the metal container. In the lantern light, Liam could see the cross on the door of the container. Corel now screamed in Latin. The man jerked his head up, and a glowing light left the man's chest.

"The Jack o' Lantern!" Liam shouted.

As the light hovered, moving in circles over the giant of a man, Liam watched Corel thrust his open palm forward at the light, which caused it to stop circling. Corel whipped his hand to the top of the container, the light whooshed into it, and Corel snapped the container firmly shut.

"Watch out!" O'Neil screamed.

The large man rushed toward Father Corel with a dagger in his hand. In an instant, Liam darted in front of Corel and thrust his sword into the man's chest. The man stopped in his tracks, and as he did, Liam pulled his sword out and finished him off.

Father Corel glanced up at Liam.

"Gracias," he said gratefully. He turned to O'Neil and spoke.

O'Neil beamed. "Father Corel said the evil spirit is contained. It is now time to bless your people."

Dunham took a sip of his coffee. The story sounded incredible, but everything now made sense—*if* one accepted the reality of the supernatural.

"Father Martin, each victim of the October serial killer has had a rutabaga jack o' lantern shoved in their mouths . . ." his voice faded. "Our criminal profiler, Dr. Gillespie, suggested the possibility that our offender believes he's possessed, and the evidence leads to the conclusion that he believes he is possessed by the spirit of Jack o' Lantern."

Martin eyed Dunham over his glasses. "And this story just confirmed your suspicions?"

Dunham nodded.

Martin sat back. "We know this evil had been terrorizing Ireland into the early Christian era, and maybe even before. According to the Vatican records, they realized it was a rouge evil spirit following no directions from the Evil One, so Father Corel wrote that he had to modify their method of exorcism."

"And the tale of Stingy Jack says he had Satan promise not to take his soul; something he later regretted," Dunham added.

"Exactly," Martin replied. "Instead of allowing it to merely find another host, the Church decided to entrap it in the container and bury it where no one would dare go—the cave, considered to be the Gates of Hell. But, as time passed, it became a tourist attraction. At the turn of the twentieth century, the Church became concerned that someone would accidentally discover it and release the evil, so they paid someone to collapse the roof in the back of the cave, further sealing the container." Martin shook his head. "Somehow, someone found out that a rare holy relic was buried there and had it illegally excavated five years ago."

Dunham shook his head. "Father Martin, this is a lot to take in." He paused. "Yes, I did see this man drop to his knees as you spoke in Latin, apparently controlling him supernaturally, and yes, the story confirms my suspicions, but I'm not yet prepared to accept anything," he took a deep breath, "or at least report anything except for our offender being a man who *believes* he's possessed." He glanced out the window. "For a practical matter, it is of no consequence since the man must be taken off the streets, regardless, if he's truly possessed or not."

"Fair enough, Dr. Dunham. I can work with that. All I'm asking is that I be there when you are about to arrest this killer." He leaned closer to Dunham. "If you don't allow it, more law enforcement officers will die at his hands. He's unbelievably powerful and agile, as you know. If I'm there, I'll be able to control this power, and you'll be able to arrest the human host." Martin sipped his coffee.

Dunham contemplated Martin's request, then remembered the McGarrity issue. "Father, we've discovered how he chooses his victims."

Caught off guard with vital information, Martin accidentally spilled some coffee. "You what?"

"Actually, a group of college students discovered it," Dunham explained. "One of them, Rob Faulks, helped me out with the Niagara Falls Serial Killer Case last year." He leaned closer to Martin. "Maybe you can make sense of it. He's selecting people from the McGarrity Family History website."

"That does make sense," Martin answered. "The village chieftain, Liam, was a MagGarraughty, which is the ancestral variant name of McGarrity." He shook his head. "He seems to be getting back at him by murdering his descendants."

That makes absolute sense, Dunham thought to himself. *Moreover, it only makes sense if it truly was a possession. How would a thief in the Cave of the Cats know about a four-hundred-fifty-year-old event only recorded in the private library of the Vatican?* Dunham nodded. "Since I am not officially part of the task force, we are violating no policy if you accompany me for the next few days."

Martin grinned.

"Halloween's just a week away, so we need to work fast," Dunham explained.

"Other than me assisting in the capture of a man who believes he's possessed, I would prefer we keep my request confidential."

Dunham nodded. "Understood. I'm not too fond of explaining the supernatural part to a task force made up of streetwise cops anyway." He looked Martin over. "Will you be carrying around a big metal box?"

Martin shook his head. "No, the spatial capacity of the container is irrelevant." He pulled out a cigar-shaped metal container camouflaged as a travel toothbrush holder. "This will suffice." He paused and stared at Dunham. "If you stay in Boston, Dr. Dunham, he will try to take your life again."

Dunham put on a slight grin. "I understand, but I now have you to protect me, right?"

Martin reached into his pocket and handed Dunham a small amulet on a chain. "It would mean a lot to me if you keep this on your person at all times; maybe even wear it around your neck. It's blessed," he held up a hand to preemptively halt Dunham's protest. "I am aware that you're skeptical about its effectiveness against this killer, but hey, you never know, right?"

"Thanks," Dunham said, then placed it around his neck and tucked it inside his shirt. "This guy threw me over my car with ease, and I don't think I'll be as lucky next time." He stood up to leave. "I'll take every advantage I can get."

chapter twenty-three

PRESENT DAY: October 27. Boston, Massachusetts—Grandma Carol's Pumpkin Farm

Ashley glanced around at the wooden shacks and stores next to the old farmhouse and grinned. It felt to her like she was taken back in time to an old western town. The warm, dark evening was the perfect backdrop for a haunted experience for a kids' Halloween party. Torches lit up the area, and cornstalks and pumpkins of all sizes decorated every nook and cranny. She leaned over and fixed a cute little girl's crown. "There you go, beautiful princess."

The girl frowned and stuck her lower lip out. "I'm a fairy godmother, not a princess!" she corrected, then ran off.

Ashley popped her head up and eyed Samantha and her two roommates and chuckled. She was glad that her roommates had agreed to volunteer with her tonight at the pumpkin farm. They wanted to be there for her and give her moral support through this stressful ordeal of being the next probable target of the October serial killer. She knew her roommate, Dayna, was not at all kid-friendly and would never have volunteered for such an event on her own. This amused Ashley greatly.

Dayna, a large young woman with short dark hair, bent over and handed a boy a pumpkin-shaped cookie from the tray she was carrying around, and at that very moment, another little boy in a skeleton costume accidentally ran into her backside. She popped straight up and turned around. "Hey!" she yelled. "Watch where you're going, kid!" She glared at the boy as he stood facing her. "While you're at it, go in the bathroom and wash your sticky little hands!" She glanced over at Ashley, frustration written on her face. "Little shit!" she mouthed to her friends.

Ashley laughed. "Only one hour to go, Dayna!"

"I'm savoring every moment," Dayna responded. "If it wasn't for me keeping an eye on you, I'd be enjoying a hot bath right now and drinking some pumpkin ale."

"Shush!" Samantha admonished Dayna, grinning. "Remember, you've volunteered because you love kids."

Dayna, still frowning, rolled her eyes, then grabbed a cookie from her tray and took a big bite to calm herself down. "And to think, women give birth to these creatures because they actually *want* them."

Just then, Ashley's other roommate, a thin, beautiful brunette named Janette, walked behind Dayna and slapped her on the behind. "Hey, save some for the kids, girl."

Dayna glanced back at Janette, who was carrying a cluster of balloons. "That's easy for you to say; you only eat salads and cottage cheese."

"Time for the jack o' lantern painting!" called an older woman dressed in a happy scarecrow costume. "Come, follow Grandma Carol!"

"Yaaaay!" the kids screamed and ran over to the long table already set with small pumpkins, water, and paint. Their parents followed them, albeit less enthusiastically.

"Parents," Grandma Carol directed, "please put the aprons on your children and stand behind them in order to make things run smoothly!" Ashley handed out kid-sized orange plastic aprons decorated with jack o' lanterns.

Dayna peeked into the refreshment building, then leaned over to Samantha. "Hey," she whispered. "Your two male counterparts aren't doing the best job of keeping an eye on Ashley."

Samantha glanced at the two men, who were flirting with a waitress. She shook her head and glared at them.

Ashley glanced over at the row of portable lavatories, then approached Samantha. "Hey, I have to use the porta-potty."

Samantha scanned the area, then nodded. "Me too, actually." She waved at the two undercover officers until they finally noticed her. They abruptly jumped off their barstools and casually approached the women.

"OK," Samantha said. "Let's go." As they neared the lavatories, Samantha turned toward Ashley. "So, how do you know Grandma Carol?"

Ashley grinned and watched Grandma Carol assisting a child. "Oh, she's been my mom's best friend for years, and she's actually my godmother. Ever since Mom and Dad flew off to Florida, she's taken it upon herself to be my surrogate mother." She beamed. "She's the best."

"She must be doing a great business," Samantha commented as they joined the lavatory line. "It's a weeknight, and there's a big crowd."

"I think so," Ashley agreed. "They've had the farm ever since I was a kid." She pointed to the other side of the lavatories at the entrance to the haunted corn maze and the line of people waiting to enter. "Ever since her sons started all these Halloween events, like the haunted maze and stuff, they've had huge crowds. Apparently, the toughest thing was getting the liquor license for the seasonal beers and hard apple cider they serve in the refreshment building."

A man at the entrance to the corn maze spotted Ashley and waved, and Ashley waved back. "That's her oldest son, Henry."

Henry pointed at the maze. "Come on, Ashley! Check it out!"

"I love haunted mazes," Samantha said. "We should do it."

"What's taking you so long?" Dayna interrupted, approaching them from behind.

Ashley and Samantha turned around. "Oh, hey," Ashley replied.

"Grandma Carol wanted me to tell you that we can take off," Dayna said. "She said she's got enough help, and they're almost done anyway."

"Sounds good," Ashley replied. "After we use the lav, let's do the maze before we leave."

"You two go," Dayna responded. "I'll get Janette, grab our purses, and hang at the bar until you're done," she said, grinning. "It's time for my pumpkin ale!"

"Perfect," Ashley replied.

Dayna left them and walked back toward the farmhouse.

"Where're you heading?" Janette asked as she approached Dayna.

"Follow me, roomie," Dayna said. "Ashley and Samantha wanna do the maze, so we're gonna wait for them at the bar."

Janette raised her eyebrows. "Oh, we have to try some of their microbrews!"

Dayna wrapped her arm around Janette's. "My thoughts exactly. Let's grab our purses, and we'll get Ashley and Samantha's stuff too."

Dayna and Janette entered the employee room, collected their things, and headed for the bar. They ordered drinks, then sat at an open table.

Janette noticed a half-dozen Halloween actors from the maze entering the bar. They all wore realistic makeup and costumes of various scary characters. "Hey, check out these monsters coming in. Oh, I love the zombies!" she gushed as the actors sidled up to the bar. "I bet they're on their break. Wonder if any of them are cute under all that stuff." She sipped her drink.

"With my luck," Dayna replied, "one of them will hit on me and I'll find out he's *not* in makeup."

Janette laughed. She noticed other people entering the bar, and one man came in wearing a hood. He stood out to her, even with all these interesting monster characters around. The man immediately met Janette's gaze, and when he glared at her, it was as if he despised her. She quickly glanced away, taking a big swig of her beer to drown her discomfort.

"Wow, that guy's an asshole," Dayna commented, having watched the exchange between her friend and the stranger in the hood. "How antisocial."

"Don't look at him," Janette whispered urgently. "I don't want him to think we want his attention. He gives me the willies."

"Don't worry," Dayna said. "He just walked out."

A few minutes later, Ashley and Samantha came in and approached Dayna and Janette.

"How was it?" Dayna asked as she handed Ashley her purse.

"Awesome!" Ashley replied. "Free too!" She grinned. "Henry takes care of me."

"Is he cute?" Dayna asked.

Ashley laughed. "Sure. You'd like him. I can set you up, if you're really interested."

Dayna nodded. "Hey, why not?" She took a drink, then looked at Ashley with a panic-stricken expression. "He doesn't have kids, does he?"

"No," Ashley replied and chuckled. "Ready to go home?"

Dayna and Janette finished their drinks, and they all left the bar, making their way through the crowd. Ashley found Grandma Carol and hugged her goodbye. As they left for their car, Ashley watched Samantha coordinating with the rest of the team regarding their exit plan. She searched her purse for the keys to the car, but her hand grasped something else instead. "Samantha!" She held up the surprise object. "Here's my old watch!"

Samantha stopped and turned. "What? That's strange."

"I can't believe it! I bet the watch fell into my purse when it broke off my wrist. I was holding onto my purse with my watch hand . . ." her voice trailed off as she mentally recalled that event. "How lucky is that!"

"Get a new band for that watch, Ashley," Janette admonished. "It's always popping off your wrist."

"At any rate, my smart watch should be ready in a couple days and I can put this old thing away," Ashley replied, slipping the watch back into her purse.

They all piled into the car, and Samantha pointed to a parked vehicle. "Ashley, follow that car. They're our backup." She pointed to a second vehicle. "Those guys will be following us."

"Sounds good," Ashley responded, easing onto the road.

* * *

October 27. Boston, Massachusetts—Boston Police Headquarters, October Serial Killer Task Force Office

Huff and Sadler hovered over the shoulders of two men and two women sitting in front of four computer monitors. Huff moved over to the far-left screen. "Is this the video feed of Ashley Geraghty?"

"Yes, sir," the woman sitting in front of the monitor replied.

Dunham entered the room. "Good evening, everyone. What do we have?"

Huff turned around. "Hi, Dr. Dunham. We're receiving a video feed from the undercover police officers assigned to Ashley Geraghty."

Dunham joined Huff and watched the video feed.

"We just got word that she, her two roommates, and Samantha Bronson—our task force member acting as an employee at the Apple Store—left the pumpkin farm and are on their way back to their home." Huff pointed at a computer screen. "This feed is coming from the undercover police officers driving behind her."

Dunham nodded.

Huff pointed to the monitor just to the right. "This is three hours of video recording of the crowd at the pumpkin farm before they left." He pointed at the other screens. "And the other two are video recordings from the mall at her work, today and yesterday."

"Have you identified anyone in the crowd who fits the description of our offender?" Dunham asked.

Huff motioned toward the woman observing the computer monitor to the far right. "Dr. Dunham, this is Anna Dragovich." Anna glanced up at Dunham. "She witnessed our offender murdering the police officers near the bridge on October 17."

Dunham approached Anna and shook her hand. "Nice to meet you, Anna, and thank you for helping."

"Nice to meet you, Dr. Dunham," Anna replied in a Slavic accent.

"Although she's not a hundred percent sure," Huff explained, "she believes she's spotted the man in the mall, standing near an escalator as Ashley was having lunch with Samantha yesterday." Sadler brought up the video recording they were referencing, and Huff pointed to the man on the video.

Anna pointed at the screen too. "He's wearing the same jacket and hood, and he looks like him."

Dunham stared at the man, suddenly feeling the hair stand on the back of his neck as he recalled his own encounter with him. "He certainly seems interested in Ashley and our undercover officer."

"Sir, we might have something at the pumpkin farm," an officer operating another computer said.

Huff and Dunham approached him and peeked over his shoulder. "What do you see?" Huff asked.

The man pointed at the screen. "Look at the man near the lavatory. This guy's wearing the same hood." He paused. "And here he is again walking out of the bar."

"Looks like him," Huff said as he watched the video. "Hold it! Go back," he directed the man in control of the video. Huff pointed at the screen. "Check this out. The hooded man approaches Ashley and almost grabs her purse." He paused. "This has got to be him."

Dunham nodded. "I agree." He stood straight up. "If this is our man, this indeed indicates that Ashley Geraghty is his next target."

"I agree," Sadler added. "Boss, we should put almost all of our resources on her."

Huff nodded. "Let's do it." He glanced over at Dunham. "Samantha Bronson will be staying at Ashley Geraghty's home tonight, then she'll ride with her to and from work."

"We've been studying her route between home and work," Sadler said to Dunham, "and we believe we've identified the most probable locations where he may attempt to kidnap her."

"How about at the mall?" Dunham asked.

Huff nodded. "There, too, especially in the parking ramp." He took a deep breath. "Kidnapping her in the mall creates many difficulties, but throwing her in his van in the parking ramp makes his life much easier."

"It'll be our best chance of catching this guy to date," Sadler commented. "Let's take advantage of it."

Huff faced Dunham. "So, Ashley leaves for work at eleven thirty a.m. and works until nine p.m.," he explained. "The detective sergeant and I are planning on being on the road just before she leaves. Would you like to join us, Dr. Dunham?"

Dunham nodded. "I certainly would."

"Excellent," Huff replied. "Be here around ten a.m."

Dunham nodded. "Ten a.m. it is. See you then, gentlemen."

Dunham left the room, made his way out of the building, and slid into the driver's seat of his car. He started it up but left it in park. He reached into his pocket, pulled out his cell phone, and tapped a recent contact.

"Father Martin," the voice said on the other end of the phone.

"Hi, Father. It's Dr. Dunham. The surveillance begins at eleven thirty a.m. at Ashley's apartment when she leaves for work. Her shift ends at nine p.m. We're confident he'll attempt to kidnap her as she leaves work, probably in the parking ramp."

"OK," Martin replied. "I'll be in and around the mall the entire day. Thank you, Dr. Dunham."

"Now, I don't want you to get caught in the crossfire," Dunham cautioned.

"You won't even see me, Dr. Dunham. I don't need to be so close," Martin explained. "If he's in the mall, I'll be able to sense him from a short distance away. Any closer and he'll be able to sense me, so I'm only going to be on the scene during the apprehension." He paused. "Good luck, Dr. Dunham, and be warned—he's unusually powerful and agile."

"Yes, I recall. Thank you, Father."

* * *

October 27. Boston, Massachusetts—Ashley's Apartment

Ashley drove into her neighborhood, nearing her apartment. Samantha was in the front seat, and Dayna and Janette were in the back. Ashley shot a glance at Samantha. "We're almost home."

Samantha peeked back at Dayna and Janette. "So, you two will need to leave tonight. We can't guarantee your safety. All of our resources must be invested on Ashley."

Dayna nodded. "We're staying at my mom's house."

Janette was staring out the window. "I wonder if the killer's out there right now."

"Or in the apartment!" Dayna blurted out nervously.

"No, the safest place for us to be is in your apartment," Samantha explained and turned toward Dayna and Janette. "When we open the front door, don't freak out. Two SWAT team members dressed in full gear are in the living room. They sneaked in a couple hours ago and have given us a green light to enter." She paused. "They plan on staying up all night as we sleep."

"Wow, this is definitely serious," Janette commented nervously.

Ashley pulled into the driveway of the apartment house, which consisted of a first- and a second-floor apartment. "Are the residents in the second-floor apartment home?" she asked Samantha.

Samantha shook her head. "No. We couldn't take any chances, so we put them up in a hotel. Told them we were from the county and that there was an urgent plumbing issue that couldn't be resolved while they were there." She smiled at the group. "Seems nobody questions a night in a nice hotel on the government's dime."

"We're here," Ashley said.

The girls got out of the car, and when Ashley entered the apartment, she could see one of the SWAT team members at the hallway entrance to the bedrooms. She turned, then spotted the other behind the TV stand.

Samantha closed the front door. "We'll keep the living room lights off for now."

Dayna and Janette packed their overnight bags, then both gave Ashley a big hug.

"You take care, Ashley," Janette said.

"I will," Ashley responded, exhaling a large calming breath. "Hopefully, we catch this guy."

Ashley and Samantha watched out the front window as Dayna and Janette got into Dayna's car and drive off.

"OK, I'm going to bed—if I can sleep," Ashley said. "I'll see everyone in the morning."

"Do you have the GPS tracker with you?" Samantha asked.

Ashley pulled it out of her pocket. "I'll wear it around my neck tonight."

chapter twenty-four

Lieutenant Huff sat in the driver's seat of an unmarked police car parked on the side of the road. He fidgeted anxiously, glancing over at Sadler, who was in the passenger seat and wearing a microphone, tuning up to listen in on the task force radio communication. Huff peeked at his watch and noted that it was 11:20 a.m., then glanced in the back seat at Dunham. "There's coffee in that thermos, Dr. Dunham. Take what you want."

"No, but thanks, anyway," Dunham replied.

Huff reached toward the back seat. "I'll take some more." Dunham handed him the thermos.

"Here we go!" Sadler announced. "They're saying that Ashley and Samantha are in their car, and they just drove off."

Huff handed his cup and thermos to Sadler, then put the car into gear. "OK, let's go." He pulled onto the road. "We'll stay about a city block behind."

Sadler glanced back at Dunham. "Ashley always parks on the first-floor mall parking ramp, so we have it packed with undercover officers. If he tries there, he won't know what hit him."

"And we'll be parked outside at the garage entrance," Huff added. "The mall is a short half-hour ride from her apartment." He pointed out the window. "As you can see, the first part of the route is a suburban residential area; the second part is a short drive on a highway; and the last part of the route is city, through Cambridge. We've identified about a half dozen locations along the route that we believe he may choose for his kidnapping attempt—that is, if he doesn't attempt it at the mall during her shift."

Sadler pointed out the window at a stoplight. "Here's one. He could block her in while at the light, pull her out of the car." He pointed to the left. "And then the highway to Salem is only seconds away."

Dunham nodded, then pointed at a vehicle parked near the intersection. "Is that an unmarked police car?"

"Sure is," Huff replied. "He's assigned here on the drive into work and back later on tonight."

They pulled onto the highway going into the city. "We don't expect much here, but the state police will have a significant presence here all day, just in case," Huff explained.

Sadler pointed in front of their car. "I see Ashley Geraghty's car a quarter of a mile up the road."

After a few minutes, Huff followed Ashley's car off the exit toward the Cambridgeside Mall. "Now we're in the city section."

Dunham stared out the window as they drove though the city. "I see quite a few possible locations. I'm sure it was difficult to decide where to allocate your resources."

Sadler glanced back at Dunham and nodded. "Very true. With only so many officers, we had to pick and choose, and a large chunk of them are at the mall and parking ramp."

Huff watched Ashley pull into the mall parking ramp. "We're here."

"She's pulling into the mall," Sadler broadcasted to everyone receiving the radio signal.

Huff parked the car on the side of the road. "I don't see any vans following her in." He paused. "I guess we wait until we get word."

Dunham glanced around to see if he could spot Father Martin, but he didn't see any sign of the priest.

Sadler grasped his headset and stared down. "Ashley and Samantha are out of their car," he said, then paused. "Nothing unusual so far." He paused again, listening. "Now, they're in the mall and on their way to the Apple Store."

Huff turned toward Dunham. "I guess you're right. Looks like he's planning on kidnapping her as she leaves."

Sadler shook his head. "No. Nothing."

"I'm still convinced our offender's going to make his move on Ashley on her way home," Dunham responded.

"Let's wait here a bit longer, but I'd like to get back to the monitors at HQ, so we can see what's happening inside the mall," Huff suggested.

"Sounds like a plan," Sadler replied.

* * *

"Nice job, Ashley," Samantha commented as the two walked through the mall toward the Apple Store.

"Even with all the protection, it's freaking me out," Ashley responded as she noticed her manager pacing at the entrance of the store, watching her, clearly concerned.

"It doesn't show," Samantha replied, then glanced at Mrs. Strassburg, "which is a lot more than I can say for your boss."

Ashley and Samantha approached the manager. "Hi, Mrs. Strassburg."

"Hi, ladies." She took Ashley's shoulders and stared at her. "If at any time you need a break today, just walk in the back."

Ashley nodded. "I'm fine." She paused. "Actually, I hope it's a busy day so time flies."

The manager smiled at Ashley, turned, and walked toward the back of the store. "You can say that again," they heard her mumble under her breath.

Ashley entered the store with Samantha, and after putting her coat and purse away, she read the daily customer reservation schedule. "It's filled, so the day should go fast."

"I'll be at the entrance," Samantha said, "so I'll see you at lunch—or dinner, I guess, since we eat so late."

"Sounds good," Ashley replied and waved to her.

The early afternoon was busy, and at one point, Ashley even forgot about being the next target of the October serial killer. Lunch break at the food court was stressful but uneventful, and the late afternoon was just as busy as earlier.

"Everything all right?" Strassburg asked Ashley.

"So far, so good," Ashley replied as she glanced up and noticed a man in his thirties or forties standing in the store, just staring at her. Chills went down her spine. His stare convinced her that he was the socially awkward type. *A perfect serial killer,* she thought. She glanced back at her clipboard, acted as if she hadn't seen him, and pretended to ignore him for minutes. She peeked back up at him and caught his eye. To her dismay he was still staring—and staring ominously. She could feel her heart pumping hard. Ashley clasped her hands together to stop the trembling. She glanced over at Samantha, who was also staring at her.

Samantha, who immediately picked up on Ashley's anxiousness, stopped what she was doing and raised her hands up. "What?" she mouthed.

Ashley pointed to the man, from behind her clipboard. She quickly glanced over at the man then immediately regained Samantha's eye contact.

Samantha spotted the man, then pointed at him, and Ashley nodded. Samantha immediately approached him, and after a quick conversation, he nodded to her and walked out of the store.

Samantha followed the man and reported the incident over the radio. A few minutes later, she approached Ashley. "Looks like a false alarm, Ashley."

Ashley took a deep breath and shook her head. "I can't wait for tomorrow."

Samantha scanned the store. "Me too."

* * *

9:00 p.m., October 28. Boston, Massachusetts—Cambridgeside Mall parking lot

Huff pulled next to the mall parking lot entrance and parked his car at the same spot he had parked in the morning. "I dunno, but my gut says this is it," he commented.

"Me too, boss," Sadler replied from the passenger seat, listening in on the radio chatter.

"That makes three of us," Dunham added from the back seat. He pulled up Father Martin's cell phone number on his iPhone and texted 'Are you near the mall?'

Seconds later, he received a text stating, 'Yes, but I have not sensed him. He still could be here though.'

Dunham popped his head up and stared outside, thinking. Then he typed, 'OK, if you do pick up anything, please text me immediately,' to which he received a text back: 'I will.'

"So far, no one's seen a van—or any vehicle for that matter—pull up next to Ashley's car in the parking lot," Sadler relayed.

"Do we have anyone in Ashley's apartment?" Dunham asked.

Huff nodded. "Same SWAT team members. They never left the apartment."

"They called in thirty minutes ago," Sadler interrupted, "and reported all quiet."

"Either we'll be seeing a van entering the parking ramp soon," Huff added, "or he'll attempt a kidnapping during her drive home."

Dunham stared out the window into the night.

* * *

Ashley watched as Samantha glanced at her watch, which she held up to Ashley to display 9:25 p.m. Into her headset she said, "Acknowledged," and she approached Ashley.

"They said everyone's in place. You ready?"

"Ready as I'll ever be," Ashley replied as confidently as she could muster. She tried to ignore the concerned looks from the others in the store. "Let's go before I get cold feet."

"All right." Samantha pulled her jacket on and grabbed her purse. She peeked in it, slid the strap up her arm, and patted the outside. "Gertie's snugly nestled in her purse holster, ready for anything. Let's go."

Ashley managed a shaky smile at Samantha's pet name for her handgun as she donned her own purse.

They walked out of the store, through the mall, and toward the parking ramp. "There are a dozen undercover officers in the parking ramp," Samantha whispered to Ashley.

"How will I know the difference between them and the serial killer?" Ashley asked.

"They won't be approaching you," Samantha answered.

"That makes sense." Ashley exhaled a nervous breath.

They neared her car, and Ashley pushed the unlock button. As they opened the doors, a man exited the mall and headed in their direction. Ashley realized that it was the same man that she was concerned about in the Apple Store. Ashley noticed that Samantha also recognized him and already had her hand in her purse. As he neared them he stared, but then he simply walked by. Ashley got into the driver's seat while Samantha stayed out of the car until the man was a distance away, then got into the car.

Ashley locked the doors. "Do you think it's him?"

Samantha kept her attention outside of the car. "I don't know, but three teams are near his car." They waited until the man drove his car out of the parking ramp before Samantha returned her attention to Ashely. "We have a team following him," she said, glancing over at Ashley and tapping her ear to indicate that they were all communicating to keep things going smoothly. "OK, let's go."

Ashley started the car, backed out of the parking space, and exited the parking ramp.

* * *

"There she is," Sadler blurted out.

"I see her," Huff responded.

Dunham stared at the suspect's car half a block down the street, now being followed by undercover officers. "The male suspect's car turned right out of the ramp, but Ashley's turning left, so it looks like a false alarm." He scanned the area. "I don't see any vans."

After a moment, Huff let off the brake and began to follow Ashley's car, keeping a short distance behind.

"Everyone along the route is on alert, boss," Sadler said. "The first probable location is four blocks away."

"Do we know if Ashley has her GPS tracker?" Dunham asked.

Sadler glanced back at Dunham and nodded. "Yeah, I heard them talk about it this morning."

Dunham texted Father Martin, 'She's on her way back to her apartment.'

Martin's text response read, 'I see her.'

Dunham popped his head up and again stared out the window. "The darkness will be his advantage," Dunham muttered aloud to himself, as well as Huff and Sadler.

* * *

"We've got people all along the route," Samantha reaffirmed to Ashley as her eyes ceaselessly scanned outside the car.

"What're you looking for?" Ashley asked.

"Vans, really," Samantha answered. "That's what he used last time."

Ashley approached the green light and turned on her right turn signal. As she drove through the intersection, the light turned yellow, then red, and the car between hers and Lieutenant Huff's stopped at the red light. She glanced at Samantha nervously. "Oops, we lost the cops behind us—is that OK?"

Samantha glanced momentarily into the sideview mirror as Ashley finished her turn. "They'll catch up when the light changes. Not a lot of traffic." She looked at Ashley and said reassuringly, "There are *lots* of other officers along the route. No worries."

Once on the street, Ashley noticed that the next light, three hundred yards ahead, was red, and about a dozen or more cars were in front of her, all stopped. She stopped behind the last car. To her right was a large parking ramp just twenty feet from the street and to her left was a large government building.

"I take back what I said about traffic," Samantha joked. "This sucks. Looks like a wait."

* * *

"Shit! We're losing Ashley," Huff growled. "Now we have to sit here until the light turns green, because this idiot in front of us is going straight," he complained. "How did that car get in front of me anyway?" He peeked to the right, down the street that Ashley drove down. "Can you see Ashley's car?"

"Not anymore," Sadler replied. "The parking ramp is blocking our view."

Dunham's iPhone beeped, and he read the incoming text. 'He's here! I can feel him!' Father Martin had texted. Dunham glanced up.

"Run the light, Lieutenant!" Dunham shouted. "We need to catch up to her now!" He pointed to the right. "That's where he's going to kidnap her!"

* * *

"It seems like this light is always red," Ashley commented, drumming her fingers on the steering wheel.

Samantha glanced up at the red light. "Probably because the other street is a major four-lane street," she surmised. "They probably get—"

SMASH! The passenger side window next to Samantha's head exploded. Frozen, Ashley watched a man punch Samantha, rip her seat belt off, open the door, and pull her out, all in what seemed like a fraction of a second. He threw Samantha's limp body twenty feet to the right, into an industrial-sized trash bin.

Ashley screamed and clicked open her seat belt in hopes of getting out of the car, but as she did, the attacker leaned in through the passenger side, grabbed her, and pulled her out of the car.

The man effortlessly threw Ashley over his shoulder and rushed into the adjacent parking ramp. He approached a Ford Taurus and opened the door.

Ashley fought to get away. "Let me go! Let me go!"

The man grabbed Ashley's hair, yanked her head back, and knocked her out with one punch.

* * *

Huff pulled out of traffic and over the right curb, drove onto the street Ashley had just turned onto, and accelerated the car.

"Shit!" Sadler screamed. "Her car door's open!"

The people in the vicinity of Ashley's car were already out of their cars. Someone was lying on the ground near the large trash bin.

Huff turned on his police lights and siren to clear a path, and then Huff, Sadler, and Dunham rushed from the vehicle.

Sadler questioned the first person he saw. "What happened? What did you see?"

The witness pointed in the parking ramp. "A man ran up to this car, punched out the window," he pointed to the person lying facedown on the ground, "threw that lady into the trash, then grabbed the driver and took her into the parking lot!"

Sadler rushed into the parking lot, screaming into his headset.

Dunham ran to follow Sadler, then stopped as he saw Samantha Bronson unconscious.

"I'll worry about Bronson, Dr. Dunham!" Huff shouted from thirty feet behind. "Catch up to Sadler!"

Dunham nodded, then ran up the ramp. When he entered the parking garage, he saw Sadler running to different vehicles.

"I need someone to track Geraghty's GPS and tell me where she is!" Sadler screamed into the microphone. He stopped, listening to the radio, then looked at Dunham. "They're saying he's already on the road! Units are in pursuit!"

"Let's get back to the car!" Dunham yelled.

They ran out of the parking ramp and saw half a dozen police officers already hovering over Samantha Bronson.

Sadler ran up to Huff. "He's already on the road, boss!"

"Let's go!" Huff yelled, then all three rushed back to their car and drove off.

"Shit! Shit! Shit!" Huff blurted out. "We can't lose her."

"Turn left!" Sadler directed.

Huff turned left, lights on and siren screaming. After a minute, he noticed three police cars blocking a Ford Taurus at a well-lit community park with a basketball court, swings, and a baseball field.

"There it is!" Sadler yelled. "They're reporting on the radio that Ashley and the driver are not there though."

Huff pulled up to the vehicles, parked, and all three rushed out. Huff approached one of the officers. "What do you have?" he gasped, motioning toward the parked Taurus with open driver and passenger doors.

"It looks like he switched vehicles, Lieutenant," the officer replied, then pointed to a pile of women's clothes. "Ashley Geraghty's."

The officer reached into the pants pocket and pulled out the GPS tracker and showed it to Huff.

Huff stared at it, then turned around and walked away. "Shit!" He approached Dunham. "How'd he know we had Ashley under surveillance?"

"I don't believe he did," Dunham answered. "The location he chose was ingenious, and he most likely would've selected it anyway." He paused. "His plan all along was to grab Ashley from her car and drag her into the parking ramp, ensuring that no witnesses would be able to see his escape vehicle."

Huff thought for a moment, then nodded.

"The only modification from the other kidnappings I've noted," Dunham continued, "was using a non-van when kidnapping her. He knew we identified him with a van."

A police officer approached Huff and Dunham with a young couple in tow. "Lieutenant, this young man and young lady were sitting on the swing set over there and claim they saw the whole thing."

Huff faced the young couple. "Great. Tell me what you saw."

The young man pointed up the street. "While we were sitting on the swings, we saw this car barreling down the street. It pulled in next to a blue van, then a guy got out of the car, opened the back door, ripped the clothes off this girl, then threw her into the van. She seemed to be unconscious." He pointed down another street. "He drove off that way."

Huff glanced up at the unusually bright park lights just above them, illuminating the basketball court and baseball field. "Are you sure it was blue?"

Both the young man and young lady nodded. "Blue," the young man said, then glanced over at the girl. "Could have been purple, but most likely blue."

"Any writing on the van?" Sadler asked.

"No," the young man said. "Nothing."

"Thank you very much," Huff said, then glanced over at the police officer. "Could you take their statements for me?"

The police officer nodded, then escorted the young couple away.

Huff faced Sadler, Dunham, and the other assembled officers. "I want every blue van heading east toward Salem pulled over and checked!"

Sadler nodded, then walked away, speaking into his headset's microphone.

Dunham received a text and glanced down to see that it was from Martin. 'I'm driving to Salem. I'll let you know if I pick up anything.'

'Great.' Dunham texted back.

"Now what?" Huff blurted out.

"Let's take a ride to Salem tonight," Dunham suggested. "Maybe we'll get lucky."

Huff nodded. "Let's go."

chapter twenty-five

Rob put his chemistry folder into his backpack and glanced toward the hall, where Sarah waved to him, her face lighting up with a warm smile.

"And don't forget that your lab report is due next class!" his professor called as the students exited the classroom.

"Wow, you're so beautiful!" Rob said as he rushed up to Sarah and kissed her.

"I like that greeting," she said, kissing him back and taking his hand as they exited the building.

Outside, Sarah bundled up her coat against the crisp autumn breeze. "Wow, those are pretty amazing," she said, pointing to an artist who was carving pumpkins in the grass, just to the left of the science building.

Rob was about to say how interesting it was that the artist was carving faces with the guts still inside the pumpkins—more of an artistic carving than an actual jack o' lantern since there would be no place inside for a candle—when he heard someone shout his name from some distance behind them.

"Rob!" Keith called again, as Rob and Sarah turned around to find their friend sprinting toward them, Nick trailing a few strides behind.

"Hi, guys," Rob answered. "What's up?

"Haven't you heard?" Nick asked. "There was another kidnapping last night!"

"What!" Rob roared. "Who? Where?"

"Her name is Ashley Geraghty," Nick answered, "and she worked at the Cambridgeside Mall. James texted his buddy to find out who got kidnapped, since they're keeping the name out of the news."

"Wow!" Rob answered. "Is her name on the McGarrity website?"

Nick nodded. "Page three."

"She was my first choice," Keith bragged.

Rob, Nick, and Sarah turned and stared at him, doubt written all over their faces.

"OK, OK, maybe not, but I remember seeing her name!" Keith replied.

Nick said to Rob, "James said that the task force figured out it was going to be her and had her under surveillance, and the guy kidnapped her right under their noses!"

"I bet they're pissed and frustrated. If it were me, I'd be all that—and depressed on top of it . . ." Rob replied, then shook his head. "So close."

"How sad for Ashley," Sarah added. "I'm sure they told her she was his next target, and she was probably stressing, only to now be in the hands of the killer. She's obviously in hysterics, probably being treated poorly, and knowing what might happen to her in two . . ."

Rob pulled out his cell phone. "We need to go to Salem now." He put on the phone speaker. "I'm calling James."

After a couple rings, James answered. "What's up, Rob?"

"James, it's Nick, Keith, Sarah, and me," Rob replied. "They just told us about Ashley Geraghty."

"I know. Sucks, huh?"

"Yeah. We need to go to Salem today. Maybe we can find Ashley before it's too late."

"My car's in the shop and won't be ready until tomorrow morning. It's available after that though."

Rob glanced at Sarah. "Well, I guess it'll be tomorrow then. Let's get together tonight and figure out what we're gonna do."

"Sounds good," James replied. "See ya in a bit."

chapter twenty-six

Huff studied the murder site map on the task force wall. He glanced to
where Sadler and Dunham sat staring at a computer monitor. "What have we
missed?" he asked, shaking his head and biting his lip. "We were *this* close, and
now Ashley Geraghty is two days from being mutilated." He cringed and jerked
his head. "Shit! Shit! Shit! We should've just had her leave town."

"Don't get yourself too frustrated, boss," Sadler said, gazing at him. "She's
not dead yet, and we need you on your game."

"Shut up, Detective Sergeant," Huff replied, harshly, still studying the map.
Then he sighed and softened. "I hate it when you're right."

"When it rains, it pours, boss," Sadler added and slid him the morning
paper. "Check that out. Someone around here opened their big mouth to the
press about us being on the lookout for a blue van. It's all over the paper, so I'm
sure this guy knows it by now."

Huff raised his hands and shook his head. "Why should I not be surprised?"
he muttered facetiously, then glanced over at Sadler and Dunham. "What the
hell're you guys looking at anyway?"

"The stomach contents of each victim," Sadler replied. "Maybe there's
something here that suggests what this killer feeds his victims while they're

being held. If it's takeout or locally foraged food, that might indicate a more specific location." He paused. "So far we don't' see anything." He glanced over at Dunham. "If he's gonna just murder these people, why is he even feeding them?"

Dunham nodded. "In most ancient cultures where they practice animal sacrifice, the purpose of the offering was to give a particular deity the best from their herd—a true sacrifice. I see our offender following this belief. He wants them healthy." He paused and stared up at the ceiling. "This does give us a small level of assistance."

Huff raised his eyebrows. "What do you mean?"

"Ashley is probably being held at a location with relatively comfortable surroundings; at least with running water, food, and a toilet, I'm sure. The food he's been feeding them contains excellent nutrition."

Huff nodded. "I see where you're going with this. She's probably not in a cave or shed, or somewhere outside chained to a tree."

Dunham nodded. "Our offender takes his sacrificial rituals, so to speak, seriously." He rubbed his eyes and stood. "If you don't mind, I'm going to take a drive to the Common. I'd like to clear my mind and mull things over."

"Anything that'll help, Dr. Dunham," Huff said. "See ya later."

Dunham left the Boston Police Headquarters and drove to Boston Common. It was a beautiful, sunny fall day, and many people were strolling around taking advantage of it. He approached a trash container and threw his used coffee cup away.

"Good morning, Dr. Dunham," a male voice said from a park bench seat behind him.

Dunham recognized the man's voice immediately.

"Good morning, Mr. Bradbury," Dunham said, turned, and made eye contact with Jonathan Bradbury, a very wealthy old man from Buffalo, New York. He'd met Bradbury last year in Buffalo during the Niagara Falls Serial Killer Case. Besides being the heir to "old money," he was grand master of the Fraternity of the Ancient and Mystical Order of the Rose Cross—a Masonic-style order even in its secrecy. "Fancy meeting you here!"

"Do you have a moment?" the Rosicrucian grand master asked.

Dunham knew immediately that this was not a chance encounter. Bradbury had access to many resources, and thus, was pivotal in closing the case on the Niagara Falls serial killer last year. "I certainly do," Dunham replied and sat next to him.

"Beautiful day, isn't it?" Bradbury commented.

"It is," Dunham answered, then glanced over at Bradbury. "So, what can I do for you?"

"Actually," Bradbury responded and grinned, "it's what I can do for you."

"Oh, how is that?"

"Well, as you're well aware, I have feelers everywhere, and I happen to know that you and your task force have collected fingerprint evidence on the October serial killer."

"Very true, but so far, we've come up with no definitive matches."

Bradbury nodded. "I believe I know why." He paused and watched a couple of pedestrians pass by. "As you may well know, many in my . . ." he cleared his throat, "financially independent social circles consider themselves above the law. They believe laws were made for the masses to keep them under control."

Dunham nodded. "I understand."

Bradbury scanned the area. "There is an exceptionally secret and well-funded organization that caters to the most ruthless of the wealthy. They perform every type of illegal task, from art theft to murder, and they are paid handsomely for their services."

"Hmm, I'm not aware of the organization," Dunham acknowledged.

Bradbury grinned. "Now, you are. You may not want to hear this, but there are certain FBI departments who do know, so if you report it, it'll fall upon deaf ears."

"How disheartening," Dunham replied.

"True," Bradbury agreed. "The people they use for these services are known for their unparalleled abilities and skills—they're called mechanics." He glanced around again and leaned closer to Dunham. "In order to ensure they don't lose these well-trained mechanics, an untold amount of money was spent eliminating any record of them in all official databases; fingerprint databases, DNA databases, and at all levels of government."

Dunham's spine stiffened, internalizing this new information. *That does explain why the offender's latent fingerprint was not a match to anyone*, he thought to himself. "Are you saying that the October serial killer is a mechanic . . . do you know who it is?"

Bradbury sat back, gazing at the horizon. "Yes and no, Dr. Dunham. I'm not one hundred percent sure, since I personally do not participate in these kinds of illicit activities, but my sources tell me so." He paused. "And no, I do not know who it is. I'm not even sure if this information will help you, but I do know that if it will, you are the person who'll figure it out. I also know that this killer has not been contracted by this clandestine organization to murder Bostonians. It seems he's gone rogue."

"Thank you, Mr. Bradbury," Dunham replied. "I have a question. Why have you come all this way to help us out?"

"Do you believe in destiny, Dr. Dunham?" Bradbury asked.

Dunham thought for a moment. "I'm not sure of my answer to that question anymore. Lately, my worldview has been challenged."

Bradbury tilted his head and laughed. "Yes, indeed. Doesn't life have a way of throwing curveballs?" He picked himself up off the bench and turned toward Dunham. "To your question, it is inevitable that our paths will cross again in the future, Dr. Dunham—actually, it is necessary. This man nearly killed you a few nights ago." He paused. "He will make another attempt on your life. We cannot let this happen." He gave Dunham a kind grin, then said, "Good day, Dr. Dunham, and happy hunting."

"Good day, Mr. Bradbury," Dunham replied as he watched Bradbury enter a waiting car. *How did he know about the offender's attack on me when I haven't spoken to anyone about it?* he thought to himself. Dunham reasoned aloud: "Father Martin must have spoken to his Church leaders . . . so Bradbury must have connections even in the Catholic Church." He grinned and shook his head. "Bradbury said, '*We* cannot let that happen.' 'We' must be referring to his Rosicrucian Order." Dunham sat back on the bench and scanned the area. He became convinced the reason Bradbury would be contacting him in the future was connected to a Rosicrucian belief, specifically, that he'd read from the ancient *Book of All Knowledge* sometime in his past.

A girl dressed in a Halloween witch costume, walking with her mother, caught Dunham's attention. He stared at the flowing costume as they walked away, his mind searching for an answer. He jumped up from the bench. "That's it!" he yelled out loud, then rushed to his car.

Dunham sat at a small table in the diner, glancing at his watch. When he spotted Huff and Sadler by the entrance, he waved them over.

"We're here, Dr. Dunham," Huff announced as he and Sadler sat down in at the table. "So, spill the beans. You said on the phone you found something, so what is it?"

Dunham glanced around the diner. "So, is this your normal lunch spot?"

Huff frowned. "Yeah, yeah, I get the roast beef sandwich and Sadler gets the meatball sub. What did you find out?"

Dunham paused. "Well, I was unexpectedly visited at the Common by Jonathan Bradbury, a multi-millionaire out of Buffalo, New York. He's a grand master in the Rosicrucian Order, and he was pivotal in the discovery of the Niagara Falls serial killer's hideout. He basically broke the case last year."

"OK, so how does this relate to our case?" Sadler asked.

"Mr. Bradbury has many connections, and he believes some information that he came across will help our case," Dunham explained. "He says there is this clandestine group that caters to certain sections of the social elite, doing their unlawful bidding, such as art theft and even murder. They contract with these top-of-the-line professional thieves—he called them mechanics—and Bradbury believes our October serial killer is one of these mechanics."

Sadler glanced over at Huff. "That would explain why he's eluded us for so long. We know the guy's brilliant."

"That's not all," Dunham continued. "The reason why we haven't matched our offender's fingerprint with anyone in IAFIS, or any other fingerprint database, is because the organization somehow deleted that information. Bradbury claims they've not only deleted information on fingerprint databases, but they've also deleted information on DNA databases—local, state, and federal."

Huff frowned and shook his head. "Then how the hell are we going to find him? Does he have an idea who it is?"

Dunham shook his head. "He has no idea who it is or even how we should go about identifying him." He slowly grinned.

Sadler grinned back. "But you do, don't you?"

"Well, the task may be monumental, but it's all we have," Dunham began. "I stand by my earlier conclusion that our offender must have had a record prior to these murders, possibly even in his teenage years. There would have been an ink tenprint fingerprint card done on him, most likely at a local police station. From the eyewitness testimony and distant video shots of him, he's most likely in his thirties or even forties. As you know, in today's digital world, most agencies use live-scan fingerprint terminals, yet many still use ink tenprint cards, then must digitize them for our IAFIS international fingerprint database."

"OK," Huff affirmed that he followed the explanation.

"In the recent past, there was a concerted effort by local, state, tribal, and federal agencies," Dunham continued, "to add to the databases by scanning latent fingerprints and tenprint cards from their old case files—even as far back as the 1960s." He sat back in his chair. "I have a suspicion that even though our offender's fingerprint and DNA information was eliminated from all databases, an old ink tenprint card with his name on it is somewhere in the basement of some police station's records department."

Huff beamed. "And all we need to do is go into their files and find it—but this could take awhile, so we'd better get our asses moving. Are you thinking we should start with the Salem Police Department?"

Dunham nodded. "Exactly."

Huff glanced over at Sadler. "While we're waiting for the server to bring our food, let's start calling all the departments."

Sadler nodded and walked away from the table, pulling out his cell phone.

"I say, after we eat," Huff suggested to Dunham, "we take a trip to Salem and get personally involved. We just might have a chance to save Ashley Geraghty."

"I was thinking the same thing," Dunham agreed.

A waitress walked over to their table and dropped off a roast beef sandwich and a meatball sub. Dunham shook his head. "I see they certainly do know you two."

Huff grinned. "We called it in." He pointed at Dunham's menu. "Hurry up and order so we can go."

Sadler returned to the table. "I have the office on it." He grabbed his sub with both hands. "Sorry, Dr. Dunham, I can't wait for you. I'm starving." He took a huge bite.

"We're leaving for Salem after lunch," Huff told Sadler.

Sadler nodded, swallowing his food. "Oh, before we leave, I wanna grab that garage door opener. Maybe we'll get lucky while we're in town."

Dunham grinned. "I like the way you think, Detective Sergeant."

* * *

October 29. Salem, Massachusetts

Retired Detective Sergeant James Gauss was at home carving out pumpkins on his back porch with his two grandchildren, Emily and Bobby. "Come on, guys!" he yelled happily. "I'm almost done. Hurry up! We've got to carve out faces sometime today."

"You're bigger than us, Grampa," Emily said. "I'm only ten and Bobby's only eight. You always finish your pumpkin before we finish ours."

Gauss laughed. "OK, OK, take your time. These jack o' lanterns are going to look great in front of the house! Last year's were awesome," he complimented his grandkids. "I can't wait to see them!"

The kitchen phone rang, so he peeked through the door and watched his wife answer it.

Bobby stopped carving out his pumpkin, frowned, and looked up at Gauss. "Grampa, can you finish mine? I can't do it."

Gauss picked up his grandson's pumpkin. "OK, OK," he replied. "Back up, young man, and watch Grampa work his magic."

"Honey," Gauss' wife interrupted. "It's the Salem Police Department—a Donna Peterson? She says it's urgent."

Gauss stared at his wife. "Donna Peterson? She's the principal clerk in the records department. I wonder what she wants." He glanced over at Emily. "Emily, help your little brother out while I take this call.

"OK, Grampa," Emily replied.

Gauss wiped his hands, walked into the kitchen, and took the phone from his wife. "Detective Sergeant Gauss."

"Hi, Jim. It's Donna Peterson," she said. "I know you weren't coming in until Monday, but we have an emergency."

"What can be enough of an emergency to call in a retired, now part-time, grumpy old detective?" Gauss asked, semi-facetiously.

"Well, you're our only latent print technician, and we have the head of the October Serial Killer Task Force along with the FBI driving here as we speak. They think we have this serial killer's fingerprints in our files."

"What?" Gauss gasped, his throat seizing up. He coughed. "I'll be there in thirty minutes." He hung up. "Dear! You're gonna have to take over. Don't know when I'll be back."

Just under thirty minutes later, Gauss entered Donna Peterson's office and saw three men speaking with her.

"Here he is," Peterson said as the three men made eye contact with Gauss. "Jim, this is Detective Lieutenant Huff, Detective Sergeant Sadler, and Special Agent Dunham."

They greeted one another, and Huff dove right in.

"Detective Sergeant," he began, handing Gauss an image of a latent fingerprint, "I'm not sure how much they've informed you, but this is the latent print of the October serial killer, and we believe there's a match somewhere in your files."

"I don't understand," Gauss responded, confused. "We've digitized everything from our files, which took me forever, I might add. It should be in IAFIS."

"We have reason to believe his fingerprint has been deliberately deleted from IAFIS," Dunham explained.

"Oh," Gauss replied, scratching his head. He studied the serial killer's latent print, then headed toward the back room. "Come, follow me."

Everyone made their way toward the room, which was filled with storage lockers and filing cabinets. Gauss stopped in front of two long rows of filing cabinets. "Here they are."

Huff stared at the filing cabinets. "Looks like this'll take awhile."

"Weeks," Sadler answered.

"Nope," Gauss interrupted confidently. "This guy has a unique feature in the epidermal ridges." He examined the fingerprint. "I see a tiny scar between a delta and a bifurcation," Gauss explained, then moved over and touched one filing cabinet. "Years ago, I cataloged each fingerprint, not by suspect name, but by epidermal ridge patterns within the loops, whorls, and arches, such as scars. In the old days, it made for a much faster search." He paused, fingering the handle. "This filing cabinet contains unique scar patterns within the epidermal ridges."

Huff glanced over at Dunham and grinned. "Excellent."

"It's the entire filing cabinet though," Gauss commented, "so it still might take a few days."

"I'll take those odds," Sadler replied.

"I'll be here day and night if I have to," Gauss said, "but things would go faster if you give me a few more latent print technicians."

"You got 'em," Huff agreed and glanced over at Sadler, who had already pulled out his cell phone.

"Phoning for backup now, boss," Sadler responded.

Huff turned back toward Gauss. "Even though we believe this guy came from here, surrounding police districts have been asked to check their files too."

Gauss nodded, then glanced over at Dunham. "Nice to finally meet you, Dr. Dunham." He grinned. "Figured you'd finally show up to Boston. Lost the bet, though. I put up twenty bucks that you'd be here last year."

chapter twenty-seven

PRESENT DAY: October 29. Boston, Massachusetts—the warehouse

Ashley woke from a deep sleep to the sound of seagulls squawking and light waves splashing slowly and rhythmically. She could smell the aroma of fish.

How strange, she thought. *My apartment's not near the ocean.*

She needed to scratch her nose, but she couldn't. When she realized that her hands were bound behind her back, reality instantly sank in. She opened her eyes as the memory of the October serial killer kidnapping her and knocking her out rushed back into her mind. She remembered how she later woke up in a moving van—naked—then him knocking her out again after he parked the van. She pulled herself up into a sitting position, then scanned the room, taking stock of her surroundings. She was in a single bed butted up against the corner of a barren room. As she thought about her predicament, her heart pumped faster, and fear flooded her senses. She wiggled into the corner, glanced around for . . . the killer—she shuddered—but he was not in the room.

She was no longer naked but had on a plastic one-piece uniform, almost like a hazmat suit, but it was made of lighter plastic. She shook her head. *If only I had time to put the GPS in my mouth*, she thought, knowing full well that the GPS was thrown out with her clothes.

The bindings were tight on her wrists, affecting the blood circulation in her hands. Her head hurt, probably from the punches to the left side of her forehead.

"Stay cool, Ashley," she whispered to herself. After some calming breaths, she stayed silent and just listened. Again, she heard waves along with the squawking seagulls, convincing her that she was on the coastline . . . somewhere. She could also hear sounds of vehicles and motorboats—maybe she was near a marina? Ashley scanned the room again. Black plastic covered the walls from ceiling to floor, with the exception of the lone tiny window, which was fitted with metal bars. The glass was nearly opaque, allowing some light in, but nothing outside was recognizable from her vantagepoint. She noticed about a dozen pieces of string hanging from the ceiling to about head level. Each piece of string had a small gourd hanging at the end. She stared and squinted at the gourds until she recognized what they were—rutabagas. As she stared at the markings indented into the vegetables, she realized that they were in the shape of faces. Ashley glanced to the left and spotted the toilet, then realized that her backside had a flap opening in the plastic outfit, which allowed her to use it. Her single bed consisted of a metal frame with bedsprings, a mattress, and plastic for bedding. Just next to the bed was a tray of food and a mug with a straw in it. She realized her captor wanted her to eat and drink. She remembered hearing that the October serial killer kidnapped his victims, kept them alive for three days, then murdered them at the sacrifice site.

"Think positive, Ashley," she whispered to herself, realizing she had two days to figure out how to escape. She twisted around to see what her bindings were and saw that she was cuffed with a huge plastic zip tie.

"Everything's plastic," she whispered. She concluded that he had used all plastic in order to eliminate any kind of trace evidence afterward.

She thought back to the attack last night and remembered how Samantha Bronson was whipped twenty feet, headfirst, into the huge trash bin. *This guy is powerful,* she thought. She wondered if Samantha was alive or not after such an impact.

Ashley heard a noise emanating from outside the room, so she rushed to the bed and positioned herself as she had been when she'd first woken. She closed her eyes and pretended to be asleep. She heard a key slip into the door, then the door opened slowly. A few seconds went by, and she heard only silence near the door. *The killer's in the room!* she thought as her heart started pumping faster. *Stay cool; remember, he's not going to kill me for another two days. Stay cool. Plenty of time to be saved . . .*

It was still quiet, but an instant later, Ashley heard him rush at her, then growl in her ear. She knew his face was only inches away, and she could even feel his hot breath on her face. Terrified, she still pretended to sleep, and she hoped she hadn't flinched when he rushed her. Her eyes still closed, she felt him place his hand over her mouth and nose, blocking her breathing. *Oh no, he's trying to suffocate me!* He pressed on her face, longer and longer. Ashley held on to the belief that his plans were to keep her alive, so she decided not to move, giving him no satisfaction of scaring her. She stayed motionless, yet he continued to hold onto her face. Every inch of her body wanted to fight to breathe, but she maintained her composure. She started to pass out, but he finally released his hand. She forced herself to breathe slowly. He giggled madly over her face. She heard him walk toward the door, exit, then lock it.

She sat up, breathing hard, then began to cry. Moments later, she replaced her tears with anger. "Get a grip; get a grip," she whispered to herself. "Don't let him beat you." She continued to draw air into her starved lungs, which finally relaxed her. She got up and examined the room again, looking for any way out. She glanced at the window. *What if I break the painted glass then scream for help?* she thought. She realized that the window was protected by metal bars, but perhaps . . .

Ashley scanned the room, attempting to find any long, thin object that she could poke through the metal bars and break the glass. She glanced back at her spring bed and studied the metal frame at the head of the bed, which had thin diagonal metal bars screwed into the frame. She rushed over and wiggled on the metal bars. After a few minutes, she gave up. "Damn!" she blurted out, then paced back and forth. She looked up and noticed a small crack in the wall next to the door, in between two large pieces of black plastic. She went to the crack to see if she could peek through it, and she discovered she certainly could see into the adjoining room. It was a large garage housing a blue van. As she scanned the garage through the crack, her view became blocked—by a person's eye! Ashley screamed and ran to the bed. She could hear laughing on the other side of the door.

chapter twenty-eight

PRESENT DAY: October 29. South Boston, Massachusetts

Dunham drove through the side streets of South Boston, following his GPS. The foggy, misty evening made it a little difficult to drive, especially with the GPS weaving him through unfamiliar Southside neighborhoods.

"You are nearing your destination," the female GPS voice announced.

Dunham spotted the house but parked his car on the opposite side, just as Father Martin had directed him to do. Someone approached the passenger door and knocked, and when he visually confirmed that it was Father Martin, he unlocked the car door.

Martin sat in the passenger seat and closed the door. "Hi, Dr. Dunham."

"Thanks for meeting me, but why here?" Dunham asked.

"You wanted to meet me immediately, and I couldn't break my plans," Martin explained, then pointed at the house across the road. "See that house? Two Boston-based priests from the International Association of Exorcists, of which I am an active member, are performing a rite of exorcism." He paused. "I promised that I would be available immediately if things go south." He glanced back at the house. "This is not just a possession by a lower-level minion demon, but one of the Evil One's arch-demons—a ruler demon." He shook his head. "They are exceptionally powerful and can do physical harm to priests."

"I see," Dunham replied.

Martin grinned. "This is a completely different world than you're used to, I'm sure."

"Yes," Dunham agreed, "although ever since I've joined serial killer task forces, I've been face-to-face with capital-E Evil more than once. Only, I used to think that evil was merely a manifestation of the human mind—subjective." He shook his head. "Lately, I've been intrigued by the possibility of an objective, external reality of evil, so meeting you here has piqued my interest." He glanced up at the house. "Can anyone be a member of the Association of Exorcists?"

Martin tilted his head. "Yes, with approval, but according to Canon Law and a document titled *Ab Aliquot Annis,* only an experienced priest or pastor," he lifted his finger, "who exhibits piety, knowledge, prudence, and integrity of life, *and* with the express permission of the local ordinary, or bishop, is allowed to perform the actual rite of exorcism. We have physicians, psychiatrists, and pious laypeople in the organization as well."

"I can see people misidentifying someone's unusual and erratic behavior as a demonic possession," Dunham commented.

Martin nodded. "In most cases we come across, there is a completely natural psychological explanation—and even if it truly is a supernatural case, it's usually demonic oppression, obsession, depression, and even infestation, but not diabolical possession." He pointed up at the house across the street. "This is as serious as it gets." He turned back to Dunham. "So, on the phone you said we may have a significant break in the case?"

Dunham nodded. "Hopefully, in the next twenty-four to thirty-six hours, we just might discover the identity of our offender." He paused. "Long story, but we believe we'll get a fingerprint match from the files at the Salem Police Department."

"Great!" Martin exclaimed.

"Upon identification, hopefully we'll get a Salem residence, which might be the location where he's holding Ashley Geraghty."

"If that happens and there's a confrontation, loss of life is a virtual certainty."

Dunham nodded. "I agree, so my plan is to text you once we get an address, and hopefully you can be there as we break down the door—at least have you in the vicinity."

Martin nodded. "I'll be there. You can count on that. Do you still have the pendant on?"

Dunham touched his chest and nodded. "I do."

"Now, there's a limit to my sensing this evil entity," Martin explained. "It's only if he's near; maybe thirty to fifty feet. The reason I sensed him when he kidnapped the young lady was because I was driving just two cars away."

Dunham nodded. "I'll keep that in mind." He paused. "Father Martin, I have a question completely off topic."

"Yes?"

"I met with a Rosicrucian grand master yesterday—the man who passed on valuable information to me that ultimately led to us searching the Salem Police Department files for our offender's fingerprint match. This same man was instrumental in closing the Niagara Falls Serial Killer Case last year."

"A good man to know," Martin replied.

Dunham nodded. "I'll get right to the point. He believes that, in my past, I read from a certain . . . *Book of All Knowledge*. The section symbolized by the Garden of Eden's Tree of the Knowledge of Good and Evil."

Martin's eyes opened wide. "Ah! I am very familiar with Rosicrucian beliefs . . . and he believes this because of your professional success in hunting down serial killers?"

Dunham nodded. "Normally, I wouldn't pay any attention to something like this, but he and I met a person last year who claimed to have read from the section symbolized by the Tree of Life. Coincidentally—or not—this guy discovered an actual, working elixir of life. This man also believed I read from this *Book of All Knowledge*."

Martin sat back in silence, considering what he just heard.

"I'm sure, as a Catholic priest, your belief is not aligned with Rosicrucianism," Dunham said. "But is there another explanation? Could he be correct?"

Martin nodded. "There could very well be an element of truth to this, even conforming to Catholic beliefs," he explained. "Though I highly doubt there is an ancient book that possesses all knowledge and that the human mind contains all knowledge—untapped or otherwise." He paused. "In the New Testament, John 21:25 discusses how little of Jesus' lessons and oral teachings were written down; therefore, many realities of faith and the supernatural are unknown to us. We call them the mysteries of faith. Scripture wasn't designed to answer every question. It's just enough to give us a roadmap to Heaven. Other flavors of the Christian faith, like the Rosicrucians, may very well have discovered some of these mysteries." He nodded at Dunham. "Now, just as they believe, I, too, believe you have a divine gift, Dr. Dunham. But, instead of it coming from an accidental reading out of a book, I believe it was a predestined gift of the Holy Spirit."

Dunham raised his eyebrows at Martin.

Martin grinned. "Another name for a divine gift is a charism, Dr. Dunham." He glanced up at the house. "I have been blessed with a charism, although it manifests itself differently than yours. As I explained before, I have the ability to sense and even control evil. Although, there is one more aspect of my charism, and that's the ability to sense charisms in others." He pointed at Dunham. "I sense something different about you, something divine, but I just can't put my finger on it yet."

Dunham grinned. "I hope it's not your ability to sense evil kicking in!"

"Ha!" Martin laughed, then grinned back. "No, it's good. I'm certain of it."

Dunham nodded. "Hmm. The mysteries of faith."

Martin opened his palm. "Take, for instance, the October serial killer. Ancient cultures may have stumbled upon realities of the supernatural. As you may now know, much of what drives his ritualistic behavior stems from the ancient Celts. As the people in the Celtic world experienced real ghostly encounters, they wanted answers—but they had no owner's manual for the spirit world. Through time, they developed their own interpretations, and after many generations, it became part of their religion." He raised his hands. "Who is to say they didn't uncover some of the mysteries of faith? Maybe it's true that the spirit world and physical world are closest at the time of Samhain, or Halloween."

Dunham grinned. "My wife would love to have this conversation with you, Father."

SMASH!

Dunham and Martin quickly turned toward the house and glanced up at the second floor. The shattered glass from a window glittered on the ground.

"Oh my!" Martin exclaimed, then dashed from the car and rushed toward the house, followed closely by Dunham. Martin and Dunham ran inside and straight up the stairway. Wind whipped around inside the house. As they reached the second floor, they saw a priest lying on the ground in the hallway, moaning and moving slowly. Martin bent down to him.

"Father!" he roared over the howling wind.

The priest pointed to the room at the end of the hallway. "Go. Help Father Carrie. Hurry."

"I'll see to him, Father Martin!" Dunham yelled.

Martin nodded, then rushed into the room, screaming a chant in Latin.

Dunham bent down to help the priest. "Are you OK, Father?"

"Yes." The priest rubbed his head. "Just shaken up from the throw." He sat up.

"How did you end up out here?" Dunham asked.

The priest shook his head and rubbed his neck. "The demon lifted me up and threw me."

Dunham turned and stared into the room from fifteen feet down the long narrow hallway. All he could see was the end of the bed and Father Martin and the other priest shouting in Latin, facing to the right at something out of his view, obstructed by the door frame and the wall. At that moment, the howling wind died. Moments later, the chants from the priests faded, and Dunham could see them approach the person in the bed.

"It looks like Father Martin is now in control," the priest said as he got up. Dunham helped the fallen priest to the room.

Dunham stopped just at the threshold, leaned against the doorframe, and peeked into the room. A young boy, about twelve years of age, lay with his eyes closed. He was panting, and his face seemed to be slightly disfigured, with pronounced eyebrows and cheekbones. The three priests stood around him in silence; Father Martin's head was down, his eyes closed, and his right hand out in front of him. Every time his hand moved, the boy would frown and his head would jerk slightly. Then, in an instant, the boy's eyes opened up and he turned and glared at Dunham. Anger filled the boy's eyes and he grinned menacingly.

It sent chills down Dunham's spine.

"You will lose, Watchmaker. You will lose," the boy blurted out in a deep, gurgling voice.

Martin chanted in Latin at the top of his lungs, which caused the boy to grimace, snap his head back, and scream. After what seemed like five minutes, the boy appeared to have fallen unconscious, and he was no longer panting. Martin faced the two other priests. "The demon is gone."

Father Carrie beamed at Martin, then glanced down at the boy. "Thank you, Father Martin. We can handle it from here."

Martin nodded, eyed Dunham, then walked out of the room. They left the home and slowly made their way back to the car. Father Martin knew why

Dunham remained silent. There was no way a twelve-year-old boy would have known he was the Watchmaker, or that he was battling an elusive, evil entity. It had to be the demon speaking directly to him.

Dunham slid into the driver's seat, but Martin stayed on the sidewalk.

Dunham started the car and lowered the window. "I think I prefer the confines of the forensic lab, Father."

"God's demand of us is never easy, Dr. Dunham," Martin replied. "We have a battle on our hands in the next two days . . . and the demon was wrong. You will win."

"I've got my game face on, Father. Keep your phone next to you."

chapter twenty-nine

Detective Sergeant James Gauss slipped another fingerprint card into the scanner interface. He rubbed his eyes and shook his head as the fingerprint image popped up on the right side of the computer screen. After a full day of comparing fingerprints, exhaustion made it much more difficult for him to compare these print cards to the October serial killer's latent print, viewed on the left side of the screen. He glanced up at the clock and decided to take a break in about twenty minutes.

Donna Peterson entered the room, stopped, and watched Gauss and the other three latent print technicians examine fingerprints on the flat-screen computer monitors. She glanced over at Gauss. "Why do I get the feeling that this is like finding a needle in a haystack?"

Gauss nodded. "It's amazing how many fingerprints are held in one filing cabinet." He removed the fingerprint card from the scanner and put in the next one.

"I'm going to make a Dunkin' Donuts run," Peterson announced to everyone. "Who wants a coffee? On me." Everyone raised their hands.

"Thank you," one of the technicians said to Peterson as she handed her a notepad to jot down her coffee order.

Peterson approached Gauss. "It's kind of exciting that we might find the identity of the October serial killer amongst all these fingerprint cards." She watched him put another card into the scanner. "I'm curious though . . . I'm curious, first, as to how his fingerprint information was deleted out of the national database, and second, how the task force figured it out."

Gauss examined the next fingerprint. "The answer to the second question is easy—the Watchmaker. The first question gives me cause for concern."

Peterson nodded and stared up at the ceiling. "I see what you mean. Who could—"

"Alec Banner," Gauss interrupted.

"Excuse me? Alec Banner deleted the information out of the database?"

"No! Alec Banner is the October serial killer!" Gauss announced.

At first, Peterson just stared at Gauss, but then, as she realized the significance of his statement, she shot over to Gauss' computer screen. She stared at the two fingerprints, then her jaw dropped. "Oh my God!" she yelled. "You did it, Jim! You did it!"

The other fingerprint techs rushed out of their seats and huddled behind Gauss, talking back and forth, clearly excited about the find.

Peterson clapped Gauss on the shoulder and handed him the desk phone. "You want to do the honors?"

* * *

"Tomorrow's the day," Huff announced as he and Sadler looked at the murder site map on the task force wall. They turned their attention to a new map with dozens of tagged locations. "I can't believe there are so many . . ." He glanced at Sadler. "What are they called?"

"Dolmens."

"Dolmens," Huff repeated. "Gates of Hell, in and around Boston." He turned toward Dunham. "Dr. Dunham, have you made a best guess as to which location this guy's gonna use for his sacrifice?"

Dunham continued to stare at the computer screen. "Well, I have a few ideas, but they're only preliminary." He stood up, walked over to the map, and pointed at the town of Lynn, located between Boston and Salem. "There is a century-old stone observatory in Lynn called High Rock Observatory. Follow me." He returned to the computer and Huff and Sadler followed. He sat down and pointed at a photo on the screen, which showcased the stone arches of the observatory.

"Wow." Sadler responded. "There's about a dozen dolmen-like features on the building, and they're made of stone."

"Not only that," Dunham began, "locals claim it's haunted. Many of our killer's murder sites were claimed to be haunted by spirits of the departed, just like the Granary Burying Ground."

Huff nodded. "I like it. What's the story behind—" Huff paused as his cell phone rang. "Lieutenant Huff," he said, then listened. His eyes opened wide. "Yes!" he shouted. "OK, email us whatever you have. Already did? Great! Thank you, Jim. Great work!" He hung up and stared at Dunham and Sadler. "They matched the October serial killer's latent print to an Alec Banner!"

"Finally!" Sadler roared excitedly.

Huff rushed to his computer. "Mrs. Peterson just sent us the information, and it should be in my mailbox. The only thing is, they couldn't find anything on an Alec Banner in their records."

"That's strange," Sadler added. "Given the fact that they still had his fingerprint in their files, he must have been arrested in their district at that time. There should be an arrest record." He sat down at another computer terminal and began typing.

"It looks like this information was taken out of their records department, just as they did with the fingerprint and DNA databases," Dunham surmised. "But apparently they believed pulling the fingerprint card was unnecessary." He paused. "To our benefit."

Huff shook his head as he pulled up his email. "Here we go again. Why do I get the feeling that we're going to come up with another dead end? Oh, here's the file . . . Yup, the only information on him has come off the tenprint fingerprint card. No address; no nothing."

"There's no Alec Banner in the City of Boston records either," Sadler added.

"Shit!" Huff stormed. "So close. There's gotta be something."

Dunham stood up, took out his iPhone, and began to type.

"I bet the FBI comes up empty-handed too," Sadler commented.

"I agree," Dunham responded, "so it's time to fight fire with fire." He turned to leave. "If you'll excuse me for one moment."

As Dunham left the room, he overheard Huff and Sadler's confusion.

"I wonder what he meant by that?" Huff asked.

"I'm not gonna ask." Sadler answered. "Let's just be happy if he finds something."

After Dunham left the task force office, he touched the Secured App on his phone, then dialed a number and put the phone to his ear.

"One Alpha Charlie," a voice answered.

"Winfall, one, eight, eight, eight, eight," Dunham replied.

"Our crypto-translators are in sync and this connection is now secured. Good afternoon, Dr. Dunham. Please ensure no one is within earshot. How may I help you?"

Dunham entered the elevator area and peeked around. "Good afternoon, Big Brother. I just texted you the name of the October serial killer."

"Making progress, I see," Big Brother replied.

"We'll see. The problem is, someone deleted all information on him from IAFIS and every other database. They've also pulled his arrest record from the Salem Police Department." He paused. "Word has it that this guy is a professional thief, or mechanic, and a clandestine group has enough financing and influence to erase him from the record at every level of government."

"Yes, I have your text," Big Brother acknowledged, "so let's see what I can come up with," he said while typing audibly. "He certainly has been deleted from the FBI's databases." He typed again. "Here's something interesting; a local newspaper article. I just sent it to you. An Alec Banner was arrested in 1984, at the age of fourteen, along with four men in their twenties and thirties, for robbing a bank."

"This conforms to the age range given by eyewitnesses of Folgers' attacker," Dunham interrupted as he opened the article on his iPhone and began to read it.

"They broke into a Salem bank one evening and successfully made off with the safe, which contained thousands of dollars," Big Brother explained, then read further as Dunham followed along. "The only reason they got caught was because one of the older members of the group bragged about it at a local bar. He later claimed that the fourteen-year-old Alec was the brains behind it. The prosecutors didn't believe him, so Alec received probation while the rest received jail time."

"Knowing that our offender became a mechanic, I bet he was indeed the mastermind," Dunham surmised.

"There's no address in the article," Big Brother commented, then typed. "Nothing else comes up, but of course, this is only a road bump in my search." He paused. "How old do you think he is?"

"Well, the article suggests that he was born around 1970," Dunham responded.

"That helps." Big Brother paused. "Let's assume he went to school in the Salem School District. It's time to check the high school yearbooks, starting with 1987." He paused again. "Found something, and I only see one Alec Banner fitting within that age range . . . yet I see no address with it."

"How about determining which elementary school he went to?" Dunham suggested. "Generally, elementary schools serve a local neighborhood, which would help us narrow down where he lived."

"Excellent idea, Dr. Dunham. And here we have it! Witchcraft Heights Elementary. What an appropriate name." He paused. "There are no Banners living near the elementary school today, but when he attended this school in the late seventies, there were."

"That might be it," Dunham replied.

"The owner was also named Alec, and the spouse was named Dorothy. Probably Mom and Dad." He paused. "Both are now deceased; died just after his high school graduation." He paused again. "Wait—this is interesting. A 1988 *Boston Globe* newspaper was flagged using the parents' names. They were victims in an unsolved murder that year. They were murdered in their bed, shot in the head with a small caliber handgun. Their son, Alec, had a solid alibi and was eliminated from the suspect list."

"Who lives in the home now?" Dunham asked.

"One second," Big Brother responded. "No one; the home seems to be owned by a local bank, and it's been empty ever since the parents were murdered. Let me see what the satellite photo of the home picks up." He paused. "The home seems to be well taken care of."

"Any van in the driveway?" Dunham asked.

"No, nothing," Big Brother answered.

"How about a garage?"

"Could be, based on the aerial view of the home's layout."

"Looks like we need to check it out," Dunham replied. "Big Brother, could you email me everything, including the rest of the newspaper articles?"

"You got it," Big Brother said, "and good luck."

"Thanks again," Dunham said, then hung up and rushed to the task force office.

"Get your coats, gentlemen," Dunham said hurriedly to Huff and Sadler. "I've got an address."

The detectives popped out of their seats, grabbed their coats, and followed Dunham out.

"Is this one of those I'd-tell-you-but-then-I'd-have-to-kill-you moments?" Huff asked.

"That's right," Dunham replied and grinned. "Although I will say this. The address I received is not Alec Banner's present address that we know of. It's his address from when he was in elementary school. The parents were murdered when he was a senior in high school. The case is still unsolved."

"Was he suspected?" Sadler asked as they got into the elevator.

"Initially," Dunham answered, "but he had an alibi; apparently a solid one." He paused. "Knowing what we know now, the first thing I'd do is re-check that alibi."

"It was him," Huff answered confidently. "Probably had the taste for blood at an early age."

Dunham nodded. "Also, our Alec was arrested at the age of fourteen for breaking into a bank and stealing the safe, and he would have been successful if it weren't for one of his accomplices having a big mouth. The others were in their twenties and thirties, yet they claimed fourteen-year-old Alec was the mastermind."

"Wow!" Huff reacted. "No wonder this elite group wanted him as a thief mechanic."

Dunham nodded. "Since the murder of the mother and father, no one has lived in the home. The bank owns it now, but satellite imagery shows it's being cared for."

"Interesting," Huff replied, then turned toward Sadler. "On the chance that he is holding Ashley in this house, we'll need SWAT involved and a ton of backup."

Sadler pulled out his phone. "You got it, boss."

They jumped into Huff's vehicle and left for Salem. Dunham sat in the back and texted Father Martin the details.

'Will be there. Leaving now,' Martin texted back. 'Have your pendant on.'

Two hours later, Huff, Dunham, and Sadler were sitting in their parked car on the side of the road, five houses to the south of the Banner house. Sadler had his headset on.

"Have they gone in yet?" Huff asked.

Sadler stared out the window, listening intently. "SWAT just went through the back window and are now clearing the first floor." He paused. "So far, they've encountered no one. Two broke off upstairs and two in the basement."

"I don't see the van," Huff added, "so I'm not surprised they don't see anyone."

Five minutes elapsed. "SWAT just gave the all clear," Sadler relayed. "They're opening the front door for us."

Huff opened the car door. "Let's go." The three made their way into the house. Huff closed the door behind them. The room was filled with what looked like the original furniture, and hanging from the walls were family photos.

"So far, we've found no one, Lieutenant," a SWAT member told Huff. "We'll keep on searching until we're satisfied."

Huff nodded. "Thank you, Sergeant."

Dunham approached the large family photo and stared at his iPhone. "These are photos of Alec and Dorothy Banner." He pointed to the young man in the photo. "This must be Alec Banner Jr., our offender."

Huff scanned the room. "It's as if the place is frozen in time from when they were murdered." He paused. "But everything is clean. Someone must be keeping this up."

"We should visit the bank and see if they're doing the upkeep," Sadler suggested.

Dunham received a text from Martin. 'I'm nearby, and I don't sense his presence at all.'

Dunham texted back: 'Thanks, I'll let you know if we find anything.'

"I see the neighbor's in his garage. I'll go ask him some questions," Sadler said, walking out the front door.

"Let's go room to room and see if we can find something that'll help us," Huff said to Dunham. "He obviously has her held up at another location, but maybe there's a clue to where this might be."

Dunham nodded.

Ten minutes later, Sadler came back into the house and found Huff and Dunham in a bedroom. "Boss, Dr. Dunham, the neighbor tells me that his son has a contract with the bank to mow the lawn and keep the exterior looking good, but he never goes in the house."

"Interesting," Dunham replied.

Sadler nodded. "He also said that occasionally a van drives up and someone goes into the house, stays for a few hours, then leaves."

"Alec Banner," Huff surmised.

Sadler nodded. "Get this; for the last few years, it's been a white van, but this year it's a blue van." He paused. "I'm sure it *is* Banner."

"Did he say when the last time was that he saw the van here?" Dunham asked.

Sadler nodded. "Last week, but only once this year." He glanced around. "Have . . ." his voice faded as he noticed the art covering each wall. "Have you found anything?" He asked slowly, realizing his question was answered by the subject of the wall coverings: scenes of Hell. "Excuse the pun, but what the Hell?"

Dunham pointed at the top of a dresser, which was covered with rutabaga jack o' lanterns. "I don't think there's any doubt that this is the childhood home of Alec Banner, the October serial killer."

Huff nodded. "The immediate problem is, this is not where he lives now, and worse—it's not where he's keeping Ashley." He glanced over at Dunham. "For some reason, the bank hasn't put this land up for sale. Why would a bank, an organization created to earn money, waste money by not selling this property and continue to pay property taxes?" he asked. "I'd like to give them a visit."

"I have the address, boss," Sadler said. "I'll go with you."

"Great idea," Dunham said. "If you don't mind, Lieutenant, I'd like to stay here and use some of my forensic skills. Maybe I can come up with something. If need be, I'll take a cab home."

Huff nodded. "I'm going to release the SWAT team and ask Salem PD to keep their distance from this house but maintain a constant surveillance. He may show up, and I'm not ready to let this asshole know we're onto him." Huff turned to Sadler. "Let's go."

"I'll see ya," Dunham replied as they headed toward the exit. He examined the rutabagas, then abruptly stopped and called out to Sadler. "Oh, Detective Sergeant? Do you still have our offender's remote?"

Sadler nodded. "I'll get it for you."

As Sadler rushed out to the vehicle to retrieve the remote, Huff released the SWAT team members. Sadler quickly returned, handed Dunham the remote, and then the two left.

After about twenty minutes, once SWAT was gone, Dunham was the only person in the house. He moved around, examining everything and taking photos with his iPhone. He stopped when his phone chimed, and he tapped to open a text from Father Martin. 'I'm at the front of the house.'

He texted Martin back. 'Come on in. The door's open.'

A few seconds later, Martin walked in and asked, "Find anything, Dr. Dunham?"

"Yes," Dunham said. "Follow me." He led Martin into the bedroom.

"Oh yes," Martin replied as he stared at the walls and jack o' lanterns. "He certainly has been here."

"The neighbor said he was here about a week ago, but only once this year."

"So, what's your next step?" Martin asked as he scanned the room.

"The fact that he visits his parents' old house periodically increases our chances that we'll apprehend him, eventually," Dunham explained. "But, our immediate efforts are to save Ashley before he attempts to sacrifice her tomorrow night. If we don't get lucky here, our plan is to continue with the surveillance of all the possible sacrifice sites."

"In that case, I'm off to the local parish for prayers," Martin said, then smiled. "Piety is power, so it's time to recharge." He started for the door. "I'll have my cell phone on me at all times."

"I'll be here for a few more hours, Father. See you soon."

Dunham watched Martin leave, then he continued his search.

chapter thirty

PRESENT DAY: October 30. Salem, Massachusetts—Pickering Wharf

"Turn here," Sarah directed from the back seat, while staring at her smartphone GPS map.

James pulled onto Wharf Street and nodded. "That's right, now I remember. This is Pickering Wharf. I haven't been here in a while." He pointed out the front window. "The House of Seven Gables and the marina shouldn't be too far."

"Hey, what do ya say we do a quick visit to the Halloween store where that Wiccan priest was found dead, before we go to the marina?" Rob suggested.

James stopped the car and pointed down a U-shaped street. "Coincidentally, it's right down there."

"Very touristy," Rob commented.

Sarah pointed out the front window. "There's the Hallowe'en Town store. Is that it?"

"That's it," James replied, then pulled into a parking spot in front of the store. When they entered the store, they encountered an older lady behind a long glass showcase counter.

Sarah stared at the walls, which were covered with black shelves, all loaded with witchcraft and Halloween items for sale. "How cool." She touched one of the stuffed black cats.

"Certainly has the feel of Halloween in here," Rob added.

"May I help you?" the lady asked in a nasal tone.

"Just browsing, thank you," James replied.

"I'm sorry for your loss," Sarah said to the lady. "It's not fair."

The old lady stared at Sarah, seemingly surprised that she knew about Ellsworth's death, but then she put on a kind smile. "Thank you, miss. He was a great man." She began to tear up.

Rob whispered to James and Sarah, "We should go," and they nodded to him.

"Goodbye," Sarah said to the lady.

The lady stared at them as they left. "You three be careful! It's not safe at the marina."

They nodded to her, left the store, and jumped into James' car.

"Holy shit!" James roared. "How'd she know we're going there?"

"That was freaky!" Rob agreed.

James pulled out and drove off. After a few minutes, the marina was visible from the road. "There it is," James said. He pulled into the parking lot and pointed to an old, well-kept building to the right. "There's the famous House of Seven Gables."

"Such great history around here," Sarah commented.

James parked the car and they got out, then approached the marina building and went in. A lady was sitting behind the counter, and they walked up to her.

She popped her head up from a book. "May I help you, young folks?"

"Hi," Rob began. "My name is Rob, this is James, and Sarah. We're students at Boston University . . . working on a research paper."

The lady nodded. "How neat. And you want my life story? My name is Myrna Petri," she joked.

Rob snickered. "Next time, maybe, Mrs. Petri." He paused. "Actually, it's a research paper on recent unsolved homicides and suspicious deaths in the area."

She nodded, realizing exactly what Rob was referring to. "Call me Myrna. You're here because of the death of the older couple on their yacht a few weeks back."

Rob nodded. "Exactly. Is it OK if we ask you about it?"

Myrna gave a kind grin and pulled out her cell phone and began texting. "Of course," she began. "The people who were docked next to them found them dead in their bedroom. They were friends of theirs." She shook her head. "Wicked shame."

"Do you know if they figured out the cause of death?" Rob asked.

"I think it was suffocation."

"That is suspicious," Sarah added.

Myrna nodded, reading an incoming text. "You're going to want to speak to my friend, Nancy. She works at the House of the Seven Gables, and she remembered the couple taking the tour that day. She thinks she saw the killer."

"Wow!" Rob exclaimed. "So, you're convinced it was a homicide?" He paused. "Is she available for us to speak to?"

Myrna nodded and waved her cell phone. "She's coming over right now . . . and yes, I am convinced."

A couple minutes later, a lady entered the marina building and approached them.

"Hi, Nancy," Myrna greeted. "This is," she paused, "Rob, James, and Sarah?" After nods of confirmation, she continued, "They're students at BU working on a research paper about mysterious deaths in the area. I told them you may have seen who murdered that old couple."

Nancy nodded. "Hi. Yes, I think I did."

"What happened?" Rob asked.

"Well," Nancy began, "the day they were murdered—" she frowned—"and don't let the police convince you otherwise."

Rob nodded.

Nancy took a deep breath. "The day they were murdered, they took a tour of the House of Seven Gables. The reason I remembered them is because I saw a nasty-looking man staring at them like he wanted to kill them or somethin'. He was wearing a hood."

"He just stared at them?" Rob asked.

"Yes, and when the couple started touring the house, this man followed them." She dropped her chin and eyed Rob over her glasses, "So *I* followed *him.*"

"That was brave," Sarah commented.

Nancy grinned. "I was angry, so I went up to him and said, 'Excuse me, sir, why are you following them?'" She placed her hands on her hips. "The guy stared at me and just growled! Can you believe it?"

"Did you tell the police?" James asked.

"No, the police already left before Nancy told me about it," Myrna said, interrupting.

Rob, Sarah, and James spent another fifteen minutes with the two ladies, asking them more questions. Rob had the feeling that they loved to gossip.

"Well, thank you very much—both of you." Then he added, "I think we have enough."

"No problem," Nancy said. "I need to get back to work anyway."

The three students left the building and approached James' car. Rob scanned the area. "To me, that sounds like our killer."

"I agree," James said.

"If true, then maybe he really is in the area." Rob paused. "I think we should contact Dr. Dunham about this."

"Do you have his number?" Sarah asked.

Rob shook his head and frowned. "No, I gave him mine, but I didn't ask for his." He paused, then beamed and pulled out his iPhone. "But my sister, Celine, might have it!" He tapped his phone, then put it to his ear. "Dr. Dunham gave Celine his cell phone number last year." He waited for it to ring, then put his iPhone on speaker.

"Robbie!" Celine's voice came over the phone. "Took you long enough to call me."

"Hi, Celine," Rob replied. "Sorry, we've been busy."

"How's college?" Celine asked.

"Great," Rob said. "I have a question. I spoke with Dr. Dunham a few days ago about the October serial killer."

"How cool!" Celine replied. "Did you say hi to him for me?"

"I did, and he asked about you." He paused. "We actually have been helping out with the case."

"Why am I not surprised," Celine interrupted. "That's my brother."

"I need to call him, but I don't have his number," Rob explained. "But I remember he gave it to you last year. Do you still have it?"

"I'm not sure . . . I'll check," Celine said. "Sooo, I hear you have a girlfriend."

Rob glanced over at Sarah and blushed. Sarah grinned. "Yes, she's here, actually. You're on speaker. Celine, this is Sarah."

"Hi, Celine," Sarah said.

"Hi, Sarah!" Celine replied. "Is Robbie taking care of you?"

Sarah snickered. "Yes, he's a great guy."

"I do have his number, Robbie," Celine announced. "I'll text it to you now."

"Thanks, Celine," Rob replied. "I'll call you soon."

"Take care, guys!" Celine said, then she hung up.

Rob received the text. "Here it is," he said, tapping the number, then putting the phone up to his ear.

"Your sister sounds cool . . . Robbie," James teased.

Rob glared at James, then realized Dunham had just answered.

"Dr. Dunham."

"Hi, Dr. Dunham," Rob began. "This is Rob Faulks. Celine had your number, so I got it from her. I hope that's OK."

"Hi, Rob. No problem. What do you need?" Dunham asked.

"Well, I think I have something," Rob answered.

"Oh?" Dunham asked. "What is it?"

Rob glanced over at James and Sarah. "James, Sarah, and I are at the Salem marina, and we believe the October serial killer is hiding out in the vicinity."

"Interesting . . . why is that?" Dunham asked.

Rob spent the next few minutes explaining to Dunham everything in detail. Dunham remained silent on the other end of the phone.

"Rob, I think you're onto something," Dunham acknowledged. "Coincidentally, I'm in Salem right now. It'll take me about an hour to get to you, but I'm going to have two members of the task force drive me to the marina. Can you wait for me?"

"Sure." Rob answered. "We'll grab a bite to eat and meet you back here."

An hour later, Huff, Sadler, and Dunham drove into the marina and parked near where Rob, Sarah, and James had requested to meet. They got out of the car and greeted them.

"Rob," Dunham began, "I told Lieutenant Huff and Detective Sergeant Sadler everything you told me over the phone."

Huff scanned the area. "Which slip was the yacht in?" Huff asked.

Rob pointed to the opposite side of the marina. "She said over in the last mooring. The yacht is still there. Apparently, family members haven't picked it up yet."

"Let's go check it out," Huff replied.

* * *

Inside the warehouse next to the marina, a man wearing a hood was pacing near a blue van parked in the middle of the garage. He moved with a deliberate pace, but then abruptly stopped and turned his head toward the small window. A piece of cardboard blocked his view of the outside. He rushed to the window, pulled up the right-hand corner of the cardboard, and peeked out. He saw two detectives and the Watchmaker speaking with three young people, all examining the old couple's yacht. He released the cardboard and clenched his fists, then started panting in rage. "Ahrrr!" he blurted out. He resumed pacing, then stopped and rushed to the back of the warehouse.

* * *

"It certainly does raise some flags," Sadler said. "If the man who followed this old couple in the House of Seven Gables was our killer, and also killed the warlock just a few blocks down, it wouldn't hurt to check out the area."

As Sadler spoke, a van caught Dunham's eye. He turned to watch the vehicle exiting the big, fenced-in warehouse neighboring the marina. The gate door opened, and the van turned right on the road. Just before it drove out of view, it passed under a streetlight, and Dunham saw that the van was blue. He grabbed Sadler's arm, causing the detective sergeant's voice to fade. "Did I just see . . . ?" He paused, then glanced over at Huff. "I just saw a blue van leave the fenced-in area of this warehouse."

Huff whipped his head around, but the van was gone. He glanced over at the window. "The window's covered." He rushed off the dock, toward the road, staring at the warehouse.

Everyone followed.

Huff whirled around toward Dunham, pointing to the front of the warehouse. "There's a garage door!"

Dunham pulled the remote garage door opener out of his pocket.

Sadler shook his head. "We can't use that one, Dr. Dunham. Remember? It's passcode protected."

Dunham stared at the remote keypad. "How many numbers did the manufacturer say is used on these remotes?"

"Three," Sadler answered.

"I wonder . . ." Dunham asked himself. He pointed the remote at the warehouse's garage door, typed in six-one-six, then pushed the button. Both the garage door and metal gate opened. The hair on the back of his neck rose.

Huff and Sadler turned toward Dunham with their jaws dropped, stunned.

"How'd you . . . ?" Huff asked.

"Remember the offender's satanic sacrifice using the numbers six, one, six—the mark of the beast?" Dunham asked.

"Ingenious, Dr. Dunham," Sadler said. "You are truly amazing."

They all stared at the warehouse. "If that was him in the van, maybe Ashley's in the warehouse right now!" Huff said loudly. He turned and rushed toward the entrance. "Call it in, Sergeant!"

"On it, boss!" Sadler hollered back to Huff.

Dunham faced Rob, Sarah, and James. "You did it again, guys." He pointed at their car. "For your safety, stay near your car." Dunham turned and rushed to catch up to Huff and Sadler. He pulled out his iPhone and texted Father Martin as he ran.

Rob, Sarah, and James approached the car. James gave Rob a high-five. "You did it, bro!"

"*We* did it," Rob corrected, smiling. "I hope she's in there," he whispered to himself.

Dunham ran through the gate, then went into the warehouse, stopped, and scanned the room. He slowly made his way to Huff and Sadler, who were standing in the middle of the warehouse. He glanced around the room again and noted how empty it was, aside from wooden pallets and trash. "This is definitely where he keeps his vans," Dunham replied.

Huff nodded and pointed to the back rooms. "That's what I'm interested in." They hurried to the back of the warehouse. Huff grabbed the door handle to the left door and opened it. They entered the room, which had black plastic on all the walls, one single bed, and one toilet. Rutabagas hung from the ceiling.

"Empty. Check the other room, Sergeant," Huff directed.

Sadler nodded and ran out of the room.

"This is clearly a room designed to hold someone against their will, but is it the only one?" Huff asked and scanned the room. "I'm sure the plastic is to reduce the DNA signature."

Dunham moved around the room, examining the bed. "Ashley was in this room."

Huff glanced over at Dunham. "How do you know?"

Dunham pointed to some scratch marks on the metal bed frame. He pointed to one particular section of chipped paint. "She wrote her name."

"Which means she was probably in that van that just left."

Dunham nodded. "That's exactly what it means."

Huff bit his lip and stomped his foot. "Shit! Shit!" He shook his head. "We're always so close, but not close enough!"

Sadler stuck his head in the room. "Boss, no one in the other room, but you'll want to see it."

Huff and Dunham followed Sadler into the adjoining room. In it was a desk covered with photos, which they all inspected. Huff glanced up at Dunham. "Sacrifice sites."

Dunham grabbed one of the photos. "That they are." He handed Huff the photo.

"Is this the observatory in Lynn?"

Dunham nodded. "We just don't know if that's the one he's going to use next. It wasn't separated from the rest of the sites. There are at least three dozen sites here," Dunham commented. He popped his head up as he heard police sirens. "Let's be thorough. I don't want to miss a thing."

Dunham reached into a basket and pulled out a rutabaga. "I would like to spend some time in these rooms and on these photos. Maybe something's here that'll confirm my suspicions about his next murder site."

"I just contacted the surveillance team watching over Banner's childhood home," Sadler interrupted. "The guy's taking her somewhere, so maybe it's there."

Huff nodded. "Good thinking, Detective Sergeant."

"An APB's already out for a blue van," Sadler added. "Maybe we'll get lucky."

"Depends," Huff answered. "If this guy had no idea we were at the marina, then maybe yes." He paused. "But my gut's telling me he left the warehouse with Ashley because he recognized us."

Dunham knew that the October serial killer would have easily recognized him, since he followed him and tried to kill him. "I believe you're correct, Lieutenant."

chapter thirty-one

PRESENT DAY: October 30. Salem, Massachusetts—Brewer Hawthorne Cove Marina

Hal Talbot sat in his favorite reclining chair in the living room, watching a movie. Ever since he turned eighty, he spent more time in his chair, especially because his knees and hips were shot. Hal enjoyed the view from his recliner: The huge TV just to the left of the huge front window—curtains always open—so he could watch his shows and the comings and goings in the neighborhood at the same time.

He heard his wife moving around in the kitchen. "I'll be there in a minute, Hal."

"Sounds great, Bethie," Hal replied. Suddenly, he saw a blue van shoot up his driveway at a high rate of speed and drive right into his attached two-car garage.

"What the . . . ?" He shouted toward the kitchen, "Beth! Someone just drove into our garage! He better not hit my Toyota!"

"That's nice, dear," she replied, her hearing having started to go.

Hal jumped as he heard the kitchen-garage door bang open.

His wife screamed.

"Beth!" He stared toward the kitchen, unable to see anything because the living room wall obstructed his view, then, slowly, a man with a deranged clown mask came into view, staring right at him. The blood left Hal's face. "Oh my God!"

The man in the mask rushed Hal and quickly snapped his neck.

The old man fell to the carpet, limp; the masked man stared at him for a moment, then went back into the kitchen, and stepped over the body of the old lady he'd just killed. He searched the kitchen and found the keys to the Toyota hanging on the wall, then grabbed them and went back into the garage. He pulled Ashley Geraghty out of the van, threw her into the back seat of the Toyota, then drove off.

* * *

Two and a half hours later, Rob, Sarah, and James, waited for Dunham at a public parking lot a short block away from the warehouse. Trees and buildings blocked their view of the marina and warehouse, but the constant stream of police cars shooting past them on Derby Street, and the police lights illuminating the entire area, kept them acutely aware that a major break had occurred in the October Serial Killer Case—and they were right in the middle of it. They sat at a picnic table in a small park area in the middle of the lot. Rob glanced up into the darkened sky, watching how the falling mist glowed from the parking lot lights. He appreciated the large tree next to them, its low-hanging branches blocking the mist. Rob straightened as Dunham approached them from Derby Street. "Here comes Dr. Dunham," he told his friends.

"Hi, guys," Dunham said as he approached them. "Thanks for waiting."

"That was the fastest two and a half hours of my life!" James commented. "This is history in the making. I wouldn't miss it for anything."

"Did you find Ashley?" Sarah asked.

Dunham frowned and shook his head. "No, but this is definitely where he kept her." He paused. "She was probably in the blue van I saw leaving the warehouse."

"I bet he saw you through the window, Dr. Dunham," Rob suggested. "And got scared—a little too close for comfort."

"I believe you're right, Rob." He turned around at the sound of footsteps. "Hi, Father Martin."

"Hi, Dr. Dunham," Martin replied back.

"Father Martin, this is Rob, Sarah, and James," Dunham introduced. "It was these three who helped us find our offender's hideout."

"Outstanding job, guys," Martin complimented. "Really."

"Thank you, Father," Rob replied.

"Since our offender's motive is satanic, Father Martin's been assisting me in the investigation," Dunham explained.

"I get that," James replied.

"It's too bad he got away," Rob said.

"He seems to be on the run," Dunham explained. "This exposes him, improving our odds that he'll be seen or that he will make a mistake. You guys might as well get back to your dorms. I'll contact—" At that moment, a fifty-gallon plastic trash can came out from the darkness and hit Father Martin with tremendous force, causing him to crash to the ground in front of the tree. The priest lay on the ground, unconscious. As Dunham watched Martin fall, time seemed to slow down. He knew immediately that the October serial killer targeted the priest first, clearing the way for him to attack his true target: him. Dunham instinctively went for his handgun, but in an instant he changed his mind and reached for the pendant inside his shirt collar. He pulled it out and turned in the direction of the projectile. Just as he turned, the attacker was upon him but screeched to a halt when he saw the pendant hanging from Dunham's neck. The attacker screamed and streaked back into the darkness.

"Oh my God!" Sarah screamed.

Dunham pulled out his handgun and pointed it in the direction that the attacker ran off. "Everyone, get near Father Martin!" he yelled.

Rob, Sarah, and James rushed to Martin's side.

Dunham followed them, backing up, keeping his attention out toward the darkness.

"Grrrr!" the attacker growled from the darkness.

"Sarah!" Dunham yelled. "Check on Father Martin. Rob! James! Be prepared for something else getting thrown at us! Block it if you can!"

James grabbed the large plastic drum and drew it up in front of him. "You got it!" he yelled.

Dunham grabbed his phone, held it next to his handgun out in front of him, speed dialed Huff's cell phone number, then put it to his ear. "I'm a block south of you at the public parking lot! We're being attacked! Send help!"

Just then, another large plastic trash drum was hurled at them at tremendous velocity. James leaped in front of Dunham with the can as a shield, and the plastic drum ricocheted off the other drum and fell harmlessly to the right.

They heard an animalistic scream in the direction the drum came from, so Dunham took a shot. The attacker screamed again, but in a different darkened location, just to the right. Just as heavier rain began to fall, a police siren blared in the distance. Moments later, a police car pulled into the parking lot, aiming its high beams right at them. They parked twenty feet away, and two police officers exited with their handguns drawn.

"What's happening?" one of the police officers yelled, but at that moment, he was attacked with lightning speed, picked up, and heaved a full fifteen feet directly into the other police officer. Both now lay unconscious, collapsed in a pile on the ground.

"Holy shit!" James blurted out.

The attacker instantly picked up one of the unconscious officers from the ground and used her as a shield, impeding Dunham's ability to shoot at him. The attacker screamed and threw the limp body at them.

Both James and Rob leaped in front of everyone and caught the police officer, but the momentum caused all three to fall back onto the ground.

Dunham got between them and the screaming man, then fired another shot. The laughter in the darkness confirmed Dunham's miss.

"Father Martin's OK!" Sarah yelled. "He's coming to."

Martin shook his head and sat up, holding his ribs, as realization washed across his face. He stood up and raised his hand. A wood pallet came flying at him, but he stumbled out of the way, pulling Sarah with him. He turned back toward the sound of the laughing attacker, lifted his hand again, and began to chant in Latin.

The attacker immediately screamed.

Dunham watched multiple police cars pull into the parking lot.

The attacker continued to scream, but in seconds it stopped.

Martin stopped chanting.

"He's gone," Martin said, panting. "He's gone." He bent over, grasping his ribs. Sarah came to his assistance, propping him up on her shoulder.

The police vehicles encircled them. Huff jumped out of his car, pulled out his firearm, and rushed toward Dunham and the others. He glanced around and noticed the two police officers lying on the ground. "What's going on?" he shouted. Sadler ran up next to him.

"We were just attacked by Alec Banner," Dunham answered. "Same hooded jacket; looked like his photo, just older; I'm convinced it was him." He pointed down a side street. "He ran off just as you got here. I think he ran in that direction."

Huff pointed to a couple of officers. "Go! Everyone! Find him!" he roared. Officers ran on foot toward the direction Huff was pointing, and two vehicles burned rubber as they sped off.

"He was unbelievably strong and aggressive," Dunham stated. "Just like the attack on the four police officers." He pointed to a drum. "He threw a fifty-gallon plastic drum at Father Martin and knocked him out." He glanced over at the downed officers being cared for. "Are they OK? He hit 'em hard."

"They're breathing," a police officer attending one of them answered. "Johnson's still unconscious, but he seems to be OK."

Huff glanced down at Martin, who was now sitting at the picnic table. "Father Martin, are you OK?"

Martin nodded. "I'll be fine, Lieutenant."

"That drum hit him hard," Rob reiterated.

"Maybe you should wait for the medical personnel, just in case," Huff replied, then glanced over at Rob, Sarah, and James, all three clearly shaken up. "Everyone all right?"

"We're fine, sir," Rob said as he held Sarah. "That guy was unbelievably powerful!"

"He threw the police officer at us from twenty feet away!" James yelled. "No one can do that!"

"Apparently, he can," Huff said matter-of-factly.

"He might be on the road right now in the blue van," Dunham interjected. "We should call it in."

"Already done," Sadler answered, even before Huff glanced over at him.

Huff glanced back at Martin, confused. "So, why are you here, Father?"

"I asked him to come," Dunham responded. "We only have until tomorrow to stop this sacrifice, and Father Martin is an expert in Satanism and satanic possessions."

Huff frowned and shook his head. "Shit! That close again!" He paused. "It seems that every time we take one step forward, we fall two steps back."

Dunham turned to Rob, Sarah, and James. "I am so sorry you three were put in harm's way. I had no idea he would come after me in an area crawling with police."

"Don't worry about us, Dr. Dunham," Rob replied. "Hey, we have something to talk about when we get back!"

"I would never forgive myself if any of you get injured, so please, go back to the university." He shook Rob's hand. "Rob, again, your assistance has been immensely helpful."

"Thanks, Dr. Dunham," Rob said.

He shook Sarah's and James' hands. "Thank you, Sarah; James." He turned back toward Rob. "Now, promise me if you do find something, just call next time and don't come."

"We promise," Rob replied, grinning.

"Guys," Huff interrupted, referring to Rob, Sarah, and James. "Before you go, come over here for a second. I'd like you to write up a statement, tell me everything you saw."

"Sure," Rob said, then the three followed Huff to another police officer.

Dunham approached Martin. "Father, the only reason why he didn't attack us was because of this pendant, and the only reason he ran off was because you regained your senses."

Martin nodded. "He is not threatened by police."

"At least he ran when the police were coming, so no one will suspect anything too unusual."

Martin nodded and bent over, rubbing his ribs. "He certainly wants you out of the picture, Dr. Dunham. I told you he was going to try again." He paused. "Do you have any idea where he'll attempt his sacrifice?"

Dunham frowned. "There are dozens of possible locations, each as likely as the next, but . . ."

"Go on," Martin replied.

"I usually don't go by intuition, Father," Dunham answered, "but my gut is telling me it's going to be at a location in Lynn. An observatory."

"Dr. Dunham, take this feeling seriously. It's your gift speaking to you," he whispered.

Dunham remained silent. It was true; many things had occurred recently that had stretched his naturalistic worldview, but he didn't want to tell Martin that he had serious reservations about possessing a supernatural gift. "The task force will most likely invest most of their resources on the Lynn location, so I hope you can be there tomorrow night."

"I already planned on it, Dr. Dunham," Martin replied.

chapter thirty-two

PRESENT DAY: 8:00 a.m., Halloween/October 31. Boston, Massachusetts—Boston Police Headquarters, October Serial Killer Task Force Office

"I thought Carnie said he sent it!" Huff shouted impatiently to Dunham, who was examining the sacrifice map on the wall.

Dunham turned and spotted Sadler entering the room with three Dunkin' Donuts coffees, then turned back toward Huff. "He said, 'I'm sending it,' which might mean in a few minutes."

Sadler handed Dunham one of the coffees. "What's he sending?"

"Thanks," Dunham said. "Jack and a team of analysts back at the FBI lab entered data on the potential murder sites into a field-proven probability algorithm. He told me it's done, and the results are listed in order of decreasing probabilities."

"Oh, here it is," Huff interrupted, staring at the computer monitor.

Sadler handed Huff a coffee and sat next to him. He studied the list, then glanced at Dunham. "Dr. Dunham, your observatory in Lynn didn't even make the top twenty." He stared back at the list. "It's number twenty-one out of thirty-six locations."

Dunham turned and faced Huff and Sadler, confused. "What? I personally gave them the parameters and assigned the weights." He shook his head. "How could I be so wrong?" He approached the computer monitor and peeked over Huff's shoulder.

"So, should we trust the FBI's algorithm or you?" Huff asked. "Personally, I'd put my money on you."

Dunham stared at the screen in silence. He shook his head again. "I wrote the algorithm, and it's evidence-based, filtered through a series of logical sequences . . . If you put your money on me, in a strange way, you're betting against me."

Sadler turned to Huff and made a sound and gesture indicating that his mind was blown.

"I see what you're saying," Huff commented to Dunham. "Your head versus your gut," he paused, "but I've never thought of you as intuitive—more like a computer walking on two legs. Could they have made an error inputting the data?"

Dunham shook his head. "Jack is the best, and besides, he plugged the data in on two separate runs and got the same results."

Huff sat back in his seat and stared at Dunham. "Your call, Dr. Dunham."

He shook his head again. "We'd better go with the algorithm results," Dunham concluded. "It's produced successful results on multiple occasions."

Huff turned back around to the monitor. "OK then, let's put our resources into the top ten, since they're spread out into six different police jurisdictions." He paused. "Good news; the first three are within a few miles of each other, just northeast of Salem in Ipswich, Massachusetts."

"Oh?" Dunham asked.

Huff nodded. "The Choate Bridge, Green Street Bridge, and County Street Bridge; all stone arches." He glanced over to Sadler. "Let's have our team disseminate this info to the field, pronto. We need each site covered yesterday."

"The team's already waiting for me, boss," Sadler replied.

"Great, then let's get on the road to Ipswich just after lunch."

Sadler nodded, then left the room.

"That'll give me enough time to get back to the FBI office and look things over one more time," Dunham said, still scratching his head.

"See you then," Huff answered.

Dunham left the room and texted Father Martin the plan for the evening, explaining why they opted not to focus upon the observatory on Lynn.

He received a text back: 'Dr. Dunham, I suggest you reconsider. I'm convinced that your gut feeling about the observatory came from your gift.'

Dunham texted in response: 'For the moment, I'm convinced the algorithms that I created are more accurate and that's what we're going to do, but I will take your suggestion seriously and think about it for the next few hours.'

He pocketed his phone as he left the room, heading for the building's exit.

* * *

7:00 p.m., October 31. Ipswich, Massachusetts—Ipswich Police Station

At the Ipswich police station, Huff and Sadler stood next to the chief of police, watching everyone coordinate the plan of action for the surveillance of the three locations. "Thank you again, Chief, for everything. It was short notice, but everything seems to be in place."

"No problem at all, Lieutenant," the chief said. "This guy's not going to sacrifice anyone in my town." He glanced over at Dunham. "Nice to finally meet you, Dr. Dunham. You're a hero in these parts."

Dunham grinned, embarrassed. "Thanks. I'm honored."

The chief stared at the video monitors broadcasting all three bridges. "Which bridge do you suspect he chooses?"

"Well," Dunham began, "probability is greatest with the Choate Bridge."

"I can see why he'd choose that one," the chief began. "It's the oldest bridge in Massachusetts and the second oldest in the country, constructed in 1764."

"History seems important to our offender," Dunham agreed.

Huff's cell phone rang, and he answered, "Lieutenant Huff." He paused. "Really! Text me the address. We'll be right there." He glanced over at Dunham and Sadler. "They found his van. He drove it into an attached garage and murdered the elderly couple living at the home!"

"Holy shit!" Sadler blurted out.

"It's right in Salem, not too far from here!" Huff explained and turned to the chief. "We'll be right back, Chief!" Huff called as he, Dunham, and Sadler headed for their car.

Fifteen minutes later, they reached the old couple's home and parked in front of it. Police vehicles filled the road and driveway. As they approached the front door, Huff gestured to the evening activity in the neighborhood. "Look at all the trick-or-treaters in this residential area."

"I hope this doesn't ruin their Halloween," Sadler commented.

They entered the crowded home; detectives and uniformed officers milled from room to room. A man approached Huff.

"Lieutenant Huff," the man said, then waved him over to the kitchen. "This way."

"Hi, Detective Anders," Huff said. "What do you have?"

Anders pointed to a woman sitting in a chair in the kitchen. "That's Mrs. Doreen Baur, the daughter of the old couple that was murdered here last night. She told me she showed up a few hours ago to check up on them, to make sure they had enough candy for the trick-or-treaters, only to find them murdered," he said gravely as he started moving toward the kitchen. "The bodies of the victims have already been removed. Let me introduce her to you."

Huff nodded.

They approached Doreen Baur, who was understandably clearly distraught.

"Doreen, this is Detective Lieutenant Huff of the Boston Police Department. Lieutenant, this is Doreen Baur," Anders introduced, then placed a comforting hand on Doreen's shoulder. "He's in charge of an important investigation."

"I'm so sorry for your loss, Mrs. Baur," Huff said somberly.

Baur nodded and looked at the floor. "Thank you." She shook her head. "Why would someone want to kill them? They were harmless."

"We believe the man that did this is the October serial killer, Mrs. Baur," Huff explained.

Baur popped her head up and her jaw dropped. "What?"

Huff nodded. "Your parents just . . . got in the way of his agenda." He paused. "He was on the run and needed a vehicle other than a van, since we'd identified it." He shook his head. "It looks like he stole your parents' car."

Baur dropped her head and put her face in her hands.

"So, what kind of car did they own?" Huff asked.

"A Toyota Corolla," Baur answered.

Anders handed Huff a piece of paper. "Here's the license plate number and vehicle information on the Corolla."

Huff passed it off to Sadler, who pulled out his cell phone and left the room.

Dunham glanced around the kitchen, then spotted a wristband with a domino-sized plastic container hanging off of it.

"Hi, Mrs. Baur," Dunham interrupted. "My name is Dr. Dunham. I'm from the FBI. Did one of your parents have dementia or Alzheimer's?"

Huff and Anders stared at Dunham, curiously.

Baur nodded. "Yes, my mother did. How'd you know?"

Dunham held up the wristband. "This is a GPS tracker made by Moto-Mon. I recognized it."

"My mom had intermediate-to-advanced-stage Alzheimer's; getting worse every day," Baur explained. "A little while ago, she went for a walk but couldn't find her way back." She paused. "Ever since, we had the GPS tracker for her in order for us to find her if she got lost again."

"Oftentimes," Dunham began, "MotoMon has package deals where they install a GPS tracker in the vehicle as well."

Baur nodded. "Yes, we did that. We have one in . . . the car." She paused, her eyes widening as the implication sank in. "Oh, I guess we can find out where the car is!"

"What?!" Huff blurted out excitedly, then glanced back and forth from Dunham to Baur. "So, how do we do it?"

Mrs. Baur grabbed her purse and searched through it. She found her wallet, opened it, and quickly pulled out a card and gave it to Huff. "Here's the information." She pulled out her smartphone. "There's an app that goes with it." She touched the screen, then pointed at the card in Huff's hand. "The card has my password on it."

"Detective Sergeant Sadler!" Huff roared and waved him back. When he returned, Huff handed him the card. "There's a GPS in that Toyota, and here's the code. All we need is the MotoMon app and we can find the location of the car!"

"I found the car!" Baur interrupted. "It shows the location on a map." She glanced up at Huff. "The car's in Lynn, Massachusetts."

Sadler whipped his head around toward Dunham. "The observatory!" he yelled.

"Shit!" Huff exclaimed. "Thank you, Mrs. Baur. You've been extremely helpful. Anders, I'll contact you later."

"Thank you," Dunham echoed to Baur. "I'm terribly sorry for your loss, but you may have just saved someone's life." He shook her hand and hurried after the detectives.

Huff, Dunham, and Sadler bolted out of the house and jumped into their car. "Next time, I'm listening to your gut, Dr. Dunham!" Huff stated with a screech of tires. He turned on the siren and sped off.

"Me too," Dunham replied, buckling his seat belt and pulling out his iPhone to text Father Martin. He knew full well that if Father Martin wasn't at the observatory as law enforcement attempted to apprehend the killer, the outcome might not be favorable.

"I've got the app on my phone, boss, and its working!" Sadler yelled. "The car's parked at the observatory!"

"Shit!" Huff yelled. "I hope it's not too late. Contact the Lynn Police Department!"

"Just dialed their number," Sadler replied.

* * *

8:30 p.m., October 31. Lynn, Massachusetts—High Rock Tower and Observatory

Little Johnny Zimmerman stood patiently at the exit to the High Rock Tower and Observatory, waiting for his dad to lock up. He'd already gone trick-or-treating with his mom, but his dad had promised to take him to the haunted house attraction in Lynn as a special Halloween trip. His friends in his third-grade class said it was the best. Johnny watched his dad talking to someone at the door of the observatory.

"Come on, Dad!" He like the fact that his dad ran the observatory, but not tonight, when there was so much spooky stuff to see and only one night to see it!

"Wait, son!" his dad called back.

Johnny shook his head, then decided to make waiting more interesting by jumping on some of the big rocks that jutted out of the ground nearby. As he teetered across them, he noticed a car parked just behind the rocks, blocked from view of the observatory. He immediately stopped in his tracks and stared. It wasn't the car that concerned him, but the man standing next to it wearing a scary clown mask. He would have dismissed it as some weirdo in a Halloween costume, but the man was watching him! Johnny shivered in fear, then froze. The scary man stood motionless, maintaining eye contact with him. He then tilted his head slowly, back and forth, still staring at Johnny.

"Let's go, Johnny," his dad yelled, waving him down from the rocks.

Johnny backed up cautiously, then turned around and bolted to his dad as fast as he could.

"Come on, son," his dad said. "Get in the car. We don't want to be late."

Johnny, who couldn't be happier to be leaving, rushed into the car, shut the door, and locked it. He decided not to say anything to his dad about the man.

"You're quiet," his dad said.

"Let's go, Dad," Johnny replied anxiously.

His dad shrugged, pulled out, and left the parking lot.

Seconds later, the man in the mask made his way up over the rocks toward the tower, carrying Ashley Geraghty over his shoulder. He stopped momentarily and glanced around. Once he assured himself that no one was in the vicinity, he continued toward the tower. He dropped Ashley on the ground in front of the tower, positioned her on her back, then reached into his bag and pulled out wheat, grapes, and a fig, all wrapped together. There was just enough light from the entranceway to the observatory to see what he was doing.

Ashley was slowly beginning to wake up, moaning quietly. He positioned the offering next to her, pulled out a rutabaga, laid it on the ground, then pulled out a large blade. He stared at it for a moment and started panting with excitement. The slight sound of distant sirens caused him to glance down the hill. He gazed at Ashley, then slowly brought the knife up over his head, aiming for her abdomen. Seconds went by, and for some reason he couldn't thrust the knife down into his target. He tried again, but his arms still wouldn't move. He drew in a breath as his muscles began to tremble, then he glanced over at the side of the tower. To his surprise, he spotted the priest glaring at him, his hand projected forward.

"Get away from her!" the priest screamed, then whipped his forward hand to the right.

The man immediately flew off of Ashley and lay on the ground writhing in pain. "Arrrrhhh!" he screamed.

Father Martin chanted in Latin at the top of his lungs as he moved closer to the man.

The man's head wrenched backward, and he still screamed and writhed. "Arrrrhhhh!"

As Martin closed in on him, he pulled out his cigar-shaped trap.

A fleet of police cars bulleted into the observatory parking lot, sirens blaring. They got out of their cars and rushed toward Martin and the killer.

"Get on the ground!" one of the police officers screamed at Martin.

Martin knew he couldn't lose his grip on the evil entity, so he ignored the policeman's order. A bright light began to emanate out of the man's chest.

A couple of police officers noticed the light, which caused them to back up.

"Facedown on the ground!" a police officer screamed at Martin. When Martin ignored him again, he rushed him and tackled him to the ground.

Martin screamed in pain as his injured ribs cracked under the impact. "No! He'll escape!"

At that moment, the light over the attacker shot back into his chest. In an instant, he leaped up off the ground, and with lightning speed, he attacked the police.

Chaos ensued, and in seconds every police officer was lying on the ground, motionless. The officer pinning Martin down simply froze where he was, stunned, mouth gaping. He glanced around, but the attacker was nowhere to be seen.

"Get off me!" Martin screamed. The police officer rolled off and Martin got up. Martin saw Ashley still lying there, and he rushed to her. "Ashley!" Ashley moved around slowly. Her eyes opened, but they were glassy, and she seemed to be oblivious of her surroundings. "Don't worry, Ashley," Martin comforted. "I'm not going anywhere."

* * *

Dunham stared out of the car's back window as Huff sped to the observatory, lights flashing and siren blaring.

He received a text from Martin: 'She's safe, but the police stopped me from completing my extraction. He attacked the police then got away.'

Dunham texted back: 'We're almost there.'

"Detective Sergeant, tell me what's happening!" Huff shouted.

Sadler listened to police chatter on the radio from his headset. "He got away, but Ashley is safe." He paused. "They're saying a priest beat them to the scene and saved her life."

Huff glanced back. "Father Martin! How'd he know to be there?"

"Banner is deathly afraid of Father Martin," Dunham answered, "and since this man has a history of defeating armed police officers, I wanted Father Martin near."

"Strangely, I get that," Huff replied, then paused. "So, why wasn't he at the Choate Bridge?"

Dunham shook his head. "Father Martin said I should have followed my gut and not my head, so he took it upon himself to go to Lynn."

"Father knows best, I guess," Huff said, then glanced at Sadler. "Check the GPS tracker again."

"Checking," Sadler replied. "But I must not be getting a good signal. There seems to be a delay or something. It's showing that the car's still parked at the observatory."

Huff drove his car up to the building. Dozens of police cars surrounded the area. He showed his ID and pulled up as close as he could get.

"Shit!" Sadler responded. "His car's on the move!"

Huff stopped and started to back up.

"Wait!" Dunham replied. "We need to get Father Martin!" Huff stopped the car again and Dunham rushed out and approached Martin.

"Hi, Dr. Dunham," Martin greeted.

"No time to talk!" Dunham blurted out. "He's on the move, and we need you to come with us!"

Martin followed Dunham to the car, and both got into the back.

"All set," Dunham relayed to Huff, and the car roared away from the observatory.

"Where is he?" Huff asked Sadler.

"He's driving north into Lynn," Sadler replied. "Turn left here. Once it dead ends into Lawton Ave., take a right," Sadler directed.

Huff turned right onto Lawton Avenue.

"The car's no longer moving," Sadler announced as he stared at his smartphone. "It's parked in the Pine Grove Cemetery!"

"Are there woods in the area, and is it fenced in?" Martin asked.

"Yes, Father," Sadler answered. "The pine forest is how it got its name. It's a huge cemetery and has an immense fieldstone wall around it. They claim it's the largest stone wall just after the Great Wall of China."

"Lots of room to hide," Huff commented.

"Thresholds and boundaries were important to ancient Celts," Martin explained. "A boundary to the Otherworld and a stone wall is ideal. It's giving him strength. Also, he feels most comfortable in wooded areas." He touched Huff's shoulder. "And, Lieutenant, he's not at all threatened by police wielding guns; rather, because of his beliefs, he is terrified of me." He paused. "I have a certain influence over him."

"I've been told," Huff replied, "and from what I've seen, I believe it."

"We need to get as close to him as possible without him knowing," Martin explained, "so I recommend you turning off your police lights and sirens in order for us to surprise him."

"We're nearly there," Sadler added.

Huff turned off the lights and siren.

"The car's in the southwest corner, butting up to the woods," Sadler relayed.

"That's where we'll go then," Huff replied.

"Go left after the entrance."

Martin leaned over toward Dunham. "In order for him to not recognize my presence," he whispered, "I'm going to have to go into a silent prayer and focus all of my attention on it." He paused. "I'll need you to slap me on the shoulder when he's close."

Dunham nodded. "I will."

Martin glanced up at Huff and Sadler. "Drive as close to the woods as possible. We won't have to leave the vicinity of the car once you park it. It's in the man's nature to attack when threatened. He won't run away, and we can take advantage of that."

Martin leaned toward Dunham again. "Leave the back door open and stand next to it. I'll stay hidden in the back seat."

"And I'll tap you just before he attacks," Dunham confirmed.

Martin nodded. "Now, when I've extracted the spirit, the host will attack me, so be prepared."

"Just like Father Corel and Liam experienced in Ireland hundreds of years ago."

"Exactly," Martin replied. "Keep your pendant hidden in your hand and show it like a badge if you need it."

Huff pulled into the cemetery and drove left on the first road they came to. Other than the illumination from the car's lights, it was pitch black due to the thick row of pine trees on both sides of the cemetery's small dirt road.

"Turn left into this circle," Sadler directed. "We should see the Corolla at the other end."

Huff drove into the circle, and on the inside of the curve the headlights revealed rows of old headstones; on the outside of the curve were the woods. "There it is!"

Dunham glanced over at Martin. His eyes were closed and his head was down, silently mouthing a prayer. Dunham pointed forward. "Park between the car and the woods, Lieutenant."

Huff parked his car in front of the other one but left the lights on and the engine running. They got out, handguns drawn.

Just as Martin had directed, Dunham left the back door open. He exited the car and slowly approached Huff. Sadler stayed on the other side of the car with the door open for protection.

Silence.

"Watch out for anything flying at you," Dunham warned.

The sound of something large crashing through the trees from left to right echoed around them; then they heard a piercing scream followed by laughter. They aimed their guns in the direction of the noise.

"I think I just wet myself!" Sadler whispered. "This guy's fast!"

Dunham moved toward the back door where Martin was praying.

In an instant, the attacker rushed Sadler and slammed his body into the car, knocking him out, collapsing his body to the ground.

Huff turned and shot at the attacker, but he had vanished into the darkness just as fast as he'd come.

"Sadler!" Huff screamed, but Sadler lay unconscious.

A large stick flashed in the headlights, flying directly at Huff, and as he ducked, the attacker pounced on him, knocking him to the ground.

"Uggh," Huff exhaled, then went limp.

Dunham slapped Martin on the shoulder, then moved away from the car, whipped out his pendant, and aimed it at the attacker, who was just feet in front of him. Just as he lifted his hand up to reveal the pendant, the attacker moved in on him. The attacker screamed and slapped the pendant with such force that Dunham lost control of it and the pendant went flying. The attacker pushed Dunham backward ten feet, causing his head to thud on the ground, dazing him.

At that moment, instead of advancing upon Dunham, the attacker dropped to his knees and screamed, covering his ears. He fell to the ground and onto his back. Behind him, Father Martin glared and chanted in Latin, holding his hand forward.

Dunham got up and aimed his handgun at the attacker. He noticed Sadler and Huff getting off of the ground.

The attacker screamed again, and his back wrenched as his chest crested off the ground in an arch.

Martin chanted loudly. He pulled out the cigar-shaped container and opened it. In seconds, a bright light emanated from the attacker and hovered over his torso.

"Holy shit!" Huff yelled.

Martin moved the container forward, and as he did so, the light shot into the container. He then closed the top and turned the lock. He shook his head, took a deep breath, then relaxed and fell to his knees.

"Watch out!" Sadler screamed as the attacker pulled out a knife and rushed Martin. Both Huff and Sadler shot the man in the chest, instantaneously dropping him.

Dunham approached the man and felt for a pulse. "He's dead." He stood up and faced Huff and Sadler. "Are you two all right? You took some heavy blows."

Huff rubbed his head and shoulder. "I'll be fine."

"Me too," Sadler replied.

Huff shook his head. "Same thing happened, though, when I got knocked out my senior year in football."

"What's that?" Dunham asked.

"I saw a bright light," Huff replied.

"I saw it too!" Sadler added.

"Did you get knocked out?" Huff asked.

Sadler rubbed his neck. "Oh yeah. He slammed my head against the car good."

"There you go," Huff explained, then approached the body of the killer and stared down at it. "So, that's the bastard who's been giving us so much trouble for the last four Octobers." He shook his head.

"Once we fingerprint him the world will be convinced," Dunham answered, "but I don't think any of us have a shred of doubt that he's our man."

"Can't say I wasn't happy to have you here, Father," Huff said. "You were our magic bullet."

Martin stared at the body. "I've been here since the beginning, Lieutenant." He glanced over at Dunham. "We have the Watchmaker to thank for this."

chapter thirty-three

PRESENT DAY: Morning, November 1. Boston, Massachusetts—Massachusetts General Hospital

Dunham, Huff, and Sadler left the elevator and walked onto the hospital floor that Ashley Geraghty was assigned to. "What room is she in?" Dunham asked.

Sadler pointed down the hall. "Six twenty-three."

"This place is going to be crowded with news cameras soon," Huff predicted. "Perfect time to visit."

They made their way to her room, peeked in, and saw that she was awake, attended dutifully by her two roommates.

"Hi, Ashley," Huff whispered. "May we visit?"

Ashley looked toward Dunham, Huff, and Sadler, then beamed. "Yes, please! I'm so glad you could come."

Huff glanced over at her roommates. "Hi, girls."

Dayna and Janette greeted the trio and made room alongside the bed for them to approach Ashley.

"How do you feel?" Dunham asked.

"I feel great, but they said I have to stay here for a few more days for observation," Ashley replied. "The psych people are going to visit, too, apparently, because of my traumatic experiences."

"You're *officially* crazy now, girl," Dayna joked.

"All the better to get checked out," Dunham acknowledged.

"I want to thank you guys for everything," Ashley said, then began to tear up. Her roommates hugged her.

"No, we need to thank you, Ashley," Huff said. "If it wasn't for you volunteering for such a dangerous task, that bastard would still be out there, terrorizing others."

She glanced over at Dunham. "Father Martin was here early this morning and said you were the reason why he was waiting for me at the Lynn Observatory."

"Luckily," Dunham began, "Father Martin listens to me even better than I listen to myself."

Sadler quietly slipped out of the room.

Huff placed his hand on Dunham's shoulder. "Ashley, if it wasn't for this guy, we'd still be completely in the dark as to the identity of the killer. Everyone owes a debt of gratitude to the Watchmaker."

Dunham blushed. "I work hard," he paused, then glanced over at Ashley, "and speaking of work, my plane back to Virginia leaves this afternoon, so, Ashley, if you ever need me, just contact Lieutenant Huff. He'll know how to get ahold of me."

"Look who's here to visit!" Sadler interrupted from the door.

Behind him came Samantha Bronson, walking on crutches and with a bandage wrapped around her head. She was smiling from ear to ear.

"Samantha!" Ashley said loudly. "You're alive!" She began to tear up again. "I didn't know what happened to you after I was kidnapped. You hit the trash container so hard."

"I'm fine, Ashley," Samantha said, approaching her and giving her a big hug. "I have a thick skull. They brought me here, and I regained consciousness the next day." She pointed down the hall. "I'm actually your neighbor, and I hear you'll be hanging with me for a few days."

Ashley snickered. "Just like old times."

Janette pointed up at the TV. "Oh look, Ashley, there's your picture on the news!" Everyone glanced up at the screen.

"How do I turn it up?" Ashley asked as she grabbed the large control pad. "Oh, here it is," she muttered, punching the volume button.

"They're interviewing the superintendent of police and Dr. Gillespie," Sadler observed.

". . . and pivotal to the case was Dr. Gillespie's discovery that the October serial killer, Alec Banner, believed he was possessed by an evil spirit," the superintendent explained to the cameras. "Eleven days later, Banner is off the streets."

The cameras moved toward Gillespie. "Is this correct, Dr. Gillespie?" a reporter asked.

"Well, yes," Gillespie began, "but this was a team effort accomplished by each police district involved in the task force, the state police, and the FBI."

Sadler glanced over at Huff and they both rolled their eyes but remained silent.

"The crowds will be coming soon, Ashley," Huff explained. "So, we need to take off."

"They can wait," Ashley replied.

"Your name is plastered all over the news, Ashley!" Sadler interrupted. "The public needs to know," he paused, "and they deserve to know. It's been a long couple of years."

They said their good-byes, then left the room and headed for the elevator. "Ready to get dropped off at the airport, Dr. Dunham?" Huff asked as he pushed the elevator button.

Dunham glanced at his watch. "Well, we have some extra time. What do you say we have a quick lunch at your special diner?"

"I'm in," Sadler said as the elevator doors opened up.

"You will be missed, Dr. Dunham," Huff replied with a wide smile. "Let's go eat."

Author's Note

Special thanks go out to my readers and editors, Nick Rastelli, Scott Benson, Gouv Cadwalader, Judy Grundy, and Jennifer Cappello. I could not have done it without you. Thank you, Anita Hawley, for being my creative filter and telling it to me straight. Tom Balk, your detective experience was invaluable.

www.ingramcontent.com/pod-product-compliance
Lightning Source LLC
Chambersburg PA
CBHW031943010726
47493CB00007B/2054